Eraserbyte

Cat Connor

Eraserbyte © Cat Connor 2015

For information regarding permission email the publisher at 9mmPressNZ@gmail.com, subject line: Permission.

Editor: Jayne Southern
Formatting: 9mm Press
Publisher: 9mm Press, New Zealand
Publication date: 2015
Country of first publication: United States of America
Current country of publication: New Zealand.

ISBN: D2D paperback: 978-1-0670072-3-2
ISBN: 978-0-69241096
ISBN ePub: 9781310400308

"The oldest and strongest emotion of mankind is fear, and the oldest and strongest kind of fear is fear of the unknown."

- H. P. Lovecraft

Chapter One.

Chasing Pavements

"You all right, Conway?"

I spun around and looked at him standing in my doorway. "Yeah, you?"

Kurt nodded. "I'm not quite sure how we pulled that off. But we did, nor did we lose anyone." He walked across the floor and lowered himself into the chair on the other side of my desk.

A smile edged over my lips. "I can't quite believe Owen still has a job."

Kurt smiled. "Supervision. She so much as breathes the wrong way, she's history."

Justice? Didn't feel like it. But compromises were made and my team still intact. Grateful for that. Very grateful.

"You never did tell me where you went and who with …"

"You know where I went. I filed a freaking report. Even on vacation I attract death and destruction."

"You and Mitch?"

"Yes." I changed the subject. "So a select committee and the Director smacked Owen across the knuckles. Should be quieter in the halls for the next few months then."

"Should be," Kurt agreed. "How much influence do you

think the CIA had on our 'enforced leave with pay, everyone's still got jobs' half-assed disciplinary action?"

"I don't know. Tierney is very supportive of this team." I tapped my fingernails on the desk. "We were lucky."

Could've been very bad for all of us.

An email alert popped up at the bottom of the screen. I moved the pointer and opened the email.

"Interesting?" Kurt asked.

"Email from a CI of mine. Suspicious activity at an abandoned factory. The CI thinks someone is being held there."

"Is this confidential informant reliable?"

"Usually. We'll go check it out." I picked up the phone on my desk and called Sam and Lee.

"We got a job."

Moments later they appeared in the doorway.

"Chicky," Lee said with a grin. "We're ready to roll."

Forty-five minutes later we stood in the rain across the road from the factory in question. It looked deserted, no signs of life.

"Let's do it," I said. "Gear up."

Gloomy, cold and drafty. Not a fan of abandoned old factories. Puddles gleamed as lightning lit the interior. There were better places to be during a thunderstorm. The structure leaked like a sieve. Another clap of thunder shook the walls and vibrated under my feet. Water trickled down the wall on my left, feeding a large puddle in the broken concrete.

My LED flashlight lit the area with white light. I

scanned the walls. Lee was with me, Sam and Kurt several paces behind us.

"On your three o'clock," I called to Sam.

The flashlight illuminated a solid-looking metal door on my right. I kept moving forward down the corridor but looked back quickly as Sam turned ninety degrees and tried the door handle. With a reverberating clang, the door hit a wall. Kurt and Sam disappeared.

Moments later, I heard Sam's voice. "Clear."

Lee looked at me.

"Our nine," he said as his flashlight shone through the doorway, onto more puddles.

"Got it."

I followed Lee into the room. He went right. I went left. Nothing but decrepit machinery, rusted hunks of metal, and more puddles.

"Clear," Lee said and we moved on.

I wanted to move on completely and go home. It was a miserable afternoon. The dank corridor stretched in front of us with no end in sight.

A door banged. The echo bounced off the walls and slammed into us, directional information distorted by the echo.

"Where was that?" I asked.

"Ahead?" Lee said, glancing over his shoulder at Sam for confirmation.

Sam nodded. "Ahead. The tip might have been right. Someone is in here."

Or a big rat can close doors?

I felt Sam and Kurt close behind us. We'd walked two abreast earlier but in single file now. Lee had point, then me, then Kurt, then Sam in the rear.

Another door closed, this time quietly.

"They know we're here," I whispered to Lee.

That was a given. We weren't exactly in stealth mode.

"Yeah, carefully does it," he replied. "They have the upper hand for now."

Counting paces helped me control my breathing and heart rate. It also meant I knew it was twenty-four feet before we saw another doorway and a closed door. Lee stopped. We listened for signs of life.

Barely breathing.

A tap or knock, so faint none of us would have heard it if we were moving at all. I needed to talk so hand signals were the way to go. I holstered my Glock to free my hand, pointed to the door, and then grabbed my wrist with my gun hand. Could be our suspect inside. Lee nodded. We stood in pairs on either side of the door. I drew my weapon.

Lee leaned forward and twisted the doorknob. The door didn't move. Locked.

I heard a distinctive metallic noise.

"Gun," I said. We leaped aside. Gunfire erupted, but bullets failed to penetrate the solid wooden door. "Handgun, not a big hole gun. Nine mil maybe," I muttered. "Or the door has a steel core?"

"We passed through fire doors at the beginning of this corridor. Looked like they separated the offices from the main factory area," Sam said, his voice low. "Think this door is just solid old wood."

He could be right. Old factory. Fewer fire codes back in the day and probably no need for more fire doors.

Sam pumped the shotgun. We were about to find out if the door had a steel core or not.

Breaching rounds.

Not a time for being subtle.

He stepped up. I covered my ears and turned away.

"Knock knock!" Sam hollered as he fired two rounds at the hinges of the door and then one at the lock. The smell of gunpowder filled the air as wood splintered. Sam gave the door a kick. It fell inward. Crashing to the ground. Kurt and Lee were first across the smashed-up door. In the corner of the room, huddled under a blanket, was a human shape.

"Show me your hands?" I yelled at the quivering form.

Kurt and Sam moved away, following sounds through a hole in the wall.

One hand came out from under the blanket, then the second. Small hands on small wrists. The blanket fell off her thin shoulders, exposing a short strappy top. The young woman remained crouched in the corner, the blanket still covering most of her.

"Are you hurt?" I asked, stepping closer. I let the beam from my flashlight rest on her; she looked cold but where she lay was dry.

"No," she said. "I am Sonya."

An accent. Not American.

"What are you doing here?" I asked.

Lee moved up and pulled the blanket away. He stood her up and searched her for weapons. She wore very little, not much room for concealment. Barefoot and in need of a shower, decent clothes and a meal, by the look of her. I'd seen better-dressed bag ladies with more meat on their bones.

"This is where I live," she replied with a strange slow deliberation, as though reading a script, but the words had no meaning.

"And why are you in America?"

"I come from Croatia for better life."

Again the same slow deliberation. Learned responses?

"How's that working out for you?" I asked.

She didn't reply. Guess that question wasn't part of the script she'd learned.

Lee signaled. The girl was unarmed and carried no identification.

She sank to the cold ground, gathering the blanket around her. Lee moved to the other side of the room. His new position allowed him to watch me and the door.

A yell from Kurt spiraled out from the dark hole in the wall. Footsteps pounded over wet ground, moving toward us.

I turned to face the sound, mirroring Lee.

Kurt's voice rang out, "Stop. FBI!"

A person erupted from the gloom, a gun clearly visible. The woman under the blanket squeaked and curled up even smaller.

"Drop the weapon!" I aimed at the disheveled mess in front of me. "Drop it!"

The gun in the person's hand wobbled from side to side. From across the room, I could feel Lee's muscles tense as he assessed the situation. It took me a moment to realize it was a woman in front of us with a gun. The gun in her hand steadied.

"Drop it," Lee said.

She squeezed off a round, which flew over my head.

"Drop the weapon!" I said.

Her trigger finger moved again. I fired. The bullet slammed into her forehead. A fine spray erupted from the back of her head and hung in the damp air before drifting downward. She buckled, collapsing onto herself and sank into a dirty puddle.

"That went well," I muttered, holstering my weapon.

Kurt and Sam stepped into the room, dodging the body as they did so.

"There was no one else. But it looks like several people were living back there," Sam said. "They're in the wind."

Kurt looked at the dead woman, then at me. "Your handiwork?"

"Yeah, how'd you know?"

"Head shot ... you still worried about zombies?" He smiled up at me as he did the customary pulse check on the body.

"Zombies are no laughing matter," I replied. "One day you'll be thanking me for my head shots."

"She had a driver's license on her," Kurt said, handing

Sam a plastic card.

Sam looked at it, then passed it to Lee. "Is this Russian?"

"Yes, and it's her."

I turned to the huddled woman. "Do you know her?"

"Yes. She keeps me."

"Are you a prisoner?"

She frowned.

"Can you leave?"

She shook her head.

I took my phone out of my pocket and made a call. "It's me. My list for this afternoon. Crime scene techs, paramedics, coroner, scene guards, and notify Homeland. I suspect we found a woman who is a victim of trafficking."

"Coroner?" Sandra repeated.

"She had a guard too."

"Sending everything to your location." I heard her pause and take a breath. "Everyone okay?"

I smiled. "Delta A are all okay."

I knew what that was about. She wanted to ask about Sam. Their not-so-secret relationship looked like a long haul thing to me. It'd been a year since I first noticed something was going on.

I hung up.

"Wrap this up. Then we're off for the weekend," I said. "As soon as our people arrive, I'll head back with Kurt and get the case file updated."

Sam and Lee nodded.

"Good result, Conway," Kurt said. "We got a live one."

It felt too easy. Or I felt uneasy. I wasn't sure which.

Chapter Two

Rolling in the Deep

At Kurt's insistence, he and I invited the team and partners out for drinks. He'd suggested it as a good way to wind down after our day. We'd definitely had a *day*. I knew better. It was a cunning move on his part. The team wanted to get to know Mitch. No one was buying my "we're just friends" line. Least of all me. But that's what we were. Friends. Close friends. This was not something I was prepared to screw up. The uneasiness from the afternoon circled like a shark looking for a free feed. It would take some effort to let it go.

Mitch smiled as he opened the car door for me. "You're quiet. All right?"

"Yes," I replied, returning the smile. "A drink would be good."

"Come on then," he said, closing the door and pressing the beeper on his key chain. The car lights flashed as the doors locked and the alarm set.

Mitch and I walked into the bar. Lee met us near the door. He went to speak but nothing audible left his lips; his jaw dropped a little. Amused, I reached over and tapped his lower jaw, "Catching flies?"

He swallowed and grinned at me. "You look different. Nice skirt? I like your hair out like that."

"Yes, it's a skirt. Thanks, I think."

Mitch interceded, his hand outstretched. He and Lee shook firmly. "Lee? I'm Mitch. Pleased to meet you."

"You too. I'd say we've heard a lot about you, but we haven't," Lee replied, slapping Mitch on the back. "The rest of the gang will be along shortly."

I slid into a booth. "Where's Tara?"

Lee pointed to the bar. "Getting drinks, what are you drinking?"

"I'll go," Mitch said. He leaned in and asked, "Margarita?"

"Please," I replied and watched as he weaved his way through the throng of people to the bar.

Lee coughed. "You okay?"

"Of course." I dragged my eyes off Mitch and settled them on a grinning Lee. "Busy in here tonight."

A couple walking in the front door caught my eye. Sam and Sandra waved, understated but still a wave. Sandra came straight over and Sam went to the bar. Lee stood up and let Sandra sit down. She slid over until she was in front of me.

"Your idea?" she asked with a smile.

"Sort of. How's Sam?"

Her smile widened. "You don't mind?"

"As far as I can tell you've been together for a while and it certainly hasn't affected anyone's performance. Why would I mind?"

"You don't miss much, do you?"

"I try to take notice of what's going on around me." I leaned on my elbows and made direct eye contact. "*If* you were in the field with us I would have transferred you out so fast, your head would spin."

"Understood."

Tara handed Lee a drink and put hers on the table. Lee wandered off toward the door. I thought I saw Kurt. Guess he did too.

"Hey, Ellie, Sandra. Kurt just came in. Regular Delta A party here tonight," Tara said. "Is there a reason?" She nudged me with her elbow and grinned. "Something we should know?"

I shook my head. "Not what you're thinking. The boys want to meet Mitch. Kurt and I decided we should all get together. No secrets. This team is too tight for secrets and ... we've drifted a little after ..." I wanted to say the words but they wouldn't come. I tried again. "We've drifted a bit after losing Carla." I took a sharp breath. Nothing crashed down over me but relief. I caught Mitch's eyes across the room.

Everything is okay.

Tara smiled. "I see, this is a team-building-strengthening Delta A night out."

I leaned back and looked at Sandra. I wanted to talk to her on Monday but no time like the present. "Can we talk shop for a minute?"

She nodded. Tara disappeared.

"Problem?"

"Not at all. I've been authorized to offer you a permanent Delta A position, what you're doing now but just for us. B and C will get their own supporting agent."

A smile bounced around her lips and lit her eyes.

"Just this team?"

"Yes."

"Even without seeing the new contract, I'm in."

I intended to shake her hand but stood up, leaned over the table and hugged her instead. She's Delta A and we hug. "Thank you," I said. "You can tell the team if you'd like."

"Can you?"

"Sure. I'll do it tonight when everyone is settled."

I waved to Tara. She'd corralled the troops including Mitch and Kurt's girlfriend, Rachel. The booth was big but not big enough.

As they all arrived, I said, "We need a bigger table."

"Over there," Sam said, pointing to a large round table.

We gathered belongings and moved. I watched the interactions for a few minutes; jovial best described the atmosphere. It was nice to hear laughter. I knew that would change the minute I spoke.

"You all met Mitch?" I asked, glancing around the table. Nods and smiles. "Now, I have an announcement ..." I found it difficult to keep my expression neutral, especially with the tension that sprang from the group. Sam sat straighter. Kurt rocked back in his chair. Lee leaned toward me.

"There will be a statement from the Director regarding Owen's tentative hold on her job." Everyone focused, their mouths set in grim lines. "She did not willingly give information to La Ford. She was a victim of his technological prowess, as were we all."

"But—" Lee started.

I shook my head. "The official line is she keeps her job. But she will be under strict supervision and operate in a limited capacity until further notice."

I knew what they were thinking. We all saw the video footage where La Ford confessed his crimes and implicated her. How could she still have a job? Sometimes justice worked in mysterious ways.

"And?" Lee asked. "There's more isn't there?"

With a small nod, I carried on, "Some changes to Delta." Kurt's chair legs hit the floor with a bang. I stifled a smile. "Sandra will be joining Delta A permanently. No more sharing our best support agent with the other teams."

It took a few moments for the news to sink in.

"Sandra is joining us. You're not leaving?" Sam said, relief flooding his words.

"You don't get rid of me that easy," I replied. "And one more thing ... I'll pick up the tab tonight. Let's welcome Sandra to the team properly."

Sam threw his keys into the middle of the table; Lee and Kurt followed suit.

"Cabs then?" Sandra said.

"Looks that way," I replied. "Mitch?"

He smiled. "I have other plans."

Lee laughed. "You think that will wash?"

"I know it will," Mitch replied.

"I like this guy," Lee announced, getting up for another

round. "Chicky, a word."

I gathered the keys from the table and dumped them into my purse before following Lee. We stopped a few feet from the table.

"Problem?"

"He hasn't taken his eyes off you for longer than a few seconds since you two arrived," Lee said.

"Really?" There was genuine amazement in my voice and a smile on my face.

"Yes. Really. Best friend, huh?"

"Talked to Kurt, I see."

"You're just as bad as Mitch ..."

When Lee spoke, I realized I was looking at Mitch.

Yeah, I'm just as bad. Friends.

Back at the table, Kurt said, "That old factory today was a damn creepy place. Would make a good horror movie set."

Lee and Sam agreed. I gave a warning shake of my head but it was too late. Lee launched into a rundown of our day. I wished he hadn't.

"Ellie pulled out another of her famous head shots," Lee said raising his glass. "Thanks for keeping us safe, Chicky."

Mitch tapped my foot with his. I looked at him. A puzzled expression greeted me.

"Head shot?"

Kurt interjected, his voice brimming with amusement, "Conway doesn't like the idea of zombies. One too many horror movies." He chuckled quietly and slammed another shot of Sambuca. "Head shot or no shot, right, Conway?"

I wondered how many Sambuca shooters he'd had. Not like Kurt to make light of a death.

"Something like that," I replied. I really didn't want to talk about the day. I sipped my margarita and let the tequila swaddle my insides in warmth.

The expression on Mitch's face told me this was not going well.

A song came from nowhere but the lyrics morphed. "It's worse than that. She's dead, Ellie." I fell head first into the Star Trekkin' music video. "We come in peace. Shoot to kill." I shook the images from my head. Mitch's eyes locked onto mine.

"You never mentioned your day," he said. "No wonder you're quiet. Sure you're all right?"

"Uh huh. It was a day."

A parade of death floated past my eyes. I swished the images with my internal window wipers and watched as they dripped from the edge of the blade. Live by the sword ... expect to get shot.

Two hours later Delta had settled in, telling stories that became wilder with every drink. I leaned back in my chair. Mitch sat across the table from me. My ankles rested on his. He smiled at me and I smiled back.

"Other plans, huh?" I whispered.

"Absolutely," he replied, his eyes never leaving mine. "You ready?"

Subtle.

"Yep, let me make sure this tab is on my card and we'll escape."

I slipped away and returned before the team noticed. Mitch stood and said goodbye. We walked away together. Side by side, not touching. Eyes followed us to the door as I knew they would. Mitch opened the door, which drew a collective cheer from my team. I waved as we left.

He opened the car door too but no one witnessed his chivalry, just me.

"Home?" Mitch asked.

"Please."

He smiled. I'd seen that smile before. Only this time it felt completely different.

***

He pulled the car into the entrance of the driveway, and the gates swung open. Before we reached the front door, the gates closed.

"You're trapped now, you know that right?" I said.

"I can live with that."

Me too. Lines blurred right in front of me. Why were there lines? Mom's voice filled my head, "Because friends don't sleep together." Advice from Mom on that subject I did not need. I snarled inwardly, you never managed to heed your own advice and expect me to do so? I pressed my key code into the panel by the front door. Mitch's car alarm beeped as he followed me inside. Mom's voice disappeared.

Maybe there is a God?

"Drink?" I asked, flicking lights on as I walked down

the hallway to the kitchen.

"Tequila," he replied.

My heart pounded. Butterflies wearing boots stomped around in my stomach; my hands shook. Deep breath. I reached into the cabinet and pulled out a bottle of tequila.

"Fruit bowl in the dining room, Mitch. Limes, please."

Gone a few seconds, he returned to two shots sitting on the counter and a knife waiting for the limes. I set a saltshaker next to the knife.

Mitch quartered the limes.

Two shots later, I was less nervous and more relaxed, leaning across the counter between us.

"Okay?" Mitch asked.

"Yep," I replied.

"You could be closer ..."

"Dangerous."

"Wrong?"

"Didn't say it was wrong." I smiled. "We could go into the living room," I suggested, which wasn't what I wanted to say at all.

"All right," Mitch replied, picking up the bottle. I took the glasses and led the way.

"Computer. Listen." I said from the doorway. "Music. Adele."

"Good choice," Mitch replied and set the bottle on the coffee table next to the pack of condoms and prescription, obviously left by Kurt. He'd called in for a chat after work. My heart sank.

Not funny, Kurt. Not funny at all.

A few hours ago, I'd pointed out to Kurt that the table was a coffee table, not a tea table, and now it was a party table.

Jeez.

He paused then picked up the pack. "Forethought?" A smile filled his voice then faded. "Something I should know? Someone I should know about?"

Words eluded me for a moment. "Ah, no, Kurt's idea of a joke?" I pushed the pack aside.

Mitch's smile returned. "You'd tell me?"

"Of course."

I couldn't think of a thing I didn't or wouldn't tell him. Sometimes I neglected the details of my day but with good reason. My day isn't always the sort of conversation people want to have. Sometimes it's me that doesn't want to have it.

Mitch poured me another drink. "You didn't tell me about the shooting today," he said, looking at me sideways.

"I didn't want to talk about it."

It wasn't that big a deal: I still lie to myself.

"You'd tell me if you were seeing someone?"

Insecure? Mitch? Really?

"Yes. I would. It's not going to happen."

"It might," he replied.

'Rolling in the Deep' flowed from the stereo, filling all the crevices of the room.

I sat on the couch next to Mitch. We were angled

toward each other, comfortable, smiling, one arm resting on the back of the couch, the fingertips of his hand touching mine for a moment before our fingers entwined. Warmth flowed from his fingers up my arm.

Breathe.

Breathe.

"Mitch?"

"Yes."

"You know ..."

He nodded. His smile was back. "Your eyes are addictive. They sparkle when you smile."

Self-control.

Masses of it.

On tap.

If I kept telling myself that, nothing would screw this up.

Chapter Three.

Rumor Has It

Sunlight slithered through a gap in the curtains. Silence filled the house. My phone rang. Rang was a misnomer. My phone blared Bon Jovi's "Have a Nice Day" as it vibrated on the nightstand. I rolled over and picked it up.

Work. Welcome to Monday. Already? Didn't seem fair. Could've sworn it was drinks at TGI Friday's yesterday.

Crap.

I tapped on the green icon on the screen. "SSA Conway."

"Agent Troy is in your office, ma'am. He insists it's important."

I groaned. I stood Delta A down for the weekend and now it was over. Agent Troy. Mentoring was never going to be a good thing for me.

"I'm coming in. Might take an hour or so," I said. Sounds of life came from the guest bedroom across the hall. "Tell Troy to wait."

I hung up and dropped my phone on the floor. It thudded onto the carpet. Rolling onto my back, I lay still and listened. My phone must've woken Mitch. Or maybe he'd set his phone alarm. It was Monday, the weekend now just a memory, and he had work too. Two minutes later, I threw the covers back and hurried into my bathroom. The day waited. The smile on my face disappeared in the steam that fogged the mirror.

The hot water helped wash away the tiredness. I didn't sleep longer than an hour all night, too aware that Mitch was in the next room. It took a lot of self-control to stay in my bed. If being determined not to screw up what we had meant no sleep, then so be it. I yawned. Extra strong coffee was imperative.

***

I sat at my desk five minutes before Justin Troy stood in front of me, desperate to share the cause of the phone call with me. I did my best to hold on to my great weekend as I listened.

"Hang on a minute. What are you telling me?" I looked up at the young agent standing in front of my desk.

"Ma'am, I don't know, ma'am." For a split second, I thought he might salute me. "But something feels wrong."

God, he was young. I wondered if I was ever that young as I looked into his solemn brown eyes.

"Okay. Walk me through this." I flapped a hand at him. "Pull up a chair."

He dragged a chair closer to my desk and sat in it.

"Five days ago I came across images on a surveillance feed. Since then I've been seeing the same three women on various feeds from all over Washington."

"Show me." He opened a file on his tablet and handed the device to me. I flicked through the images, noting date stamps and locations. A few minutes later, I handed the device back. "Who are they?"

"I don't know yet."

Learning curve coming up.

"You should know who you are dealing with by now. You've been watching these women for five days."

"Yes, ma'am. Sorry, ma'am."

Sharp bend ahead.

"Could be tourists minding their own business."

His eyes flashed at me. Whoa. He didn't think so.

"Do you think that?"

I smiled. "You know what ... follow this. Let me know where it goes. Keep me informed. Don't piss anyone off."

"Ma'am."

I sighed. "Enough with the ma'am already. SSA is better."

"Hey, you" was better than ma'am.

He nodded. "SSA."

"First, find out who they are and where they hail from. Then follow that until you know why they're visiting places like The Department of Energy. And while you're at it, I want to know how the hell they got past the barriers and into the structure."

"Yes, SSA."

"Away you go. If you need anything that you can't find, ask Sandra. She has magic fingers and ways of finding information that we can only dream of." I smiled at the nervous-looking young man. "Agent Troy, you have twenty-four hours to bring me a reason for these women to be in a high-security area and on your radar."

He pushed the chair back as he stood, nodded and

hurried away.

I summoned Sam. He lurched through the doorway with a grin on his face.

"You wanted me?"

"Not really. It's just … this mentor program is great but goddamn, they're young."

Sam rocked on his heels. "I hear you, Chicky, I hear you."

"Agent Troy is looking into some suspicious behavior by three women in various places around Washington."

"Anything to it?"

"Could be. They've been photographed in places they shouldn't have been, over the course of five days. I'll let him run with it for twenty-four hours. If he finds something worth a closer look, then we'll help him."

"Okay."

I reached across my desk and picked up my cell phone just as it rang.

Picking up the phone before it rang was now a habit. Without looking, I tapped the screen and answered the call.

"Caine," I said.

"Ellie," he replied.

Knowing who was calling without looking was the new normal.

"Up for some traveling?"

"Sure, reason?"

I saw it hovering in the middle of the room. A head. Just a head. No body. Gruesome.

"Dismembered heads," Caine said. I imagined the corner of his mouth twitching in time with a stress twitch in his left eye.

"How many?" I could only see one, seemed smart to ask. Knowing I shouldn't be able to see any at all wasn't helping.

"Twenty," Caine replied.

"That's a lot of heads."

"And they're waiting for you in Wellington, New Zealand."

An American flag fell over the head I saw suspended in the air.

"Why?"

"Because that's where they are."

I smiled and rephrased the question. "Why *us*?"

"They're American. Or at least the ones identified so far are."

"We're packing," I replied.

"Sandra is making travel arrangements."

"Talk before we leave," I said and ended the call.

Sam waited.

"What's up?"

"We're going back to New Zealand."

"I'm up for it."

Not sure I am.

The country held too many memories and they all ended in screaming and pain; not me screaming but definitely my pain. Although my most recent trip was a lot more fun than the previous two, but there was still the whole dead-body-on-the-beach thing. A sigh dropped from my lips.

Cursed? Maybe.

"Can you get the team in here for a briefing? Caine should have sent the file through by now."

"Yes." He walked toward the door then stopped, turned to face me and said, "And the other thing?"

"I'm sure I'll cope. Me mentoring a young agent, what could go wrong?"

"Chicky Babe ..." he replied with a subtle shake of his head.

"Work," I replied and shooed him away.

I checked for the case notes from Caine and shoved the mentoring thing away. Not an issue. We were leaving the country.

Can't mentor from New Zealand.

I knew that wasn't right. Mentoring didn't have to be in person – we could FaceTime or Skype for that matter, or we could implement good ol' fashioned phone calls.

Linking the waiting file to the team, I started reading. Not much to go on.

I noted Faye's name, the detective attached to the case in Wellington. My eyes flicked to the clocks on the wall as I picked up the phone receiver and pressed buttons. Almost a minute later, I heard Faye's voice.

"Faye, it's Ellie Conway. You got something for me?"

"I do, Ellie. Not the best of presents, mind you."

"Fill me in?" I scrolled through the notes on the computer hoping Faye had some insight not included.

"With pleasure." She paused for a moment and I heard a door close. "Last night I got a call from customs. They were doing a routine search of a container ship in the harbor and a customs dog indicated a large box in the ship's hold. No one seemed to know anything about it."

"Manifest?"

"Not listed."

"Well, that's quite the oversight. And the heads are in it?"

"Yes, twenty heads. Male and female." She swallowed audibly. "Some things you can never unsee or unsmell."

"Not frozen then?"

"They may have been once but not when we found them. They were sealed in heavy opaque plastic and some bright spark cut one of the bags open."

Ewww.

"The ship came from?"

"Indonesia."

"Nationality of the heads?"

"We've identified nine so far, using facial recognition software. They are American citizens. We still need DNA confirmation."

"Last known whereabouts?"

"So far, of the nine people we've identified, two were last known to be living in Algeria, one in Saudi Arabia. The others were last known to live in various European countries. France, Italy, England, Spain, and a few in Germany."

"That's quite a scattering."

Americans, but not living in America. Curious.

"You're telling me."

"Do you know how or when they died?" I asked, swinging in my chair.

"Another oddity," Faye replied. "I can't find any death certificates."

"That's not good."

"Similar to what I said, but I used expletives," Faye said.

"Estimation of how long they've been dead."

"The ship took three weeks to get here and they were possibly frozen at some point. Could be a month, could be longer."

"If these aren't natural deaths then some people somewhere are missing family and friends ..." I couldn't imagine how they'd be natural deaths. People tend to die with their heads attached. Well, mostly.

"Twenty is a lot of missing people," Faye said. "You'd think someone would notice."

"Why were they on the ship? Where were they going?"

"No idea. The box wasn't listed on the manifest at all. I'll let you know what our forensics people pull off it by way of evidence." Faye cleared her throat. "The label on the box said basketballs."

"Someone had a sense of humor," I replied and smiled as Kurt walked into my office.

"We'll be on our way as soon as we get a flight. Looking forward to seeing you again."

"Send me flight details. I'll pick you up."

"Will do," and hung up.

Kurt sat in a chair reading his tablet. His eyebrows rose as he looked at me.

"What's with you and dismembered bodies?"

I shrugged. "The box wasn't addressed to me. Caine just said we were investigating it. That makes a nice change."

"Yes, it does."

Sam and Lee entered one at a time.

"Interesting case," Lee mumbled, taking a seat. "Heads. Makes a nice change from hands, feet and ass."

"Not addressed to me, not me being photographed holding body parts," I replied. "Let's not forget that."

Sam grinned. "We're never going to forget."

Sandra knocked on the doorframe then walked over to my desk.

"E-tickets already sent to your phones. Hard copies can be picked up from my desk on your way out. Visas approved. State Department is aware and will assist with whatever you need."

A shimmering image appeared, suspended in the air, above everyone. I watched with fascination: two young women escorted to a waiting van by four balaclava-clad men. The women appeared unwilling but weren't struggling; I couldn't see their faces. The men doing the herding were armed and everyone had heads. As they pushed one of the women into the back of the van, she looked up and I recognized her as the woman from the abandoned factory. The second young woman hit the man holding her arm and made a break for freedom. Short-lived. Another male caught her and forced her into the van affording me a glimpse of her face. The women could've been sisters. The image faded from left to right.

"Ellie?" Kurt said.

I blinked. Sandra watched me. Kurt leaned over my desk. Sam and Lee frowned. Something was up.

"What?"

"Did you hear Sandra?" Kurt asked.

"I don't know. What'd she say?"

He stood up straight and ordered everyone from my office.

Really? Unnecessary.

He shut my door. "What happened?" Kurt asked, beckoning me to walk to him.

"I was thinking," I replied. "This is overkill. I'm okay."

"You weren't thinking, Ellie. You were looking at something. Watching something."

I steadied my writhing innards. "I'm okay, Kurt. Don't go all doc on me now. I am okay."

"It's part of my job description. In case you forgot, it is *Doctor* Henderson not just SSA Henderson."

There was no forgetting. Ever. His eyes penetrated mine. I felt them searching for clues, probing my brain, looking for a reason that made medical sense. I noticed his hand reach into his pocket.

"Take your hand out of your pocket. If that horrid little freaking flashlight of yours comes near my eyes, you will pay ..."

He smiled and left the flashlight in his pocket.

Wise man.

"Do you have a headache?"

"No."

"Holes in your vision?"

"No."

"Flashing lights?"

I smiled. "I'm okay. I promise."

He sighed. "Then what happened? Because from this side, it looked very like something I've seen before." He peered into my eyes harder. "In Lexington."

No, not Lexington.

"I'm not living in two worlds. My memory is intact." As far as I could ascertain.

"I'm waiting for your explanation."

I knew I had to tell him something. "A dragonfly. I saw a dragonfly."

He glanced around the room. "We're on the fifth floor and the windows are shut."

"Must've been outside, a shadow or something."

His eyes narrowed, disbelief flooded his voice, "A dragonfly? That's all?"

"Yeah."

Sure, that's all. Certainly didn't see two women forced into a van at gunpoint. That'd be nuts. Just like I didn't recognize the woman getting into the van as the one we rescued on Friday.

"You got some migraine Synergy with you?"

"Yes."

"Maybe you should use it. Just in case."

There was no point arguing. I took the vial from my drawer, tipped a few drops into my hands, rubbed them together, cupped my hands and inhaled the vapors. It was a little trick I learned to make the inhalation more effective. If I told him what I thought I saw, he'd schedule an emergency MRI. Synergy was easier.

"You want to continue the briefing?" Kurt asked.

"We'll do it later. We've got seventeen hours of flight time. We can do it then." I screwed the top onto the Synergy and dropped it into my drawer. "Send everyone home to pack."

"You too, go home."

Kurt opened the door. He paused and turned back to me. "You're sure you're all right?"

"Absolutely."

No, not at all.

Chapter Four.

Turning Tables.

It was early evening when I lay on my bed with my phone in my hand in front of me.

Mitch smiled at me from the screen as I told him about our upcoming trip.

"New Zealand again?"

"Yep."

"Don't suppose it will be as much fun as our trip?"

"Nope, don't suppose it will. For one thing, I won't be in Marlborough and for another you won't be there."

His smile widened. "It was good, wasn't it?"

Yes, it was.

I nodded and hid a yawn behind my hand.

"Tired, El?"

"Little bit." Another yawn, "Might be a messy case." I didn't want to think about New Zealand or the case. I wanted distraction. Desperation crept in. "How's work?"

"Really, you want one of my work stories?"

"Yeah, go on."

"Remember the other day I said my printer wasn't working?"

"Uh huh."

Mitch launched into a story about how the IT guy came to fix his printer. I covered a yawn with my hand but he caught me.

"Am I boring you?"

"No, life is short and I was wondering if is there was point to this story ... and please tell me it's not that the IT guy fixed your printer."

He smiled, "Have you heard the one about the pig?"

"The pig who fixed the printer?"

"No, the pig who walked into a bar."

"Enlighten me." Anything is better than more work stories.

"A little pig walks into a bar, orders a drink and then asks directions to the bathroom. The barman tells him and the pig hurries off to relieve himself. A second little pig comes in, orders a drink and asks for the bathroom. Again the barman tells the pig where to go and the pig hurries away. A third little pig then appears and orders a drink. 'I suppose you'll want to know where the toilets are,' says the barman. 'No,' replies the pig. 'I'm the one that goes wee-wee-wee all the way home.'"

Laughter trickled over my phone, covering Mitch in sparkling chuckles.

"That was much better than one of your work stories!"

"I thought that was a good one," he replied with a laugh. "I have another ..."

"Go on then."

"A redheaded man walks into a bar and sits next to another redheaded man. He orders a Guinness. The second redheaded man turns to him. 'I'm guessing from that accent you're from Dublin?' he asks, in an Irish brogue.

'Of course!' the first guy exclaims, 'here, bartender, get this guy a Guinness, too.'

Their exchange continues.

First: Lemme ask you, what street did you grow up on?

Second: St. Catherine Street. And you?

First: St. Catherine Street, same as you!

Second: Here, bartender, get this guy a Jameson! What school did you go to?

First: St. Joseph's Boy's Academy.

Second: Son of a bitch, I went to St. Joe's too! Bartender, get this guy a Jameson!

This continues, as they find they had the same teachers and knew the same neighborhood kids. They get louder and drunker until a guy at the other end of the bar asks the bartender, 'What's up with those two?'

The bartender shrugs and says, 'It's the O'Shaughnessy twins, they're drunk again.'"

"No more, Mitch! I don't think I can cope with another joke."

"When do you leave?" he asked changing the subject.

I picked up the paperwork next to me and read it.

"Flying into San Fran tomorrow." I liked SFO more than LAX.

"When do you get to SFO?"

"Nine in the morning." I heard his fingers tapping on keys.

"You're not flying out again until three?" He'd already checked out our connecting flight. "Presuming you're on the next flight to New Zealand, the three p.m."

"Yeah, that's the one. Long day at the airport."

I smiled. It was impossible not to; he was smiling at me.

The screen in my hand blurred. Mitch's face fell apart and reassembled as four men forced a young woman to sign a piece of paper. Beyond the men, another young woman cowered by a wall. The same women again.

Mitch's voice shot through the image. Cracks appeared. The people crumbled into a pile of pixels.

"Hey! Ellie!"

"Uh huh," I replied, shaking my head to dislodge the last remnants of the picture.

"I lost you for a few seconds. You okay?"

"Of course."

"Where were you?"

"Wishing you were coming to New Zealand with me," I said with a smile.

"You are all right?"

"Yes. Just daydreaming about hanging out with you."

His smile faltered then cemented. "That's always fun. No doubt about it. But that's not what that was ..."

Crap. With powers of observation like his, he should be in law enforcement.

"I don't know what it was. I saw something. Probably nothing," I said. Hoping it sounded like nothing, because I wasn't convinced.

"Are you really okay?"

"Yep, I'm okay."

"We'll talk soon. And we'll talk about whatever that

was," Mitch replied. He was still smiling but didn't look convinced.

"Talk in a few days," I said.

"Looking forward to it," Mitch replied. "I'll have more work stories for you by then."

"Can't wait."

I hung up, reached into my nightstand and hooked out a notebook and pen.

Twice in one afternoon, I'd seen things I shouldn't be able to see. Twice I'd seen the same women. Writing it down seemed smart. Starting with the women, men with guns and the nondescript white van. I wrote fast. When I read the paragraphs back, I knew it was something. I also knew it somehow connected to the heads. But how and who were the men and why take the women? As usual I had more questions than answers.

I read it again. Nothing jumped out and screamed. That was a blessing. There's no telling how my hallucinations will manifest. As yet there'd been no screaming ones. No songs emerged as a soundtrack. I leaned back and closed my eyes. The pictures weren't random. A new case, then images – definitely linked. I just needed to figure out how. My eyes pinged open.

I scrolled through contacts in my phone and found the CI who'd called me with the tip-off about the factory and made a call. "Hey, it's Ellie. Can you talk?"

"Yes."

"What do you know about the woman at the factory?"

"Nothing. I told you everything."

"No, you didn't but you're going to. Meet me in forty minutes at Vienna Metro."

"I ... um ... I can't ... it's dangerous."

"Suit yourself, but this avenue of income is about to dry up."

He paused. I could almost hear his mind working. "All right. Jeez. Vienna Metro. Where exactly?"

"Up top. By the entrance to the platform."

I hung up, rolled off the bed and dragged on my boots. On my way out of the house, I made another phone call. "Kurt, Vienna Metro. Now."

"Why?"

"CI. Think he neglected to give me all the information regarding the factory."

"I'll see you there."

I parked my car and walked across the dark street to the entrance of the metro station in Vienna. From the corner of my eye, I saw Kurt walking toward me. Unmistakable even at night. He fell into step with me.

"Who is the CI?" Kurt asked.

"Arnie Arthur. His *friends*, using the term loosely, call him Double A."

"Slimy little guy who was mixed up with a trafficking ring a few years back?"

"That's him."

My eyes scanned the area as we crossed the covered walkway and entered the station. No sign of Double A. I'd planned to be there well before him. We stood with our backs against a wall, facing the entrance, waiting.

Ten minutes had passed before I saw a shape approach the doors at the far end of the walkway.

"We've got company," I said, pushing myself off the wall and standing straighter.

"I see," Kurt replied.

Watching Arnie zigzag across the walkway made me feel ill.

"Is he drunk?" I whispered to Kurt.

"Nope, don't think so. He's zigzagging, not staggering. Maybe he thinks he's being evasive."

I heard the smile in Kurt's voice.

"Hey, Arnie. Just walk," I called. "You look like a candidate for a short bus."

He stopped and stared at me.

Now what?

Glancing over his shoulder once, he started to run toward us. Kurt grabbed my arm and pulled me around the corner. I could see Arnie barreling toward our position.

"I don't like this," Kurt whispered.

Panic escalated on Arnie's face.

"Rob ..." He never finished his sentence. Arnie fell. Red mist billowed from him. His head smacked into the concrete with a sickening thud. Dust puffed into the air as bullets hit the wall near us.

"Bad," I muttered. "Very bad."

I seated my Glock firmly in my right hand. Gunshots came from the end of the walkway then from the windows. Glass flew into the internal spaces. At least there were no people around. We needed another way out. Stairs. I tapped Kurt's shoulder.

"There are stairs, over there." I pointed to a hallway that led to toilets. A rumble came from below us. A train.

Oh crap. Trains mean commuters.

Which meant buses and taxis would pull up any minute by the parking lot. From the direction of the platform, I heard, "Orange line. Vienna. Doors opening, right side."

People would spew onto the concourse any minute. How many people would get off the late train, I had zero clue. No civilian casualties seemed a good rule to go by.

More bullets hit the wall. A few rounds flew past us into the great beyond. No cover. We'd have to cross the gunfire to get to the stairs.

Crap. Pinned down. Not ideal. What about into the station and down to the platform? Same problem but more cover.

"Can you see the shooter?" Kurt asked.

"No. No target."

"Parking lot. Rifle," Kurt said. "Whoever it is, they're sure not using a handgun."

"We're fucked. Calling in backup," I said, leaning hard against the wall as another round flew into the open space in front of us. "We need to stop people coming up here from the platform."

Kurt nodded. I made a call to SWAT.

"What's my favorite Special Agent up to?" Andrews asked as he recognized my voice.

"Oh, you know, being shot at by some dickwad with a rifle at Vienna Metro."

"You alone?"

"With Henderson."

"Watch your six, Conway, cavalry is inbound."

I hung up and shoved my phone back in my pocket.

"We good?" Kurt asked as another round hit the wall.

"They're coming."

"You reckon we can make it to the stairs and get out?" Kurt leaned out from the wall. Another round blasted by. I pushed him back. Another round fired. Different angle.

"Depends whether you want to end up as Swiss cheese or not." I watched the walkway. "I think there are two shooters."

I heard people. Walking. Talking. Bustling along. No clue what they were walking into, just keen to get home.

Taking a deep breath, I swung out from my covered position and fired two rounds down the tunnel, jumping back beside Kurt before return volleys smashed the last of the glass in the windows. Now all the disembarking passengers knew there was something wrong. I hoped they'd immediately go back down to the platform. What I hoped and what people did were often at odds.

Footsteps kept coming. More rounds smashed into the wall sending dust and plaster flying.

I yelled, "Federal Agents. Go back down to the platform!"

The footsteps became stumbles and panic.

"Calmly, go back!" Kurt hollered. "Keep down, take

care of each other."

Panicked screams and cries wafted into the night.

I checked my watch. An eerie silence fell as the commuters descended to the safety of the platform below.

We waited. Every few minutes, more bullets fired in our direction.

Tiresome.

"What do you suppose Arnie meant by Rob?" I wondered aloud.

"Know any Robs?" Kurt asked leaning next to me.

"Not that I can think of. Rob. He's never mentioned anyone called Rob. What was he trying to tell me? Rob. Robert. Robbie. Robber. Nope, coming up blank."

"We'll grab his cell phone when we can, might be a Rob in that somewhere."

I nodded. "Worth a look."

Rotor blades thwacked the air outside. A bright light illuminated the interior of the building we were in. Gunfire erupted. Semi-automatic. Rifle shots. More semi-automatic fire. Booted feet ran, dark shapes headed toward us down the walkway, flashlights almost blinded me. Familiar voices and sounds brought a level of comfort and security that few outsiders understood. Men in tactical gear equal safety in my world.

"Conway!" Andrews called.

"Down here," I yelled back.

Feet pounded the concrete floor, double time.

"You good?" Andrews asked, coming to a stop in front

of us. Men on either side of him scanned the area for potential trouble.

"We're fine. Thanks. Civilians down on the platform."

"I'll send a couple of men down to explain and make sure everyone's okay," he said. He pressed his shoulder and gave orders to his team. A few seconds later his attention turned back to us. "You need anything?"

"Just to get to the dead guy," Kurt replied.

"Go for it," Andrews replied. "Both shooters have been detained."

Kurt hurried to the body as I watched from where I stood. He patted Arnie's pockets. Removing a wallet, cell phone, car keys ... and a little baggie. He held the baggie up to the minimal light.

"Crystal meth," he said. "Arnie was a user."

That was news. Or that was new. Or someone wanted us to think he was a user. The way things were going, I suspected the latter.

"Who are the shooters?" I asked.

"No idea. No doubt you'll find out once you get them back for questioning," Andrews said.

My phone rang. I knew it was Mitch. I wrestled the phone from my pocket, walked away a few feet and answered his call.

"You all right?"

There was no stopping my smile.

"Strange thing to ask."

"There was a disruption in the force," he replied. From anyone else that would've been weird, from Mitch it felt right.

"I'm okay. Shouldn't you be asleep?"

"I nearly was, then something happened and all I could see was you."

I swallowed hard.

"I'll tell you about it tomorrow. Meanwhile, go to sleep. There won't be any more disruptions in the force tonight."

Mitch laughed softly. "As long as you're okay."

"I am. Goodnight."

"'Night, El."

With my phone back in my pocket, I rejoined Andrews and Kurt. Neither commented on my obviously personal call. Smart men.

Chapter Five.

Set Fire to the Rain

"Houston we have a problem," I mumbled sitting behind my desk and firing up my laptop. "Why kill my CI?"

Kurt watched me from the couch in my office. "Can't answer that."

"They can, the shooters. We'll let them sit for a bit then go have a chat."

Kurt smiled. "Coffee?"

"You buying?" I glanced at him.

He nodded. "More fetching, we'll have to make do with the overcooked coffee from the break room." Kurt stood up, smoothed his suit jacket and left the room.

He returned bearing our coffee mugs containing a black liquid impersonating coffee. Unpleasant but caffeine loaded. It'd have to do.

Twenty minutes later we were in the first interview room with candidate number one. I dropped a file on the table.

"Jan Trudenca," I said. He didn't look up, his gaze held by a small mark on the table surface. "We need to have a little talk about Arnie Arthur and his demise." I flipped open the folder and spread out photos of Arnie, dead.

Trudenca said nothing.

Spinning the folder to face me, I read from the sheet of paper inside. "Jan Trudenca. Thirty-four years old. Born in Warsaw, Poland. Family immigrated to the USA when you were five, making their home in New Jersey. Your father is a doctor, your mother a nurse. You have three siblings. All younger. Two sisters and a brother. Both sisters are in medical school. Your brother died in a car crash two years ago. You were driving."

I looked at him. This time he made eye contact. "Killing your brother must be hard to live with."

His eyes sought the mark on the table once more. His expression gave nothing away.

I carried on. "You served eighteen months of a three-year prison sentence for aggravated robbery when you were twenty-two."

Nothing.

"Stand up," I instructed.

He did, fixing his eyes on the wall behind me. I gave the table a shove, moving it out of the way.

"Sit."

He sat in his chair. I grabbed another chair and dragged it over to sit in front of him.

"Now, let's talk."

As soon as I spoke, he pulled his feet under the chair, hooking them around the legs. He ran one hand through this hair, then pulled at the neck of his tee shirt with the same hand before dropping it into his lap. Not as cool calm and collected as he first appeared.

"Your partner is talking," I said. "He's having a nice long chat with my partner about how who you work for and why you shot Arnie and fired on us."

"Bullshit."

"You wish." I paused, listening to Kurt speaking via the comms link I wore in my ear. His partner was indeed talking. "He's quite the Chatty Cathy."

Trudenca lifted his head and stared at me.

"I want a lawyer."

Crap! An internal snarl bounced off the walls of my skull.

"Great, I'll arrange that for you now." I stood up, picked up the file and photos from the table and left the room.

Kurt met me outside the door.

"He wants his lawyer," I said.

"His buddy was too stupid to ask. We have information but still don't know who hired them. Ashwyn Cox is saying Trudenca was the one who took the job and he didn't tell Cox who hired them. All Cox knows is they were told to take out Arnie Arthur before he met you in Vienna. They got extra if they killed you."

"Nice."

"How'd they know Arnie was meeting me?"

"That I don't know. Cox didn't know. His information was limited."

I was beginning to see why. He couldn't be trusted to keep his mouth shut.

"Did he know a Rob?"

"No."

"I'm calling the DA. If Cox and Trudenca took a contract to kill Arthur and were offered extra cash for killing me in the State of Virginia ... we may be able to put the death penalty on the table." My experience is that people tend to talk when faced with the death penalty.

"Extra cash for the death of a Federal agent sounds like a contract hit to me," Kurt said. "I'll make the call to the District Attorney."

Kurt and I walked back to our offices. He left me at the door to mine and went to make the calls. I swung my door open to find Agent Troy waiting for me.

"Can I help you?" I asked, moving past him and sitting at my desk.

"Yes, ma'am ... I mean SSA. I ... have something to show you," he said, passing me his tablet.

"Have you been home?" I asked, leaning back in my chair with his tablet in my hands.

"No, SSA."

I smiled. Maybe he'd make a good agent. He seemed dedicated enough. I viewed everything he'd found. Unease filled me again. Unease was the new normal.

"This is starting to look like tradecraft," I said, reaching for the phone on my desk as I checked the clock on the wall. Late. "Or it feels like tradecraft with a smattering of tourist thrown in to throw off the casual onlooker."

I stretched my arm and pressed a series of numbers. It was too late to expect Iain to be in his office, so I called him at home. A few rings later, his answer machine kicked in.

"It's me. Pick up."

The phone clicked.

"What's up?"

"One of my agents has found something you need to look at."

I glanced up to see Troy smile proudly. He stopped when he saw me looking at him.

"You in your office?"

"Yes."

"I'll be right over."

I hung up and spoke to Troy. "Get comfortable. He won't be long."

The dark night beyond the windows of my office captured the light from within and swallowed it whole.

I picked the phone up again and made another call. I knew Caine was still in his office. He was almost always in his office, or a meeting; dedicated. The FBI was his life and his family.

"Change of plans, I've got something here. We're talking national security."

Caine snapped, "I need someone on the ground in New Zealand."

"Lee and Sam can handle it. I want Kurt with me."

Not so much want as need him with me, there was something very odd going on in my head and for me to admit that meant it was very strange indeed.

"Done. Get them on that plane first thing. I want a full briefing on this new issue A-sap."

"As soon as I know what this is, you'll get it."

Sam rocked through my doorway. Didn't even need to

use the bat signal, guess his trouble radar was active. He should have been home packing or sleeping or something.

"Chicky?"

"You and Lee are on the flight. Troy here has uncovered something sticky. Kurt and I will stay." I decided not to mention our evening. Until I knew for sure, Arnie's death and the shooters were a different situation. I felt my stomach roil.

That's not evidence.

"Okay. We'll see you when we get back."

"Stay in touch."

Sam grinned. "See you on the other side."

"Sam?"

"Yeah?"

"There's something hinky with the head thing. Extra care."

He tipped his head to one side and looked at me. "Song?"

"Not this time, just call it gut instinct. Almost feels like we're being distracted."

"We'll be careful." He straightened his head, a thoughtful expression in his eyes. "If you're right, then you and Kurt ..." He didn't finish his thought. He didn't need to.

"The woman from the factory, where is she?"

"Immigration and Customs Enforcement have her. She's an illegal."

"ICE. Homeland. Campbell is with Homeland now."

"So I heard. What's with the interest in the woman?"

"I can't explain it. But you should talk to her. It might have something to do with the heads."

"All right. I will. I'll try and get to her before we leave."

"Good."

"Eyes wide open, Chicky."

"Alert and safe."

"Always," Sam replied and left.

Troy crossed his legs then uncrossed them.

"Go get a coffee if you want," I said as I opened a new case file. "I wouldn't say no either. Black, strong, go."

He disappeared. I felt a smile settle on my lips. This mentoring thing might not be so bad. A few seconds later, I went out to Sandra's desk.

"Might be a long night, you up for it?" I said. There wasn't really room for debate but I was willing to listen to any concerns or issues posed.

"Without question, O fearless leader."

"You already said goodbye to Sam?"

"Yes. He'll call before they take off."

"Great. This could be a long night."

"I'm here, just let me know what you need."

I walked back to my office and made the most of Troy's absence by building a case file. By the time he got back with coffee, the file was ready to go: everything he'd come across so far included, and some of my own hurriedly sourced information.

Having friends in the State Department hurried a few queries along.

"Coffee, SSA," Troy said setting the take-out cup on my desk.

"Thanks," I replied motioning him to sit. "I've added you to the new case file so you can access the information and work within the file." My eyes rose over the laptop screen. "Do you know who these women are?"

"Yes. I tracked them back to their entry into the United States."

I knew that. But as far as I could tell, he hadn't gone beyond that. They entered via Canada on New Zealand passports. There was a beginning to this story and it needed investigating.

"Have you seen the airport footage?"

He frowned. "No, SSA."

"Would you like to?"

"Yes, SSA."

I swiveled my laptop to face him. "Press enter when you're ready. The highlighted file follows them from their origin airport all the way through to La Guardia a week ago."

He watched in silence. When he was done, he looked up at me.

"They weren't flagged at all, at any point," he said with a small sigh.

"Nope. Would their behavior trigger anything in you?" I asked. I'd seen the footage. Nothing stood out but something wasn't right. As a teaching tool, the video seemed innocent and useless. My gut said otherwise.

Troy shook his head. "What does that mean?"

I didn't know if Troy's question required an answer or not. Being his mentor meant I should explain if in any doubt. "Either they're very good, it was an oversight, or they're tourists."

"Which do you think?" Troy asked. This time he wanted an answer.

"They're close. The blonde women are in protection mode, and that indicates the dark-haired woman is important to them."

"What does that mean?"

"I can't answer that at this point." Leaning forward, I pulled the video back and replayed a section. "Look, here," I said pointing. The dark-haired woman and one blonde woman stood waiting at Toronto International Airport. "She how she's standing?" I pointed to the brunette.

"Leaning on a wall with her ankles crossed and she's looking at her phone," Troy commented.

"She's secure, safe, feeling good and trusts her traveling companions."

"All that from one image," Troy whispered.

"Feet don't lie. Standing like probably means she doesn't feel any sort of threat. She's not in a ready position, she can't move easily to evade or attack." I made a mental note to get Troy on one of our in-house body language courses.

"But the blonde has a different stance."

"That's right. Right foot forward, left foot back, legs apart. She's not as relaxed." I played it again. "She's alert and ready."

"What could this be?" Troy asked.

"One person relaxed, the other constantly looking for trouble," I replied. "Trust and protection. The blonde's job is to protect her and the brunette trusts her to do just that."

I watched Troy's face, wishing I could see his legs. Legs and feet don't lie. They're governed by the limbic brain, not the thinking brain. Faces lie or mask. Game face. Feet don't.

"So the dark-haired woman is someone who needs protection."

"Yes."

He watched some more. "Do you think they have connections here?"

"Yes, I think so. What sort of connections, I don't know. But I'm in a betting mood and my money is on them having people on the ground that they know."

His hand reached out to the laptop. I heard a key press. Then again. And again.

"SSA?"

"Problem?"

"The file disappeared."

The video was supposed to be streaming from the airline site.

I spun my laptop back so I could see the screen. A black square and an orange traffic cone marked the spot where the file should've been.

"Erased," I muttered. "Not good."

I picked up my phone and called Sandra.

"Hey, a file just got deleted from an airline site, can you work some magic?"

"I'll certainly try. Email the deets."

Four keystrokes later.

"Done," I said.

"I'll get on it. Back to you shortly." Sandra hung up.

Chapter Six.

I'll Be Waiting

Campbell knocked on my door and entered without waiting for a response.

"How's it going?" I asked, looking up from my laptop. "This is Agent Justin Troy. Troy, Iain Campbell."

They shook hands then Iain grabbed a chair and set it next to me.

"Rolling out favors in all directions for the FBI tonight," Iain said with a smile. "Sam wanted to talk to the woman you found."

I nodded, pleased that Sam made the call.

"Got something I want you to see." I crossed my fingers.

"Show me."

"Files are being deleted. Pretty much as soon as I see it, it's deleted. Sandra is on it." I clicked the mouse button. "But these I downloaded earlier."

I played the selection for Iain, who watched with interest.

"What do you see?" I asked.

Troy leaned forward eager, waiting.

"I see a protection detail disguised as friends or traveling companions," he said at the end of the viewing time. "They're up to something."

"So we thought. Now, my question - can we get a

drone?"

Iain grinned. "Within D.C. airspace? You want a drone?"

"Yeah. Can't rely on traffic and surveillance cameras if someone is hacking in and erasing the files." Not that I could confirm that was the case, yet. "A drone would provide us with our own feed."

Catching sight of Troy's intent interest in our conversation, hairs rose on the back of my neck. My limbic response interested me. Why did Troy's interest in his own case cause a chill/fear response in me? Filing it for later examination, I gave Iain my full attention. I wanted a drone.

"And again, an Unmanned Aerial Vehicle in Washington D.C. airspace?"

"Yep, and Northern Virginia."

"Three major airports feed into this particular piece of sky, not counting private airfields and helicopter companies. Dulles is the second busiest international gateway to the Eastern seaboard."

"Is that a problem?" I found it harder and harder to maintain my innocent countenance, knowing damn well I was asking the impossible, but who better to ask?

"The FAA has not approved UAVs for use within the District or Northern Virginia."

"Well, I know that. I'm not talking FAA approved flights here. I'm talking borrowing a CIA drone."

"They still need permission to fly."

"But you could get it, right? National security and all

that?"

"You're going to make me have that conversation with Tierney aren't you?"

"Yep. He hasn't set foot in my office since I shot his wife." There was no way to make that sound good. She was a liability trying to kill an asset. Simple, really.

"He supplied some hefty help not so long ago, I recall," Iain said. "You could ask him?"

"It's been awkward since the shooting. But he has been there for me. He was there watching my back when that idiot chopped up my ex-brother-in-law."

Troy shuffled in his chair.

"Problem?" I asked.

"Just. No. No, SSA." He shook his head. "No problem."

"Baptism by fire for the new guy?" Iain said with a grin. "Guess he hadn't heard the stories."

"I have, sir. Didn't think they were true," Troy said, moving his chair back a little. He tugged at his collar then rubbed his jaw. Nervous?

I smiled; it was more of a smirk and I knew it. I'd heard that before. Seems the stories float around the halls at Quantico but no one really believes them until suddenly they do.

"Iain?" I said. "Will you?"

"Yeah. I'll drive out now and visit Tierney. He owes me a coffee." Iain glanced at the Rolex on his wrist. "If it gets much later this will be a breakfast meeting."

"Thank you."

Iain stood up, put his chair back, said goodbye to Troy,

waved at me and left.

"Will he really try to get you drones?" Troy asked. His hand rubbed the back of his neck.

Something bothered him. I watched his reaction as I spoke again.

"Yes. Yes, he will. We need to find those women. We need our own feed. You heard my argument."

Troy's fingers pulled at his collar, then adjusted his tie. He nodded. "Now what?"

I moved away from the drone subject. "Now, you need to add everything you have to our file."

He stopped fidgeting. "Yes, ma'am, I mean ... SSA."

"You can use my office. When you've finished, go home get some sleep. I'll be back here by six a.m."

"Yes, SSA."

I picked up my phone and holster from my desk before leaving the room. From the doorway, I said, "Hope we get the drone."

Troy rubbed his neck and said nothing. Something about the drone made him unhappy. Halfway down the hallway I paused and made a call. While I waited for Mitch to answer, I slid the paddle holster into my waistband and adjusted my jacket.

"Hi, awake?"

"Yes. Where are you?" Mitch said.

"Escaping the office for a few hours. Coffee?"

"Yes. Come over."

"On my way."

Seventeen minutes later, I walked up the path to

Mitch's front door. Security lighting flooded the area in a brilliant white glow. The door opened.

"It's late, you okay?" Mitch asked, ushering me across the threshold and into the dimly lit hallway. I stepped into his embrace, exhaled, and relaxed, in no hurry to move. "Didn't think I'd see you until you got back from New Zealand."

Leaning back a little in his arms, I smiled. "Plans changed. Kurt and I are staying. Lee and Sam are going."

The smell of freshly brewed coffee wafted down the hallway. Hand in hand we walked into the kitchen.

Before I could take the cup Mitch held out to me, the room shimmered, disappearing. My right hand hit the counter as I tried to find something solid. The cold marble countertop jolted the shimmer into submission but the images stayed. I saw the dark-haired woman from the surveillance tapes standing outside the White House and the word 'renegade' painted across the lawn surrounded by glowing roses and vegetables.

An urgency in Mitch's voice made me look up. His eyes searched mine. "What was that?" he asked. "Something happened."

I felt his hand tighten around my arm.

What was that? There was no good answer.

"I slipped?"

"No, you didn't. What was it?" he said. "Sit down."

Mitch watched me, his smile gone. I heard The Joker and recognized the voice as Heath Ledger's, "Why so serious?"

Not now.

Mitch's head shook just a little. "El, sit down."

I did as he asked. My mind ran in circles trying to figure out what happened and why I saw that woman. That woman. One of the three on Troy's watch list.

The White House.

Could be nothing. Could be nothing, except the Secret Service called the President 'Renegade.' The roses came back into view. Glowing. Radiant.

Nausea circled. I breathed until it subsided.

Radiance and Rosebud were Renegade's children. The vegetables. The First Lady, FLOTUS, had a vegetable garden. The Secret Service called her Renaissance. Obviously, that was a hard word for my mind to depict.

Could be nothing?

"Ellie? Talk."

I looked at Mitch. So worried. "It's okay. I'm sorry. Guess I'm tired."

"Nah, not buying it. What happened? It looked like you saw something."

He shouldn't have to buy it. That's not fair of me. Need to be better at this relationship stuff than I have been before.

"I did. I saw something." That wasn't as scary as I thought it would be. Going for broke seemed like a good plan. "The room shimmered and I saw a target of ours outside the White House ... the word 'renegade' was written on the lawn and surrounded by glowing roses and vegetables."

He looked into my eyes for about twenty seconds before speaking. "Were the vegetables glowing or just the roses?"

I smiled. "That's it?"

His smile came back. "No, but I knew it would make you smile. So what was it?"

"Hallucination?"

"Hmmm and it means?"

That I need another MRI.

"Maybe something, maybe nothing."

"Is it nothing?"

My head shook. "No, but I can't prove what my gut is saying until we find the women we're looking for."

"What's it saying?"

"That the First family is in danger and that I might be right thinking that one of our targets is 'someone.'"

"Wow."

"I know, right? Could also mean that I need another MRI ... and my brain has finally short-circuited."

"How do you feel?"

"To be fair that's not a very good indicator, Mitch. I'm always okay."

"Yeah, you are." His eyes studied mine. "You look better. Before, your eyes were dark, the sparkle gone."

So seeing things has a physical manifestation. Imagine that.

"I'm waiting for a colleague to get something authorized for me. Then maybe I can prove or disprove this new crazy." I picked up the coffee cup in front of me.

The coffee was still warm. "Can I stay tonight?"

He smiled. "You need to ask?"

"No ... that was me being polite. I need to be back in the office by six and I don't want to be alone."

Breaking down walls. Admitting I don't want to be alone, big!

A hint of suspicion crept into Mitch's voice. "Is that something to do with the hallucination?"

I nodded. "It's not the first one this week, but it is the first one that could show a possible threat to national security." I saw the concern in his eyes before he could mask it. I needed to shut up.

"The others?"

"I think they're related to the case in New Zealand, and the discovery of a woman at an abandoned factory. Overall impression is that it's connected with trafficking and is possibly a distraction. Lee and Sam will figure it out. If it were a distraction, it wouldn't be the first time, and also only half the team is going." I leaned on the counter. "Enough work talk ... it's making me sound more and more insane."

"Your mind is definitely not like other peoples, but it's not insanity."

"That's not insane?"

"No. You're observant. People's bodies speak to you."

"Thanks. It feels like insanity."

"You also have the ability to tap into something out there ..."

"That's not insane?"

"No more insane than you and I knowing what the other is thinking, or awake ..."

"You heard those words, right?" I smiled. "When you start hearing the same songs as me you might change your mind about the sanity of the situation."

"You mean like Adele's 'Set Fire to the Rain' at four this morning?"

"Ha, snap!"

"I'm already there ..."

What were the chances of us being on the same wavelength?

"What is it you need to do to prove that woman is a threat?"

"I need to find them. Every time we get them on a camera, the feed disappears and we don't know where they are. The pattern so far suggests they're mainly interested in Washington. I know where they've been, can extrapolate that information and project it into possible places they'll end up."

"Soft targets or hard?"

I blinked. "Excuse me?"

Jargon? Mitch?

"Do you think they're going after soft or hard targets?"

"It's D.C. We're still scrambling fighter planes at the drop of a hat. And since the Navy Yard shooting and that woman who rammed the White House gates in 2013, security is even tighter. Is there such a thing as a soft target here anymore?"

"Good point. Where have they visited so far?"

"Smithsonian, reflecting pools, Monument, White House, The Mall. Capitol Hill, the Department of Energy …"

"Okay."

No, not okay.

"What's with the questions and the jargon? That's not like you." I set my cup on the counter. "Don't think you can pass this off as spending too much time with me, or being in my head."

He smiled. "We've been working on a Defense contract for the last year. There's a prototype drone in my office. It's so small it doesn't need FAA approval." He held his index finger and thumb apart about an inch. "It's the size of a hummingbird."

"A hummingbird? How am I just hearing about this now?" I asked.

"We have lots of contracts for various things," Mitch replied with a grin.

That was true. He and his brother owned a company that designed and manufactured electronic components for all manner of applications and, apparently, made drones.

"Who designed the hummingbird?"

His smile widened. "It's my design."

"Thought you were more into management these days?"

"Me too. Couldn't resist the challenge."

That was Mitch. He was all about the challenge and doing things right. Sometimes doing things right meant doing it yourself.

"And it's tiny, this drone, the size of a hummingbird?"

"Yep. There is a catch – you have to follow it, and keep within a mile. The range isn't great. We won't be flying these things in Iraq from here."

"That's the only catch?"

"Not exactly. We're looking to field test the hummingbird so we would collect data." Mitch paused then carried on. "The plus of this little toy is … it's capable of going into buildings."

That was a definite design advantage.

"And if someone spots it and swats it against a wall?"

"The FBI gets invoiced for quarter of a million dollars."

"That seems fair."

Yeah, covering the destruction on the tiny drone would blow my quarterly budget straight to hell.

"Let's hope it doesn't get squished."

If we could get the bigger drone from the CIA to do the initial locating of these women, then we could deploy the hummingbird to follow them more closely. I liked it.

Chapter Seven.

Take It All.

My phone alarm went at five. I woke to the smell of coffee.

"Morning," Mitch murmured as he leaned down and kissed me. "Coffee is ready. About to make breakfast. Hungry?"

"Starving." My stomach rumbled.

"Your phone's being going nuts for the last twenty minutes," Mitch said and passed it to me. My fingers pressed the button on the top of the case. The screen lit up. Missed calls, text messages, and emails. I pressed the button again and let the blackness swallow the colorful commotion.

My eyes didn't want to focus on anything but Mitch. I knew I had to, but not until after my coffee and after breakfast. My stomach grumbled again.

Mitch laughed. "Sleep well?"

"Yes," I said with a smile. "You?"

"Yes, always when you're close."

Me too. One day soon we'd be really close.

"Mind if I have a shower before breakfast?" I said. My phone buzzed in my hand. I didn't look. Instead, I put the phone back on the nightstand. "They can wait."

"Go for it. You know where everything is."

Ten minutes later, showered and dressed, I joined

Mitch in the kitchen.

"Omelet?" he asked as he broke eggs into a bowl.

"Please."

We ate without talking, because we didn't need to. After breakfast, I checked the messages on my phone.

"We got the CIA drone," I said, reading a text from Iain Campbell. "Lee and Sam are on their way to New Zealand. Kurt couldn't find me. Troy thinks he found something." I paused and looked at the rest of the messages. "Troy thinks he found something times three and Kurt's getting worried."

Mitch grinned. "Can no one live without you?"

"They're jumpy, that's all," I replied.

I knew why Kurt was worried. He didn't buy my explanation for the weirdness in the office the other day. And then there was the being shot at thing. I read an email from Kurt. The DA made a decision to hold Trudenca and Cox on murder charges for the death of Arnie Arthur and the attempted murder of two federal agents. Their lawyers were trying to get them released on bail. Kurt thought if they were released, they wouldn't last long and we'd never find out who Rob is or was.

"Something is going on in D.C. and we don't know what it is," I said.

"Sure ... that's the reason."

"Funny man."

"Who's flying the drone for you?"

"CIA, I presume, it's their toy."

"Let me know if you want to use the hummingbird."

"Who'd control it?"

"I would," he replied without hesitation. "Prototype, can't let anyone outside the company control it."

"And you have to follow it?"

"Yes, it's a limited-range vehicle."

Seemed weird thinking of something very small as a vehicle.

"So you'd be in the field with me?"

"Yes."

There was no stopping the smile as it spread across my lips. Then there was: in the field? With me? That was a whole new scenario filled with potential hell. "What ifs" circled like seagulls after a free feed.

"You okay?" Mitch asked, refilling my coffee.

"Not really. I'm not keen on you being in the field with me. Too many variables."

"It's surveillance. I don't carry a gun. I won't be entering any unsafe situations. I'm controlling a drone," Mitch mustered his patient voice. I knew that wasn't easy for him.

I shook my head. Life had a way of fucking everything up.

"My focus will shift if I know you're in the field."

Honest. Very honest. And true.

"You worked with Mac—"

I saw the look on his face as soon as the words left his mouth. "Bad analogy," I said, taking a sip of my coffee. "Bad analogy."

"That wasn't your fault—"

"It's okay."

No sense in getting into that or arguing what was or wasn't my fault. But it's okay. It won't happen again. Live and learn.

"It's surveillance, El, I won't be in the line of fire." He smiled to reassure me. "And anyway, I know you'll be there."

"My focus ... it's about *my* focus. If I'm thinking about you, I'm not thinking about potential issues."

"Okay. It's your decision. I respect that. But just let me ask you something ..."

I didn't like where that was going but nodded.

"Last week you were involved in a situation, yes?"

"Yes."

Situation. Ha. Lunatic with a hostage. Good word *situation*.

"What were you thinking about when you entered that building? Honestly."

Oh, that's not fair. He knew. He could feel my thoughts when they involved him. How did that even happen?

"You."

"Uh huh."

"That's not the same. You weren't in danger."

"No, but you were and you still focused despite me being on your mind." He smiled. "You can do this, Grasshopper."

"I can do this. If you get hurt ... I'll kill you."

His eyebrows rose. "I guess that's fair?"

"Don't get hurt."

"I'll be out of the way, flying the drone, nowhere near the targets."

That's what you say now.

"They better not be famous last words." I finished my omelet before I asked another question. "What's your security clearance?"

Mitch's eyes met mine. "TS/SCI."

"Top Secret, Sensitive Compartmented Information." I let his acronyms roll around my head. "Special projects?"

He nodded.

Chapter Eight.

I met a boy.

"I need authorization for a civilian to conduct surveillance for us," I said, sitting on the edge of Caine's desk and sliding the paperwork across to him.

Caine read the name on the paperwork, "Mitch Iverson."

"Yeah."

"Clearance?" he asked.

"Defense. TS/SCI."

"You said civilian." His eyes met mine. A distracting twitch in the corner of Caine's mouth caught my eye. Stress.

"He is. His company has a contract to develop some hardware for our military."

"I see."

"Just do it ..." I said with a smile.

"Keep him out of the line of fire, Ellie. A lawsuit we don't need."

"I'll do my best."

Caine twitched again. "I want a protective detail with him. Delta A is down two."

I saw that coming. "I'd be happy to ask for volunteers from SWAT."

"Do it." Caine narrowed his eyes. "I'll authorize this but he doesn't go into the field without SWAT with him.

Got that?"

"Yes."

His all-seeing eyes scrutinized my face for a moment. "You all right? Last night was unfortunate."

Unfortunate. Yeah, that's what it was.

"Kurt and I are fine. My CI not so much."

"So I heard." Caine's eyes disappeared into the creases of his face. "As long as you're all right. Carry on."

My next visit was to the SWAT tactics room.

I knocked twice. "Y'all decent in there?" I called and opened the door.

"Come on in, Ellie," Andrews hollered from across the room. "Cover up boys, lady on deck."

I laughed. As if anyone was wandering around naked; tactics room, not locker room.

"I need a favor, Andrews. Two men for a protection detail."

"Volunteers or do you have people in mind?"

"I have two of your men in mind. But warn them, it's a surveillance job and possibly quite boring." My fingers crossed all by themselves. Boring is safe. With Mitch on the team, I wanted as much boring as a person could handle.

"Names?" Andrews asked.

"Jerry Dixon and Kris Gibson."

"You're in luck, they're both on today." He turned around and scanned the room. "They should be in the armory. Wait one, I'll get them."

I checked my phone while I waited. An email from

Mitch. He said he was ready when I was. A warm glow spread through my stomach matched only by the smile on my face. I typed a reply explaining I was getting him a protective detail.

I looked up to see Kris and Jerry walking toward me, carrying large bags and H & K MP5 assault rifles.

"Hey, Conway," Jerry said setting his bag down and shaking my hand. "Got a job for us?"

"Yeah, did Andrews warn you ... might be a bit boring? We're doing a surveillance job and I need a protection detail."

"He did warn us. I'm sure we'll cope. Who are we protecting?"

"Mitch Iverson." I couldn't even say his name without smiling. I bit my lip. "He'll be controlling a tiny drone for us. Don't let anything happen to him."

Jerry grinned. "That smile just then ... he's the cause, yes?"

No use denying it. I obviously couldn't hide it. "Yep. Just look after him."

Kris grinned at me. "Risky, taking someone special into the field."

"Yeah, hence you two. Delta is two men down. You good to go now? I'll brief you with the team."

"We're good," Jerry replied. "Let's do it."

Andrews called out his goodbyes.

We walked down to my floor, taking the stairs, not the elevator. I saw Kurt in Sandra's office and stopped in the open doorway. "Either of you heard from Campbell?"

Kurt nodded. "He's waiting on you. Permission to fly was granted – the window is limited."

"How limited?"

"You need to locate those women within an hour of the launch and follow up with the hummingbird."

"Okay."

Sure, an hour to locate three women in D.C. Easy? Hell, yes.

"Our meeting room twenty minutes. Can you notify Campbell and Troy? I'll get Mitch."

I motioned to Kris and Jerry and pointed them to the meeting room. "Go in, make yourselves comfortable. I won't be long." I headed down to my office while dialing Mitch's cell phone.

He answered on the fourth ring. "Hey, how quickly can you get here with that toy?"

"Ten minutes," he replied. "Where should I meet you?"

"I'll wait for you at the visitor entrance on Pennsylvania."

"That's the main entrance, right?"

"Yep. Once the CIA bird is airborne, we'll have an hour to locate the women."

"I'll bring everything I need with me."

"See you soon," I replied.

"You will," Mitch said. I heard his smile. The warm feeling in my stomach flooded back.

I hung up and sat at my desk. Without warning, a clawing cold replaced the warmth in my stomach.

Breathe.

Icy tendrils eased through my nervous system.

Nothing bad is going to happen.

Breathe.

The hair on the back of my neck prickled.

Breathe.

I glanced at the clock on my wall. Ten minutes.

Time enough to access the file I'd set up for this case, Operation Visitor. I didn't believe they were tourists any more than I believed in Santa or the Easter Bunny.

Troy added his information to the file. I scrolled through images of the women and their entry cards, matching faces and names. I printed pictures, placed them inside a manila folder and then sent the photos to our phones and to Mitch's.

The phone on my desk rang. I pressed the speaker button. "Conway."

"Chicky Babe," Sam crooned from my desk.

"Hey, how goes it?"

"Just landed at SFO. Everything okay your end?"

"So far so good. Deploying drones very soon."

"Dammit ... and we're missing the geeky tech good times."

"You are. While you're sitting around twiddling your thumbs, can you run some names by Faye in New Zealand?"

"Your case has a New Zealand connection too?"

"Oh yeah, starting to see what I'm seeing?"

"I am. You want us to come back? If this is a decoy or a distraction ..." He didn't finish his thought. He didn't need to. If someone just successfully split Delta A, then I'm freaking glad to have a couple of SWAT guys with us.

"Run these names by Faye ... it won't hurt to check even though I don't expect anything. Ready?"

"Yep, fire."

"Trudi Welsh, Susan Hollows, Danielle Lane."

"Got them," he replied then repeated the names back.

"I'm out. Need to get this show on the road."

"Stay safe, Chicky."

"I intend to."

I hung up, picked up the folder and walked into the meeting room.

"These are the women we're looking for today," I said, sliding the file across the table in the center of the room. "I'll be back."

Chapter Nine.

Lips of an Angel.

My cell rang. I answered it, watching Mitch enter the atrium, a smile settled on his lips. He carried a metal case. I returned his smile and signaled for him to wait by the desk for me.

"Caine?"

"Cox and Trudenca were released on bail."

"What?"

"I see your reaction was the same as mine and the DA's."

"How the hell did that even happen?" Stunned.

People hurried past or stood around in small groups talking. Busy as usual. I listened to Caine tell me they had no idea how Trudenca's lawyer managed to get them out on bail. Or how a lowlife like Trudenca came up with the two million dollars the judge set as the bail amount. I imagined his parents helped.

My thoughts were dark and my gut told me Trudenca would be dead by morning. I thanked Caine for the heads up and walked over to the desk.

An odd awkwardness descended over me as I signed the visitor log to allow Mitch access to the building. We hadn't worked together before and I wasn't sure how we would handle it.

The agent manning the desk handed me a visitor's

pass. I clipped it to Mitch's lapel.

"You need to sign in," I said, pointing to the log.

He signed the book adding relevant data to the appropriate lines. Mitch Iverson. Iverson Technology.

"Sir, are you carrying any weapons?" The desk agent asked.

"No."

"What's in the case, sir?"

I stepped in. "He's with me, agent. The case is classified."

"Yes, ma'am."

I turned and pointed to the stairwell door. My heart pounded. It was hard being that close to him and not touching. No kiss hello. No hug. Working. It was strange.

It was a relief to be in the stairwell, just us.

"Okay?" Mitch asked as we paused on the first landing.

"I think so," I replied. "I think so."

His hand touched my arm; warmth spread from his fingers. "You need to be sure, El."

"I'm okay. It's just, this is … this is different."

"Harder than normal us," he said.

"Professional distance is no fun."

We continued the climb.

"Breathe, it'll get easier. It'll be fun like usual."

"I'm breathing."

"Do I know anyone you're working with today?"

"Only Kurt and Sandra," I replied. "Sandra will stay in the office and be on hand for queries, et cetera."

Four landings later, we reached our destination floor. I

opened the door for Mitch.

"Now where?" he asked.

"Right, about three-quarters of the way down the corridor. We're using a meeting room."

"Do I get to see your office?"

With a smile, I replied, "Absolutely." We walked in silence to the meeting room. I swung the door open. Kurt, Iain, Sandra, Troy, Kris and Jerry all looked up from their conversations. "And we're all here. Introductions." Mitch stood next to me. "Easiest way is often the best. This is Mitch Iverson, left to right, go ..."

"Kris Gibson, SWAT."

"Jerry Dixon, SWAT."

"Think you know me. Hi, Mitch," Kurt said with a grin.

"Me too," Sandra said. "Nice to see you, Mitch."

"Iain Campbell, Homeland."

"Justin Troy, FBI."

"Nice to meet you all," Mitch replied and sat down next to me.

Our thighs touched for a moment.

Breathe.

"Let's do this thing," I said. "We have limited time. I've sent photos of the targets to your phones ... apart from Jerry and Kris. I don't have your cell numbers, so you have hard copies. Everyone familiar with the targets?"

An affirmative murmur followed.

"There is a pattern of sorts in the targets' movements. We still do not know where they are staying. I don't think it's within the District. Pattern so far, the women arrive in the city before ten in the morning and have been seen on Metro cameras. Sticking to the pattern means they'll be on a train about now. I think they'll take the Green line today. My money is on The Navy Yard as their destination."

Iain took his phone out of his pocket and made a call.

We waited, listening only to his side of the conversation. Moments after making the call, he hung up.

"Had to check," he said. "No one from New Zealand has applied for permission to be in the Navy Yard this week."

"I doubt that will stop them. No one asked for permission to go inside the Department of Energy complex either," Sandra said, "I'll tap into the Metro cameras and see if I can see something before we lose the feed. I guess if we lose the feed then we know we're on the right track."

Something on the wall caught my eye. A still-life painting. A bowl of oranges.

Yeah, that's normal.

I knew it wasn't there when I walked into the room.

What should be there? The Delta team seal. Not oranges. The painting changed and now a child sat at a table eating an orange.

Breathe.

"I can't base this on anything other than my overwhelming desire for an orange, but I think they'll change lines at L'Enfant Plaza," I said. I blinked, trying to clear my vision. Everything was orange. Orange. The orange became a single line.

Metro orange line ran from Vienna in Fairfax County, Virginia to New Carrollton, Maryland. "I think they're in Virginia somewhere."

I felt Mitch's questions and Kurt's eyes studying me from across the table. Neither of them said a word. For that, I was thankful.

The orange faded. Our seal returned. Fidelity, Bravery … 'I' for Integrity, not insanity.

Sandra's pen moved at speed across her notebook. She looked up. "Based on that, I'm going back to my office. I need to be watching the cameras at L'Enfant Plaza. If you're right and they switch lines there, then we should get a good clear series of images. I'll let you know." She stood up, said goodbye, and disappeared.

"How sure are you?" Kurt asked me.

"I could be wrong …"

"One day maybe, doesn't feel like that day is here."

"I hope not." I glanced around the table. "Iain, the drone should be deployed to cover the area from the Navy Yard Metro stop to the Navy Yard."

"That's a compact and very specific area. You don't want to widen that?"

"Not at the moment."

"We've only got an hour from the minute we launch the vehicle," he reminded everyone.

"I know."

I knew. I was putting all my eggs in one basket because it made sense. The Navy Yard made sense. But not if they were planning to attack the President only; it made sense if they intended to use a multifaceted approach. Terror was best deployed to terrify as much of the population as possible and to confuse a situation. The list of potential targets in D.C. was extensive.

"Okay. As long as you're aware," Iain said.

"I am aware. Now, once you locate the women with the big drone, Mitch will send in the hummingbird. We need to be close for that. Kurt and I will be on the ground, guided by Mitch. Kris and Jerry will be with Mitch at all times." I looked at Kris and Jerry. "You do not leave him. Got it?"

"We got it," Jerry said with a small smile. "It might even be fun."

I hoped not.

"Let me know when you want the drone in the air, I'll be liaising with flight comms," Iain said.

"Waiting on confirmation from Sandra ..."

As if on cue, my phone buzzed.

I read the text. "Visual confirmation of the three women at L'Enfant Plaza." I glanced at my watch. "We have seven minutes before they get on a green line train."

My mind is a scary place full of numbers and dates and apparently train timetables.

Iain made his call to deploy the drone and get it into position.

"We're moving out. Iain, you and Troy can use my office. Everything you need should be there, if not Sandra will locate it for you."

"Your office will be fine."

"Jerry, take one of the Delta SUVs, Mitch will ride with you. At this point, we are heading toward the Navy Yard. If anything changes, we'll inform you." I looked at the SWAT guys. "Need your cell numbers." I slid my phone across the table to Kris. "Add your number then give it to Jerry. Add me to your phones but phones are not our primary communication device."

Kurt set a black case on the table and opened it. "We're using these." He unpacked familiar-looking comms equipment. "Channel four. Emergency channel is one."

Kurt passed the in-ear bone conduction headsets and control units around the table. "SWAT has been using this tech for a while now, I believe," he said.

"Yes, we have," Kris replied.

"This is a plug-and-go system," Kurt said for everyone else's benefit. "I won't go as far as to say idiot-proof, but it's pretty damn close. Push to talk is a T-switch, low-profile and a silent press. You can wear it on your vests or your palm." Kurt looked at Mitch. "Palm probably easiest for you?"

"Yes."

"You okay with that?" I asked Mitch.

"Yes, if not, I'm sure Jerry or Kris will help me out."

"Okay, one last thing. Radio code."

Kurt smiled. "I got it," he said, taking a piece of paper out of his pocket and reading aloud, "Ellie is Nutcracker. I am Rook. Mitch is Blue Jay. Jerry is Crow. Kris is Magpie and Iain is Raven." He looked around the table.

"As a collective we are Corvid. Blue Jay, Crow, and Magpie are collectively Mobile Nest. Everyone okay with that? Anyone need a repeat?"

Heads shook.

Nutcracker? Are you kidding me?

"Okay. We're going," I said and stood up.

My heart pounded so hard I thought it was trying to find a way out of my chest. It did not feel good. Nervous. Shouldn't be. A giant cloud of doom encroached. I shoved it away.

Mitch touched my shoulder.

"Breathe," he said in a low whisper. "Focus."

"I got this," I replied with a smile. "See you out there. Be safe."

"You too."

I left before my heart threatened to cartwheel out of my mouth and followed Kurt down the hall. Behind us, I could hear Kris, Jerry, and Mitch talking as they walked. We reached the elevator before I realized I couldn't hear them at all. I could hear Mitch and he wasn't talking, he was thinking.

Just Mitch.

I liked it.

Chapter Ten.

Carry On.

Before we got near our destination, the voices changed. Iain broke in, "Go for Nutcracker and Rook. Eyes on the targets. Looks like you were right, Nutcracker. Targets have emerged from the Metro and are walking toward the Navy Yard. Over."

I pressed the push-to-talk button on my vest. "Good copy, Raven. Stay with them. Can you see who is on the gate? Over."

"Go for Nutcracker. Wait one ... Over."

I waited, scanning the gray sky through the windscreen for any signs of the drone.

Campbell's voice erupted in my ear, "Go for Nutcracker. Police," he said. "No wait, rent-a-cop. Over."

Should be a marine. That's not a public accessible gate. A ball of tightly wound dread formed in my stomach.

"Good copy, Raven. Out."

Kurt glanced at me.

"All right?"

"You heard Iain. They're going to walk right in, rent-a-cop on the gate."

"No way should that happen, especially after the 2013 shooting here."

"Five bucks says he lets them in," I said.

Kurt was right; it shouldn't happen but I knew it

would.

"Not betting against you."

No one ever does.

"I could be wrong."

"Yeah, that's not today."

"So sure?"

"Yes."

"Why?"

"Because so far you've been right."

"Pull over. We're going in on foot."

I called NCIS at their office inside the Navy Yard. A familiar place; not only had my father worked there but we had a good relationship with Noel Gerrard's former NCIS team. The last time I was in the Navy Yard was to remove evidence from Christopher Doyle's office, former Director of NCIS, after his arrest. The Washington Navy Yard and I had history.

"It's SSA Conway. Can someone meet me at the 6th and M Street gate?"

The gate on M Street and the 6th Street was for Department of Defense Common Access cardholders and military personnel only. To get to the public access gates, we'd have to go around to N or O streets, taking time we didn't have.

"Sure. What time?"

"Five minutes." I looked up the street.

Didn't seem like much of a hill from where I stood but I knew it was a little more than a gentle slope. Rain splattered the windshield. I opened the car door and walked around to the sidewalk removing my vest as I went.

I slid my left hand through the elastic band that held the push-to-talk button, and adjusted it, making the button comfortable in my palm. I depressed the button by closing my hand around it. "Go for Corvid. Heads up people. Kurt and I are on foot. Where are the targets? Over."

Iain's voice was crystal clear in my head.

"Go for Nutcracker and Rook. Long message. From your position, they are fifty yards back in a doorway. One was looking at a phone before they ducked under the awning to shelter from the rain. Can't get this big bird low enough to see what they're doing now. Over."

"Good copy, Raven. We're going to stay ahead and go in first. Keep us posted. Nutcracker Out."

I turned to Kurt. "Pop the trunk. Leaving the vest."

He did as I asked. Our FBI vests and jackets would draw too much attention. From the trunk, I took my jacket. Kurt did the same. I'd expected a modicum of the usual protest when I ditched my vest. This didn't feel like a shooty or stabby problem. Felt more explody. A vest wouldn't help if that were the case.

A smoky haze filled the air. I blinked but it stayed. Flames. Smoke. Sirens. Screams. I leaned on the car and closed my eyes. When I opened them a few seconds later, the smoke was gone.

"Conway?"

"Henderson?"

"What was that?"

"The street filled with smoke," I replied, throwing nonchalant into my voice and hoping it stuck.

"Smoke from?"

This is a perfectly normal conversation to have.

"I don't know, but I suspect an explosion at the Navy Yard."

My phone buzzed. I looked at the screen. A text from Mitch. I read it twice.

Mitch: Where did the smoke come from?

We were ascending to new levels all the time. This didn't feel like too big a step.

Me: Did you see it?

Mitch: Yes

Me: I'll explain later. Let's do this thing first.

Mitch: a smiley face.

I pocketed my phone and turned to Kurt, who watched me with a mix of amusement and concern. Normal then.

"Camera?" I asked.

Kurt patted his jacket pocket. "Yes." He shouldered his backpack.

"Let's go," I said.

Iain's voice broke into our conversation. "Go for Nutcracker and Rook. They're moving toward you now. Over."

Kurt replied, "Copy that, Raven. We're on our way. Out."

We walked and didn't look back. Iain was right; there was a rent-a-cop on the gate. He asked for our ID but didn't really look at it. Beyond him, I saw Jen wave. She and another special agent I recognized as Kathy stood waiting for us.

"Hey, what's going on?" Jen asked. The four of us stepped back behind the guardhouse. Off the sidewalk and not quite on the road.

"Just visiting," I replied with a smile.

"We need to be out of the way but with line of sight to the gate," Kurt said, looking around.

"Because you're just visiting ..." Kathy's disbelief echoed in the air. "Over here." She moved away and we followed. Standing across the road in the shadow of the building, we could clearly see the street and anyone approaching. Rain dripped steadily off the guttering above us.

I turned away slightly and pressed the talk button.

"Go for Blue Jay. They're almost in. We're ready for the hummingbird. Over."

Iain replied, "Go for Nutcracker and Rook. The big drone is being recalled. The video feed is downloading now. Over."

"Copy that, Raven. Nutcracker out."

Mitch's voice sounded in my ear. "Go for Nutcracker. Good copy. Out."

I turned to Kathy and Jen. "Three women will enter the gate on foot in a few minutes. The women are foreign civilians and about to enter a restricted gate. We also have a car coming onto the base."

"The car is just visiting too?"

"Something like that."

"You think there is a briefing we missed?" Jen said to Kathy.

"Think so."

"Gerrard might have bought this ..." Jen said.

No, he wouldn't. He would have crucified me as soon as he realized I hadn't shared information.

"Our targets are entering the base. We need to use our own surveillance," I said.

I saw the women. The rent-a-cop stopped them. One of them flashed something and he let them through.

Dammit. The drone would've been able to see what she flashed.

"You going to let our car in?"

Mitch spoke in my ear.

"Go for Nutcracker. Hummingbird is up, picture is crystal clear. Over."

I pressed the talk button. "Copy, Blue Jay. You didn't happen to see what the woman showed the guard? Over."

"Copy that Nutcracker. Passport. Over," Mitch said. "Helpful? Over."

"Affirmative, Blue Jay, thank you. Out."

"Go for Nutcracker and Rook. By the way, I have a Defense CAC. We're good to enter this gate. Out," Mitch said.

"Copy that, Blue Jay. Out."

I smiled at Jen. "Never mind. We don't need authorization."

"You have someone in that car with DoD clearance,"

she said with a small smile. "Well played, Ellie."

Well played indeed. Who knew?

I signaled to Jerry to pull over as the car drove through the gate unchallenged. I went to talk to them. Jen and Kathy joined us. Jerry wound down his window.

"Let the women go ahead, we don't want them thinking we're all following them. They know they shouldn't be here and they must know they shouldn't have used that gate. Let them think it's all good," I said. "Mitch, you okay?" I peered into the backseat where he sat, focused on a laptop screen.

"Yes. The targets are still walking. Bird is performing well. Ticking all the boxes."

I smiled at him, his eyes flashed to mine for a second. Warmth.

"I'll leave you to it and brief NCIS. Then Kurt and I will go for a stroll."

"Be careful, El."

"Always."

I stepped away and talked to Jen and Kathy, filling them in on what we saw as the situation, conceding I could have briefed them sooner. They accepted that I didn't know for sure that the Navy Yard was the destination of the day until they arrived at the nearest Metro station and started walking toward it.

The four of us walked down the street. We were in no hurry. Somewhere ahead of us, the tiny drone watched and listened to the women as they chatted. Every now and then, I heard Mitch. I couldn't tell anymore if he was using comms or I could just hear his thoughts. Either way, it worked for me. He warned us the women had stopped at a bus shelter. We slowed our pace.

I pressed the talk button. "Go for Crow. Must be getting close to the edge of the range for the drone. Bring the car down to the NCIS building. There is parking out front. Over."

His voice came back in my ear. "Copy that, Nutcracker. Moving now. Out."

A few moments later, they drove past.

We walked on. Twenty yards later, we passed the bus shelter. Walking and talking and taking no notice of the women, other than we saw them and I nodded on the way past.

Two had backpacks. The third carried a shoulder bag.

Backpacks. Carried by tourists and terrorists alike.

I smelled smoke. Haze filled the street. My eyes darted around the area. No obvious cause for the smoke. No origin. The smoky haze meant something. Questions erupted: the navy brat that I was pulled a short list together. What was the point of being in the Navy Yard? The Navy Band? That was doubtful. Chief of Naval Operations? Possible. NAVSEA - that seemed likely, Navy Sea Systems Command. I paused over that thought, trying to remember how many warfare centers that encompassed. Nine. Two undersea and seven surface. Taking out NAVSEA could be why they're here? Nothing cemented to say I was on the right track.

"Jen, what's here apart from NAVSEA that could be a

target?"

"Navy Band?" she smiled. "No?"

I shook my head. "You'd have to really hate brass instruments."

Her tone changed, serious, now. "Naval Reactors, JAG, us, a few classified facilities. The Navy Museum?"

JAG, Judge Advocate General's office. Didn't feel right. Classified facilities. Maybe.

"Naval Reactors?"

"That's the office responsible for the operation of our nuclear propulsion program."

A definite maybe on Naval Reactors then. The thought of propulsion systems reminded me that the decommissioned destroyer *USS Barry* was now a museum ship and moored at the Navy Yard. She'd make a big splash. I pulled out my phone and rang Dad.

"Quick question, The *USS Barry*, what is she?"

"A museum," Dad replied.

"Not what I meant." I sighed. "What class is she?"

"Destroyer. Forrest-Sherman from memory," Dad said. "Everything all right?"

"Yeah. Just trying to figure out something. *Barry*'s propulsion system?"

"Steam turbines."

"Thanks, Dad." I pocketed my phone and discovered all eyes were on me. "Thinking, that's all," I said and went back to my musing. NCIS headquarters? A large building right next door to NCIS housed the Navy Museum. Smoke thickened.

Mitch's voice but I couldn't tell if it was via comms or not. "El, more smoke?"

I went with comms and pressed the talk button. "Blue Jay? Over."

Thoughts muddled. More smoke. What if ... what if it was today? What the hell is *it*?

"Copy, Nutcracker. Today? Over."

My heart pounded so hard I felt dizzy. I didn't know how to answer him, so I ignored his question.

"Go for Blue Jay. What are they doing? Over."

"Copy, Nutcracker. Still in the bus shelter. Having a picnic. They're eating. Over."

"Blue Jay, a picnic? Over."

"Affirmative, Nutcracker. Sandwiches by the look of it. I need to move the bird away a little bit. They'll notice it soon if I don't. Over."

"Copy, Blue Jay. Out." I turned to Jen. "Okay to go into the NCIS building? If we stay outside, we're too obvious." A black cloud of holy fuck descended. Outside felt bad, unsafe, I wasn't sure that inside was any better.

Jen smiled and nodded. She and Kathy led the way.

Once inside, I rested against a desk and waited. Words climbed the walls in my mind and tumbled to the cold ground.

I knew I had to say something about the potential POTUS threat thing and the smoke and the possibility that something horrific could happen today. I saw it. It wasn't something that I should keep to myself. Words. I needed some that didn't sound like I required an MRI.

"Kurt?"

"Yes?" He turned away from the window and faced me. "Something I should know?"

"Yep. Now that I've broken the ice with my orange line observation and I was right ... there's something else. I think the target here is the presidency."

Did I really think that? Yeah, I did. Whatever was about to happen at the Navy Yard wasn't the main event.

Silence.

Not even breathing sounds.

Damn.

"That's big, Conway. You got anything to substantiate that?" Kurt asked.

"Nope. Not a thing. But wait there's more." I took a breath. "Twice now I've seen smoke coming from here. I can't explain it, but it feels like a terror attack. It feels like explosions."

"So based on nothing, you're going to put that out there?" Kurt said. "You think the president is under threat and the Navy Yard is going to go bang?"

"Yes," I said. "If I don't say something and I'm right ... then what?"

"Then ..." Kurt looked at me. "We can't go there. That's not an option."

"Those women, Kurt. What's in those backpacks? We have no reason to stop them and conduct a search."

Kathy coughed, letting us know she heard our conversation. "You don't, but we do. They came in a restricted gate. Let *us* do this."

"Do it," I said. Then pressed the button in my hand. "Go for Blue Jay. Anything? Over."

"Negative, Nutcracker. Still eating. Over."

"NCIS are going to talk to them. Over."

"Copy, Nutcracker. I'll bring the bird back in. It's done well. Out," Mitch said, the lightness in his voice spoke volumes. He was pleased with his prototype's first field test.

"Go for Mobile Nest. Thank you. I want you three out of here. Meet you back at the office. Out."

Jerry spoke, "Good copy, Nutcracker. Mobile Nest on our way as soon as the little bird is stowed safely. Out."

Kathy and Jen waved as they left the building. Kurt and I waited. We saw Mitch open his door and pick up something small from the ground.

Two minutes later the car pulled out. I watched them. The car stopped.

I pressed the button in my palm by closing my hand. "Go for Crow, you need to leave. How copy?"

"Good copy, Nutcracker. Deploying the drone for one last look. Over."

"Negative, Crow. Move the Nest. Now. You're too close. Out." I heard my words and they made no sense. Too close to what? "Move *now*. How copy Mobile Nest?"

Mitch broke in. "Nutcracker, it's up and, we're moving. Breathe. Out."

Breathe.

I stood in the doorway as the car disappeared from view. Everything felt wrong. At the pier, I could see the

USS Barry. Gray ship on a gray day. Ghostly. It just needed fog to make a perfect horror movie set. A shudder vibrated up my backbone.

"Go for Blue Jay. Can you see anything? Over."

"Copy, Nutcracker. Be more specific. Over." His voice smiled.

Something was counting down.

A flash lit the corner of my eye. As I turned my head to the left, the building shook: I lost my balance and hit the wall behind me. Debris flew across my line of sight. Hunks of metal slammed into a parked car. Smoke and dust filled the air. Large chunks of brick, concrete and metal crashed from the sky.

"Break-break, Nutcracker!" Voices in my head belonged to Jerry and Kris.

"Loud and Clear, Mobile Nest. Get Blue Jay out of here. Out," I replied, turning my attention to the room we were in as I used the wall for support. "Kurt?"

"You can be wrong any time now," he replied, taking a step toward me. "Okay?"

"Yep. You?"

"Yes."

Another massive explosion rocked the building. We hit the ground hard. I looked up in time to see a car crash down onto the pavement outside. I blinked. Mitch was just there. Bile rose.

My hand closed around the button in my palm, "Break-break. Massive explosion in Naval Yard. Request emergency services." I paused then pressed the button again. "Go for Blue Jay. It's today. Out."

I struggled to my feet and grabbed for the door handle. Another explosion shook the area. Glass spewed from the destroyed windows, shards spearing desks and chairs. Screams followed. I spun around. Screams from where? There was no one in the bullpen. Where was everyone?

"What building was it?"

"I don't know. Museum?" Kurt replied. He took my hand off the door handle.

"Maybe museum. Where is everyone?"

"I don't know. You ready?"

"Yep."

Kurt swung the door open.

Silence.

A thick blanket of smoke and dust fell over the area. We couldn't see anything in front of us. We couldn't hear anything. Seconds ticked by then from under the cloud, I heard a cry, then another and another.

"Kurt, there are kids in there."

He held my arm as I moved toward the sounds. Every breath caused coughing. The thick polluted air threatened to choke me. "Wait. They'll have gas masks in here," Kurt said.

He pulled me back inside and shut the door. Smoke crept through the broken windows, rolling over wrecked desks, like dry ice at a concert. The sound disappeared. We scanned the walls looking for the telltale emergency arrow and spotted one. Kurt rifled through the cabinet and found two gas masks similar to those our SWAT teams wore. We pulled them on.

"Let's do it," I said. "You can hear me?"

"Yep. Voice box amplifier is working," Kurt replied.

"Yours too."

"Stick close, Conway. I don't want to lose you out there."

Kurt stepped in front of me. I placed my right hand on his shoulder and squeezed, ready for him to move.

Sixteen paces into the thick smoke, we almost tripped over a dismembered leg. Kurt kept going. My foot hit something - it dislodged an arm from under the rubble. A few stumbled steps later dead eyes stared at me. A deep breath shook my rib cage: time to push the horror away and concentrate on finding the living. After a few more yards, the carnage barely registered. I couldn't let it. Sounds of life, albeit struggling life, found its way to us. Kurt tapped my hand.

"Right."

I followed.

Chapter Eleven.

Whole Again.

Twelve hours later, Kurt and I stepped out of the elevator and walked down the corridor to my office. Drained. Exhausted. Unable to process all I'd seen. We hadn't spoken since leaving the Navy Yard. There was nothing to say. We'd seen it, all of it. Touched. Smelled. Vomited. Tried to piece people back together. Held children while life drained away. Lied to parents. Bagged limbs. Consoled the inconsolable. Picked our way through rubble and death to find the origin.

The wreckage cried out, muffled, lost, broken.

We'd soon realized where a lot of the people from the NCIS offices were. There was a special celebration happening in the museum. Navy personnel, partners and children.

The bombs were in the museum. Coat check.

I opened my office door. Mitch jumped to his feet. I didn't expect him to be waiting.

"Is the hummingbird okay?" The last I knew it was airborne when the first explosion hit.

He nodded. "It'll need some repairs but it mostly survived the blast wave."

Robust little thing.

I dropped my comms set on my desk, wiped my hands down my filthy jeans and stepped into his arms.

"You're all right?" he whispered into my ear.

"No. I'm really not."

His right foot stepped back, creating a gap between us. Mitch looked into my eyes.

"Ellie?"

"I'm not hurt," I replied. His arms tightened around me as he pulled me close again. "Take me home."

"You don't need to do anything?"

Yeah, I do. I need to figure out how those bombs got there and what the women had to do with it. Jen said there was nothing but tourist stuff in the backpacks and their phones. No calls made, or texts sent within half an hour of the explosions. Jen and Kathy were the only survivors of their team. I felt sick all over again.

"I need to go home."

"Done."

I saw Sandra on the way out.

"I'm going home." I looked down at my filthy clothes and noticed brown stains smeared down the thighs of my jeans among the general dirt. Blood. "I can't work like this."

I couldn't work. I couldn't breathe. Sandra disappeared into a haze. I took a step, my foot connected with something soft. Not concrete. Not metal.

I knelt down on my right knee to get close enough to see what it was. Something sharp stuck into me. A gap in the haze formed. Just enough for me to see a little boy. I pushed wood off him. He didn't cry. He stared with wide eyes. I scooped him up. So light. My mind stopped. I held him in my arms. His head tipped back. His eyes stared up at me, not blinking, not reacting. Maybe my mask scared him? All of a sudden, my brain kicked back in and tried to make sense of his small battered body. Where were his legs? My head turned. Vomit sprayed across the wreckage at my feet.

I could hear Mitch. "Ellie?"

I blinked. There was no smoke. There was no little boy.

"What was I doing?" I asked, looking at my hands. Where was the little boy? My hands shook as I tried to control the rising tide of bile. I tried to wipe the blood off my hands by rubbing them on my jeans. "I got it."

Breathe.

Forcing away the panic, I said, "Sandra, find out if those women were on the base at any time prior to today …" My voice cracked. Another slow breath. Think calm. I felt warmth from Mitch's hand in the small of my back. "See if they've been anywhere twice - even days apart. And where are they now? NCIS …"

My throat tightened. Don't think.

I carried on. "Double check with Jen and Kathy at NCIS, I don't think they got anything usable from the women when they spoke to them, but check for me. Everything fell apart."

"I'll let you know as soon as I have something," Sandra said. Why was she still looking at me? "Are you all right?"

I shook my head. Mitch draped his jacket around me. The warmth from his jacket seeped into my shoulders. The shaking needed to stop.

It seemed to take forever to get home. I caught sight of my reflection in the hall mirror on my way upstairs. Soot, blood, dust, dirt. I looked like crap. It was comforting to know I looked as good as I felt.

Mitch went ahead of me. I walked into my room seconds after him and the shower in the en suite was already running.

"Thanks," I said passing him his jacket and my holster.

"I'll be right here."

I peeled off my clothes and dropped them in a heap on the bathroom floor, destined for the garbage, not the laundry. Standing under the hot water felt good. The grime washed down the drain. Images of broken bleeding people swirled in the bubbles from the soap circling the drain and finally falling in. Screams faded into gurgles. I leaned on the wall, letting water pour over me. I don't know how long I was there. Until I was warm again. Until I could breathe without feeling the claustrophobia that came from hours of wearing a gas mask. Until I couldn't see the images anymore.

By the time I turned off the water, all I wanted was Mitch. To be lost in his eyes and safe in his arms.

I wrapped a robe around me and padded into the bedroom leaving the day at the bottom of the shower. Mitch lay on the bed. He smiled.

"Hey," I said. Lifting the bottom of the robe so I could crawl across the bed. I lay with my head on his shoulder. His left arm curled around me. Safe. I slipped my hand inside his shirt. Warm. Alive. My fingers traced the outline of his muscles enjoying the sensation as his body responded to my touch.

Mitch slid out a bit and rested on his left elbow. Lost in his eyes, I smiled. Mitch's lips met mine. My eyes closed. His kiss breathed life back into my aching body. I felt his lips on my neck, light butterfly kisses. Sinking into Mitch, I tilted my head, exposing more of my neck. As he kissed me, his hand moved the robe away. My skin flamed as his hand ran over my stomach. My teeth sank into my lip. I rolled toward Mitch and slid my arms around his neck, drawing him closer, legs entwined. I reached down and undid his belt.

Mitch kissed me again ... long, loving kisses. A need burned deep within me. A hunger for his body. Something almost primal in its urgency. My arms tightened around his neck as I pulled him closer.

He whispered, his voice husky, "We've got all the time in the world."

That was all I needed to hear.

I kissed him, long, slow, warm, savoring the taste of him. I was exactly where I wanted to be. Nothing else mattered. I looked into Mitch's eyes and saw the rest of my life.

"You're smiling," he whispered.

"So are you," I replied pushing him gently until he rolled onto his back, taking me with him.

His heart beat with mine.

"I love you," he said, his voice husky, his breath ruffling my hair.

His words took my breath away. There was nothing in the world but us. Just us.

Emotions I never thought I'd feel again sprang from the deep. "I love you too."

I melted into Mitch as his arms tightened around me.

Chapter Twelve.

Something I need.

I heard the alarm but didn't want to get up. I knew what was waiting out there and I didn't know how to stop it. Lying curled around Mitch felt the best place to be. Warm. Comfortable. Safe from the world.

My phone blared. Bon Jovi's 'I'll Sleep when I'm Dead' bounced off the walls and smashed into the bed.

Bon Jovi?

Caine. Work. Destruction and mayhem waited for me.

I wriggled out from Mitch's warmth and answered the phone.

"Yep."

"You all right, kid?" Caine's customary growl was less teddy bear and more rabid dog this morning but he still called me kid. I knew that meant he was concerned.

"Yes." I sighed without meaning to. I was okay until the phone rang and it all came flooding back.

"How many agencies are we working with us on this Navy Yard situation?" Caine asked.

"Two." Can't count CIA. They weren't supposed to be involved. Support role only.

"Is this an extension of Operation Visitor?"

Honestly, I had no idea. I thought so, but I had no real clue.

"It's possible, probable even."

"I want you to brief the Directors. Set up a meeting."

Brief them on what exactly? I don't know anything. Not that I can prove. As I tried to focus on the day ahead of me, I saw our office building collapse. What the hell?

"It'll be off-site. I'll let you know where when I do."

Time to think. A safe place. Off the grid.

"When can we expect you at the office?"

"Be there as soon as I can. Advance warning ... I need all SWAT teams and bomb disposal units on standby." I paused, then asked, "I'm lead on this case, yes?"

A hint of amusement circled his words. "Yes. Delta A has point."

"Good. Cancel all leave. I want as many agents available as possible. Alert all hospitals that there could be more mass casualties. Tell the Secret Service they'll be read in this morning."

"Secret Service – Homeland will take care of that."

I rolled onto my back and stared at the ceiling for a second before replying. "I *need* to do it. Where's Renegade?"

"At the Castle," Caine replied, his voice taking on a new pitch. "Do you have evidence that this is about Renegade?"

That was the tricky bit. I didn't. None. Not a scrap.

"No. I have ..." Just say it. "I have a gut feeling that there will be a lot of distractions in and around D.C. while whoever is behind this makes a move against Renegade."

"Get evidence, do it fast."

"We're working on it."

Well, everyone but Kurt and me. We'd taken time out to recharge. Experience told me I was no good to anyone if I didn't look after myself. Mistakes now could be catastrophic. "Meanwhile, tell the Secret Service to increase security around the entire family."

"How much video did you get yesterday?"

"I don't know ... I'll let you know when I do."

"Straight to my office when you get in."

"Yes."

I hung up as a horrible feeling of powerlessness descended. Washington was going to burn and I had nothing. Nothing.

I heard a car on the driveway.

Outside most people's houses that would be normal but not mine. The only cars that could be close enough for me to hear belonged to Delta, my father, or Mitch. The front door opened and closed.

"Visitors?" Mitch asked kissing my neck.

"Kurt," I replied. "I think."

I heard the person walk through the house. A smile edged across my mouth as Mitch leaned over me. "Seems a shame but ..."

"... time to go to work," I said finishing his sentence. At that moment I realized I might not be back for days; it didn't feel like I could do that. Not now. "One second ..."

I reached for my phone, noting how many missed calls I had before calling Kurt. A phone rang somewhere in the distance.

"You up?" Kurt said.

"Just hitting the shower. Making coffee?"

"Yes, as it happens."

"Not tea."

"It's coffee, Conway. Full of caffeine. You'll be jacked up all morning."

"I'll be down in fifteen."

I hung up and swung my legs over the edge of the bed just catching Mitch's smile as the covers fell away. My phone rang. Insistent. I glanced at the screen as Mike Fisher's image flashed with the words 'incoming call' across the bottom of it. Damn.

I reached down, picked up the phone and answered it.

"Wifey. I've been calling you since the news broke yesterday," Mike said, injecting calm into his voice but failing at removing the raspy edges of concern.

"Sorry, Mike. I was ... it's been ..."

"You all right?"

"Kurt and I were there. The explosion. We were there."

Silence for a beat.

"I've been watching the news coverage." Disbelief flooded his voice. "No one's claiming responsibility?"

"To be honest, Mike, I have no idea what's being reported. But we'll find who did it."

"Lee? He's not answering his phone."

"On his way to New Zealand. Your brother is safe, Mike, he's with Sam."

"You and Kurt?"

"Not hurt." Not hurt but it's going to take a while to scrub our minds and deal with what we had to do. I

110

sighed. "Thanks for calling, Mike."

I hung up and dropped my phone back on to the floor.

"Shower," I said. "You coming?" I extended my hand to Mitch. He stood up, stretched, and took my hand.

I turned on the shower and stepped under the water. He smiled. I reached out pulling him under the water with me.

Our warm bodies slipped across each other under hot running water. Mitch slid an arm around my waist holding me close, leaning his free hand against the wall. His muscles rippled as he moved against me. A storm gathered. One hand on his shoulder, the other arm around his neck.

Blue eyes searching blue eyes.

Smiling. Hot water, cascading down our bodies. Steam rising.

I felt his tongue between my lips and I forgot to breathe.

Chapter Thirteen.

Can you hear me?

I leaned against Caine's desk and ran over the little I did know in my mind while I waited for him to finish his phone call. Sandra had some information for me; she'd worked her magic just as I knew she would.

Caine hung up. "Must you lean?" he grumbled.

"I don't want to sit," I replied, standing up and turning to face him. "I have a list of all the places those three women visited. As far as we can tell, using surveillance that is fast disappearing, they didn't visit the Navy Yard before yesterday."

"And there was nothing on them to suggest they'd detonated a bomb?"

"Not a thing."

"What's your gut saying?"

"It's saying they're involved somehow. But I have no reason to pursue that line of investigation."

"That's never stopped you before," Caine replied.

True.

"I'm going to bring them in regardless. They were there yesterday ... maybe they saw something."

"I hope so," Caine said. "Have you located them?"

I shook my head. "Kinda hoping they'll turn up in the city and someone will spot them." Long shot. If I'd been a tourist at a destination that exploded, I wouldn't be in a hurry to go back into the city. Something told me these three would.

Why? No damn idea.

"BOLO?"

"Yeah, asked Sandra to put one out this morning. Wanted for questioning. It's gone out across Northern Virginia as well as D.C."

"Why not Maryland too?"

"Because I think they're in Virginia. Somewhere on the orange line."

Sandra was doing her best to find out where. She'd contacted hotels and asked them to check their registries. It all took time. If we could just get an area, we could work on narrowing it down.

"I'll leave the Director briefings to you. Find a location, set it up, do it quickly."

"Yes, sir."

I left his office and passed the chief on his way in.

"Let me know when the briefing is, Conway."

"Yes, Chief."

As tempting as it was to run down the hallway to get away, I didn't. I walked. Crossed my fingers and hoped I didn't run into Assistant Director Owen.

The buzz from the bullpen floated in the air, enveloping me as I walked down our corridor. Everyone was working. Phones rang. Chairs moved. Fingers tapped on keyboards. I didn't need to go in and disturb anyone. Both SSAs from Delta B and C were in there. Their cases now in limbo. The terror attack on the Navy Yard took precedence.

Safely back in my office, I started going over the video footage from the CIA drone and the hummingbird. Mitch and Iain had downloaded all their footage to Sentinel while Kurt and I were ... we just were and that's where my thought stopped. Not productive to go to back there.

What was I looking for? Someone else. Someone with a cell phone in their hand just before the explosions. A needle in a haystack. A message flashed up on my screen: Sandra found something from the day before. She sent me the link and the time stamp.

I clicked play, then dragged my mouse along the bar at the bottom of the window to the appropriate time and let it play.

Troy.

I stopped the video and enlarged the image. It was Troy. No mistake.

What the hell was Troy doing at the Navy Yard the day before the explosion?

I picked up my phone and called him. He answered on the fourth ring.

"I want you in my office A-sap."

"Is something wrong, SSA?"

"Ah, yeah, the Navy Yard exploded yesterday. Slip your mind, did it?"

He bristled. "No, SSA. I was following a lead."

"And that lead led you where, Agent Troy?"

Sandra appeared in my doorway and waited.

"It went nowhere. I thought I could locate the women.

I was wrong."

"My office, now."

As soon as I put my phone down Sandra spoke, "I don't understand why he would be at the Navy Yard."

"Me neither." I swung in my chair. We'd had no business at the Navy Yard until we were sure the three women were headed there. There was no link prior to that. "He's on his way to my office. Have you seen him today?"

She shook her head. "I thought you'd given him instructions, to my knowledge he hasn't been in."

She'd know. Sandra knew who came in and when. No one slipped past her.

"I want you to go over all our surveillance ... you're not just looking for the three women, you're looking for someone with a cell phone prior to the explosions and Troy."

I leaned back in my chair and watched Sandra leave.

Shit just got messy.

The Directors' briefing needed a venue. I tapped on my laptop keyboard and checked on the various safe houses belonging to the combined Delta teams. Two in use. But all the Delta A houses were free. I booked out one of the houses and attached the case name and number. My gut told me to make sure Troy thought he knew where we would be. It also told me to hold the briefing somewhere else.

Kurt's name flashed in the bottom corner of my screen. I clicked and typed into the window. *Road trip in twenty*. I stared at the words and wondered why on earth I wrote them. I wasn't planning on leaving.

Sandra barreled through my door in a cloud of perfume and sparkles.

"They're at the Extended Stay hotel in Fairfax, on Lee Highway."

And suddenly the road trip made sense. Another random act of weirdness from my synapses.

"Room?"

"No idea. My powers are great but even I can't access an actual handwritten guest book."

"Seriously?"

"Yep. The sort you have to sign, with a *pen*," she replied with utter disbelief. "Bookings can be made via email but they don't appear to use any computer-based booking system that I can find."

"Wow. Doesn't matter, we can find out when we get there. When you see Troy, do not let him leave the building." I twisted in my chair. "Every time I hear his name my stomach tightens. There is something wrong."

"Got it, O goddess of all things spooky."

"He can use Sentinel," I said with a smile. "In fact, suggest he works from the bullpen. Do not upload any of the video with him in it to Sentinel."

"Got it."

"Kurt and I are going."

I jumped up from my desk, shoved my holster back into my waistband and pulled my jacket on.

From the doorway of the bullpen I whistled. Kurt

looked up from whatever he was doing at the other end of the office.

I swirled my index finger in the air. Rally up. It was my belief that we should employ more SWAT hand gestures in the office.

Claude saw it and strode across the floor. "Do you need help?"

"Not at this point. You carry on here. I'll get local police backup. If I think we need them."

"Yell out if you need us."

I smiled. "You know I will."

Kurt joined me.

"Road trip early?" he said.

"Yeah, we know where they are."

He smiled. "Let's go, I'm driving."

"Only because you know we're going to need flashers to get out of D.C. this morning."

"Not just lights, we're going full noise. Have you seen the chaos out there?"

I laughed. "You are starting to sound like Sam."

He shrugged. "I feel like having some fun."

We walked down the corridor and stepped into the elevator.

No sign of Troy.

In the car, I filled Kurt in on the Troy thing and told him I made it look like I was going to brief the Directors at a safe house. He voiced what I thought. "Another person we should be able to trust fucking us over?"

"It's not looking good."

"Directors?"

"We'll do it at Langley. I'll set it up when we find these women." Langley was the safest place I could think of and out of D.C. The chances of Langley exploding into a fireball were very slim.

My head rested on the window. It felt good. Cold. Soothing. The last week and the strange way the case unfolded irked me. A strange realization settled over me: something was missing. Something I needed. I missed Chance. I missed Mac. I missed the insight and frustration of their appearances but they were ten times better than the hallucinations I'd seen all week. My honest admission stunned me.

Blocking out the siren and lights, I closed my eyes, still tired.

Thick black outlines appeared, colors dimmed, and the world around me flattened. There was a door in front of me. I waited, barely breathing. Who would open the door? That was the moment I realized that my world became the pages of a comic book.

Familiar.

The page turned revealing an open door. Christopher Chance stepped through the doorway and into my office. He wasn't a cartoon.

"Long time no see," he said picking up a piece of paper from my desk and looking at it. He shrugged and put it back. "That's interesting." His fingers tapped the piece of paper.

"That's one way of putting it," I replied, swishing the

paper around to face me. It was a list of names. A list of seventy-four people killed in yesterday's explosions. Some were colleagues, some were friends, and a lot were children.

His smile drifted away. "Tough day," he said.

"Where you been, Chance?" I asked, leaning back in my chair and watching him.

"Around." His pale blue eyes lit with amusement. "You look different."

"So everyone says." He didn't; he looked the same. Blond, chiseled, charming. "You dropping in for a particular reason?"

My fingers crossed. I hoped so. I really hoped this wasn't just a daydream. I missed my talking interactive hallucinations. As much as I hated to admit it and sure wouldn't tell him, but I missed Chance a lot. I hadn't seen him since Carla died.

"What's his name?"

"What makes you think ... never mind. His name is Mitch."

He grinned. "Lucky man."

"Thanks." I leaned one elbow on my desk. "Now why are you here?"

"Everyone thinks you're nuts, so I figured I'd come push you over the edge ..."

Dimples, sparkling pale blue eyes, boyish. Yep, he had all the things that could push me over the edge.

"I appreciate the sentiment," I said with a smile. "And really?"

"The women are almost what you thought. Tourists but not really, but not terrorists." He paused. "Scratch that, I'm not convinced about all of them. They're officially on a research trip. One of them is an author."

"Of *Human Target* episodes or comic books?"

He laughed. "No, but she has written a few screenplays along with about twelve novels, all set here on the East Coast."

"Should I know this?"

"Yes, you should."

"Why?"

"Because her main character is you."

"She's what now?" I smiled indulgently. "In case you missed the memo, I'm a real person."

Chances displayed his dimples; his eyes danced with amusement.

"Me too."

"Nah, you're an actor playing a role. I'm just me."

"Look into it, Ellie. She writes about you, the name is different but it's you."

"Gimme a title ..."

"I can rattle off several. *I See You, Gemineyes, Satellite*. Think there are another couple as well."

"Great, I'll look into it. I don't have time to read books right now though. You know what with shit going down in D.C. an' all."

He nodded and perched on the edge of my desk playing with a pen he'd found. "Could be that they're handy scapegoats. There is something else going on and even I can't see what it is. I think one of them knows something. But the scapegoat thing means—"

"Someone could be monitoring their communication and movements to make it look like they're involved, or one or more of them *is* involved."

"Look at you being a grown-up special agent."

"Smartass. Don't suppose you have any joyful insight regarding Troy?"

"Do you trust him?"

"No."

"There's your insight. Gotta go, Ellie. Take care."

Chance pocketed my pen and walked toward the door then paused and looked at me. "You know how sometimes firefighters become arsonists?"

"Yeah, I am familiar with that phenomenon." The penny dropped. "Thanks, Chance."

He waved and stepped through the doorway. The ink bubbled then ran. Dripping down the walls and pooling on the floor, the colors mingled before fading away. I smiled. As insane as it probably was I felt happier with the familiar. Chance was familiar. Music was familiar.

It was strangely quiet in the car. Sirens were off. Nothing indicated our lights were still rolling. The view out the window told me we were in Fairfax County. All quiet on the eastern front.

Could Troy be involved because he wants to play hero and make a name for himself? Possible. Stranger things have happened. Except, he failed.

He didn't make it to hero status: people died. Maybe

Chance was wrong.

"Hey?" Kurt said, tapping my knee with his right hand. "You with me?"

"Yeah."

"Okay?"

"Yes."

"Do I want to ask what the smile is about?"

I looked at him. He watched the road, his eyes shooting sidelong glances in my direction often enough to concern me.

"Eyes on the road," I whispered. "Chance is back."

His head turned for a moment.

"Did you just say Chance is back?" he asked. "Do I need to pull over so we can have a conversation?"

"No. It's good. I understand him."

"You do hear the words coming out of your mouth? Because I'm hearing a reason to schedule an emergency CT."

"You would. And I heard the words, smartass." Hard *not* to hear them when I said them. "The women, one of them is an author. You ever read a book called *I See You*? No idea which one of them wrote it."

I knew Kurt read a lot. His house was full of books. His nightstand had so many they were piled on the floor as well. How'd I know that? A little bit of pre-Christmas snooping last year, that's how. Okay, it might have been a bit of pre-Christmas breaking and entering. Not proud of it.

"Conway, we're five minutes away from the hotel,

we've been in the car for an hour and your phone hasn't rung ... this is what? Information from thin air?"

"I told you, Chance is back," I said quietly. "Have you read that book?"

"I have. The author is Caro Clancy. I've read her books. That's not a name associated with this case. You sure about this?"

I nodded. Chance has never been wrong before. "Let's say one of them is this Clancy woman, just for fun."

"I had no idea she was a New Zealander," Kurt said.

Maybe she isn't.

"And? Anyone familiar in it?"

He parked at the far end of the hotel parking lot, undid his seat belt and angled toward me.

"Familiar? Yes."

"And you never mentioned it?"

"Ellie, I read it before I met you. I read it before I was Delta A."

"And again ... you never mentioned it."

"What was I going to say ... hey, Conway, you're just like this character in a book I read?"

"Yeah, that."

"We should get in there and find these women," Kurt said, opening his door.

"Ya think?" I muttered. "Go in the side door, trip the fire alarm, cause an evacuation ... everyone will pour forth from the hotel, we'll be able to get them easily and they won't have time to destroy anything."

"Sneaky."

"Up here for thinking," I replied tapping my head. "Let's go."

Anything that didn't require knocking on two hundred doors worked for me. I already knew they hadn't checked in using any of their names. But maybe they were using the name of the author.

I went through the front door into the reception area while Kurt used a side entrance and located the nearest fire alarm.

Attracting the attention of the duty manager, I said, "Excuse me. I think a friend of mine is staying here?"

Polite but firm, he replied, "We don't give out guest information."

Damn. He wasn't going to play. I could see the guest register on his desk. I tried one more time.

"Caro Clancy, does that ring a bell?"

He shrugged apologetically. "We have a lot of guests."

"Never mind," I said, changing tack. "What are your rates and do you have a non-smoking room available for a month from early next week?"

Just as he was telling me what he had available the fire alarm almost deafened me. He pointed to the door.

"Please go into the parking lot," he said as he headed for the stairwell.

Staff came running. I heard them go room to room on the ground floor making sure people were leaving then entered the stairwell.

I left the building and waited near one of the large pillars with a clear line of sight to the doorway. Kurt would stay by the other door. Sirens resounded. I saw the lights in the distance coming closer. Good to know the alarm was connected to the fire department. Panicked people emerged from the hotel. For a minute, I thought I smelled smoke.

Nah? Yeah?

My phone rang.

Kurt.

"Anything yet?"

"Not so far," I replied as another group of guests filed through the doors.

Kurt disconnected the call. I moved around the pillar a little and spotted the women talking among themselves as they exited the building. One of them I thought might be Trudi went over to the first fire truck that arrived and spoke to the firefighters. She pointed back to the hotel. Interesting. Leadership role. As she turned back to the other two women, I saw an emblem on her tee shirt. A Fire Department tee shirt, but not an American one.

I called Kurt and told him all three were out. Content to watch the interactions, I waited for him to arrive. The women were together again, still talking, animated. They each carried cell phones and purses.

Kurt appeared next to me.

"How do you want to handle this?" he asked, leaning close to my ear.

"I don't like our chances of getting them back into D.C. in a timely fashion. We need a venue, and if they are being watched we need to appear innocuous." That might be a big ask. Kurt screamed FBI in his dark blue suit, white shirt, and blue striped tie. I opted for more casual, as usual, cowboy boots, boot-leg jeans, a button-down long-sleeved blue shirt and a lightweight tailored jacket.

"There's a bar over in the mall," Kurt replied. "Champps." He checked his watch. "Almost lunchtime. Well, after ten-thirty. Invite them for a drink. They probably need one after yesterday."

I smiled. "So we invite them for a drink?"

"Why not," he said.

"Let's try that then." I looked at him out of the corner of my eye. "Did you light a fire in there?" I could still smell smoke. Images from the day before wound around a smoky haze in my head. Not good. The little boy's eyes stared up at me. I blinked him away.

Focus.

Kurt smiled and winked.

"All about authenticity."

"Delta A better not be getting a bill for fire damage, our budget is probably shot to shit after the hummingbird got caught in that explosion."

"It survived didn't it?"

"Kinda. I'm making a point here. Don't need a bill from a hotel!"

Kurt's smile grew.

Chapter Fourteen.

Cold shoulder.

"Hi, this is exciting, isn't it?" I said with a wave at the fire engines as I approached the group of women.

"Not after yesterday," the blonde woman I'd seen talking to the firefighters replied. She watched the goings on near the fire trucks.

Another blonde woman spoke. "There are people in the stairwell, just standing there. Bloody ridiculous."

The first blonde nodded. "I had a word with a firefighter about that."

"Oh?"

The second woman said, "We're Fire Service from New Zealand."

I nodded, smiled and rolled back to her earlier comment. "What happened yesterday?"

The first blonde shook her head as she spoke, "We went to visit the Navy Museum at the Navy Yard. Luckily, we stopped at a bus stop for lunch. There was an explosion."

I nodded. "Oh, wow. You were there? All over the news last night and today. Must've been terrifying."

"We'd just been talking to an NCIS agent. Very scary," she replied still distracted by the firefighters.

"Apart from that how are you finding it here?"

"Magic," the other blonde woman, replied. "Everyone

is really friendly."

"I'm Ellie. This might take a while." I turned to look at the third engine that rolled into the parking lot and wondered if Kurt had set fire to the hotel. "Buy you all a coffee over at Champps?"

"Sounds good," the first blonde said. "I'm Trudi, this is Susan and that's ..." The dark haired woman flashed her eyes at Trudi. A warning? Fascinating. Trudi carried on, "That's Ca ... Danni."

I heard her change her mind. What was she going to say? Caro? That's where my money lay.

The women said hello. Two blondes and a brunette. I matched their live faces to the photos I had in my head. Trudi and Susan looked similar. I figured Danni was the writer, just needed confirmation.

Then from nowhere a question from Danni. "Which agency are you with?"

"Excuse me?"

"Which agency?" she repeated with a smile.

"FBI," I replied.

"And you just happened to be staying here?"

I detected something in her tone.

"No, just making inquiries for a colleague."

"I see."

Okay, now I was curious. "Why?"

"I thought the FBI used a hotel in D.C. for out of town feds, a Marriott."

Yeah, we do. Big fan of the Marriott at Metro; stayed there a few times over the years. Chances of someone from New Zealand knowing we used the Marriott? Not high, I wouldn't have thought. My gut said if any of them was a writer, it was her. Danielle Lane, Danni also known as Caro Clancy.

I shrugged and didn't comment. Kurt sauntered over and nudged me.

"Introduce me, can't leave you alone for two minutes before you start mingling and looking for drinking buddies?"

Implying I have a drinking problem. Nice touch. Might have been almost true once. A tequila bottle rolled into view. I stifled a chuckle. It wasn't easy for a rectangular bottle to roll. Looked like it was drunk. Been there, done that, made friends with the worms.

"I suggested coffee, smartass. Ladies, this is Kurt Henderson."

They introduced themselves while I pretended to have forgotten their names.

"Where did Ellie suggest?" Kurt asked, charming the group with his smile.

"Champps," Susan replied. "Today was a recharge day for us, Champps sounds good."

I noticed a few looks between the three of them. Questioning maybe? Secretive looks. My phone buzzed. I fished it out of my pocket and glanced at the screen. Mitch. I bit my lip trying to contain my smile.

"Champps it is then," Kurt said, he homed in on Danni and fell into step with her. He was chatting. Mostly small talk. I noted she asked a lot of questions.

My mind actively sifted and sorted information. I wanted to hurry things along but that wasn't the smart approach. The BOLO needed rescinding. Having a police officer try to pick up the women while I was with them wouldn't help us get information. I had a feeling I'd get more from them by being friendly, than I would back at the Hoover Building in a sterile interview room.

I let myself fall behind the group as we walked across the Seers parking lot and called Sandra. She took care of the BOLO and added a 'do not approach interview in progress' comment. Just in case. While I lagged behind, I made a quick call to Mitch.

"Hey," I said. "You okay?"

"Yes." One word and I could hear his smile.

"Just wanted to say hi," I said, watching the group move away. The ground shook. I stumbled. The air filled with thick smoke. Choking me. "Mitch!"

"I'm here." His words cut a channel in the smoke. "What's wrong?" I could see Kurt and the women, hazy shapes in the smoke moving away. No sign that they'd felt the ground shake.

"Did you feel an earthquake?" I asked. Knowing it wasn't an earthquake. They were rare in Virginia. I'd never forget the last one: images of buildings evacuating into the streets, overlaid with fresh images of rubble and destruction. Facades fell into crowded streets. People screamed. Smoke billowed.

Breathe.

"Ellie? There was no earthquake. What happened?"

The smoke disappeared.

"The ground shook and the air filled with smoke." Panic flowed in. "Where are you?"

"At work."

"Go home, please."

"El, come on, I'll be fine. There was no earthquake."

I closed my eyes. Mitch didn't see the smoke this time. Maybe he would be fine. Maybe's ass. It didn't happen until I talked to him.

"I know it wasn't an earthquake," I replied. "Something is going to happen."

"El, I'll be fine. I'm at work."

Yeah, I'm sure that's what everyone at the Navy Yard thought too.

"Humor me, please. I'm asking. Get out of D.C. Go home." Smoke wafted across my line of vision. "Go to my place."

"Ellie, I'm working."

"Mitch, please ..."

Silence.

"All right." Reluctance filled his voice. "I'll work from your place. I can do this remotely."

"Thank you." I realized I'd been holding my breath as I exhaled and tension left my shoulders.

"Be careful, El."

"I will. Go home now, Mitch. Don't wait." I smiled, but it was more from relief than pleasure. I knew he heard it. "See you soon."

"You will."

I hung up and the smile and smoke left. Something else was going to explode and I didn't know where, except that it could be near Mitch's office. I ran to catch up. No one had missed me, or if they did, they didn't say anything. Kurt remained engaged in conversation with Danni.

Trudi and Susan weren't talking. They were listening. There was something about those two. Curious.

The mall was busy, bright, and overly warm. Dodging shoppers was the only way to get through and up to the restaurant. A super-efficient server seated us. He seemed to know the women. All smiles and sweetness as he offered to bring their usual. Trudi declined, stating they'd like coffee.

She ordered for Danni and Susan. The two woman accepted that, so I guessed it was normal.

Kurt and I ordered coffees.

As I listened to Kurt talking to Danni, I was acutely aware of the other two and what they were doing. They were watching not just Danni and us, but the bar in general. Curiouser and curiouser. I expected a white rabbit to race through the place at any minute muttering about how late he was.

I listened to Kurt chatting about D.C. and asking where they'd come from and why they were here. All very friendly. The replies however were stilted and felt rehearsed. At the mention of research, I was all ears. For the first time, Danni had said something that felt true. All thoughts of curious white rabbits disappeared.

"Research did you say, Danni?" I rested my elbows on the table.

"Yes, for a series I'm writing."

"Oh, you write?"

Her posture changed. I felt sure she hadn't meant to mention research or writing at all. Her arms crossed, hands holding her arms. Restraining herself?

"Yes, I write."

Trudi looked up and smiled. "Danni writes thrillers, set in Northern Virginia and D.C."

"Would I have read them?" I asked Trudi, getting ready to ask if Danni used her own name or a pen name.

Danni's hands gripped her arms tighter.

"Maybe," Trudi replied.

Danni's fingers relaxed a little. "I write a thriller series, my publisher calls it the Gabrielle Connor Series."

"Really?" Kurt asked. He inserted a good deal of surprise and mingled it with unrestrained joy. "That's great. I've read all the GCS books." He turned in his seat to face Danni. "Caro Clancy writes them?"

"Yes, she does." With a small smile, Danni extended her hand to Kurt. "I'm Caro Clancy, pleased to meet you." They shook.

Kurt bumped me. "Remember that book I told you about?"

"Which one again?"

"*I See You.*"

"Yes, I do recall that one." I gave it a second for effect. "So, you write under another name?"

"Yes."

"And *I See You*, is that the first in the series?"

"Yes, that's the first in the series," she said.

"Nice. Kurt here was raving about your book," I replied. "I'll have to look for them."

She beamed. Movement caught my eye and smoke poured out of the walls. I blinked, the smoke cleared. This smoky hallucination thing wasn't ideal.

Kurt launched into more about that book and mentioned others. Either he was cheating and using his phone to glean information from the internet or he'd genuinely read them all and hadn't let on.

I watched and listened. He'd read them all, all right. Oh my God. He was into the main character big time. Wasn't she supposedly me? We did share the same first name, Gabrielle. I shuddered. No one uses the G word.

A smile wandered over my lips. It was pretty funny that Kurt liked the main character so much. Our timing sucked. We came close to being a couple once or twice, but it would've broken up the team. Longevity of Delta A was more important than any relationship. My job was more important.

Right then, I knew that was no longer true.

Mitch was more important than Delta A and that was okay, because he'd never make me choose. I flipped back to the conversation and Kurt babbling about scenes from the latest book. That was new. I'd never seen Kurt babble like that. Fascinating, just fascinating. Kurt was capable of fan-boy behavior. I loved it.

Trudi and Susan looked on. Their coffees arrived. I saw the server walking our way with more coffees. Three this time. Impressive. I waited until he left. I saw something shiny around Danni's wrist when she reached for her coffee. A bracelet? Her hand moved to take sugar from the container in the middle of the table. Shiny, yes. Bracelet, yes. I caught sight of a black edge on one side and suspected it was a pretty shiny bracelet that concealed a flash drive. Bet whatever was on that made fascinating reading.

We needed to get to the bit where we could ask about the bombing and their movements and the possibility they were being tracked. We needed to get to that bit.

Impatient? Yes. Lives were at stake.

I adjusted my jacket and pulled my ID wallet out of my pocket. I opened it and set on the table. Silence fell. I folded the wallet and put it back in my pocket.

Serious voice now. "This is great but we need to get to the bottom of a situation that you may not be aware of, but involves you three."

I watched. Who would speak first?

Danni.

"What situation?" She was calm. Calm is good. I preferred calm to the freewheeling alternatives.

"The bombing of the Navy Yard," I replied. "You three were there. To us, that's suspicious. You entered a restricted gate. Again suspicious."

At the mention of the gate, Trudi and Susan looked at each other. I knew that look. Surprise. They didn't know.

"Danni? Did you know it's restricted access through the gates on M Street?" Kurt asked.

She nodded. "It was raining and crappy and the guard let us in."

"We know. We were there. Now is probably a good time to tell you we've been watching your movements for a few days. Your behavior triggered a flag," I said.

"How so?" Trudi asked.

"Well, until the Navy Yard exploded, we were trying to figure out what you were doing visiting places like the Department of Energy—"

"And after?" Danni said.

"After the Navy Yard, a BOLO went out on the three of you. Wanted for Questioning."

Danni nodded, as if she expected my answer. She probably did – and she didn't ask what a BOLO was.

"We're here researching for new books," Danni replied. "While we were in New York we went to a book launch at the Mysterious Bookshop. Talk to Michael Connelly or Reed Farrell Coleman or Sara J Henry, they were all there. They can tell you who I am."

"I know who you are now," I said. "I'm interested in your companions and your movements and in whoever is watching you."

Trudi and Susan looked at each other and then at Danni.

Danni smiled. "They're my Admins," she said. "Why is someone watching us?"

"What do admins do?" I asked, ignoring her question

for the time being.

Trudi replied, "Not a bloody thing." She and Susan laughed.

Danni smiled. "That's not true."

I knew it wasn't true. I'd seen them watching her and watching the bar. They protected her. But why?

"So, tell me Danni, what do they do?"

"They watch my back. They travel with me. They bring me wine and chocolate when life is shitty. They are my two best friends."

Trudi nodded. Susan smiled.

"Any of those things lead to exploding buildings?" I asked.

"No," the blonde women replied in unison.

"That's ridiculous," Danni said.

No, it wasn't. Something happened when I asked that question. Nothing I could put my finger on, but something changed. And saying something is ridiculous is not denial.

"How many times have you been near the White House?"

"About three," Danni replied.

"Have you been on a tour of the inside?"

Kurt dropped his hand onto the seat between us and tapped my leg, once. He saw something. "No. We've walked right around it twice."

"Shame you haven't signed up for a tour. The White House is well worth the effort. Tours can be organized months in advance." They could be organized months in advance: foreign nationals wanting a tour were subject to a Secret Service background check and had to apply through their embassy.

Kurt tapped me again.

"We'd have liked to visit the White House," Trudi said.

"Why didn't you organize a tour?"

Trudi's eyes flicked toward Danni for a nanosecond, one blink, and I would've missed it.

"Ran out of time," Danni said, attempting to end the conversation with her tone.

"Maybe next time," I said with a smile and made a mental note to check with the Secret Service and find out if any of their names cropped up on tour requests or tours. "Okay, anywhere else you've visited more than once?"

"My turn," Danni said. "Who is watching us?"

Okay, that was fair.

"We don't know. We need to find out. Have you noticed anything?"

The three of them shook their heads. "Let me know if you think of anything. Now back to my question, where have you visited more than once?"

Danni pulled a notebook from her bag and flipped through several pages. "Capitol Hill, Department of Energy, two museums, the Hard Rock Café and the Smithsonian Castle," Danni replied. "And the Hoover Building."

I looked at Kurt.

The Hoover Building. Fuck. Bad enough that The Hard

Rock Café was right across the road from work without them also lurking at the offices.

"We don't do tours, so what were you doing at the Hoover Building?"

"We took a lot of photos from outside," Danni replied. "A lot of me outside the building, at various entrances."

"Okay. Which museums in particular?"

"The Museum of Natural History and Newseum."

I smelled smoke and scanned the room. Nothing.

Newseum. Mitch's office was nearby. Seeing the smoke when I was talking to him now made sense and I didn't like it.

"Okay. Drink your coffee. We'll talk more in a minute." I stood up and left the table. From the few feet away in a quiet corner, I called Sandra.

"The list is ... White House, Capitol Hill, Department of Energy, Hard Rock Café, The Castle, Natural History Museum and Newseum. Our building. Soft targets get swept first ... I want EDD teams in The Hard Rock Café, The Castle and Natural History Museum first. Get those places swept for explosives. Now."

Security-wise, the other locations were harder for people to access, or there were multiple security measures. Metal detectors, bag-scanning machines, hands-on bag searches by trained personnel. I knew they had metal detectors at the Natural History Museum but it was still, in my eyes, a likely target, especially if the bomber wanted to hit the public. And kids. The timing of the Navy Yard bombs weighed on my mind.

"Sending the alerts now, Ellie. Anything else?"

"Yes, get hold of Tierney at Langley. Tell him we need one of his conference rooms for a Director-level meeting."

"Doing it. What time?"

I looked at my watch. "Two hours. I want the Directors there in two hours. We'll meet them in Langley."

"And the women?"

"Need them watched, but I want them to carry on doing their thing. I need to monitor them and find out who is watching."

"Setting up surveillance teams now."

This is why we offered Sandra a permanent position in Delta A. She just does it. Whatever I asked she did, God alone knows how. The woman is gold.

"Close surveillance and protection, Sandra." I wanted two teams but realistically I could only assign one. "Get Kris and Jerry from SWAT into plain clothes and put them on this." I trusted them with Mitch, so I trusted them with this.

"Already on it, my esteemed leader."

I laughed.

"There's something else. Who do we know in the Secret Service?"

"Charlie Prendergast," she replied. "You want me to set up something?"

"Please. Tell him I don't care where or how but we need to meet today."

"Consider it done, O Genie of the Bullpen."

"See you this afternoon."

I slipped my phone back into my pocket, took a breath, and sat back in my chair at the table.

"I have nothing to base this on, but I don't think you three were responsible for the Navy Yard, I think someone would like me to think you were." That was a lie but not a really big one. Chance's comments cemented in my mind. I doubted Trudi or Susan were responsible for anything but there was something dark lurking under the surface with Danni. As soon as I mentioned the Navy Yard, I saw it again in her. Uncomfortable? Maybe. It was something.

No one spoke.

"This is what is going to happen. You're going to put my phone number in your phones. You're going to carry on being tourists. If you see anything that doesn't feel right, if you see a person you've seen before while you're out and about, if you think someone is following you, call me."

They nodded.

"You won't be alone. Don't think for one minute I'm turning you loose. You will be protected." I crossed my fingers under the table. "Nothing will happen to you."

Danni looked at me. "You can guarantee our safety knowing there is a terrorist out there?" She sounded sincere and worried. There wasn't anything to tip me to her being part of the situation, yet I wasn't convinced.

"Absolutely."

Liar liar pants on fire.

"I doubt that, but either way, this is our trip and we still have stuff to see," Danni said. She wrote on a clear page in her notebook. I wanted to get a look at that book and her flash drive.

Trudi and Susan agreed with Danni that they had places to see. I passed out my cards and watched them put the numbers into their phones.

"Now text me your names so I have a record of your cell numbers, please."

They did. My phone chirped as the texts arrived. I added them to my contacts.

"Enjoy your coffees, stay close to Fairfax today. Tomorrow resume your sightseeing. Any clue where you'll go?"

"We wanted to go to Rosslyn and walk over Key Bridge then up M Street to Pennsylvania."

"Okay, that sounds good. Enjoy." I paused. "You want to photograph the Starbucks on M, don't you?" I said to Danni. "You know the history?"

"Yes, I do and yes, if you mean the triple murder in nineteen ninety-seven."

I looked up as Chance strolled toward me. A speech bubble grew from the side of his head. I read the black comic sans words. *She knows about you being shot near the Firehook and Lee's shooting outside Ford's Theater.* Chance winked and walked right past.

"Anywhere else you want to visit because of acts of violence?"

She smiled. "Yes, Ford's Theater and the Firehook

Bakery."

"What specifically draws you to those places?" I was pretty sure it wasn't the assassination of Abraham Lincoln.

"I know that an FBI agent was wounded going back from the Firehook with coffee."

I nodded. Yes, I was. Not fun. Having Danni say that was confirmation of what Chance told me, in case I needed reminding how helpful my hallucinations are.

"And Ford's Theater?"

"The same agent saved another agent's life outside Ford's Theater."

And again, yes I did. Not something I wanted to relive.

"Well, only one of those events is public knowledge and that was the coffee shop shooting."

Thanks to some idiot journalist who splashed the story all over the internet. We would watch these women and closely. I didn't like my chances of getting another drone airborne, so I hoped our surveillance teams could handle the task. They'd never let me down before. This cannot be the first time.

Kurt kicked my foot with his. He was not happy.

"Stay in public, like the mall or in your hotel room for the rest of today. Can you do that?" I said.

The three of them nodded.

"And tomorrow?" Trudi asked.

Thought we'd covered tomorrow. Maybe she was rattled.

"Business as usual, you travel via Metro? Train from

Vienna?"

"Yes," Trudi said. "We're usually on the train about nine-thirty."

I knew that.

"Good. Have a nice afternoon. We'll talk again."

I stood up and moved away, waiting for Kurt by the door.

We glanced back once and saw their heads bowed in conference. There was a lot to discuss. I had their phone numbers. I filled Kurt in on our need for more surveillance. He agreed and made a call to Judge Reinhardt to get a warrant sent straight to Cyber.

I made a call to the office as we went back across the parking lot to the hotel and our car.

"Cyber," I said and waited.

"How can we help?"

"It's SSA Conway. I need some roving bugs installed on the following cell phones, please." I read out the numbers.

"We should be able to do that, are they all smartphones?"

"Yes, they are. Two iPhone 5's and an android."

"We have some new software that will look like Facebook updates."

"Great. Fire away. A-sap."

"They'll be up and running within the hour. You have a warrant for this surveillance, I assume?"

Never assume. It makes an ass out of you and me.

"Not quite." I crossed my fingers and looked at Kurt.

144

"Any minute now."

"I need the warrant, Conway."

"I know, it's coming." So is Christmas. I hoped the warrant wouldn't take that long.

Kurt smiled and gave me a thumbs up. He put his phone in his pocket.

"It's on its way to you now."

"Excellent. Where shall I send the links?"

"Send to my phone and SSA Henderson's phone."

"Sure thing, Agent Conway."

I hung up as we reached the car.

"How're we doing for time?" Kurt said, unlocking the doors.

"Not great. Head for Langley," I replied, opening the back passenger door and grabbing Kurt's laptop. "Mind if I use your laptop? Mine is sitting on my desk at work. I'll write that briefing on the way."

"Go right ahead." Kurt grinned. "Last minute?"

"Well, I didn't know anything until now."

"True."

My phone rang. Caine's grumpy face flashed on the screen. I tapped the speaker icon.

"Writing the brief now," I said. "But that's not what this call is about is it?"

Caine huffed and snapped, "Cox was found floating in the river. Gunshot wound to the head."

"Dead?"

"Yes."

"And Trudenca?"

"In the wind. There is a BOLO out on him."

"Did he kill Cox?"

"No way of knowing that at this point."

"This is getting very messy."

"Watch your six," Caine grumbled. "Nothing good is happening here."

He hung up.

Kurt and I looked at each other for a split second.

Nothing good was happening anywhere.

Chapter Fifteen.

Sittin' on a Fence.

Jonathon Tierney met us at the main doors. I looked down at the seal on the floor as we crossed it. Still preferred the FBI seal. The white eagle on the CIA seal appeared menacing. Fitted the agency behind it, I suppose.

"I've set up a conference room for your use," Tierney said.

Yeah, he didn't, his minions did. He gave orders. His hands rarely touched anything, yet his fingerprints were on so many things. Including my life.

We followed Tierney through the building down long corridors and into a spacious conference room. Nice. I slid the laptop onto the large dark-stained table in the center of the room.

"Need anything else?" Tierney asked.

"I'll let you know," I replied. "This is one helluva situation, Jonathon."

"Worse than our last one?"

"Hard to know. Nukes versus a lunatic bomber intent on God knows what?" I didn't add anything about his wife. It's not as if I can kill her twice.

His beady eyes brightened. "About the same then."

"We get all the fun."

"You attract it, Conway, you always have. That's what

makes you so good at this," he replied.

"Is there a printer I can use?" I asked, ignoring his comment.

"Yes," he replied, pointing to a counter by the far wall and a printer. "It's wireless. Your laptop should connect to our network automatically. The printer you want is Conference four." Tierney scurried away, leaving me wondering if he'd handed me a compliment earlier or if he was just passing a comment.

I fired up the laptop and sent the short brief to the printer. Kurt walked over and waited for the paper to spew forth.

I checked my phone. Nothing. I expected - I didn't know what I expected. I called home. The phone rang ten times before Mitch answered.

"Ellie Conway's residence."

"You're there." I breathed a sigh of relief. "Thank you."

"'You're welcome' doesn't seem right. You okay?"

"Yeah, keep an eye on the news. I expect a bomb near the Newseum or in it."

"That's a ballsy move. Security is tight at that particular museum. You can't even get to the store inside without going through scanners and having your bag X-rayed and searched."

True. Security was tighter at that museum than the Navy Yard. Bizarre.

"All true. But in a world where terrorists hide fissile material in ventriloquist dummies ..."

"Point taken. I'm staying in. Do you think you'll make

it home for dinner?"

"If you're cooking ... I will do my best."

"Be safe, El."

I smiled as I hung up. Home for dinner. I hoped so.

Caine called. I put him on speaker. "More bad news?" I asked.

"Trudenca turned up dead in the Anacostia River near the Sousa Bridge."

That was a yes to the bad news question.

Kurt spoke, "Gunshot to the head?"

"Yes. ME thinks it was the same caliber round as the one that killed Cox. No gun recovered."

"Potentially the same weapon?" Kurt asked, coming closer.

"Yes."

"Someone's cleaning up," I said. "We'll be in the office as soon as we've finished briefing the Directors."

I disconnected. Messy didn't even begin to describe the situation now. Someone was cleaning house. Made sense that it could be the person who hired Trudenca to take out my CI and me.

"Not loving this," I mumbled under my breath and to no one in particular.

"You okay?" Kurt asked. He was back on the other side of the room.

I nodded. Okay. Yeah. Sure. Why not?

My phone buzzed. I looked at the screen. A Voxer message from Mitch. Voxer? I pressed play: Mitch telling me he loved me.

Pressing the talk button I held the phone in front of me and sent the same message back. Kurt pretended not to hear but the grin on his face was hard to miss. I ignored it. The Voxer thing spun around in my head until I felt dizzy. Voxer held possibilities I hadn't considered before.

I lifted my phone and opened Voxer. GPS. Tapping the message Mitch sent showed the location he sent from on a map. He was at my place.

"Kurt, we can use this."

"Voxer?" he asked.

"Yep. Let's see if any of our new friends use Voxer."

"What are you thinking?"

"I'm thinking if I get them Voxing me then we know exactly where they are. It can't hurt." It didn't hurt to have multiple ways to pinpoint someone's location. Things were screwy with this case or these cases. Nope, case. I was sure what seemed like separate incidents were connected, somehow.

"Liking that."

Finding Susan and Danni on Voxer was pretty easy. I sent them both text Voxer messages. They replied within minutes. I tapped the screen and revealed their location.

"They're not in Fairfax," I said to Kurt showing him the map on my phone. "Disobedient tourists."

"Ah, crap. Pennsylvania Ave."

I made a call to Kris to find out what was going on. Pacing up and down the room as the phone rang and rang. When I was about ready to give up he answered.

"Conway?"

"Got eyes on those women?"

"Not yet. We're on our way."

Dammit. I expected them in position by now.

"Give me a Sit-Rep A-sap when you have eyes on them."

"Problem?"

"Potentially. Either the electronic surveillance is screwy or they're not where they're supposed to be."

"I'll be in touch."

I hung up and stopped pacing.

"How far away are the Directors, do you think?" I asked Kurt. "We need to get into D.C."

I heard a light cough and turned around to find our Director standing in the doorway.

"Give me the brief and go," Cait O'Hare said. She walked to the table and placed her laptop bag on the polished wooden surface. "You have a brief?"

I nodded in an effort to stop my head shaking. Sort of. Yeah. Really, it was crap.

"Right here, ma'am," Kurt said placing piles of papers on the desk. "Everything we know, and everything Ellie suspects."

Cait picked the pile in front of her up and looked through them.

"This is it?" She looked at me.

"Yes. I think something is going to happen in D.C. now or very soon."

That's it and it's mostly conjecture.

"Go. Keep in touch. Let me know what you need. I will carry on here and do the briefing."

"Thank you," I said and closed the laptop.

"Stay safe, Ellie."

"Yes, ma'am."

Kurt and I left Cait O'Hare to explain how my gut was responsible for stopping all leave and for putting everyone in D.C. on standby, and increasing security throughout the city. And how I was too late to prevent the Navy Yard. Not to mention why I demanded all the Federal Protection Service Explosive Dog Detection teams be at my disposal. It's a lot to pin on a twingy gut. The overtime alone will severely dent everyone's budgets.

In the parking lot, Kurt paused by the car door.

"Where?" he asked as I put his laptop in the back seat.

"The office."

"Okay. You *see* anything, tell me."

"Sure."

Nah. Maybe. Dunno.

I called Sandra. "We got anything from the EDD sweeps?"

"Bomb squad has gone into Hard Rock Café. Dogs found a cell phone."

"A cell phone?"

"That's all I know so far. Waiting on the bomb squad report."

"Keep me posted. How wide is the evacuation?"

"Limited."

"Our building?"

"Not at this point."

"Okay. We're on our way back."

Sandra's words rumbled in my head as I dropped my phone into my lap. A cell phone? The dogs found explosives in a cell phone? That wasn't going to bring down a building. It was an annoyance find. A decoy. Another distraction.

My phone was in my hand as the next thought surfaced. What about a cell phone bomb in the White House? Now that could cause pandemonium. I called Sandra back.

"I need a number for Charlie Prendergast."

Kurt passed me a pen from his pocket as Sandra read out the number. I wrote it on my hand, thanked her and said goodbye.

Moments later I waited for Charlie to answer his phone.

"This is Charlie Prendergast."

"Charlie, It's SSA Ellie Conway, FBI." I didn't wait for him to acknowledge me. "There's a situation unfolding in D.C. I need some information."

"Sure. Fire away."

Poor choice of words.

"Can you run three names, Trudi Welsh, Danielle Lane, and Susan Hollows? I want to know if any of them applied for a White House tour." He typed. "They are foreign nationals from New Zealand."

The typing continued.

"Not seeing any applications and they're not on this

month's approved visitor list."

"Try Caro Clancy, see if anything comes up."

Typing.

"I have a Caroline Clancy but she's a US citizen living in Virginia."

"And she's on an approved visitor list?"

"Yes."

"Has she been on the tour?"

"Yes, two days ago."

"Do you have surveillance tapes of visitors arriving or on the tour?"

"The rooms are monitored by cameras and yes, the grounds' cameras capture visitors."

"Can I see the video of the day Caroline Clancy visited?"

"Sure. Come to my office whenever you're ready."

"Thanks, Charlie. See you later this afternoon."

My gut twisted, turned, flopped and churned until I felt sick.

Chapter Sixteen.

The Vision.

Standing on Pennsylvania across the 6th Street intersection, I watched rubble spew into the street from the Newseum. Traffic in all directions slowed, some cars stopped, a truck hit a light pole on the other side of the road. The ground rumbled under my feet as walls collapsed and fell into the street. Dust, smoke, particles of building material billowed. I coughed into my elbow. Kurt grabbed my arm and pointed. People stumbled over rubble, wounded, bleeding, disorientated.

We're here again.

Kurt's backpack hung over one shoulder. I wondered if he'd added gas masks to his kit, as I heard sirens and horns. Flashing lights broke through the smoke. Two men ran past me in full SWAT gear. I turned as more spilled from a truck nearby. A voice under the crashing crumbling chaos spoke my name.

"Conway!" I shook the cobwebs from my head and turned to the voice.

Andrews. He ran toward me carrying two flak jackets and helmets.

"Put it on," he said, thrusting the jacket into my arms and jamming the helmet on my head. "Do it up." He peered past me to Kurt. "Here, put it on."

Kurt nodded. He dropped his backpack and pulled the

flak jacket over his head, fastening the Velcro at the sides. Andrews dropped a helmet on his head.

"Thanks."

"You just get here?" Andrews asked.

"Yeah, we were walking toward the museum when it exploded," Kurt replied. "I need to get to the wounded."

One swift hand signal and Kurt had a two-man SWAT escort.

"Conway, with me," Andrews said.

My head shook. "I'm going with Kurt. I just need to do something first. We have three people helping us, they could be in there." I pointed to the rubble-spewing building. Another violent rumble toppled more of the building. "Kurt, wait?"

"Of course," he replied.

I checked Voxer and audio messaged Susan. "Where are you?"

I waited. Hardly breathing. Breathing hurt anyway. Too much smoke, not enough oxygen. I needed a gas mask but didn't want to feel trapped again.

A text message came back via Voxer. "In Fair Oaks Mall." I tapped the screen. Nope, it came up as Capitol Hill. Holy crap, it was getting worse.

I replied, "You're not near the Newseum?"

This time she replied immediately, "We're in the Redskin store."

"All of you?"

"No, just me and Trudi."

"Where's Danni?"

"At the hotel."

"Something just happened in D.C. Stay put."

I pocketed my phone just as it rang again. It was Kris.

"Eyes on Hollows and Welsh – they're in Fair Oaks Mall. Cannot see Lane."

"Hollows told me Lane is back at the hotel."

"Will confirm A-sap."

"Thanks."

I hung up and this time my phone stayed silent as I shoved it into my pocket.

"Right, let's get in there and do this thing," I said to Kurt.

More wounded, confused people stumbled past us to a triage center that had popped up by the SWAT truck. Medical personal in scrubs and paramedics wearing flight suits directed the wounded. The only thing I felt grateful for at that moment was that everyone listened. We had people who knew what they were doing on the ground within minutes.

As we approached the building, emergency personal sprouted like mushrooms. High-Vis vests in all directions, both yellow and orange. People barked orders. Some yelled. The wounded we saw said nothing and made no noise. Shock. Disbelief. Horror. Terror.

I didn't want to go into the building.

Suck it up, Princess. You're doing this and dealing.

I kept pace with Kurt. Ahead of me a figure I recognized emerged and clambered with sure feet over unsteady hunks of stone, eventually jumping to a patch of clear ground. Blood trickled from Claude's forehead. He wiped if off with impatience.

"If you're going in, I'll come with you," Claude said. "But I don't advise it."

Kurt responded, "We need to. You okay?"

"Yeah. It's nothing," he replied. "Flesh wound."

"How'd you get here so fast?" I asked. "Where's the rest of Delta B?"

"I was already here and on my own." He wiped away more blood. "I just wanted to be sure of their security measures."

Kurt dropped his pack. He took out iodine spray, sterile wound pads and a sticky dressing. "Close your eyes. This will sting," Kurt said as he sprayed the cut, wiped the area with the wound pad and then stuck a dressing over it.

"That'll do for now," he said, closing his pack and slinging it back on his shoulder.

"Thanks, I think," Claude replied, wiping residual iodine spray off his face.

"Let's go," Kurt said.

I took a breath and climbed over the rubble following Kurt and Claude into the dusty, smoke-filled interior toward the sound of choking and tears.

Chapter Seventeen.

Into the Daylight

I slid down the wall of a building on 10th Street, across the road from the J Edgar Hoover Building and drew up my knees. My heart raced, nausea came and went. It took vast amounts of effort to control my breathing and bring everything around me back into focus. My phone was in a death grip in my filthy hands. I saw Mitch's picture on the screen, below it a green call button. I touched the call button and waited. Breathing and counting.

"Talk to me for a few minutes?" My voice steady enough to speak when he answered.

"Of course. You okay?"

"No, yes, maybe."

Breathe.

"El?"

"I will be."

Mitch started talking and I breathed. "Today I worked from home. Your home. It was nice being among your things. Comforting."

Everything slowed down as I listened to Mitch's voice. I loved his voice.

"I'm cooking us dinner. Roast chicken. Stuffed it too. Homemade stuffing. Nice bottle of Pinot Gris chilling. Ellie, you doing okay?"

"I'm doing better. Keep talking."

Mitch talked. I listened to his words, letting them take over my being and settle the crazy in my mind. "Mom rang. She was worried when she couldn't reach me at my desk today. I switched the news on about two this afternoon. Thank you for insisting I go home. You were right. Is this what this is about?"

"Newseum at one fifty-three this afternoon, and ..." I checked my watch. "Five minutes ago a large chunk of the Hoover Building landed on Pennsylvania killing a woman as she walked by."

"Are you safe?" Mitch asked.

"Yes," I replied, crossing my fingers. I had no idea. But I hoped so. "I'm trying to figure out how two of those women were at the Newseum and near the Hoover Building today as Voxer indicated when they messaged me this afternoon. Our bugs say they were still in Fair Oaks Mall. They said they were in Fair Oaks mall when I spoke to them and that was confirmed by my surveillance team."

What the hell? It made zero sense.

I took a shaky breath. Then another and another. Just keep breathing. Don't think. Just be. The answers will come.

"Are you alone?"

I looked around. "Yeah, I am." I had no idea where everyone was. "I should go find Kurt and Claude and the rest of the Delta teams."

"Come home, El?"

"Soon. I'll find Kurt first and I have to meet with a

Secret Service agent this afternoon." I looked over at our building. Chaos. Utter chaos. "I gotta go."

I ended the call. The bedlam in front of me was an all-too-familiar scene now. My mind sifted images and compartmentalized everything. To survive the day, I needed to mentally step back. I couldn't be emotionally tied to anything I witnessed.

Sitting on the cold ground with a solid building against my back didn't feel as soothing as it once would have done. Getting back to a place where D.C. felt safe would not be easy. Someone broke my city and it would take time to fix it.

Deep breaths. Calming thoughts.

Mitch's voice in my head.

With some distance achieved, I scanned the area. Looking for anyone familiar, maybe someone I'd seen at the earlier bombing or maybe at the Navy Yard. Someone like Agent Troy.

I doubted whoever was responsible had left. The person may even be helping. I remembered what Chance said about firefighters lighting fires.

Where was Troy?

If he was intent on being a hero and this was his handiwork, then surely he should've stumbled upon the bomb and played the hero? Three bombings in twenty-four hours. That's some serious shit.

There were people everywhere. It was hard to see individuals and focus on faces. My phone rang. I looked at the screen: Iain Campbell.

"I have the drone airborne. I can see you. You okay?" Iain said.

"Yeah. What else can you see?"

"Having to fly low, lot of smoke and particles in the air, scanning the crowd, checking out bystanders."

Bystanders. Rubberneckers. The worse the incident, the bigger the crowd. People have a perverse need to view the unfathomable.

I looked up and spotted the drone hovering in the sky at the corner of the building I leaned on. I waved.

"Do your best, Iain. If you get eyes on Troy, let me know. He's been missing all day."

"Where do you want me to download the feed?"

Good question. Not my office.

"You got my home number?"

"Yes."

"Call home, talk to Mitch. Send the feed directly to my PC."

"Good thinking."

"Hey, does that drone of yours deliver food?"

"A picture of food maybe ... hungry?"

"Yeah, for a poppy seed bagel with cream cheese and smoked salmon."

Iain laughed. "Carnage will do that to a person. I've got Mitch on the other line. Talk soon."

I didn't move. That confused me. Why wasn't I standing up and looking for Kurt and Sandra? Why wasn't I coming up with avenues of investigation? Because I didn't know where to start. And then I remembered the C4 inside the Beretta that I found in our bullpen once. The only way to get explosives into our building was if the person was supposed to be there and/ or carrying something that could conceal the explosive. Not a backpack and not a briefcase, not unless they were supposed to be there. That thought swirled, making me feel sick. I could walk in carrying Semtex without anyone blinking, especially in an evidence bag or in a box with other evidence or even in my shoulder bag. Hell, I could just carry a couple of pounds of the orange shit in my hand.

Would anyone challenge Troy?

No. He was an agent. Mentored by me.

Holy enabling Batman.

I was on my feet and running toward the entrance we usually used on 10th. If it was someone, anyone, who was comfortable in the building, why blow out one section only? To focus attention away from something? No one stopped me as I ran through the doors and up the stairs. Running without thought, I felt I knew something I didn't or couldn't know and had no explanation.

I swung open a smoke-stop door and stood in the quiet of the corridor that led to my office. Quiet? It wasn't quiet. From deep within the walls that surrounded the Delta team bullpen, I heard the tapping of a keyboard. No one should be here. I took my phone from my pocket and switched it to silent.

My hand tightened on the grip of my Glock and I released it from my holster. Gun in hand, I approached the bullpen. There was a sudden draft. I glanced over my shoulder as the stairwell door slowly closed. Kurt walked toward me. I signaled him to be quiet and pointed to the bullpen. He fell in behind me.

Ten feet.

Breathe.

At the doorway, Kurt's hand squeezed my shoulder twice, indicating he was ready to move. I was right. He was left. I tapped his hand and stepped through the doorway focusing on the right side of the room, checking for hazards. Clear.

From a secure position, I faced the interior of the room. Kurt had his weapon trained on Troy.

Our missing agent.

What a surprise.

I walked toward them. "You want to explain why you're in an evacuated building?" I asked, as Kurt stood Troy up and took his weapon.

"I was trying to find a link between the bombings," he replied. I detected a tremor in his voice. Not so sure of himself then?

"How's that working for you?"

"The only link is the women."

"The three women. Well, let's bring them in then," I said. "Do you know where they are?"

He said nothing. Kurt repeated my question.

Troy shook his head.

"Walk," Kurt said, giving him gentle encouragement toward the nearest wall. "Assume the position." Kurt patted him down and removed two flash drives from his suit jacket pocket. "Catch." He threw them to me one at a time.

"What will I find on these?" I asked Troy.

"My notes," he replied.

Two flash drives. I looked at them carefully. Two eight-gig flash drives: seemed like he required a lot of storage for his notes. Maybe he expected to be using them for a long time.

"Let's have a look shall we? My office."

I let Kurt take Troy and lead the way. I paused by the computer he'd been using and read the screen. He had the Operation Visitor case file open. I checked to see what pages he'd looked at and if he'd added notes. He had. He'd surmised that the only link between the bombings was the three tourists from New Zealand based on not much. I scrolled down the screen.

Ah, crap.

He said the women were in the city today and in the vicinity of the Newseum prior to the explosion. Why would he think that? He didn't know about our electronic surveillance because only Kurt and I could see the feed and in any case, our surveillance program put them firmly in Fairfax County not here in D.C.; Voxer put them here. He didn't know about Kris and Jerry either.

Where was Troy getting his information?

I took a screen shot of the information and filed it. Then amended the case notes to say I had doubts about the women's involvement, based on a short interview. It was time to lock Troy out of the case file.

In my office, Troy sat still. His gaze fixed on the wall behind my desk.

"Why do you think the women were in the city today?" I asked as I plugged the first of his flash drives into my laptop. Two seconds later, a box on my screen asked for a password. "Password, Troy?"

"Tourist," he replied.

A complete copy of the Sentinel case file scrolled down the screen. I shook my head.

"You copied a case file. How fucking stupid are you?" I glared at him over my laptop. "That's a career ender."

"I thought I could work on it at home."

"Never occurred to you to log in remotely and work on it?"

Of course, that would leave a trail. And Sentinel would recognize the remote access and block all attempts at downloading or copying the file and its contents. Safeguards are necessary. People are stupid. So he knew enough not to try remote access but Troy didn't seem aware that Sentinel logged all changes to case files with the agent's name and ID. It would've logged the download and tagged the file. I'd see it as soon as I logged back in. That information was above his pay grade.

Troy's mouth set in a firm line. He wasn't feeling chatty. Shame. Because I was.

"Are there any more bombs in this building?"

He said nothing.

"Troy. If you have any hope of redeeming yourself then

you need to talk to me. Now."

A psychic twinge made me check my phone. The screen was full of missed calls and messages. Dammit. I turned the volume back on. Three of the calls were from Campbell.

"I need to make a call," I said to Kurt. "I'll be in the hall."

I closed the door, leaned on the wall and called Campbell.

"You wanted me?"

"You all right? You took off in a big hurry. Thermal imaging suggested a person in your bullpen and I saw you run into the building."

"You sent Kurt?"

"Yes. You're welcome."

"We found Troy in the bullpen downloading files."

"Idiot."

"Yep."

"Let me know if you need anything. It's still crazy out here."

"Thanks, Iain."

I checked the text messages next. One long one from Mitch. I replied to tell him I was fine and I'd be home when I could get there. Caine's messages weren't such easy replies. I ignored them. I had no answers yet. Director O'Hare's message required a response. I texted her saying Delta was safe. The explosion took out empty offices.

Empty offices.

I pocketed my phone. The next floor down directly under us were conference rooms. I went back into my office and checked the second flash drive. No password this time. It contained video footage. I clicked on the first video. It was one I'd seen before. I clicked the next and the next ... I had fourteen videos open and flicked from one to the other. These were the deleted videos.

"Talking would be smart," I said, looking at Troy.

"I don't know what's on that drive," he said, his voice cracked.

Was it enough to arrest him on suspicion of terrorism? No. he never left the damn building with the flash drives, but he intended to. There was a ledge and I suspected legal would go nuts if I rappelled over it.

How'd they feel about me pushing Troy over the ledge?

"Special Agent Troy, you are required to explain your behavior to SAC Grafton and me at the earliest possible time. You may bring a support person with you." I opened the Delta calendar and scanned for suitable time and date. "We are not done here but you are. You will be in SAC Grafton's office next Monday morning at eight. Until then you are stood down."

He slumped in the chair.

Kurt spoke, "Badge and ID on the desk, now."

Troy did as he was asked.

I entered data onto Sentinel, updating Troy's agent status. He would no longer be able to access the building freely. I marked him "escort required." If I were proven wrong, I'd apologize. I hoped I was wrong, even though his behavior did nothing for my trust issues.

Smoke.

I glanced at Kurt. A fine haze filled the room. It smelled like death. That was wrong. We weren't anywhere near the explosion site.

Kurt's eyes met mine he started to speak, his words lost in a roar. Everything moved. My desk tilted and my chair tried to roll into the wall behind me with me on it. I fought to stay within arm's reach of my desk. I pocketed the flash drives, shut my laptop and jammed it into the case that sat next to my desk.

"Leave it," Kurt said.

"No." I took the case with me.

The three of us made it to the hallway. I turned to see the wall behind my desk collapse. My chair flew into the air. My office disintegrated.

Shit.

We ran for the stairs. At the first landing, I wondered how far we would get before there were no stairs. Two floors down smoke rose from below. I pulled open a smoke-stop door and stepped out of the stairwell followed by Kurt and Troy. Another massive rumble shook the building. I lurched into a wall. Something hit me from behind. Glass in the door we'd come through smashed all over the hallway. I switched hands with my laptop case. Troy fell. Kurt helped him to his feet. Smoke billowed into the corridor. We moved fast in the opposite direction, heading for another set of stairs. It seemed to take forever to get out. Emergency services were all over the ground, high-vis everything in all directions.

"Stick with us," Kurt said to Troy. He had his hand on Troy's arm. "I mean it."

"Yes, sir."

I stood on the corner by the Hard Rock Café and surveyed the confusion in front of me. My eyes and brain tried to make sense of the destruction.

"That's the painting that was on my wall," I said pointing at something that spilled from the masonry before more wreckage covered it. "That was a close thing."

"Too close," Kurt replied. His hand touched my shoulder blade. It twinged a bit. "You've got a piece of something sticking out of your back. Should've left our vests on. Just your luck, Conway."

"Crap. Can we just leave it and let it work its way out?" I knew that wasn't going to happen. But it was worth a try.

"Turn a little toward my hand," he said, touching my right shoulder.

I did.

"What is it?"

"Wood. Probably a piece of door."

"Bad?"

"Don't think so ... I need to get in there and have a look."

There were people everywhere. I didn't really feel like taking off my jacket and top. There was no triage tent yet but I could see medical personnel, so I knew there would be soon.

"Into the Hard Rock, they have enough room in the bathrooms. I've got my gear," Kurt said.

Yay. But he was right about the large bathrooms. Kurt told Troy he was coming with us. That didn't impress me much.

"You are staying outside the bathroom door. Do I have to handcuff you to something?" I said as we went into the Café.

Kurt spoke to a staff member.

"You don't," Troy said. "I'll wait."

"Good that your brain finally kicked in," I replied.

We followed Kurt up the stairs and to the women's bathroom. It was empty. Troy stood outside.

Kurt opened his backpack and I stopped watching. I knew what he was going to do and it didn't thrill me.

"You'll need my help to get your jacket and shirt off. You ready?"

"Sure. Just do it."

I felt the thing in my back move when Kurt lifted the fabric from my jacket out a little. He cut the hole bigger. I took one arm out of my jacket, Kurt lifted the fabric off the wood, and then I took out the other arm. The jacket ended up on the floor.

"Same again but with your shirt. Undo the buttons first."

That bit was easy enough. Kurt pulled the fabric away from the wood and cut, then eased out my arm and lifted the fabric off the wood. My shirt landed on top of my jacket.

"We good now?" I asked.

"Yep. It looks like a smooth piece of wood, so I'm not expecting splinters but I need to get in there and look. This is going to hurt."

"Thanks for the warning."

"Let's sit you down." I sat on the floor. Cold from the tiles seeped into my jeans. I shivered.

"Not ideal, Conway, but we can do this. You ready?"

"Yes."

No, not at all.

He sprayed something cold on my back. Iodine. I sat up straighter as the wood moved from side-to-side.

Jeez. He wasn't kidding about it hurting.

My mind mumbled inside itself searching for a happy place before he yanked the wood right out. Mitch. I closed my eyes and went to Mitch. He was checking on the progress of tonight's dinner. Whistling. Whistling. I liked that he whistled. I felt Kurt's fingers grip the wood. Mitch turned around. He looked right at me and smiled.

With one hand on my other shoulder, Kurt pulled.

Violent, sharp pain shot through me.

"Fuck," I groaned and took a slow, shallow breath.

"Sorry, Conway. A few more minutes, the wood is out, here." He reached around and handed me a two-inch piece of wood that resembled a knife blade. It was about three-quarters of an inch across at the widest point. Nice splinter.

I fought my way back to Mitch. He looked at me and

frowned then picked up his phone from the counter.

My phone rang.

Weird.

"What happened?" Mitch asked.

"Got a bit of wood in my back." Talking wasn't easy. Kurt was poking around in the wound and it hurt. "How did you know something happened?"

"I heard you."

Once upon a time, that would've made no sense at all.

"Can't talk long," I said. My reasoning stayed within my mind because it made little sense now. I have to go because I don't want you to hear how hard it is for me to talk normally while Kurt is sewing up my back.

"You are okay?"

"Yes. Just uncomfortable." I changed the subject. "How's dinner?"

"Looks good, be ready soon."

"Don't suppose you could slow down the cooking process?"

"I'll do my best," Mitch replied.

"I'll try to be there before the chicken shrivels."

I hung up as the suture needle made its first pass.

Ten minutes later, with the wound on my back covered with a waterproof dressing, I had my holey shirt back on. Kurt helped me with my jacket.

"Thank you," I said.

"You're welcome. Everything feel okay?"

I moved my shoulders and stretched a little. "Yep."

"Go easy on those sutures, Conway. No acrobatics until

I take them out."

I smiled. "Deal."

"Now let's go get a head count and make sure all our people are accounted for."

We took Troy and left the delicious aromas of the Hard Rock Café behind.

I looked around for Caine. A hand went up from down the street amidst the disarray and waved. Caine. A smile grew. He was okay. He made his way to us – I was in no hurry to go near the mess. I was almost part of it. My thoughts stopped at that. 'What if' is not a game that should be played.

"Where were you?" Caine asked. "You didn't answer your phone."

"In my office," I said. I saw a piece of my desk. "And now it's there." I pointed.

"Everyone is accounted for, except Troy." Caine looked over my shoulder. "I see you found him."

He stood beside Kurt; shell-shocked aptly described his expression.

"About that. We have a disciplinary meeting with Troy next Monday. He had the entire Operation Visitor case file on a flash drive and all the deleted video footage on another."

Caine's lip twitched. "We've been here before," he said. His attention turned to Troy, his tone hostile. "For your sake I hope you can explain this come Monday. Go home, agent."

Troy said nothing. He turned and walked back up the

street.

"Surveillance," I said. "I need people on him twenty-four-seven until Monday."

We were pushed to the limit. I needed to call in some favors. Again.

"We've activated an emergency terrorism protocol. FBI have point on this investigation but all policing agencies are involved."

I leaned forward and whispered, "Renegade?"

"Angel," he replied.

So he was on board Air Force One and would be airborne until further notice. I blinked to clear dust from my eyes. Looking back at the rubble-filled street in front of me, I saw flames trailing behind a plane. A fireball raced through the cabin and a chunk of wreckage landed by my feet. Not good.

"That could be what they want."

My internal screen flicked to another scene. A missile fired. It tracked something in the air. The plane? Air force One?

"Ellie?" Caine motioned for me to walk with him. We walked up the middle of the road until we were level with Ford's Theater. "Explain, could be what they want?"

"Ground to air missile, just thinking out loud," I said, hoping he didn't ask for more of an explanation. I didn't have one.

"The plane is escorted."

I knew that. But still I saw flaming wreckage.

"What if they don't care? What if there is more than

one missile tracking the plane? What if the escort is taken out?" My fingers tightened around the handle on my laptop case.

"Where is this coming from?" Caine's lip twitched.

My phone rang. Iain Campbell. "I need to take this ..." I said, holding my phone up. Caine nodded.

Iain's voice flowed from the phone in my hand, "You're okay, good. Drone above you. I saw what you said to Caine. If you're right ..."

"Saw?"

"Drone can see with amazing clarity and I can lip read."

Of course.

"If I'm right, now what?"

"Now, I make a call. Time to play hide and seek with Angel."

"Thanks."

"Don't mention it."

I hung up and smiled at Caine. "We're being watched." I pointed to the sky. "Campbell will take care of the potential angel problem."

"Good, now surveillance for Troy. Give it to Transit."

I frowned. "Transit?"

"Yeah. Transit."

"Okay."

"Hand the surveillance job to Transit and then go home, Ellie."

"I can't go home ... have you not seen the state of the city?"

"It's an order. Go home."

"I need to meet with someone over at the Secret Service first. Send Kurt home too."

"Take Kurt with you to your meeting then both of you are to go home. I'll be in touch and let you know where our temporary office is in the morning."

"Are you planning on using the Washington field office?"

"All going well. Otherwise, we'll cross the river and come set up at your place."

"Thanks." I smiled. "That idea isn't top of my list." Wouldn't be the first time my place had become a temporary base but I'd prefer it not to be. "Let's use the field office."

Caine twitched. "Now, hand over the surveillance job and get to that meeting."

We walked back to the throng of orange and yellow jackets, crime scene tape, triage areas, flashing lights and noise. Kurt was in a triage tent. It's what he did and who he was.

"Hey, we've been ordered home but first a meeting with Secret Service."

I waited for the argument. Nothing. Damn. Whole new level. Rachel. That's why no argument. Rachel. My how our priorities have changed.

"I'm ready to go," he said, handing paperwork to a woman wearing a flight suit.

"Where's Rachel?"

"My place with Olivia."

"We had a car. Where the hell is our car?" I looked around hoping something would jog my memory.

"On Penns," Kurt replied. "Come on."

That's right, we left the car on Pennsylvania and walked to the Newseum. The walk down Pennsylvania to find the car was slow going. We found the car then started planning a route out. Getting out of the area would be fun. So much destruction. People everywhere. Car and trucks abandoned by their owners. Emergency service vehicles with rolling lights. Thankfully, no sirens. Barricades in place, preventing people getting too close to the Newseum. Most of the intersection blocked.

My eyes scanned faces, searching for familiar people on the sidewalks. At one point, I thought I saw Danni Lane. Odd.

I let the face drift in my mind. The next thing that caught my attention was a black Sharpie. It drew the outline of a room. An office. A glass-topped desk and leather chair. A laptop. The room shimmered and the outlines filled in. Color flooded the scene. When the chair turned, I saw Chance. He grinned.

"Hey, Ellie, my office this time. Nice to see you in here."

"Nice office, don't know what I expected but not this ..." Stylish, modern, light.

"You had a question?"

I nodded. "What sort of research do authors who write thrillers do?"

"You mean how hands on is the research, don't you?"

"Yeah, and also how realistic is Lane's writing?"

"That's a question for Kurt, he's read her. As for research, I thought they mainly interviewed people and maybe fired a gun or two."

"Kurt, yeah, and thanks."

"You all right?"

"Think so."

"Take it easy."

The room faded; Chance waved before he disappeared.

Kurt reached out and turned on the radio. News. Public service announcements: Washington effectively closed.

"I have a question," I said.

"I'm listening."

"How realistic is Lane's writing about the FBI, and me in particular?"

His head nodded as he frowned. "She's close, very close. The reactions of her main character are very similar to yours. And she's got a good handle on how we work."

"Fascinating." I leaned back, trying to get comfortable.

"Back okay?"

"Yeah, just feeling bruised." I thought about what Kurt had said and what Chance said for a few moments. "Okay. How is she so accurate?"

"Research?" Kurt offered.

"Of course," I replied. "But how is it conducted?"

"Interviews."

"Yeah well, I've never been interviewed."

"Maybe she's a stalker?"

"Shit, you're funny."

Kurt laughed.

Thirty minutes later Charlie ushered us into his office.

"Crazy out there?" he asked, pointing to chairs in front of a bank of screens. "Have a seat. I imagine you're quite busy."

I smiled and nodded. "Renegade is still airborne?"

"Yes." He didn't query how I knew.

"Show us the tapes from the day Caroline Clancy visited the White House."

"They're ready to go," Charlie said and reached past me to press two keys on the keyboard in front of me.

We watched in silence until a dark-haired woman approached the gate and admitted at a security checkpoint. I paused the video.

Kurt looked at me.

"That looks like Danni Lane," Kurt said leaning forward for a closer look.

"Yeah, it does," I agreed.

Charlie intervened. "We have a copy of her photo identification." He flicked through some paperwork on his desk and handed me two sheets of paper. "Virginia State ID card and a current Virginia driver's license."

I looked at the pictures.

"What did she enter the White House with? Do you know?"

He nodded and picked up another piece of paper. "Cell phone, wallet, car keys."

"And she left with?"

"Cell phone, wallet, car keys."

I stared at the image on the screen. Screened. Searched. She had three things with her.

"Can we see the footage from inside, please?"

"Sure." Charlie pulled up another camera, same day, ten minutes later.

Watching Danni and two other people walk through the public areas of the White House was a yawn-worthy exercise until Clancy knelt down to re-tie her sneaker lace. As she stood up, she used a desk as support. A Secret Service agent nearby said something to her and she appeared apologetic and moved away.

"What is that?" I asked, pointing to the desk.

"A desk that belonged to one of the First Ladies."

She touched it.

She *touched* it.

I rewound and watched the shoe tying again. She took something from between her laces and the tongue of her shoe.

What?

"Has that desk always been there?"

Charlie thumbed through more papers. Then opened a filing cabinet and pulled out a file. More thumbing.

"I found it. It was recently returned after resurfacing. It's been back in that room for eight days."

"Where did it go?"

"A restoration company in New York."

"I need the address and everything you have about that

company. Also, no one goes in that room until the bomb squad clear it."

Charlie leaned on the desk, a frown creasing his brow, worry filling his green eyes.

"We sweep for bombs, bugs, and electronic devices three times a day."

"Humor me, it's better than going bang."

He nodded.

I picked up the phone on his desk and used it to call the bomb squad. So very pleased that POTUS was airborne.

"I have another question …"

"Go ahead," Charlie said.

"How fucked do you think we are right now?"

Charlie grinned. "About as fucked as it gets."

That's what I thought and yet, Caine had ordered us to go home.

"Keep in touch, Charlie. Keep your head down and stay out of that room until it's clear."

"Will do."

We left.

My mind rolled scenarios like cigarettes.

How could Danni Lane be Caroline Clancy? One was a New Zealander and the other an American.

It didn't make sense. The week didn't make sense.

Kurt broke into my thoughts. "Let it go, Conway. I'll check on our electronic surveillance and the surveillance team when I get home."

"How'd you know I was thinking about her?"

"Really?"

"Nah."

Chapter Eighteen.

Just Give Me a Reason

Opening the front door, I gave in to the urge and called out, "Honey, I'm home and I've had a hard day."

Mitch emerged from the living room. His laughter bounced off the hallway walls.

"I'm glad you're home."

We met in the middle of the hall. Again, I was filthy, covered in masonry dust and blood smeared. This time some of the blood was mine. He hadn't seen that yet. Mitch held his arms out. I didn't step into his arms right away.

A small frown creased his forehead. "Okay to hug you?"

"Yeah," I took one step forward. "Just ..."

"I'll be careful." His arms encircled me, avoiding the cut on my back, and everything melted away.

I don't know how long we stood like that. It could've been a minute; could've been ten.

He whispered, "You've got time to clean up before dinner."

I laughed. "Subtle."

Mitch's chest vibrated as he laughed with me.

"How's your back?"

"It's okay. I'm going to shower."

"Need a hand?" I leaned back in his arms to see his

face. Yeah, that wasn't great. I attempted to hide a wince and failed. "Yeah, you do," Mitch said without waiting for my reply.

My muscles were achy. The wound site felt bruised, it probably was, and I wasn't sure how much movement I had in my right shoulder.

Half an hour later I sat at the dining table with a plate of the best-looking slightly dry roast chicken and roast vegetables I'd seen in ages and a glass of Pinot Gris. I rolled the stem of the glass between my fingers and thumb, swirling the contents. In the background, I heard a song. I smiled as I recognized it. "Angie." I closed my eyes and listened for a bit.

"This is wonderful." My eyes flicked to Mitch. His smile lit up his eyes and his whole expression softened.

"It was my pleasure."

The song changed. "Far away eyes."

Mitch transformed my house into a sanctuary from the storm that raged in our world just by being in it. My phone sat on the table by my right hand. The screen flashed then the phone rang. Kris. I was still waiting to hear from him about Danni's whereabouts. I answered it with an apologetic smile at Mitch.

"What's up?"

"We cannot confirm the whereabouts of Danni Lane."

Crap!

"You haven't sighted her at all?"

"No. The other two women are in the hotel room now. Lights are off. Have not seen Lane."

"Thanks, Kris. Get some sleep. We'll pick this up again tomorrow." I hung up, walked into the kitchen and put my phone on the counter. I hoped Lane was in the hotel room but I wasn't counting on it.

I returned to the dining room and sat back in my chair. The music washed over me and filled the room, insulating us from the horror of the outside world.

My phone buzzed on the kitchen counter. Loud, insistent, like a blowfly fighting its inevitable but excruciating death. I didn't even look in its direction, just willed it to stop. No more interruptions tonight. I let The Rolling Stones "Beast of Burden" override the buzzing until all I heard was Mick Jagger.

"Excellent choice in music."

"Thought I remembered you liking the Stones."

He remembered everything. Every detail.

We ate and talked and talked and ate and drank our way through a bottle of wine. In the kitchen doing the dishes together, "Wild Horses" came on. Mitch turned it up, took my hand and pulled me close. Slow dancing in the kitchen to the Rolling Stones. My head on his shoulder.

And nothing else mattered.

An hour or so later we lay together in bed, enjoying the moment and each other's warmth. The house was quiet. No distractions. No rush, no urgency. I silenced my mind and quieted the insistent voices that demanded I go back to work. If tomorrow never comes, all you have is now. There was no guarantee we'd be here again.

Mitch's heart thumped against my hand. The constant beat was comforting and reassuring. I knew that we were meant to be. This was working. The world as I knew it might be exploding but I finally got something right.

My mind wandered into a safe space. There was nothing else, just Mitch and me. I drifted into an exhausted sleep.

Chapter Nineteen.

Hey Ya

A scream.

Startled from sleep, my eyes flicked open. Disoriented.

My heart pounded too fast and too loud and made swishing noises in my head. I touched the bed next to me.

Cold. Empty. Confusing.

Where did the scream come from?

Was I awake? My hand hit the base of the bedside light. A warm glow illuminated the room.

The room. Not *my* room.

Where was I?

From the bed, I could see two closed doors, one window, a nightstand, a set of drawers and a mirror on the wall. No artwork. Nothing of mine. Nothing familiar. I pushed the covers back. A hospital gown?

I looked around the room again.

It wasn't a hospital room. Or was it?

My legs worked. I swung them over the side of the bed and dropped to my feet. Standing was okay. Nothing hurt. My arms were free of tubing. These were good signs.

"Mitch?" I couldn't see anyone. He always heard me when I called.

No one came.

"Mitch!"

I twisted the door handle on one door. It came off in my hand. I dropped it on the ground and it disappeared. Weird. I tried the other door. Locked or stuck. I tried again. This time shaking the door handle. It didn't budge.

The room shimmered. I walked back to the bed and sat down. The walls bulged and heaved. Not good.

Thick black outlines appeared around the furniture, the doors and window. Everything flattened. I closed my eyes for a second. A door opened then closed.

"Mitch?"

"No, Ellie. I'm not Mitch."

I opened my eyes to find Chance standing in front of me. Could've been worse but he wasn't who I wanted to see.

"Where am I?"

"I told you they said you were close to the edge, looks like you jumped right off," he said with a grin and sat next to me. "You okay?"

I shook my head. "No, when I went to sleep last night, I was at home with Mitch. This doesn't work ..." I waved my hand at the flat scene we sat in. "I don't feel right being in a comic."

He grinned. "You'll get used to it. It's just like when you visited me in my office but ... different."

"Why are you here?"

"Troy."

"I suspended him and removed his security clearance pending an investigation."

Chance nodded. "Troy met with someone last night."

189

"He's under surveillance."

"But this won't look suspicious. He met with someone from the legal division."

"So, he's getting advice. Smart."

"No, he's discussing the case with someone."

"Friend or co-conspirator?"

"I'm guessing the latter," Chance said.

"Ah crap, it's not just him."

Not that I thought it was.

"Ellie, you should lie down."

"Why?"

"You're bleeding," he replied, pointing to my abdomen.

I looked down. The gown had stuck to me; blood seeped through the fabric creating a large red wet area.

"Oh, that's probably not good."

"Lie down."

The ceiling undulated as I lay back on the pillow. Chance leaned over me. His hand pressed on my stomach. I knew what I needed.

"Mitch!"

"Ellie, he's not here," Chance said. His hand pressing harder. Blood bubbled through his fingers.

"He'll come," I replied. "He'll come."

"How can you be so sure?" Chance's voice faded into the ether.

My eyes closed.

"Because he *loves* me," I whispered into the cold darkness. "Please come, Mitch. There's something wrong and I'm cold. So cold."

I had no idea whether my eyes were still closed or if they were open. There was nothing but dark.

Glowing letters circled above me. They twisted and joined.

Words.

Speech marks.

My name.

A line. It wasn't a line it was a sentence.

"Ellie, I want you to wake up." More glow in the dark words made another sentence. "El, open your eyes."

I saw the words and heard the voice. I was right. I knew he'd come.

My eyes opened and blinked. Light. It hurt. With a rush, I pushed the blankets off me. No hospital gown. No abdominal wound. Naked. Hands pulled the blankets back up.

"Hey, you were dreaming," Mitch said.

"Dreaming?"

"Yes, you woke me up with a scream. Lie down?"

I didn't. Mitch sat in bed next to me.

"Chance told me to lie down."

"Who's Chance?"

"Too hard to explain."

"What were you looking for when you woke up?"

"Abdo wound."

"Did he tell you about that?"

"No. Yes."

Mitch chewed his lip. "You saw it."

"Yes."

"El, what exactly did you see?" Worry lines etched across his forehead.

Go me. Wake him up with a scream then scare him with my craziness.

I tried to smile. "It was a nightmare."

"A nightmare," he repeated, unconvinced. "El, you see things and they happen."

"It was different. It was a nightmare, not me seeing smoke or anything while I'm awake." I tried the smile again. "And you didn't see it?"

He shook his head. "I didn't see it. Are you sure it was just a nightmare?"

Do I lie? Not to him.

"I think I just saw my death."

He slid an arm around my shoulders and pulled me close until we were lying together again. Skin on skin. Hearts beating as one. The life I wanted stretching in front of me. Finally safe. No one is taking this away. Not now.

I let Mitch's heartbeat soothe me. Steady, strong, life affirming. He held me close and kissed me. So loving and sweet. From that place, I could afford to let things line up in my mind.

I shuffled everything to do with the case until it was in order. I checked and double-checked.

What was this case about?

Terrorism.

What did it have to do with New Zealand?

Nothing.

Troy called me with his suspicions hours before we were supposed to leave for New Zealand. I never told him we were leaving.

Did I tell him?

No.

Did he access my case notes?

He wasn't cleared for my notes.

This can't be about Troy.

It's something else.

Delta separated.

Why?

Why send Delta so far away?

Not to divide us but to have the whole team at the bottom of the world. If that was the plan, it failed.

The target changed. To get to POTUS, they'd have to incapacitate more than just Kurt and me. Something about the potential threat to POTUS didn't feel right but it spun Danni Lane in the limelight. The question I'd asked Kurt and Chance sat front and center in my mind. Research? All about me? Studying me in various situations?

A small chuckle escaped.

"What's funny?" Mitch asked, his voice thick with sleep.

"For a minute I thought this case was all about me."

"It's not always about you, El," Mitch replied with sleepy amusement.

"Not when you're around, Mitch."

Not when you're around.

Backup.

Delta expanded. We grew up. We have lives and partners. This has something to do with all of us.

I reached out and picked up my cell phone.

"Sleep, El," Mitch said.

"In a minute."

I sent a text message to the whole team. It sounded nuts, it probably was, but if there were any truth in it, I couldn't ignore it. I closed my eyes when I opened them again the crazy text was still sitting on the screen:

'Delta A may have become targets of whatever this is in D.C, just because of what we do. I believe the original intended target was Renegade.'

I pressed send. Slid my phone back onto the nightstand and curled up with Mitch.

Chapter Twenty.

Seek and Destroy

Morning didn't creep in under the curtains and lazily waft across the room. It blasted its horn and hammered on the front door.

Mitch groaned, rolled out of bed and pulled on jeans. He searched in the semi-darkness then straightened up and dragged a sweater over his head. Barefoot, he left the room. I heard him running down the stairs. The man liked to run up and down stairs. He just liked to run.

The pounding continued.

Kurt could let himself in, so could Sam and Lee ... they were still away. Dad could let himself in, but didn't if he knew I was home. He didn't pound on doors. Aidan did. He had a gate code but couldn't let himself into my house. Trust issues after the time he poked through my stuff and published my poetry.

Aidan's voice. He sounded agitated. Damn. I was going to have to get up.

"Where is she?" Aidan's voice floated up the stairs and down the hallway to my room.

"In bed," Mitch replied. I had to listen for his reply. He was in calm-Aidan-down mode. It reminded me of when we were kids. I fell back on the pillows. The clock next to the bed showed five-thirty. Too early for Aidan and drama. Way too early.

"Ellie, get up! We have to talk!" Aidan hollered.

Mitch's voice followed. Quiet, determined, steering Aidan away from the stairs.

I took the opportunity to shower. My brother's hysteria could wait. Also, I knew if I showered first, coffee would be ready by the time I got downstairs. Priorities.

When I joined the men in the kitchen, coffee was waiting. Aidan had calmed down and Mitch smiled. All good.

"What's happening in D.C?" Aidan asked.

"No, good morning Ellie, how'd you sleep?" I replied, filling my coffee cup.

"Yeah, yeah, good morning, now what's going on?"

I smiled at the coffee maker and hoped the smile had gone when I turned to face Aidan.

"We're having some problems."

"Ellie, I'm an insurance assessor. Problems? Ya think? These problems are going to cost my company a rather large fortune."

"Shit happens, Aid." How much it would cost his company wasn't my concern. "Might pay to keep out of D.C. for a while," I commented. "Unless you like delays, rubble in the streets, explosions and panic." He didn't. My messy world was not one Aidan enjoyed.

"I intend to. Who is behind it?"

"Don't know. Part of my job is to find out."

"The city looks like a war zone." His voice was flat.

"I know, Aid, I know."

The taste of the dust in my throat and seeing offices

disappearing to the street below were things that wouldn't go away.

I sipped my coffee and watched Aidan and Mitch.

"We'll be okay, Aid," I said, pouring more coffee into everyone's cups.

"You can't know that," Aidan replied. Still flat.

"Nah, I can't. But let's pretend we will be. Trust me on this, okay?" Just like when we were kids. It was my job to make everything better.

"How many bombs in how many buildings, Ellie?"

I did a quick count. Navy Yard - multiple bombs, Newseum - one bomb we thought. Hoover building - multiple bombs. The non-event of a cellphone IED in the Hard Rock Café and judging by the messages I missed yesterday, the same sort of devices in the Natural History Museum and the Castle.

"Three buildings were badly damaged. It's unknown at this stage exactly how many bombs." Best to avoid any talk of the people killed or injured. My brother could cope with building damage but not when it came to people.

"It feels like it's just getting started," Aidan said with a heavy sigh.

"I'm rather hoping it's finished," I replied.

Hope and reality, two very different beasts. I glanced at Mitch. He leaned against the kitchen counter, watching me. Our eyes met. He smiled. A thought wandered into my mind.

I can do this. We'll be fine.

"Ellie?"

"Aidan?"

"When did this happen?"

"What?" When I looked at him, his eyes jumped from me to Mitch and back again.

Oh, *that* this.

Mitch grinned.

"It's been coming for a while now," I replied.

"A long while," Mitch agreed. "Problem, Aidan?"

Aidan shook his head. "No." He smiled. "Guess that explains why Mitch isn't wearing socks and his sweater is inside out."

Mitch glanced down and laughed. It was inside out.

"Back to topic, Aidan, as much as I hate to talk about it. You need to keep out of D.C, tell Holly and Dad. Don't go into the city, not until we know what's going on and we can control it."

"My office is in the city," Aidan replied.

"Use the Fairfax office, Aidan. Yours is inside the cordon anyway, so you can't get in there."

"There's a cordon?"

"Nah, Aid. We let people blow up whatever the fuck they like in the Capitol and have no regard for the safety of the public and the Federal personnel working in there. What do you think?"

"Don't be like that," he grumbled.

"Then don't be stupid."

Mitch's expression changed. He frowned, not much, and it was fleeting but I saw it and I remembered when we were teenagers and how much he disliked name calling.

My phone rang. Mitch's phone rang. The kitchen phone rang. I answered mine as Mitch answered his. The kitchen phone rang on. I pointed to Aidan. He answered it.

Stupid.

I walked into the hallway talking to Caine.

"How bad is it?"

"I need you in my office."

"You still have one?"

"Nope. Washington field office. A-sap."

"Can I drive into the city?" I had a feeling the answer would be no.

"Sending a helicopter for you."

Crap. That was bad.

"When?"

"You should hear it soon. It'll land in the field at the end of your street."

"Thanks."

I hung up. From the doorway, I could see Mitch still talking on his phone. Life as we knew it was over, of being able to be home and feel safe, over. I didn't know when I'd be back. Images from the night flashed into my consciousness. I didn't know *if* I'd be back.

Eyes watching me. Mitch.

He shook his head. *Don't think that.*

He heard it?

The smile on his face told me he did. He *heard* my thoughts. Mitch put down his phone and walked over to me. He took my hand and pulled me close, wrapping his arms around me. A shield against the evil in the world.

Breathe.

"You're coming back," he whispered. "I'll be here when you do."

"So sure?" I whispered back.

"Yes."

Right there, that moment, wrapped in his arms, feeling his heart beating, I believed him.

Chapter Twenty-one.
Creeping Death

Parts of Washington weren't recognizable from the air anymore. Sad. Yes, that's how I felt flying into the city. Sad. The fight had been close before. September eleven sprang to mind. This was different, I couldn't explain how I knew that, but it was. I'd always felt safe in D.C. The irony of that thought swirled around me. Shot in the city going for coffee, yet I always felt safe?

The part of the city worst affected was under a cordon. I spotted Marine uniforms and Army uniforms, and more police than I'd ever seen in one place before. Emergency personnel still worked at the Newseum site. Dogs and handlers. I wondered if they were rescue or cadaver dogs. It didn't pay to think about that too long. The Hoover building hadn't fared too badly considering. Dogs were there too. We wouldn't be allowed back in anytime soon.

Triage tents dotted the area.

Something caught my eye. I looked toward the Mall. A blinding flash lit the interior of the helicopter. We tipped right, then left, then right again. The pilot's voice was clear through my headset.

"Brace for impact. Mayday, mayday."

The ground tilted then disappeared. Tossed around like a kid's toy for what seemed like minutes, but I think it may have been seconds, we spiraled ever lower. Dizzy.

Sick. My brain couldn't process the changing view from the windows.

"We're going down."

I couldn't see the ground anymore. My head hit something hard as the helicopter lurched sideways. Thick black smoke streamed past the window. Another violent lurch, followed by a crunching metal sound. Mitch's voice in my head telling me I'd be back faded but I could see his face, the last thing I saw before the nothing took over.

The nothing shook and hollered.

It vibrated through me and smelled like fire and fuel.

I heard noises that sounded like words but I couldn't see them in the dark. I tried to turn my head. A little bit of panic edged in when my head wouldn't move. My arms? I moved my fingers. They flexed. Good sign. My right hand touched my face. I couldn't feel my face. Something pushed my hand down again.

A moan came from somewhere. It sounded close. Me?

More words. This time a bright light. Bright. White. In my face. How did I know? My eyes were open. The light hurt. It moved, came back and then disappeared. I knew that light.

More words.

If my eyes were open why couldn't I see who held the light?

Nothing made sense and it was all too much work. I recognized my name and my eyes wanted to close.

"Ellie, stay with me."

My eyes closed. The nothing came back. I liked the

nothing.

Dark, soothing, quiet.

I liked the dark. The light couldn't get me.

Chapter Twenty-two.

For whom the bell tolls/Mitch.

I sat down at Ellie's desk, laptop in front of me, and coffee in my hand. I'd only been there about two minutes when I stood up again. I placed the cup on the desk and picked up my phone.

Nothing. No messages. No email. Why?

The clock on the wall ticked. Would she be there yet? I did a quick calculation. Yes, she should be.

Pausing. Phone in hand. Something was wrong.

I sent Ellie a text.

Back at the desk, I leaned back in the chair and looked at the screen in front of me. Nausea rose as I stared at a blank screen.

Smoke. Spinning. Nausea. What was happening? Then the dark. Why was it dark?

My phone screen lit up. Not Ellie. I ignored it.

Seconds later, it lit again. Ellie.

I answered it.

"Mitch?"

It wasn't Ellie's voice. It was an older sounding male.

"Yes, who's this?"

"It's Caine Grafton, Ellie's SAC." He paused. "The helicopter crashed. Ellie is injured. We don't know how badly. She's on her way to Inova Fairfax."

"Did it crash in Virginia?"

"No, D.C."

"Then why bring her back? A hospital in Washington would be closest."

"Trauma centers are full. D.C. is stretched to the limit. Fairfax has room," Caine replied.

"Her father, Simon?"

"He's been notified and will meet you at the hospital."

"Thank you."

I hung up and finished the last of my coffee while concentrating on Ellie and breathing. There had to be a way through the dark that surrounded her.

Nothing.

The nothing hurt. It crushed my chest.

I shoved my phone in my pocket and found my car keys.

Twenty minutes later, I parked in the Gray parking lot at the hospital and walked into the emergency room. I saw Simon before he saw me and hurried over.

"Have you seen her?" I asked, noting there were a lot of police around.

"Not yet," Simon replied. "Thought I saw Kurt going into a level 1 trauma room, but I can't be sure." He leaned back in his chair. "We've been here a few times, Mitch. I know this is new for you, but for me, welcome to life with Ellie. It's never dull."

I took a breath. There was still darkness when I tried to see Ellie. That wasn't right. I could always see her or feel her unless she blocked me. This time I doubted she was blocking me. It felt bad.

"Do you know what happened?"

"Crash investigators are still at the scene. A bystander described a flash from the ground before the helicopter crashed."

"It was shot down?"

"That's where my money is, Caine's too."

"So this could be something to do with the situation in D.C?"

"I'd say so, wouldn't you?"

I nodded. It made as much sense as anything else.

"The pilot? Was anyone else onboard?"

"The pilot is dead ...died at the scene."

The pilot died. Ellie didn't.

I hung onto those thoughts for a minute.

"It was a marked helicopter?"

"Yes, a black Eurocopter AS350 with FBI written on the tail."

"Where did it happen?"

"In the street, not far from the cordon. The flash appeared to come from the direction of the Mall."

I nodded again and wished someone would come and tell us we could see her. I needed to see her. To know what was happening and why it was all so dark.

The dark wasn't right. It wasn't Ellie. She was light. Rainbows of light.

Somewhere in my head, I heard a gasp. Small shards of light cracked through the darkness.

I looked at Simon.

"She's trying to wake up."

He frowned for a second. "How do you know?"

I gave that some thought but didn't come up with much of an explanation. "Not sure. I just know. It's been dark, too dark to see her and now there is a sliver of light. She's trying."

Simon regarded me. "You're aware how that sounds, I take it?"

"Yes. Yes I am."

I was very aware how it sounded.

"You sound like Ellie."

"I know."

"That's beyond finishing each other's sentences, Mitchell," Simon's voice dropped to a husky whisper. "Ellie's brain is no place to hang out."

"It's not a choice I made, Simon. It just happened."

Ellie's voice filled my head. *Mitch*! I looked at Simon and then beyond the reception desk at the corridor and the many sliding curtained glass doors opening off it. She was in one of them.

"What's the matter?" Simon asked.

"She's calling me. Where did you see Kurt?"

Simon stood up and beckoned me to follow. "This way."

We strode along the corridor and stopped outside a glass door. It was shut but the curtain wasn't. Through the glass, I saw Kurt standing near a bed. Lights, machines, nurses, doctors. Crowded. I knocked once and opened the door. A doctor looked up and told me to leave.

"No," I said. "I'm not going anywhere."

Kurt looked over.

"He stays," Kurt said. "Come closer, Mitch, but don't get in the way."

I nodded. He pointed me to a gap near the wall from where I could watch and Ellie could hear me, if she were capable.

"Will she be okay?"

"It's Ellie, she's tough," Kurt replied, then under his breath muttered, "I hope so."

"Can I touch her?"

He moved over a little and allowed me access to her hand. I lifted her pale cool, almost lifeless hand from the bed and held it in mine. She didn't react.

"El, I'm here."

Nothing. No sign that she could hear me or knew I was there. I looked at Kurt.

"She's breathing, that's a good thing," he replied. "Let me run down the list. Brain injury. Rib fractures. Spleen injury, which may require surgery." Kurt glanced at a machine near him. "I'm not happy."

Kurt moved away and consulted with the other doctors in a low voice. I didn't listen. Instead, I concentrated on willing Ellie to get well. He came back, perched himself on the other side of her bed near the equipment, and checked a printout from one of the machines.

"Now what?" I asked.

"We wait. We watch. We hope," Kurt replied. "If you pray, that wouldn't hurt."

I wasn't happy with that. I watched Ellie's face. Her eyes moved under closed lashes.

"The reason she isn't waking?"

Her eyes flickered, not opening but not fully shut either.

"Trauma to her brain," Kurt replied.

"Not the first time?" I asked, paying close attention to Ellie as I spoke. One eye closed properly. She *was* reacting to my voice.

"No."

"How bad is this, Kurt?"

"Her GCS score is shocking."

"And that is?"

"Glasgow Coma Scale."

"Tell me?"

"It's a score out of fifteen made up from three different criteria. Eye response, verbal response, motor response. In very basic terms, three is wood and anything under eight we intubate."

"And Ellie?"

"She scored six out of a possible fifteen. If I didn't know Ellie, if this were a stranger, I'd say we're looking at severe brain injury and a possible non-recovery situation."

That seemed like a roundabout way of saying vegetable or death were the only outcomes. That wasn't helpful thinking. I pushed it away.

"How is Ellie different? This isn't her first head injury, isn't that more dangerous?"

"Yes. Medically, I can't explain why she's different. It's Ellie, she just is. She always comes back."

Kurt seemed convinced she'd be okay. Just as I was going to ask about her chances of full recovery, an alarm sounded. Ellie's eyes pinged open. Panic flashed across her face. Her eyes shut, the alarm continued. Another doctor and a nurse joined Kurt on the opposite side of the bed.

"Her blood pressure is dropping," the doctor said. "We need to get in there, she's still bleeding."

"Now," Kurt agreed. He moved equipment, the portable equipment now balanced precariously on the gurney. The doctor made a phone call then looked at Kurt and nodded.

"We're taking her to theater. You scrubbing in?"

"Yes," Kurt replied.

I leaned down as they unlocked the wheels, kissed Ellie's cool cheek and lay her hand across her stomach. The dream she'd told me about come flooding back.

"Spleen, upper abdomen?" I asked Kurt.

"Yeah, under the ribs, between the ninth and eleventh ribs on the left-hand side.

Nausea rose in waves as I willed her to be okay.

"Right here. I'm right here," I said, kissing her again. "Don't be long."

Nothing. No reaction. No thoughts. No images.

Words wouldn't form. Breathing hurt. My chest felt tight, as though my heart was being crushed. No air. An asthma attack without the asthma. The darkness had closed back in.

I watched the gurney leave then turned back to the waiting area and found Simon standing behind me. With his hand on my shoulder, we walked together.

"You all right?" Simon asked as we sat down.

I couldn't speak. I nodded. Suffocated by the world.

"Shattered," he replied, looking at me. "You're not all right."

I struggled to find words and project them audibly.

"I'll be fine," I said, my voice sounding rough even to me. So much emotion. It hurt. "As soon as she wakes up. I'll be fine."

She will be fine and I'll be right there.

"We all will," Simon replied. "We will all be fine."

"Where's Aidan?" It didn't occur to me before that I hadn't seen him. My emphasis and energy centered on Ellie.

"I don't know," Simon replied his voice low and quiet. "I called him, he knows what's happened. As for where he is? It's Aidan. He doesn't cope well with hospitals."

I tilted my head and looked at Simon.

"Really?" Unbelievable.

He nodded. "If he shows, he shows."

I shook my head. Aidan's attitude made no sense. His sister badly hurt – and he couldn't get over himself and show up at least to support his dad?

My thoughts roamed until I reined them in and put an end to the speculation. This was all about Ellie. The thoughts became an internal pep talk. Positive reinforcement. She'd be fine. She'd make a full recovery and I would be there every second. Nothing else mattered. The words spun through my mind, repeatedly. She'd be fine.

Every now and then, images followed the mantra. Life-affirming images of Ellie. Laughing. Stretched out on the couch watching a movie. Smiling. Walking next to me through the city. Looking at me over her coffee cup at the Firehook café. Her smile lighting her eyes.

Simon nudged me. Jolting me back to the stark surroundings of the hospital waiting room. He held his phone out to me. "Your mom."

"How?"

"I called her as soon as Caine told me what had happened."

I smiled and took the call. "You could've rung my phone Mom," I said.

"Thought it best to talk to Simon first in case you were unable to answer your phone," Mom said. "Any news?"

"No, but she'll be fine. She's tough," I said, forcing positivity into my words.

"She will be and she is. What about you?" Mom said sending my positivity back to me. "How's my Mitch?"

"I'm good, thanks. Waiting."

"Not easy. Do you need anything?"

"No." I just need Ellie to wake up and be okay. "I don't need anything, Mom."

"We'll be in soon, let me know if you think of anything you need."

"Thanks, Mom."

I hung up and gave Simon back his phone. "Mom and Dad are coming over."

Simon nodded. "I figured they would. Family. This is a time for family."

Made Aidan's absence stand out even more.

The main doors to the emergency department opened. Caine walked in, stopped, looked around then walked over to us. He pulled up a chair and sat opposite us.

"News?" he asked.

"Surgery," Simon replied. "Internal bleeding, they're repairing her spleen."

Caine's mouth set in a straight line. Grim. He looked grim. I wanted to tell him that wouldn't help but resisted.

"Her phone has been going non-stop this morning. This Voxer thing. I can't get to grips with it," Caine said, looking at the phone in his hand.

"Voxer?" I said.

"Yes. She keeps getting messages. I don't know how to reply or what's going on."

I held my hand out. He dropped the phone into it.

I checked her notifications. He was right. Lots of Voxer messages. I touched the first notification and opened the app.

"Ellie was using Voxer to keep an eye on those tourists. She thought someone hacked either the Voxer app they were using or had planted something on the phones that would throw her off," I said reading the messages. "These are all from the same person. Danni Lane. She's one of the women, the tourists."

"Can you reply?" Caine asked.

"Yes, but this is work. I'm not a Fed. I shouldn't be involved."

Caine's mouth twitched. He growled, "You have a higher security clearance than most of my agents."

"It's project specific," I reminded him.

"So this is just another project. Didn't you use your drone on this?" I nodded. "Then you are part of this case."

"Okay. What do you want me to say?"

"Let her think you are Ellie, and just answer the messages as best you can."

"Okay." I scrolled through the messages and gave Caine an overview, "Danni says they were going to Rosslyn this morning. They wanted to walk M street from Georgetown. So they planned to cross Key Bridge on foot. But they don't know if they should because of the news and the explosions in the city. Then there is a very recent message saying they heard that an FBI helicopter was shot down in the city."

"Damn reporters. We're not convinced the helicopter was shot down, yet. It's highly probable, but we're not making statements yet," Caine said. "Tell her to carry on with their planned route. For whatever reason, Ellie set this up, so let it run. Don't confirm the helicopter crash."

Dangerous game.

I replied to Danni and let her know they should carry on with their planned outing. I also suggested they avoid

Pennsylvania Avenue near the Hoover Building and the Newseum.

"Okay, done."

Then it occurred to me that the message had GPS coordinates attached. If Danni tapped the icon she'd know the message was sent from Inova Fairfax.

I glanced at Caine. "She might figure out this is coming from the hospital."

Caine grimaced. "So be it. Can you take over the communication with these women until Kurt is out of the OR?"

"Yes."

Could I? Of course. For Ellie? Absolutely.

"Good man," Caine replied and stood. He returned the chair to its rightful place and spoke briefly to Simon. I heard them discuss Aidan. Caine was about as impressed as I was but unlike me, he wasn't surprised.

I spoke to Caine before he walked away. "Do you know where Iain Campbell is?"

Caine nodded. Minimalistic at best but still an affirmation. "He'll be here soon. He's coordinating the investigation from Homeland's perspective. You'll be briefed."

I'll be briefed? He knew I'd be involved?

"I'll be here. He can reach me on Ellie's cell."

The corner of Caine's mouth twitched. "I'll let him know."

And he was gone.

I leaned back in the chair, stretching my legs in front

of me, and read the rest of the messages on Ellie's phone. I had something to do, something else to occupy my mind. Piecing together what she'd told me about the case and what I gleaned from her phone, I could see where Ellie was going with the investigation.

She thought the women were being used. That their presence was convenient. I wanted access to her files.

I made a call to Iain Campbell. He answered on the fifth ring. "Ellie?"

"Nope, Mitch. Any way I can access the case files for Operation Visitor?"

"Mitch? You want access?"

"Yes."

"I can't give you access to Sentinel but I know Ellie and she kept backups."

"Can I get them?"

Silence.

"Iain?"

"Thinking. This is not straightforward. This is a complicated ongoing investigation. There are red-tape issues. What's your clearance again?"

"TS/SCI."

I heard fingers on a keyboard.

"You're already attached to this investigation. Yes, you can access the case files but you'll need access via the master file. Ellie was wearing the files. She always does. Yellow flash band on her wrist."

"I'll see if I can find it," I replied and hung up.

She always wore the yellow band. A smile edged onto

my lips. Except in the shower. I held that image close for a few minutes. When I let it go and remembered why we were here it hurt all over again. My chest tightened.

She'll be okay. Everything will be fine.

I stood up.

"Where you going?" Simon asked

"I need to find her things. The flash band."

Simon stood too. "I'll come. My old body doesn't sit well these days."

I understood that. I needed to move. Sitting. I don't do sitting. Not for long anyway.

Restless.

We approached the front desk. Simon asked about patient personal effects. The unhelpful receptionist glared at him and flapped a hand as though she had better things to do, like file her nails or drink her tea.

"Ma'am, this is important. Where would Agent Conway's personal items be?" I said, leaning over the divider and smiling. I hoped I was smiling; to be honest it felt more like a sneer.

"You'll have to wait until she is out of surgery," she replied, I wasn't much impressed with her tone.

"Where will she be taken after theater?" Different tactic this time, but same smile.

"Intensive care probably, she won't come back here."

"Thanks."

I started to walk down the long corridor to the elevators at the end. She called after me, "They won't have her things."

I turned back. "Who will?"

"They would've gone to theater with her. They'll be there until they move her."

Simon thanked her. I couldn't. I walked away.

He caught me up by the elevators. "Theater Suite?" he asked.

"Yes."

Silence descended. A welcome silence. I needed to hear Ellie's voice in my head. The darkness lifted for a few moments and I heard her. Her voice was clear and light.

I breathed.

The elevator stopped. We stepped out into a quiet place. A reception desk was the first thing I saw; behind it a woman in scrubs. Beyond her, to the left were double sliding glass doors. The theater suites.

"Can I help?" she asked.

Simon stepped forward. "My daughter, Ellie Conway, is having surgery. I need to pick up her belongings."

"Sure. Mr. Conway. If you could show me some identification."

Simon fished his wallet out of his pocket and produced a card. I smiled as I caught sight of it. NCIS. Retired.

Nice touch. Could've gone with his driver's license.

She took three large paper bags from under the desk and stacked them on the top of the counter. Simon scooped them up. We retreated to chairs that lined the wall behind us. She called out, "There is a waiting room. Coffee and tea are available." I followed her line of sight to a door that said 'waiting room', all too obvious for us to see.

"Thanks," I replied with a smile.

Simon and I entered the room. The smell of institutional coffee filled the space. I poured coffee into Styrofoam cups and Simon went through the paper bags. He carefully laid things on the table.

Her Glock still in its holster. Handcuff case. Identification. Badge. Wallet. Business card holder. Jeans. Boots. Shirt. Underwear. Socks. Jacket. A small plastic bag containing jewelry. Her laptop, still in its sleeve. He tipped the last bag upside down and shook it. The silicone flash band fell to the floor and bounced.

I breathed a sigh of relief.

"Any chance the laptop fared better than her clothes?" I asked as Simon held up her jeans. They'd been cut off.

"It didn't have to be cut it off her so you might be lucky."

I reached for the laptop. In the zip pocket on the outside of the sleeve, I felt the power cord. Helpful.

I slid off the case and inspected the laptop.

"Seems okay. No cracks." I opened the lid and powered it up while I unraveled the cord and looked for a wall outlet. There was one right behind my chair.

"It goes," Simon said on hearing the Windows music. He handed me the flash band. "Cross something."

While the laptop finished powering up, I thought about other ways to get information that might help the case.

Prism.

NSA.

If the women were really involved in something, we could get information both recent and stored by using Prism. I plugged the flash band into the USB port on the laptop and searched for the case files. It took me a few minutes to figure out the password Ellie assigned to the files. My name.

Thirty minutes later I'd read through the case notes and found out exactly what Ellie thought. I wasn't happy about her notes regarding Troy. Looked like the right decision to suspend him and pull his security clearance. No mention of trying NSA. Notes at the bottom of one page told me she thought the bombings were distractions, she also considered the case in New Zealand was a distraction, a way of removing Delta A from D.C. There was some mention of her feelings regarding POTUS being a target. Ellie had added with careful notation that she had no proof yet. She'd had executable roving bugs installed on the women's cell phones. She'd also made notes about the possibility of the Voxer app on their phones having a virus that makes the GPS controllable remotely.

That would explain why the roving bugs recorded one location but the GPS within Voxer recorded another. Ideas rolled around. Is it possible to deconstruct the Voxer program and locate the altered program components or extra components? That idea was worth pursuing. I shelved it for a moment and thought again about Prism. Who did I know who could help with that?

I took my phone from my pocket and scrolled through the contacts list. Had to be someone.

Scroll. Scroll. Scroll. Bam. Nigel.

Gotcha.

I gave him a call. "Hey, it's Mitch. How's your day?"

"Good. Bit crazy in the city. You heard?"

"Yes. Crazy. Good description."

"What do you need, Mitch?"

"Information for the FBI."

"For?"

"Yeah, for. My girlfriend is ..."

"Supervisory Special Agent Ellie Conway," he said with a small laugh. "We all put two and two together. The whole gang."

"Great. I still need some information."

"Give me names, email addresses, and phone numbers."

"I'll email the information to you. How long will it take?"

"A few hours."

"Thanks, Nigel. I appreciate it."

"No problem." I hung up.

Simon was smiling. "You're pretty good at this," he said.

"We'll see."

I was smiling. I knew it. I liked the challenge. This was new. New is exciting. I was being useful. I liked that.

"Now what?" Simon asked.

"Now I need someone who can pull the apps on their phones apart and look for extra program lines."

"Bet there is someone in that phone of yours who can do that."

"Probably, but doesn't Ellie know someone?" Outsourcing would be a security risk. If she knew someone, it would be better. I had no choice but to outsource information gleaned via Prism but deemed NSA trustworthy. Nigel was an old friend.

Simon thought for a few minutes. Someone knocked lightly on the door. We looked up at the same time. Simon smiled.

"Speak of the devil. Come on in, Sean."

"Hello, Simon. I heard. Thought I'd come on in and see how it was going." Simon started to stand. "Stay where you are."

"This is Mitch Iverson. Mitch, Sean O'Hare. He's the man you need."

I was already on my feet reaching for his hand. "Pleased to meet you."

Sean smiled. "So you're Mitch. Heard about you."

"Have a seat," I said. "You're a friend of Ellie's?"

"Yes." Sean sat on the sofa opposite me.

"O'Hare? Like the Director?"

"Uh huh. She's my twin."

"Ah, yes, Ellie has talked about you." Focus. "Ellie thinks someone planted some code inside an app on the phones of the three women she's investigating."

"This has something to do with the bombings?"

"Yes."

"Can you get me the phone number of one of the phones?"

"Got those right here."

I wrote Danni's number on a piece of paper and handed it to him.

"Cheers, I'll see if I can access the phone and the apps."

"There is an FBI roving bug in there. Ellie noted it was disguised as a Facebook update."

Sean nodded. "Good, I won't go near that."

So that was done. Ticking things off the list. I leaned back a little bit and scanned more notes. Sean talked to Simon about Ellie. No one knew anything. It was a short conversation that ended in silence. The waiting drove me crazy. I buried myself in the case files again. Hoping that something else would jump out and wave a flag, so I'd know where to go next. It didn't but I had a feeling she was on the right track. We needed to know why and we needed to stop any more explosions.

I shut the laptop, slid it to the coffee table and stretched.

"Anyone need anything from anywhere?" I asked. "I need to walk a bit."

"No, thanks," Simon said. "Go, I'll call you if I hear anything."

"Won't be long."

I wanted to go for a run but I knew that would take me too far away and I needed to be close. Close but useful.

The elevators were in front of me as I walked down the corridor but on the right was a stairwell door.

With a small smile, I pulled the door open. I ran down the stairs to the ground floor, then back up. On my third descent, a phone rang in my pocket. Not my ringtone. It was Ellie's phone. I stopped running and answered the call.

"Mitch Iverson."

"Looking for Special Agent Conway?" A male voice said.

"You reached her phone. She is unavailable at the moment. Can I help?"

The call dropped.

Interesting. I made a mental note to do a reverse search on the number when I got the chance. I resumed running and the phone rang again. This time it was Simon on my phone.

"She's in recovery. Kurt is here. We're waiting for you."

"I'm on my way," I checked the number above the landing. I ran up. At the door to the intensive care floor, I paused to collect my thoughts.

Positive. Positive. Positive.

I opened the door and stepped into chaos.

What the hell?

People in various colored scrubs swarmed like ants. Gurneys moved. People talked. Machines beeped. The nurse on the desk was frantic. I scanned the room looking for a way through the madness to the room we'd been using. An opening appeared. I took it. Dodging people who stepped into my path.

"Excuse me. Sorry, just trying to get to the waiting room."

I walked through the open door still looking over my shoulder at the scene behind me.

"What happened?" I asked.

"Another bombing," Simon replied.

I shook my head. Not good news. Kurt sat with a coffee, still in green scrubs. Sean had gone.

"Ellie?" I asked. "How is she?"

Part of me didn't want to hear what he said next and the rest of me focused so hard on the positive that I almost missed it.

"We repaired a tear in her spleen. She'll make a good recovery from the laparoscopic surgery."

I could feel the *but* hovering there.

"But?"

"She's not waking."

My heart twisted in my chest. Positive. Think. Remember. And I did. A memory surfaced. Not something from Ellie but something I remembered Aidan telling my mom about Ellie and a head injury she suffered during a case. It pointed to why he wasn't here now. In my opinion, he still needed to man up and be here for his dad and Ellie. No excuses. It's not about him.

"This has happened before, yes?" Kurt nodded. "How low was her GCS last time ... it was a while ago? Four years or more back?"

"That's about right." He picked up a thick folder that

was on the ground next to him and flipped through the pages. "Four. She scored a four out of fifteen."

"You said she's a six this time?"

"Yep." Kurt looked at me. "I know where you're going with this. She survived a four but Mitch, since then she's had a couple of moderate head injuries … they compound." Kurt sighed. "You need to be realistic and prepare for the worst."

All the air rushed out of my lungs. I felt as if I'd been hit by a truck. No air. Just crushing pain. It won't be like that. She'll be okay.

She'll be okay.

The door opened and a familiar face entered the room. Mom.

I met her half way across the room and hugged her.

"I brought sandwiches, you and Simon need to eat," Mom said. She looked past me at Simon and Kurt. "Took us a long while to get here. The world has gone mad. Where's Aidan?"

"No one knows, Mom. He hasn't shown up."

Simon greeted Mom, "Joan. Thank you for coming all this way." He kissed her cheek.

Mom smiled. "Someone needs to make sure you boys eat," she replied. I took the basket she carried and set it on the sideboard that held the coffee maker and electric kettle.

Simon ushered Mom to a seat. Dad appeared moments later, looking harried. I met him in the middle of the room. We had a brief hug.

"All right?" Dad asked me and joined Mom.

"Yes. I'm fine."

He turned his attention to Simon, then back to me and Mom.

Dad talked about the drive over and the crazy traffic and how hard it was to find a parking space.

I could hear Simon and Kurt talking but I didn't know what they were saying. My mind filled once more with images of Ellie laughing. Amidst the laughter, a curtain parted and light flooded in. What was I seeing? She was waking up. Ellie called my name so strongly and so loudly I expected to see her walk into the room.

I interrupted Kurt and Simon, "Where is Ellie?"

"Recovery," Kurt replied.

"I need ... she needs ..." Words failed me. I could see her. I could hear her. She needed me. Mom was on her feet.

"Mitch?"

"Mom, please just stay with Dad. I need to see her."

Kurt stood up. "I'll take you in."

I glanced at my parents. "I'll be back soon. We'll eat then."

I didn't even ask if Simon was coming. I assumed he would and he did. Kurt led the way through the craziness outside our small sterile sanctuary. People and pain. Not good. Outside a set of large glass doors, Kurt stopped.

"Turn off your cell phones. Usually, I wouldn't care but this area is super sensitive. She's in the fifth bay on the right," Kurt said, leading the way. "She's on a ventilator.

We're giving her a break. Hard work breathing when your brain isn't functioning like it should."

The word ventilator hung in the air.

Kurt entered the bay first. I paused, took a breath, forced a smile onto my face and followed him. He indicated I should go to the left of her bed, away from the machinery.

So still and pale. Intubation tube in her throat hooked to a machine that breathed for her. An IV tube running from a pump to her arm. Heart monitors. Wires. Sensors. Finding somewhere that didn't have wires or tubes to touch wasn't easy.

I lifted her hand, careful to avoid a cannula in the back of it. Cool. Unresponsive.

"El, I'm here." I forced the words through my tight throat as I leaned down and kissed her forehead. "You need to open your eyes. I'll be right here until you do."

Her hand moved. I felt a slight pressure from her fingers.

"My mom and dad are in the waiting room. They brought sandwiches. I know you love my mom's ham sandwiches."

Her fingers tightened around mine.

"El? You in there?"

She responded with a strangled groan.

Kurt leaned over. "You're okay, Conway. Intubated and on a ventilator but you're okay. Gimme a minute, I'll turn the machine off."

Her eyes opened.

Chapter Twenty-three.

Victim of Changes

I looked up at Mitch. His eyes glistened. A tear escaped and dripped onto my face as he kissed my forehead.

"Welcome back, El," he said, his voice clouded with emotion.

I wanted the tube out. I couldn't even smile properly. So annoying. My mind darted about, trying to piece things together. I was pretty sure he'd said his parents were here and there were ham sandwiches. He looked amazing. Felt like I'd been away for a week. Where had I been?

Talking was impossible, I could barely make any sounds at all. Struggling to let Kurt know I wanted the tube out wasn't working for me.

Kurt's hand touched my shoulder. "Come on, Conway, relax. You know the drill. I need to check your oxygen level after you've been breathing by yourself for a little bit." I rolled my eyes. "I'll take the intubation tube out once I know you're capable of breathing through it unaided."

Relax. Sure. Easy.

Idiot.

It felt like forever before Kurt said he was ready to take out the damn tube.

Kurt told me to cough, carefully. It hurt and I couldn't.

Total muscle weakness. What the hell? He pressed gently on my upper abdomen and told me to cough again. As I did, he pulled the tube from my throat. Gagging. So attractive. Right up there with drooling, pretty sure I did that too.

Mitch smiled. I smiled.

Kurt shook his head in wonderment. "Don't try talking," he warned. "Ice chips first."

I remembered from last time I was intubated. Sucked that I had that memory at all but at that point, I was just pleased to have memory. It could've gone again. And it didn't. Which felt like a very good thing. I sucked ice and watched Mitch's face. He looked …

I'd never seen that look before.

What was it?

All my memories of Mitch's facial expressions paraded past. I decided I was looking at a combination of happy, relieved, and still a little concerned.

He wasn't the only one. I could think, I knew that. But could I talk? Could I still communicate with the world? I swallowed the cold ice. My throat felt raw.

Time to give the speaking thing a whirl.

"Mmmm … itch."

Not great, but hey, a word. I'll take that.

"Right here," he replied.

Good, a recognizable word. Even better. Bit early to celebrate.

"I … know. Not … blind."

Mitch smiled. "Glad you're not blind. I like the way you

look at me."

Kurt groaned.

And I was back and the words kept coming.

"Can I ... sit up more?" I asked, knowing Kurt could hear me.

"A little bit. Go easy. Fractured ribs are not fun. And you had surgery on your spleen. You will be in bed a couple of days."

No, that wasn't going to work.

"Nah, I'll be fine."

"In about half an hour we're going to take you up to a ward. It *is* in intensive care."

"Intensive care? I'm fine."

Mitch smiled. Kurt laughed.

"Yeah, we know," Kurt replied. "Intensive care for thirty-six hours unless Leon clears you sooner."

"Leon is a neurologist," I said.

"Well done, Conway. I see you are returning faster than expected," Kurt commented. "You have a traumatic brain injury."

"You said spleen and ribs."

I'm pretty sure I'd remember if anyone had mentioned head injury. Or would I?

"I didn't tell you everything," he replied. "Go ahead, shoot me."

"I would but someone took my Glock."

Dad spoke, "If you two kids are done ..."

"Are they always like this?" Mitch asked, turning toward Dad.

"Pretty much," Dad replied. "At least he isn't wearing bruises this time."

"You'll need to explain that," Mitch said with a small laugh.

"Later," Dad said. "Let's get Ellie settled first."

I am settled. Sounds like I've been settled a while. Time to shake things up.

"I need clothes." Experience told me mine were now rags, and I'm not really a grunge person. The bag lady look didn't impress me much either. "Also, someone get Caine in here. I want to know what's happening with my investigation. Where's my phone?" I inspected the tube in my arm. "And this thing here … it can go. I'm capable of drinking … I don't need IV fluid."

"That's true," Kurt replied. "But you're receiving more than fluid, so it stays."

I grumbled under my breath. "Don't be like that. I need to work."

"Don't make me sedate you," Kurt replied as he leaned in close. "Because I will."

"I need to work this case. Sam and Lee aren't here. This is on me."

"What am I? Chopped liver?" Kurt replied.

Mitch cleared his throat. "Enough. Come on."

Kurt threw his hands in the air. Surrender. "Mitch is right." Kurt used his special calming Ellie's-going-to-lose-it voice. "I'm not arguing with you anymore. We'll go up to intensive care and we'll talk about how much you think you can do *from a bed*."

Mitch's head made the slightest shake from side to side as I readied a response. I swallowed it and behaved. Not easy but he knew that.

I smiled as our eyes met and I heard his thoughts. *Better than you know yourself.*

My only thought was a comment on his very fine backside. *Smartass.*

Half an hour later, which seemed like days, I met the intensive care staff and moved to one of their beds. I'm not going to say that went smoothly. Because it didn't. It hurt. Ribs hurt. A lot.

Mitch's parents came to visit me. They were allowed to stay a whole ten minutes Mitch walked them down to the front foyer but was back in double quick time. Work needed to happen. Terrorists weren't going to wait around for me to be fully functional again.

"I still need my phone and laptop," I said through clenched teeth. "Do I even still have a laptop and a phone?"

Kurt topped up the pain relief while he talked, "I believe you have both. Neither will be used in here. You'll to have to wait, Conway."

"People are dying. This is not a waiting situation." A groan escaped as I tried to move. Moving wasn't happening.

"You were nearly one of them," he replied. "You will allow your body time to recover."

"I'm okay. Just let me try."

"Conway, you're not okay and you will rest." Kurt was

serious. He looked at his watch. The room floated. Damn. What the hell did he give me?

"What'd you do?" I asked as he floated up to the ceiling.

"Topped up your pain relief," he replied from the light in the middle of the room.

"Bastard. You gave me something else as well."

He smiled at me as he swam across the ceiling. "Promethazine hydrochloride. So the pain relief doesn't make you sick. You don't want to be sick with fractured ribs and an injured spleen."

Sounded like a good reason. Promethazine hydrochloride? It was familiar. It had another name. Phenergan. Ah crap! This was sneaky sedation.

"Okay. I hate this ..." I looked at Mitch, he swayed in and out of focus.

Phenergan combined with pain relief. Dammit.

"What do you hate?" Mitch asked pulling a chair closer to me.

"I can't focus. He gave me Phenergan."

Kurt smiled at me as he swam back across the ceiling.

"Your brain still works, Conway," he said as the light glowed behind him like a halo.

Mitch rubbed my arm. "Sleep. Close your eyes. I'll be here you when you wake up and we'll talk. Everything is moving forward in the investigation. I promise. Now please, sleep."

"For someone who wanted me to wake up you're awful quick in wanting me to go to sleep again," I mumbled as my eyes closed.

"How'd you know?" Mitch whispered.

"I heard you telling me to wake up," I replied, listening to my words slur. "It was dark and you seemed a long way away but I could hear you."

And I never got a ham sandwich.

"Sleep."

Dad's voice cut in as I drifted. I wasn't asleep but I wasn't capable of joining the conversation. Anyway, it was more fun to listen and let the words create images in my brain.

"It sounds like you two can hear each other's thoughts," Dad said.

"I think we can," Mitch replied. "More than that though. I see what she sees if she lets me."

"Explain."

I really wanted to hear the explanation. Part of me hoped Mitch had figured out what I couldn't, how and why it was happening.

"Before the Navy Yard explosion, Ellie saw the street fill with smoke. So did I."

"How often has that happened?" Dad asked.

"A few times over the last week."

"Anything else?"

"I hear the same music as she does."

I couldn't see, but I imagined Dad nodding sagely. As he always did when my craziness surfaced. But it wasn't just my craziness now. I'd spread it around. Mitch caught it. Maybe it was viral?

Kurt's voice joined the conversation. "You ever have a head injury, Mitch?"

Typical Kurt, looking for a medical explanation. Couldn't just be a thing, oh no, had to have some kind of brain issue behind it. Can't we just be on the same wavelength?

"Yes. When I was teenager."

"Notice anything like this before, this thought sharing, song hearing, and hallucination thing?"

"No. Only when Ellie and I became close ..." His voice lowered. Harder for me to hear. I had to listen. "More noticeable since we, um, got together."

Oh, he didn't want to say anything else in front of Dad. I hoped I hadn't smiled. I wanted them to think I was sleeping so I could hear the interactions and work out what was going on. Because something was. Fighting sleep and brain fog made following the conversation a little more entertaining that it would otherwise have been.

"Extraordinary," Kurt replied. "You're sure you didn't hit your head in the last week?"

"Positive."

"Okay, good. We can rule out head injury then."

"So what is it?"

"A connection," Kurt replied. "A very strong one."

No one spoke for a few minutes. In the silence, I wondered what would happen if I thought specific things, directed at Mitch. So I tried.

I can hear you talking with Kurt and Dad about us.

He looked at me. How did I know he was looking at me? I could feel him.

"You're not asleep," Mitch said. I heard the smile in his voice. "Enjoying the conversation?"

I smiled but kept my eyes shut. I was sleepy, just not sleeping.

"Okay, that's it. She needs to rest. We're taking this outside," Kurt said.

No. Don't leave me, Mitch.

"I'm staying. I'll sit right here and be quiet," Mitch said. I heard Kurt try to argue.

"She can communicate with him no matter what, Kurt. It really doesn't matter if he's in the room or not. Or did you not grasp that?" Dad said.

"I got it," Kurt replied. "Where's her phone?"

"Here," Mitch said.

"Right, I'll take it and check on the investigation. I'll be back in an hour. Encourage her to rest."

"I will," Mitch replied.

The room felt different. Less crowded. Dad had gone with Kurt. Just me and Mitch now. I let myself fall through the clouds and into real sleep.

Chapter Twenty-four.

Unwell

Mitch and Kurt sat by the wall when I woke up. I could see their legs without turning my head.

It occurred to me that Mitch should know I was awake. Why didn't he know? Or did he?

I couldn't trust my voice. My throat was still raw and dry. Instead of speaking, I moved my hand.

"El, you okay" Mitch asked. He was watching. He was always watching.

"Mm."

"Drink," Kurt said. "She needs a drink."

A straw touched my lips. Cool water. Nice.

Made it easier to talk. "Thanks," I said to Mitch.

He smiled and just like that, the world brightened.

"All right?" he asked.

"Yes." I was. I felt pretty good considering the fog in my brain. Trying to think through a Phenergan hangover; not fun. I rallied my thoughts and concentrated them, stopping them from wandering away while I tried to get them in order. Thinking, I could manage, maybe. Moving, not so much. No one needed to know that.

"Take it easy. You sure you're okay?" Mitch said, putting down the glass.

Absolutely. I'm not about to run a marathon. My mind wandered to our last run, early morning along the

Potomac. The sensible part of me knew that wouldn't be happening again for quite a while. The rest of me wanted to go now.

Concentrate on what you can do. Questions. I had plenty and no answers.

"Tell me about today. What happened to the helicopter? Where's the pilot? Any more explosions?" I took a few shallow breaths. Cracked ribs and breathing didn't go well together. "Where are Danni, Trudi, and Susan? Did they carry on as planned today? Anything from Sam and Lee? Where's Renegade, is he safe? What about Troy?"

"Conway, *slow* down," Kurt said.

"I'm in bed, this *is* slow," I replied with careful enunciation. "This *is* slow. Time is ticking. We *need* answers. "Can I use my phone and laptop in here?"

"Wait, please. Just wait a bit longer before you launch yourself into orbit working."

I saw the look on his face. I saw the look on Mitch's face. I knew they wanted what was best for me. I couldn't just switch off. Answers. I wanted them. My job required me to find those answers.

I measured my thoughts to one question at a time. Slow. Calm. Considered. "Where's the pilot?"

"Died at the scene," Kurt replied.

I refused to let myself think about his family, there would be time for that later. With a shove, I closed the door on the human tragedy aspect.

"What happened to the helicopter?"

"Crash investigators are still working at the scene. Eyewitnesses reported a flash and smoke from the ground seconds before they saw flames and smoke coming from the helicopter."

"A flash?" What did I remember? Nothing. I closed my eyes. I remembered taking off; that was it until I woke up in hospital.

"Rocket launcher of some description," Kurt muttered. "Could even be a homemade thing. We'll know more once they're finished with the wreckage."

"Where was the flash seen?"

"Reports came from near the Mall."

I thought about the possibility of someone using a Shoulder-Launched Multipurpose Assault Weapon in the National Mall. Dangerous to use, they required a lot of clear area behind the weapon. The Mall had plenty of area but it was usually full of people. A well-used space.

"Backblast," I said and it wasn't easy. Pain – coming back in spades. Breathe. "It can be lethal to ninety-eight feet. That's a big fucking area. Someone would've been killed or badly injured. Any reports?"

"No," Kurt said then tempered his answer. "Not that I know of."

Mitch spoke, "A soft launch would diminish the backblast."

I closed my eyes for a second and when I opened them Kurt and Mitch were watching me. I swallowed.

"You talking about a Predator?" I asked Mitch.

"Yeah, a Predator Short Range Assault Weapon. It'd fit

the bill with its fire-and-forget system. It has fire-from-enclosure capability."

I smiled. Everything hurt all of a sudden but I still smiled. I loved that Mitch's expertise extended to the field of weapons.

"Can we find out if there are any SRAW's unaccounted for nationwide?"

Kurt made the call before I'd finished the sentence. I let my eyes close for a few minutes. I think it was minutes, might have been seconds, could've been an hour.

Kurt's voice cut a passage through the murk in my mind. "I sent out an alert to all agencies and the armed services asking them to check for reports of any missing short-range missiles."

"Good." I was fighting a thick gray cloud and still had questions. "If a Predator hit the chopper, why am I alive?"

"Because you have nine lives, Conway, but I swear they're running out."

Good point. Time to be more careful with the few I have left. Yeah, because that was an option? It's not as if I do these things to myself. I attract aberrations and often they want to drastically shorten my life.

"People need to stop shooting at me."

"Agreed," Mitch and Kurt said.

"Phone and laptop, can I use them in here?"

"Yes, you can. This is an isolated room," Kurt replied.

Well, that was clever of him. It occurred to me that

asking if I could use them was a long way off being capable of doing so. That frustrated me. I was still wearing sensors and still had an IV. Annoying. I had a feeling if I complained too much I'd end up asleep again, though part of me considered that might be a good idea. Breathing hurt. The longer I fought to function, the more pain I felt.

"The women?" The effort to speak was exponentially greater than before.

Mitch moved his chair closer. "Caine asked me to keep tabs on the three women. They arrived in Rosslyn, crossed Key Bridge on foot and last I heard they were walking up M." He looked into my eyes and shook his head. "El, you all right?"

I nodded, a little nod, and found more words. "Any more explosions?"

"Yes, while you were in surgery. I don't know where. Kurt?"

"Smithsonian Museum of Natural History."

A shiver ran up my spine. An image of a woman under a blanket sprang into my mind. It seemed out of place but it had to be something. Give it a minute. I let my thoughts settle.

"Kurt, that woman we rescued, where is she?"

"I don't know. ICE took custody. She's an illegal."

"Is she being returned to ... where was she from?"

"Croatia and I presume the intent is to return her."

"Find out ... when ... has she left?" My heart raced. Pain surged through my rib cage. She wasn't what she seemed to be. She wasn't. What was she? A bomb. No, it would've exploded by now. Or would it? She wouldn't have left, not yet. She's connected.

"Conway, you need to calm down," Kurt warned. He was watching the monitor by my bed and shaking his head.

"There is something wrong with her ... too easy to find." I knew I needed to calm down. I also needed the pain to stop so I could think properly and breathe effectively.

"Chill ... now ... or I sedate you again." Kurt's voice took on a stern tone. I didn't care for it.

"What if she's a bomb? Get me Iain!"

"She would've gone bang by now ..." Kurt said. He didn't sound convinced.

I stared at him.

"Not if she wasn't a bomb but now is ..."

"Jesus!" Kurt exclaimed. "You've just woken up. You're injured. How could you know?"

I gave him a look. "Really, you wanna ask me that now?"

Kurt suppressed a smile. "Yeah, maybe not. But will you calm down, please?"

Mitch called Iain Campbell and handed me the phone.

"You're still with us, Ellie, good, pleased," Iain said with a smile in his voice.

"Yeah, I'm great. That woman ... the Croatian. Where is she now?"

"Being held by ICE, I think. I'll check."

"Please do, also find out who has visited her ..." I paused giving myself breathing space. "And how long they were with her." Not as easy as I thought to talk. "She's not a prisoner? She's a victim, yes?"

"I think so."

"So less security?"

"Yeah."

"Iain, find her ... I need that information on visitors." Slow breaths. "Also, any requests she's made for asylum or anything else."

"You sound bad, Conway, try resting. I'll get back to you in twenty."

I hung up and gave Mitch the phone. He put it in his pocket and sat back down next to me.

"To what end?" he asked.

"The woman being a bomb?" I queried.

"Yes."

"More destruction." I took a few shallow breaths before speaking again. "It depends on what she's asked for, how much damage she could do." Kurt looped tubing over my ears and positioned a nasal cannula in my nose. "I can breathe," I grumbled.

I'm not great at it but I'm doing it.

"The oxygen level in your blood is dropping. You're not breathing well enough," Kurt replied. "You need to calm down and rest."

"She could've ... been meant to explode ... in our building," I said looking at Kurt as he adjusted the oxygen flow.

"Then someone got it wrong, we're not ICE."

"Yeah." I thought about it. You wouldn't get that wrong. Maybe she isn't about us. "We need to know ... who she is."

"Conway, this could be drug-induced ramblings," Kurt cautioned, but he didn't believe it, I could tell by his tone.

"Could be ... get Sam on the phone, Kurt, please."

"Sure." He used his cell and called Sam. After a quick conversation in which he explained I'd been in a helicopter crash, he handed me the phone. "Don't be long. Keep calm. Breathe."

I sucked up the urge to flip him off and spoke to Sam, hoping my voice didn't sound as pain-filled as I felt.

"You two okay over there?"

"Chicky babe, good to hear your voice. We're good. Not entirely sure why we're here."

"Delta was requested." I needed a few breaths before continuing. "Some of the heads were American?"

"Oh, all of them are. It is a shipment of heads destined for cremation."

"Say what?"

"Yep, we ran the biometrics and they are all from donated bodies and were supposed to go to Chicago from a research facility in South Korea. Some joint American-South Korean research project."

"Donated bodies ... South Korea ... sure, that makes sense." Not.

"Yep."

"Why and how did they end up in New Zealand?"

245

"Ah, Chicky, the million-dollar question. I'm not kidding. Someone paid a crew member damn near a million US to make sure this box was in the cargo and not on the manifest on this ship when it left Indonesia."

"Who and by whom?"

There was silence for a beat before Sam said, "We're coming home. We'll brief you in person. No phones, no electronic communication."

Ah, crap. That was bad.

"How soon can you be here?"

"Booking flights now, see you in about twenty-four hours. Will you still be in hospital?"

"I don't think … I have much choice. Stay safe. Thank Faye for me."

I tried to hand the phone to Mitch but missed his hand. He caught it before it hit the ground. A combination of the crash, surgery, pain, and what I knew was a fairly decent concussion, took their toll.

I hurt. My head swam. Failure hurt. It hurt more than any physical pain. Physical pain ended. Sooner or later it stopped. The pain felt from failing to exact justice never left.

A door opened and someone came in. I couldn't see who it was. Panic set in, then Mitch's voice inside my head said, 'Open your eyes.' I tried but they wouldn't open.

The person introduced himself to Mitch. I knew his voice. Leon Kapowski. My long-suffering neurologist.

Blinding pain shot through my head.

Chapter Twenty-five.

Raining Blood

Voices.

Low murmurings and quiet conversations. I knew they were close. One of them was Mitch. I felt his presence. He was closest. Probably within arm's reach. My eyes wouldn't open. Probably a good thing. I moved my hand. Mitch's hand covered mine and squeezed. I still couldn't see. Disobedient eyes.

"You're waking up," Mitch said. "Good. It's been a few hours."

Hours? That didn't seem right. Hours? My eyes struggled to open. The light was dim but still hurt. The other voices murmured a few more times and vanished.

"How many hours?" My voice sounded wrong, husky. Oxygen. It's drying.

Mitch held a straw to my mouth.

"This will help. Iced water."

He was right. "How many hours, Mitch?"

"Almost an entire day. El, your body is a bit broken. You need to mend. Too much too soon, not good."

It was a little easier to breathe and talk, maybe sleeping had helped. I was still wearing sensors but the IV had gone. I just had a port in my left hand. Progress.

"All right?" Mitch watched me.

"Any more explosions?"

"No."

"Good. Did they find the Croatian woman? Sonya, I think that was her name."

"Yes. Kurt's interviewing her here. He left just as you woke up. She was admitted with abdominal pain an hour or so ago."

"Here?"

"Uh huh."

"Do you know if they did an ultrasound before Kurt got near her?" I could feel something horrible brewing and it was hard to keep that from my voice. "Mitch, did they?"

"I don't know. I'll call him, right now."

Mitch pulled my phone from his pocket and called Kurt.

I held my hand out for the phone as soon as Mitch said hello. "Hey, don't go near her," I said. A fine red mist filled the air. "Don't, Kurt. Don't."

"Conway. It's fine. She's sick. I'm just going to have a conversation with her."

"No! She's not sick. Kurt. Please!"

"Calm down."

"Stop." I took a painful breath and controlled the shaking in my voice. "Come back."

"Conway, put Mitch on."

"Doc, please. Come back."

Mitch took the phone when I held it out to him. Seemed like a good opportunity to try to sit up. My hand hit a something in the bed. Controls. I sat the bed up. Pain coursed freely through my body. I felt nauseous, swallowing hard and hoping I didn't throw up. Throwing up would hurt. It would really hurt.

"Kurt, I saw what it was that upset Ellie. Red mist in the air," Mitch said. For some reason it sounded less insane when Mitch said it than when I did. "She's trying to get out of bed."

All of a sudden, Mitch thrust a white plastic container into my hands. I vomited. The room spun. The back of the bed moved down a little. I wasn't going anywhere. Large black dots floated in front of my eyes.

"Enough, Ellie. You have to rest," Mitch said, taking the container. "No more moving."

He was serious.

There was a knock on glass and the door slid open.

"I'm back. Explain," Kurt said walking over to my bed. "While you're at it, explain what the hell you thought you were doing." He glanced in the container that Mitch showed him. "That's not good."

"Did they do an abdominal ultrasound before you went to see that woman?"

"They were waiting on a radiologist. I was going to have a quick word before she went to radiology."

"Why?"

"She asked for you. She wanted to see the agent who saved her."

My blood turned to crystals. "You knew I thought she could be a bomb—"

"Yes. I did. I also have a list of her visitors and how long they were with her. She's been in custody. ICE aren't in the habit of letting people walk into their facilities carrying explosives."

"We don't either," I replied as another wave of pain crashed over me. "We don't either, Kurt, but it happened."

He had no comeback. Instead, he took his phone and made a call and put it on speaker. I listened.

"This is SSA Kurt Henderson. I need a Bomb Squad to Inova Fairfax hospital. A-sap."

"Kurt, it's Tony. I'm on the way." He whistled.

I knew what followed. He had their attention, now it was instruction time. He'd circle his index finger in the air. Rally up. "What are you dealing with?" I could hear movement. Feet on the floor. Doors opening and closing. A truck starting.

"Possible suicide bomber."

"Crap-a-doodle-do. I hate that shit."

"Not my favorite either."

"Tony, ETA?" I said.

"Hey, Conway, glad you're still with us. Thirty minutes. Precautionary measures until then. Get the potential threat isolated."

"I'll meet you, Tony. At the entrance to Emergency," Kurt said.

"See you then." The call disconnected.

Kurt looked over at me. "Happy now?"

I couldn't nod and speaking wasn't great. "Isolate her." I paused for breath. "Get ICE to do it. I need you here."

He didn't argue or question why. He just made another

call, paced the room, then hung up and spoke quietly to Mitch. So quietly, I couldn't hear. I concentrated on Mitch. Nothing. What? Kurt still talked to him, preventing any shared images from configuring. Clever. But it also meant they didn't want me to know something.

Not cool.

"Secrets. Rude," I muttered under another upsurge of pain.

Kurt was right there. "On a scale of one to ten, Conway, ten being worst possible. How bad is the pain?"

I contained a grimace and let a small smile replace it. "Five."

"You're done. I'm getting Leon in for another consult and looking at stronger pain relief."

Mitch frowned. Kurt noticed.

"She said five?" Mitch said. "Doesn't seem like five from the outside looking in?"

"That's because it's Conway. Her five is a normal person's nine."

Mitch smiled. "That's not surprising."

"No, it's not."

My head hurt, my ribs indignant, and the stupidity of trying to move caused fiery pitchforks to jab me. It occurred to me that I wouldn't much like hell. Hopefully, that's not where destiny would lead me. I closed my eyes.

When I opened them, Leon was in the room.

"What made you vomit?" he asked.

"Moving," I replied. "It was a reaction to more pain."

Maybe five wasn't quite right.

"You're certain? You didn't feel sick before you tried to move?"

"No, I was okay."

I was awesome, ready to go for a run.

"How's the head?"

"Sore."

"What year is it?"

"Nineteen eighty-two." It wasn't easy keeping a straight face but I did.

"And you are a wiseass as always. Name?"

I sighed.

"Gabrielle Conway."

"Where are you?"

I sighed again, a little too heavily, and the fiery pitchfork was back. Instead of fighting it, I went with the pain. Breathe. Aware that Leon, Kurt and Mitch stood watching and waiting for me to speak, made me uncomfortable. Breathe. As the pain subsided, I glanced around the room, a small smile lurking on the edges of my lips.

"Looks like a space station."

Leon shook his head. "Play along."

"Hospital. Are we done?" I paused to steady my breathing. "Twenty questions is not my favorite game. So unimaginative. Just accept I'm not suffering ill-effects from a head injury."

That may well happen, but it ain't a thing yet.

Leon smiled. "She's fine. Go ahead and increase her

pain meds. Sedate if you need to."

"Thought you were supposed to be on my side?" I said. And saw his little torture light in his hand. "You can put that away. No light."

"I'm your neurologist. Do you have any idea how much fun that isn't?"

"There is still no need for you to suggest sedation." How rude.

"When you're feeling better I want to run through the Epley maneuver with you again," Leon said. "I'll wait until you can move. BPPV is probably going to be an issue again. The sooner we get it treated the better."

"Okay." Benign Paroxysmal Positional Vertigo. I was well used to that unpleasantness but was pleased he didn't want to attempt the Epley maneuver now.

"Also, there's something going on with you. We've witnessed non-verbal communication. There could be an underlying trauma issue responsible."

A smile trickled into my voice. "No, it isn't. I'm just observant. Nothing more."

"And Mitch as well?"

"Yes. That's why we get on so well."

Telepathy? No. That didn't feel right. We definitely had some kind of cerebral connection happening though. Empathic accuracy was a good description. Yes, that fitted. We could accurately infer each other's thoughts and feelings. I leaned my head back. How did I know what it was? Before the crash I had no idea. I just knew I knew stuff and not just about Mitch. I have always been able to sense when people were holding back and able to pull information from places untapped by most people. It didn't explain the hallucinations. It didn't explain how Mitch could see what I saw.

How could I project images like that? Or open my mind so he could walk in? How did I see Chance and how did he help me know things?

Accept it, don't think about it.

My eyes closed without my bidding. Mitch's voice flowed over me.

"We're close. We sense things about each other," he said. "It's our thing. Don't make it something it's not by trying to give it a name."

"Pain relief," Kurt said, putting a kidney-shaped dish on the bed, containing two full syringes, one bigger than the other and a silver packet. He ripped open the silver packet and cleaned the port in my hand. I watched with interest as he took the needle cap off the smaller syringe with his teeth. He held the port with one hand and the syringe in the other. "This might be a little uncomfortable."

I didn't notice if it was or wasn't. When the syringe was empty, he recapped it and dropped it into the dish before picking up the second syringe.

"What's that?"

"Saline flush. I want the medication in your blood stream, not in the tubing."

Fair enough.

"All done. Ten minutes and you should be a lot more

comfortable."

"You didn't mix any Phenergan in this time, did you?"

"No."

"Thank you."

"I used a different anti-nausea medicine, doesn't have a sedating effect. Don't make me regret it."

The room went quiet. Mitch sat close enough that he could touch me. Our fingers linked. His voice chased away the pain as he talked to me, telling me how Kurt had gone to meet the bomb squad and that Dad was having a coffee. The last thing I remembered hearing as I drifted into a pain-free ether was him saying everything would be okay.

Chapter Twenty-six.

The Number of the beast

I moved the back of the bed a little, enabling me to see more of the room and feel more like an active participant in anything that happened. Mitch said I'd slept for four hours. The day was over. In some ways, that was a blessing. Kurt topped up my pain relief and said Doug was coming in to talk to me.

I figured I must be almost fully recovered judging by the amount of sleep I'd had since my arrival in hospital. Shame my body didn't agree.

Doug's hulking figure ambled through the door of my room. He was one of the most seasoned Delta C agents. Mitch stood up, his eyes flashed from me to Doug. I smiled.

"Doug this is Mitch, he's my ..." I looked at Mitch for help. We hadn't defined us. It was all new, we'd moved from best friends to this new thing.

Mitch grinned and shook Doug's hand. "The word she's looking for is 'beau.'"

Such an old-fashioned yet fabulous word. Yep, beau. That worked.

Mitch and Doug exchanged greetings. Mitch sat in a chair by the door, allowing Doug access to me.

Doug sat heavily in the closest chair. "It's mad out there," he said. His voice rattled like a freight train arriving at a station.

"Not great in here either," I replied.

"Your two-man protection slash surveillance team is still in place watching those women. We're liaising with the Transit team who are watching Troy. It's one helluva juggling act to make surveillance happen in the current climate." He pulled out his phone and checked the screen, then he stopped and said, "Can I ask you a question?"

"Sure."

"You worked the Hawk case, yeah?"

I nodded. Funny how it will always be the Hawk case even though we knew the real identity of Hawk. Do we really need to go there again?

"How'd he blow out the back of that young woman's head?"

Do we want to go *there* again? Do *I*?

I skimmed the image forever chiseled into my mind and answered quickly. "C4. He'd filled a hollow metal hair barrette with C4 and added a small remote detonator. It was enough to turn her skull into shrapnel."

Doug's foot hit the chair leg. I jumped. My heart raced. Everything came back into focus. I was in a hospital bed, not a stadium. Somehow, that wasn't overly comforting.

"You all right?" Doug asked.

"Uh huh, why the question?"

Kurt might be closer to the truth than I'd care to admit with the PTSD comments he'd been making for the last year or so.

"You didn't seem to be with me here," Doug said.

Well, I can't be everywhere at fucking once, can I? Seemed smart to keep that observation to myself. I saw Mitch move closer. He frowned and shook his head a little. I knew that look.

Mitch leaned toward me. "You sure you're all right?"

"I'm okay." I wondered if he saw the explosion because I went there again. The look in his eyes told me he did. I wanted to hug him and tell him I was sorry. It would have to wait.

My attention reverted to Doug. "Why'd you ask about the woman in New Zealand?" I didn't want to say her name. But I couldn't help but think it, Gloria.

"Because one of those musical cards arrived at the office the morning of the explosion, addressed to you," he said.

"And?"

"It contained enough C4 to kill you and make a hole where your desk was."

There is a hole where my office was.

He pulled an evidence bag from his pocket and handed it to me. I read the front of the envelope and noted the name on it was mine. Supervisory Special Agent Conway, but the address was care of the Federal Bureau of Investigation, followed by the street address. It didn't stipulate Delta Team, criminal investigation division. Whoever addressed it either didn't know how to get it directly to my desk, or didn't care.

The bomb in a musical card was clever. Hard to detect, wouldn't show up as anything suspicious on the X-ray, just a musical card. I had thought about ways to smuggle explosives into our building after the explosion. Musical greeting cards. God. I willed my heart rate to return to normal as I concentrated on what Doug said.

"The return address caused suspicion. Know anyone in the Czech Republic who'd be sending you a card at this time of year?"

"No. I don't know anyone in the Czech Republic." I looked at the writing on the envelope. "I guess the return address is fake?"

"Yes."

"And no, I don't even know anyone currently traveling in Europe who'd send me a card."

"That's what SAC Grafton said. He called that Russian you work with."

I rounded up my bizarre thoughts about singing Christmas cards and creepy Santas. Where they came from, I had no idea. Once I'd dispatched the Santas, I determined the card situation was serious and more than likely related to the bombings. Caine must've thought so too if he called Misha.

Doug started speaking again. "The Russian, Misha Praskovya, got one too, a few days ago. Someone in his office opened the card ... there's a sticky hole where his assistant and her desk used to be."

Robin and Batman stepped out of the wall and a speech bubble grew from Robin's mouth.

I read it aloud. "Holy people-goo, Batman! That's a job for crime scene cleanup."

Robin turned to Batman with a theatrical flick of his crusader's cape, and they ran through the opposite wall.

Mitch suppressed a smile.

Doug's eyes widened, he wisely ignored my people-goo comment and carried on, "There was a C4 theft in France over a year ago. It's possibly some of that. We'll know more when the lab has finished."

That could take anything from a week to six months. Our laboratory backlogs are legendary and now we had even more pressure on the system. I'd heard about the theft, everyone who had anything to do with security knew about the seventy-eight pounds of missing C4 and the missing detonators, presumed stolen from a depot in Lyon, France. C4 was often the terrorist explosive of choice and especially true if it didn't contain taggants. This left an explosive with no smell that was hard to detect, stable, shapeable, and super easy to use. Just ask the survivors of Pan Am flight 103, back in nineteen eighty-eight.

Some of the missing French C4 had turned up in IEDs in Afghanistan over the last six months or so, targeting troops and civilians alike. I knew that because the French C4 contained taggants. It conformed to current protocol regarding the marking of plastic explosives.

"The stolen C4 contained taggants."

"I'll look into it and make sure." Doug wrote in his notebook.

"Poke the lab ... we need to know if there is a detection taggant in the musical card C4. Because if there is one in there, how did it get through the mail centers and airline screening?"

More writing in his notebook.

"Also, I'm interested in the identification taggant. Let's find out who manufactured this shit if we can. It might not be the French C4."

"Anyone got any ideas as to why Misha and I are targets?" A cold sick feeling crawled around my stomach looking for a corner to hide in. It told me my gut was right all along.

This was about us. Why? That was the body-exploding question. Me, sure I can see that. It's not the first time some fucktard has targeted me, but all of Delta and Misha too?

Doug's expression turned super-serious and he quietly asked, "You think Hawk could be back? Could he be behind the bombings?"

I willed myself not to smile.

I shook my head. "No."

"You're sure?"

"Oh, yeah. Trust me," I replied.

Very sure, the Abbasi brothers have left the mortal realm.

I had a feeling convincing the FBI that Hawk/Abbasi wasn't back might prove a problem. I came up with a possible solution.

"I'll give Caine a call and get together with him to go

over the possibilities," I said. Mitch gave another minute shake of his head. Yep, supposed to be resting. I got it. I can do this. I'm good here.

"Delta C reopened the file on Hawk/Abbasi," Doug informed me. He sounded as if there was no doubt Hawk was responsible. Wrong. This isn't about Hawk. Dead men don't exact revenge.

"Director O'Hare know?" I oozed nonchalance as I spoke, while leaning my head back and trying not to let the pain take over.

"I wouldn't think so."

She will as soon as I can get hold of her. Apart from me, she was the only other person from our agency present that day to witness his demise. I moved in some scary circles at times

I had a few things that needed taking care of and a call to O'Hare was now first on my list.

"My money's on Semtex for these explosions," I said, more to myself than to Doug.

"Could be," Doug replied. "We haven't had anything back from the ballistics lab yet. Still sifting through wreckage at all the sites except the Navy Yard. Let me check." He made a call while I thought about Semtex and where it could be sourced.

"Ellie?" Doug's voice reverberated. "There were no markers in the Navy Yard explosion. None. It wasn't C4."

Or maybe it was old, pre-marking. Or maybe it was manufactured especially for someone without any taggant at all.

"Dogs found a small amount of explosive at the Hard Rock Café ..." Thoughts spilled from my mouth unchecked. "Whoever is doing this could be using a mixture of older Semtex and newer stuff. If you wanted a bomb found ... you'd give clues and use something the sniffer dogs could find. Decoy. If you wanted to kill people and cause utter fucking chaos and had access to older stock of Semtex, you'd use that, right?"

Doug nodded.

The room tilted to the left, knocking the conversation out of my head. I watched my words fall to the floor and melt into small puddles. They shone like liquid silver. In one of the silver puddles, I saw Mitch's reflection. A vibration disturbed the pool. His image blurred. My eyes searched and found him, standing at the end of my bed.

He took my breath away.

Mitch looked worried. Made me wonder why. His head turned as if he was looking at someone else for a moment. He spoke but I couldn't see the words, they flew away from me. Maybe we weren't alone?

Then I heard him. His hand touched my arm. I felt myself relax.

"El? You okay? Did you hear Doug?"

"No. Yes. What?"

It took a great deal of effort to drag my mind back to the present situation, concentration a deliberate act.

"Did you hear Doug?" Mitch's voice was gentle but firm.

"No." I struggled to remember why Doug was in the

room. Bits and pieces of our conversation came back. "Gimme a minute." I breathed as deeply as I could while the missing pieces jumped into a scrabble tray. All of a sudden, they were little yellow ducks. It was impossible not to smile as my ducks lined up. "Okay, my ducks are in a row, continue Doug."

"There have been some rumblings about that woman Delta A rescued," Doug said without question. "An anonymous tip came in a few days ago, it was only just now deemed of interest."

Not surprising - a lot of things are of interest now we have acts of terror inside D.C. A duck quacked.

"I'm listening ..."

"The tip-off suggested she isn't Croatian."

The room revolved. I heard Cher singing 'Woman's World.' Confused, I listened to the lyrics as the song played, complete with images rolling past my eyes. I might be strong enough to rise above being torn up, busted, and taken apart but I suspected someone wasn't. A woman? The woman? The revolving increased. With a bang, the room stopped dead and flattened. Inked thick black lines appeared around everything in the room. A comic strip enveloped me. The glass door opened and Chance sauntered into the room.

"You okay?" he said, perching on my bed.

"What do you think?"

He grinned. "I think you're lucky."

"What do you know, Chance?"

"I know she's not Croatian. Explore Czech Republic or

Slovakia as options. And that she's being used by someone set on revenge."

"Seriously? That's not just my drug-addled brain?"

"Sorry, Ellie. It's the truth." He glanced sideways. "But what's with the ducks?" I followed his gaze. Little yellow rubber ducks all in a row.

"At least they're in a row," I muttered. "How am I supposed to announce the woman might be Czech or Slovak and is somehow being used by someone?"

He grinned. "It's you, you'll figure it out. You have to. You need to get them looking in the right direction."

"You know I have a head injury, right?"

"Probably accounts for the ducks," he replied. "You can do this."

Chance grinned and faded into the background. The color faded, the black lines ran, then spiraled into the ground.

"Ellie?"

I cleared my vision and focused on Mitch's voice.

"Yes."

"Okay?"

"Yes."

She was a Czech or Slovak and Chance was back again. Completely normal. Yep. Completely normal.

I tended toward Czech, simply because the card came from the Czech Republic. My gut agreed. To be honest, it would probably agree with anything. It hadn't been fed for what seemed like days. It occurred to me that realizing I hadn't eaten meant I felt better.

"I want someone to do a thorough background on the woman, she might be Czech. She might also have some kind of link to us," I said to Doug.

"Czech?" Doug questioned. "A link?"

"Humor me, Doug." Sometimes I even surprise myself. Some random facts jumped to mind. "I happen to know there are about a hundred and twenty thousand pounds of unmarked Semtex still in Czech armories. Their security can be a bit shit."

"I'll get on it, Ellie. When are you expecting Davenport and Jackson back?"

"Any time now, I think." I glanced at Mitch, who nodded. I was right. Good. "You better get back, Doug. Thanks for the heads up and for helping us out."

"We're all in this together, Ellie. I've never seen agencies pull together like they are right now."

Good to know.

I watched Doug leave before I asked Mitch for my phone and called Cait O'Hare.

"It's me. They're re-opening the Hawk case."

"I'll have it quashed. How you doing?"

"I'm okay and thank you." I had another question. "Did you know Misha and I were both sent exploding cards?"

"No. I did not."

"Shit just got way closer to home." Having the war so close made it that much harder to deal with.

"Was close enough to start with. What do you need?"

"A body that isn't so banged up. To get out of this

hospital. To go back to work."

I heard the amusement in her voice. "You're too like me for your own good. Work from your hospital bed if you have to but do not leave until you're discharged. Got it?"

"Yes, ma'am."

"Kurt is to stay with you. As soon as we get some spare bodies I'll assign a security detail."

"I'm fine. I don't need protecting."

Cait laughed. "It's like looking in a mirror."

She hung up.

Mitch took my phone and put it out of reach. His eyes met mine, a fire burned deep within me.

"Enough. You need to rest," he said.

Probably, but that wasn't what I wanted. Not at all what I wanted.

"No, I need ... I want ..." I chewed my lip. The state I was in I doubted it was even possible. Kurt's pain relief cocktail had blurred the edges of reality. Something else popped into my head and momentarily overrode my desire. "I have a question."

"Let's hear it."

"Did you see someone walk in while Doug was here and sit on the bed and talk to me?"

"No. It was you, Doug, and me. No one came in."

"Okay, good." I didn't want to question why Mitch couldn't see Chance. "Moving right along. You're a little too far away and wearing way too many clothes ..."

"Really?"

I smiled. "That was supposed to be inside my head, it wasn't was it?"

"Nope." Mitch smiled. "You need rest."

Mitch closed the glass door. Beyond the glass, the ICU was a hive of activity. I was a prisoner in a goldfish bowl. A tired prisoner with a mind that wouldn't stop thinking about being alone with Mitch. *Alone.* Mitch pulled the curtains then disappeared to the other side of the curtain with a piece of paper in his hand. I heard the door open and then close. A few minutes later Mitch reappeared smiling.

"We won't be disturbed for an hour. I told the staff you're resting and want to be left alone. I told Kurt too, he's not far away. But he won't come in, think he's pleased you're actually resting." He dimmed the light, by turning off the main lights and dimming the light above the bed.

I smiled. "Thank you."

"Don't mention it ..."

I blinked, he sounded so much like Chance.

"Mitch?"

"Yep, last time I looked," he replied, as his fingers wrapped around mine. "All right?"

I wanted to put my arms around his neck, lose myself in his touch and forget everything.

"Yes."

I was higher than the clouds. It was possible that none of this was real. But I wanted and needed to be lost with him.

Mitch sat down at my side, his legs stretched out beside mine. I could feel the heat from his body through the covers.

His eyes shone in the dimmed light. Mitch's lips hovered a fraction above mine. I wanted to reach up and pull him closer but my left arm was uncooperative. He kissed me softly.

"Rest. I'll be right here."

My head rested on Mitch's chest. He held me close.

"If I keep talking I think I can get you to fall asleep," he said, his fingertips stroked my arm.

"Maybe."

Breathing in his warm scent, wrapped in safe arms. I listened as he talked. His voice low and soft, lulling me to sleep. My eyes closed. I could hear his breathing, his voice, the warmth in his words as they flowed, washing over me. Filling the crevices of my mind with smiles and laughter, and nothing else mattered.

Chapter Twenty-seven

Angel of Death

I woke to the sound of deep voices rumbling around the room like thunder in a spring storm. Aware that Mitch was still next to me in the bed, I didn't move. I didn't want to move.

He was talking. I could feel the vibrations of his voice. My head still lay on his chest.

Nice.

The rumbling around me sounded like Sam, Lee and Kurt all comparing notes.

"All right there, Conway?" Kurt asked.

"Yep. What's happening?"

"You missed most of the briefing. We have a few names for you. Think you might find them interesting," Sam said.

A duck quacked. I couldn't see a duck.

"Names, give 'em to me."

"You want to sit up a bit and take part?" Kurt asked.

Did I? Not really. Well, no, I did but I didn't want to sit up. I was comfortable and for the first time in what felt like days was not in pain.

"No, I'm good. Names?"

"Trudi Welsh and Susan Hollows," Lee said.

Ah, crap.

"What about Danni Lane?"

"Her name never came into it," he replied.

"And Welsh and Hollows did what exactly in relation to the heads in New Zealand and what we're dealing with here?"

"Trudi Welsh was the crew member paid to ensure the heads were in the cargo and not on the manifest. We traced the money back to Susan Hollows."

"Okay, they're the same people we've dealt with here? New Zealand citizens here on a research trip with Danni Lane?"

"You tell me," Lee said, handing Mitch his phone. "Gallery, NZ folder."

Mitch found the photos. He showed me. Impossible.

"That's from the ship?" I asked. I was looking at a head shot of Trudi Welsh.

"Yes. Crew records."

"How? She's here."

"She wasn't on the ship when it sailed. She was supposed to be but never showed."

"She was an actual crew member? The captain knew her, other crew members knew her?"

"That's where it gets interesting."

"It's pretty freaking interesting already ..."

"Four crew members swore they knew her and that she had worked on the ship for two years."

"Four? Two years and only four crew knew her?"

"Most of the crew was new. The four who knew her had been on the ship for six or seven years."

"And?"

"They were paid to vouch for her." Sam grinned and rocked on his heels. "We're good at what we do."

I flicked to the next picture and sighed.

"And Susan Hollows?"

"It looks like she transferred the money from an account in Switzerland. She was never in Indonesia, as far as we can tell. In fact, as far as we can tell, neither of them were ever there. Still waiting for confirmation from Interpol about the Swiss account and if Hollows has ever traveled to Switzerland and if she has an account with the bank in question."

I needed a fully functional brain and body. The case just twisted the shit out of itself.

"Well, fuck." I moved against Mitch trying to sit up a little.

"Hold on, I'll help," he said reaching for the bed controls. "How far?"

"Sixty degrees."

The bed moved slowly and with it a wave of pain. My breath caught in my throat.

Mitch stopped the bed moving. "That's far enough. Okay now?"

I exhaled with care. "Yeah." I looked up. Kurt was on his feet reading my chart. He glanced at me over the clipboard.

"I'll get you something for that," he said. "Don't go anywhere."

"And here's me thinking I'd tango down the corridor ..."

He left.

Mitch chuckled. "Tango?"

"I tango." I replied with a smile. I do a lot of things. I turned my attention away from Latin American dances and back to work. "Sam, did Faye have anything to say about the women?"

"If you're ready to hear the rest?" Sam replied opening his notebook.

"Tell me."

"Susan Hollows and Trudi Welsh are New Zealand citizens and volunteer firefighters with the NZ Fire Service. Trudi is a Station Officer and Susan a senior Fire Fighter. They have day jobs as well. No criminal records not even speeding tickets. Danni Lane is a NZ citizen but there was very little information about her. Fay found a record of her holding a Private Investigators license but nothing to say she worked as a PI."

Didn't really get us anywhere.

"Lee, where are the women now?" I asked.

"At the field office, waiting for us."

"The author chick?"

"Not here, she's back at the hotel. We still have a protection/surveillance team watching her."

"Kris and Jerry?"

"Yes."

"Okay, good."

"And the Sonya the Czech, Slovak, Croatian?"

Sam laughed.

"We have her, ICE handed her over. They didn't want

anything to do with relocating a possible terrorist."

"Is she a bomb?"

"Not now."

Jeez. I was right. "Did she know?"

"No, or at least we don't think she knew."

"How?"

"Tampons. She was wearing one and had another two with her."

"Exploding tampons and she didn't know," I said.

"They looked normal and like they'd come straight from a box, still in the wrappers. The only thing difference was the Semtex core and detonator."

Jeez. I'd heard about the idea. It was developed as a way round the body scanners and sniffer dogs at airports. The mythical bomb had a kill radius of sixteen feet and detonated by pulling the string.

"Who is she really?"

"We still don't know. Getting there, Ellie, getting there. There is an awful lot going on."

I nodded and regretted it. "You need to find out where those tampons came from. I don't want to hear they're on shelves anywhere." I paused. "As far as I know Al-Qaeda are the only group to have developed exploding tampons. They called them Sempax. It's relatively new. I didn't think they actually existed – we didn't have any proof."

"We've got Delta B on tracking the manufacturer and running the list of visitors to our young lady."

"Good. Make sure they're aware that this technology was claimed by Al-Qaeda."

"I will."

"Okay, this is what we're doing. I'm getting out of here." I sounded a lot more convincing than I felt. "I'm going to talk to our foreign friend and then we're going to go talk to those women … tell me they are being held separately and that someone said the word terrorism, so I don't have to deal with their State Department interference and have these women screaming for lawyers?"

"You're not. We will talk to them all. They are being held separately and yes, terrorism was mentioned," Kurt said from the doorway. I saw the syringes sticking out of the kidney dish in his hand.

I smiled. "We'll see …"

As he walked toward me, I saw the uniforms outside the door. They were supposed to keep anyone from getting to me not me from getting out.

"Behave, Conway," Kurt cautioned as he went through the procedure of injecting pain relief into the port in my hand.

The machine next to me, which had monitored my vital signs since I'd arrived, was silent. And pushed back against the wall. It was off. The sensors were gone. The only one left was a glowing red sensor on my finger. I followed the wire to something that looked like large digital watch on my wrist.

"What's with the sensor and the watch thing?"

"Keeping an eye on your blood oxygen level and pulse rate for another few hours," Kurt replied. Dropping the last syringe into the dish. "It's a portable pulse oximeter and it sends data to my phone."

Great. Portable is good.

"Why so interested in my oxygen levels?" A few things really annoy me and the biggest is being fussed over.

"If your lung collapses I want to know fast."

"Excuse me what?"

"You heard."

"Yeah, but no one's mentioned a collapsed lung as a thing that could happen—"

"Chest trauma, abdominal trauma, being on a ventilator, surgery, it's a possibility exacerbated by your build ... tall and thin. You have risk factors. This is precautionary."

I choose to ignore the notion of collapsed lungs. It sounded like something I didn't want to know about.

"What else have you got?" I asked Sam.

"A get well card from Faye," Sam replied handing a red envelope to me.

Trepidation pulsed as I held it in my hands. It felt bulky. A musical card? What were the odds?

"From Faye?" I knew my voice conveyed some of the trepidation.

"Yes. Problem?"

"Probably not." I couldn't bring myself to open the envelope. Staring at it didn't magically give up its secrets. "Did Faye give it to you herself?"

Sam's brow furrowed and his head shook.

"Give me the card," he said, holding out his hand.

I placed the envelope in his hand. He turned and walked away. Lee followed him.

I watched them leave knowing what came next. My thoughts turned to prayer, well my version of prayer: Now's a good time to prove you exist. You listening God? Don't let my men go bang. I don't mind if I never get another birthday, Christmas, anything card, in my life.

Chapter Twenty-eight.

Breathe

Sam and Lee were with the bomb squad regarding my not so cheerful get-well card. Kurt paced outside the door. He had his phone in his hand. By the grim look on his face I guessed he was talking to Caine.

"Do I have clothes?" I asked Mitch, then thought I should clarify. "Wearable ones?"

"Yes."

"Will you help me?"

"Do I have a choice?" he asked.

"Not really. I need to shower."

"Then I'm your man." His smile widened.

"Pleased about that." I adjusted my position, sitting up a little more. "Something's are much more fun with you around."

"You're pretty flirty for someone who can hardly move," he commented.

"Problem?"

"Not at all. Just want to make sure you're okay."

"You think this contraption on my wrist is waterproof?" I asked, inspecting the glow on my finger. Yep, I felt like ET. I pointed at Mitch. "Phone home."

"Very funny. Let me have a look at the thing."

He took a closer look at the device on my wrist and declared it waterproof.

"Great."

"You sure you're all right?"

"I'm fine. Let's go try out the shower."

I figured if I could walk to the shower under my own steam then I could go back to work. It may not have been the best plan but it was the only one I had. As awesome as Kurt, Sam and Lee were, they weren't the ones who should be talking to a woman who had an explosive tampon inside her body. Just no.

"Whenever you're ready, El."

I hadn't moved. Funny because I thought I had.

With care, I shifted to the edge of the bed. My hand connected with the remote. I lowered the bed about six-inches, intent on making standing as easy as possible.

"Okay. How far do you think the bathroom is?"

I was looking for something to focus on. Counting steps would do.

"Twelve feet."

Easy. Yeah, easy.

Chapter Twenty-nine.

Symptom of the Universe

I sat uncomfortably at my temporary desk in the Washington Field office and listened to Caine brief me on the current state of play. None of it was good. Lee and Sam questioned Trudi and Susan. As I suspected, they had no knowledge of any of the Indonesian connection. I wasn't surprised to find Hollows say she'd never been to Switzerland and didn't have a Swiss bank account. I wondered about Interpol and if they'd confirm that.

Danni was missing. For the life of me, I couldn't understand how that happened. Except that things were confused, communication was a struggle at times and as far as we all knew there was still a bomber loose in the city. Because Danni wasn't implicated in any of the scenarios, my surveillance team were re-prioritized. We had to rely on the electronic surveillance I'd had installed on her phone. The situation irked me. My gut said she was involved in something but that wasn't enough to take Kris and Jerry off their SWAT duties t follow her. My gut also said the electronic surveillance was hinky as all hell.

"I can monitor her myself," I said.

"And you need to delegate more," Caine countered.

"I have been. You know I have."

"I know that you shouldn't be here," Caine replied.

"You need me."

He nodded. "Didn't say we didn't, but you shouldn't be here."

"But I am here, so use me."

His lip twitched. "What do you see?"

"I see a mess. I see this being about three different things that overlap."

"And they are?"

"An attempt on the President, bringing terrorism to D.C. to cripple the seat of power, and an all-out attempt on Delta A."

"No one's getting near Renegade after that movie came out. You know the one, *Olympus has Fallen*. You saw that right?"

"I did." Gerard Butler was in it.

"The Secret Service doesn't even want him in the bunker. He's being moved around. The Secretary of State too and the Vice President."

"Together?"

"No. The VP is at Camp David. The Secretary is out of the country."

"Okay, so the President is safe. That leaves terror and the crippling of the seat of power and justice. So far quite successful, wouldn't you say?"

Caine nodded. "We found another bomb, this time in the Capitol building mailroom. Another card, addressed to Senator Robinson."

"Why?"

"We don't know."

"I got two, lucky me. Praskovya one and Senator

Robinson one?"

Robinson. Rob. Was Arnie trying to tell me Robinson?

"That is what I was told," Caine confirmed.

"The senator ever come to our attention for anything before?" Trying to make that sound like a casual inquiry.

"Not that I am aware of. Nothing flagged when his name came up."

"So I need to find the link between me, Praskovya, and Robinson." I didn't remember ever meeting Senator Robinson. Every time I thought Robinson, I heard Arnie saying Rob. That was something I needed to look into. Praskovya's connection to me I knew. He was our FSB colleague and a member of Delta A when necessary. That connection was easy. He was one of us. "Did anyone else receive cards?"

"Not as far as I am aware."

"So that begs the question, why was I singled out from Delta A to receive cards?"

"Good question, Ellie. Although Sam and Lee did travel with your second card. It could well have been meant to take them out but failed."

"Kurt?"

"Him too. You are all together often ... there's a good chance one card would either kill or maim all of you at once."

Nice thought.

"Was the detonator faulty?"

"The chip was fried. The signal never got through."

Not killing us was an accident. So, the woman could've

been the backup, or the card.

Okay.

Breathe.

"Where's Mitch?" It occurred to me I hadn't seen him for half an hour. It felt odd not having him in the room.

"I sent him home—"

"And he went?"

"He had no choice. Kurt is with him."

"Hang on, Mitch had no choice. My Mitch?"

His lip twitched twice. "Your Mitch is stubborn. I see why you two get on so well. He's gone home to get some rest. Kurt will stay with him. No one associated with Delta A is to be alone."

I smiled. Stubborn. Hell, yes. Although I preferred to think of Mitch as driven not stubborn. Semantics.

"Home?"

"Your place."

Fantastic. A few hours rest would be good for them. I slowed my breathing and heard Mitch's voice in my head telling me to be careful. That I could do.

"Right. I'm going to talk girl-talk with the woman we rescued. She's here?"

"Yes, interview room down the hall. She's not giving any information."

"That could be because men keep asking her. She recently found out she had a bomb inside her. How would you feel? And she's got her period. I mean, really? That meant whoever held her captive had her long enough to track her cycle."

283

I willed myself to stand without wincing. Not easy but I did it.

"Good points."

I thought so. I also wasn't keen on using tampons any time soon. Okay, ever again.

Standing was good. Easier than sitting.

"I'll check in later," I said moving with care toward the door.

"Go easy, Ellie."

I smiled and let myself out.

I knocked on the interview room door. A female agent opened the door from the inside.

"Ellie, you're back," she said with a smile.

"Maryann, how are the kids?"

"Growing too fast," she replied. "I'll introduce you, then leave you to it."

"Thank you."

She turned to the young woman at the table, who had been reading a magazine but now looked at me.

"Alexandra, this is SSA Ellie Conway. She's going to spend some time with you. I'll be right outside. You can call me if you need to."

The woman nodded but said nothing. Maryann left and closed the door behind her.

"Do you mind?" I asked as I pulled out a chair opposite Alexandra. She shook her head. "Thank you."

Sitting hurt. I regretted my decision but standing was too intimidating.

"Alexandra, yes?"

She nodded.

"Do you speak English?"

Again she nodded.

"Will you talk to me?"

Nothing.

"You have a family?"

She nodded. A tear slid down her face.

I waited.

She looked like she was going to speak. The look faded.

I watched her eyes as I spoke. "Mother, father, brothers, sisters?"

She flinched.

"Where is your family?"

"We were taken."

"Taken?"

"From our family home."

"Who was taken?"

"My sister and I."

"Do you know where she is?"

She shook her head. "They took her away a week ago. I am not to see her again unless I do what they say."

"Why did they take her and leave you?"

"I do not know."

"Why did they take you both from your parents?"

"I do not know."

"What does your father do?"

She shrugged. "He is working for government. I do not know what he does."

"Your mother?"

A small but fleeting smile crossed her lips. "She is teacher."

A teacher and a government worker. My money was on the unknown government job as a reason for the abductions.

"What is your father's name?"

"Eduard Dobrovolný."

"Thank you. You are Czech?" I needed confirmation.

"Yes. From Prague."

I emailed his name to Lee with a note that he should run a background check and confirmation that Alexandra was indeed Czech.

"Mother's name?"

"Alena Dobrovolný."

I smiled. I emailed that name to Lee as well. I felt her becoming more relaxed.

"Would you like some tea?"

She nodded. I stood, took a moment to breath then walked to the door and swung it open.

"Maryann, any chance someone could get Alexandra some tea, please? And something sweet to eat. Chocolate?" I glanced at Alexandra. She smiled.

"Of course. I'll do it. Everything okay?"

"Yes. We're making progress."

I closed the door and sat down at the table. Not as easy as it sounds. Used to take sitting and breathing for granted, now, not so much.

"Tell me about your sister?"

"Anastazia is born after me. She is younger."

I rechecked her initial story. "She was taken with you?"

"Yes. We were together in the place you found me."

"Then what happened?"

"They take her away. The men. The next day the woman shows me pictures of Stazia. She is wearing only underwear and a man is holding a knife to her throat." Another tear ran down her cheek. "The woman tells me it will be bad for my sister if I don't do what they tell me."

"What sort of bad, did they give you details?"

She nodded. "They say they will sell her to highest bidder but first they have their fun with her." She swallowed hard.

"Why did you say you were here for a better life? When we found you?"

"I was told ... what to say."

Which is what I'd thought.

"Where are your parents?"

"I do not know. Home. Worried. I do not know."

"Did anyone make contact with them that you know of? Ransom demands, anything?"

"I do not know."

"Have you ever heard the name Rob mentioned?"

She shook her head.

"How about Robinson? Did that name ever come up? Did you ever met anyone called Robinson?"

She shook her head, then stopped. She looked at me. "No. But I heard them talking about someone called R."

My mind wanted to jump ahead and make two plus two equal five. After a few moments of internal battle, my mind conceded I needed more information. I needed proof that R was Robinson.

Our tea arrived. We drank tea and visited. Alexandra talked of her life and her sister. Normal family things. Normal family life. Nothing that stood out. I was no closer to discovering why they were taken or where the sister was by the time I'd finished my tea and said goodbye.

Chapter Thirty.
Cowboys from Hell

"Are you sure it's Seamus Kennedy you saw?" I asked Lee as he lowered himself into a chair by my desk.

"Yes. He was in the Mall, pretty sure he was with Tim Jones."

"They're back, the quasi-UN?" I said. The first time we met, I dubbed them the quasi-UN, also, the International Rescue Squad because that's what they were. They were in D.C. to find someone and reunite that person with her parents and here they are again, right when we have two women taken from their parents. Coincidence? I don't believe in coincidences. "We've got Kennedy and Jones, how about Holmes and Praskovya? Are they here?"

Lee shook his head. "I don't know. But it looks like our old pals have reunited for something."

"This has to be related."

"That's what I thought."

I picked up my phone and scrolled through to find Seamus's contact details. I had an email address. I emailed him, not mentioning that Lee saw him and asked if he knew of any terror groups in Croatia, Slovakia or the Czech Republic.

Twenty minutes later, my phone chimed. Incoming email.

"It's from Seamus and he's just implied he is still in the

UK. He obviously doesn't want anyone, us, knowing he's here." I thought for a moment. "I want surveillance. If he's not talking, there's a reason. My gut says it's related."

Lee grinned. "Your preferred approach?"

"What do ya bet Kennedy is staying in the same house as last time?"

"Worth a look."

"You and me. You up for it?" I asked.

"I'm fine. It's you we're all worried about."

I shrugged and it didn't kill me.

"I'll be okay." I crossed my fingers. "I'm walking and talking. It's all good."

"Mitch and Kurt are not going to like this ..."

"You scared?" A smile settled on my lips. Lee scared? Have I ever seen that? Nope.

"Fucking terrified, Chicky. Kurt I can handle but Mitch, I'm not so sure."

Interesting and amusing.

"If we're going to do this, let's do it now." Before Kurt or Mitch can put an end to it. It needed doing and I wanted to do it.

I knew my idea wasn't brilliant. I wasn't on form and yet I was keen to partake in a little bit of breaking and entering to try to find out why Seamus was in town. Ask? Yeah, no, not him. Stonewalls and cinder blocks talk more than Seamus Kennedy. Something was up and I was pretty sure it had to do with the current climate in D.C.

An hour later Lee parked down the road from the

house we knew Kennedy had stayed in the last time he was in town.

I made my way up the path and bashed on the door. No answer. Excellent. If anyone had answered, I was ready to spin a story depending on who it was. If it were one of the quasi-UN, I'd demand information.

I waited a few minutes before bashing again, just in case someone was there but otherwise occupied.

Nothing.

Waiting a sensible few seconds longer, I wondered if there was an alarm system: no outward advertising if there were. I glanced about not wanting anyone to creep up behind me as I stepped into the second part of the plan. From my pocket, I pulled a small leather case and took two thin pieces of metal.

I tumbled the lock and let myself in. No alarm and no one home. I checked the entire house and wondered how often he did a bug sweep. The house was tidy and clean. Nothing left lying around. Disappointing but not surprising. I'd danced with Kennedy before and knew where to look. We bought some of our more interesting pieces of furniture from the same specialist cabinet maker. In the living room was a solid old hutch dresser. I recognized it as the piece I wanted a look at by the workmanship.

The front cabinet opened with ease. I kneeled down and looked inside. Empty. Using the tips of the fingers of my right hand I carefully pressed the far right side of the back wall. It popped open about half an inch; hooking my fingers behind the secret door I pulled it fully open. Inside I found mail. I looked through some letters which confirmed he was living in the house. Mostly they were in English but some were in an odd mix of English and what was possibly a Slavonic language. Not Russian. I guessed at Czech because that fitted with some of what was going on. They seemed to be communications from an employer, and that was about all I could glean. For me, that smacked of a reason for him to be here. There was nothing in the letters that looked like Rob or Robinson that I could find.

My eyes drifted to the signature at the bottom of the page. Signed not printed. I snapped a photo of the signature. It was difficult to make out but looked like a name I'd heard recently: Dobrovolný.

A small white box bearing an apple logo sat on the shelf below the letters. I took it out for closer inspection. It once housed an iPhone. This was a good find. Inside the box I found a cardboard wallet that used to house a micro SIM card. The barcode on the back had the phone number printed underneath it. I added the number to my phone and returned everything to its rightful place then closed the cabinet. Using the dresser as support I stood with care. A few deep breaths and I continued on my mission.

Keen on placing GPS devices in the clothing in his closet I walked into Kennedy's bedroom. Knowing Lee was outside waiting in the car didn't help settle my nerves any. The longer I was in the house, the more dangerous my position. A quick search of the bedroom highlighted nothing of interest

Footsteps. The very last thing I wanted to hear.

I looked around the bedroom. They got closer. I ducked into the closet and took the opportunity to force the tiny tracking devices into the seams of jackets as I moved to the far end behind several long overcoats.

Standing still, barely breathing at the very end of the closest, pleased that I'd managed to get the trackers into as many jackets as possible. My fingers closed around the grip of my gun. I wasn't going to shoot Seamus. Was I? That simple action slowed my heart rate from pound to thump. I glanced at the oximeter on my wrist. Oxygen was okay, heart rate up. No problem.

The feet stopped. Then moved on, fading. I took a breath. They came back. I held it. My eyes wanted to close. If I couldn't see, then no one could see me.

The door opened. Light filtered through the clothes but didn't quite reach me.

A hand took a jacket. The door shut.

I didn't dare breath. Footsteps moved away. I took a breath.

Without warning, both doors swung open. A hand pulled a cord in the middle of the closet. Light flooded every nook and cranny.

Frozen.

Unblinking.

Hands rummaged on the shelf above me.

Mutterings followed more rummaging. Little puffs of

dust floated in the light.

The bulb flickered. A hand pulled the cord. It clicked. A grayish semi-darkness blanketed the closet.

The doors shut. I heard movement outside the doors.

My nose tickled and eyes watered, and I could still hear him moving about the bedroom. The urge to sneeze grew exponentially. I willed him to leave. Movement came close to the closet again.

Just leave.

If I sneezed, it'd kill my ribs. A little voice inside my head told me to lick the roof of my mouth. The urge vanished.

The footsteps walked away. A heavier door opened and closed. The front door maybe.

I waited.

Without warning I sneezed.

"Oh crap!"

My left-hand pressed on my side trying to stop the pain. I couldn't breathe for a minute. My right-hand stayed closed around my gun. I waited. No running footsteps. No sound of movement. I waited a full two minutes. Not because I wanted to but because I couldn't move.

Cautiously I opened the closet door and peered into the bedroom. No one.

I sneezed again and let loose an involuntary yelp. Shit it hurt.

I crept from my hiding place, keeping close to the walls as I left the bedroom and made my way to the front door.

I looked out a front window and saw Seamus.

Crap.

He stood at the end of his path talking on his cell phone.

I called Lee's cell phone. "He's at the end of the path. I'll go out the back. Meet me."

"I'm coming."

I moved quickly and quietly to the backdoor. It didn't open. I took my lock picks from my pocket and worked on the lock, listening carefully for sounds behind me. The lock tumbled. I could almost breathe again. I opened the door and closed it gently behind me. Standing in a backyard with high wooden fences and no place to take cover wasn't going to work. A tree caught my attention. The display on my wrist said my oxygen levels were falling. Not much but I bet it was enough for Kurt to want to investigate. Which meant he'd tell Mitch.

I looked at the tree and back at the door. It would hurt. Climbing would *really* hurt. I climbed up the trunk of the tree, not wanting to stretch too far. Slowly and with care, I climbed up until I was level with the high fence that bordered the properties. A bird tweeted in annoyance as I nudged its nest. I apologized as I straddled the branch containing the nest and then eased over another branch. Faced with zero choice, I dropped down into the adjacent yard. Landing heavily, I couldn't stand up right away. One glance at the pulse oximeter told me things were not good. It took a minute before I could catch my breath, straighten up, and move on. Hugging my side helped a bit. I kept my left arm wrapped around my ribs.

Another prayer to the great unknown: please don't have a dog.

I stayed close to the fence and walked as quickly as I could to the back of the property. Faced with more fences I almost gave up. Using the corner where the two fences met I scaled a six foot fence and semi-dropped, more fell, into the yard behind. The fall forced air out of my lungs. Breathing hurt. A lot. I hugged my ribs.

Someone yelled from a window as I half-tripped over a kid's toy while trying to run down a driveway. I made it to the sidewalk. In the distance, I saw Lee's car. I kept walking until he was level with me. I scooted around the car; the door popped open and I gingerly angled in.

"Okay?" he asked.

"No."

Adrenaline pumped through my muscles. Pain rampaged. I looked at my wrist. Heart rate was through the roof, oxygen levels down.

"Chicky, you never say no."

"I need Kurt." It hurt more than ever to breathe. I hoped he'd seen my oxygen level fall and wasn't far away. GPS is a wonderful thing, not only did our phones send GPS data but our cars did too.

"We're on our way." He flipped a switch on the dash. Blue and red lights flashed. "Did you bug him?"

"Yep." I tried to get more comfortable and failed. "I attached bugs to every jacket I could."

Slow, shallow breaths were all I could manage. "He took

one while I was trapped in his closet."

Lee glanced at me. "Good job. Try to relax, it'll be easier to breathe."

A car caught my eye. Danni Lane was driving it. My brain whirred.

"I think ..." Suddenly it hurt a lot to talk. I paused for a moment and tried again. "Danni, one of the women ..." Shallow breaths. My eyes flicked to the oximeter on my wrist. My oxygen level was at ninety-five per cent and falling. Not ideal. "She was driving the Ford Focus that just went by."

A little yellow duck quacked as it wandered in circles.

I pulled out my phone and noted the license plate. Weird. What was she doing out here? I opened the app that would monitor the bugs I'd planted in Kennedy's clothing. The one he'd taken was already collecting information. I hoped we'd get enough to tell us what was going on and what Kennedy had to do with it.

Getting air was hard work. Mitch filled my mind. I fucked up, Mitch.

"Ellie? Okay?"

"No. Lee ... Inova, please."

His finger pressed a button. Our siren wailed. He picked up the handset for the car radio.

"Break-Break ... SAA Lee Davenport, 4509. Request escort. Under lights and siren. Agent seeking urgent medical help. Over."

The radio crackled. I closed my eyes. Just for a minute. Just to regain some control.

The next thing I heard was Kurt's voice over the radio.

"I'm right behind you. Pull over."

"Roger that."

My door opened, hands caught me before I fell. And the dark wafted in.

Chapter Thirty-one.
Pull the Plug

"You've done plenty of crazy things, Conway, but climbing a fucking tree and scaling fences, really?" Kurt was not happy. He wasn't known to curse. "At what point did you think 'this is going to end badly'?"

I blinked. It was bright. I was lying down looking up at Kurt. Two seconds later, I knew I was in the emergency room for the second time this week.

"When Seamus was standing on the path," I said. My voice felt strained but I was breathing. "What's wrong with me?"

"Partially collapsed lung."

That sounded bad. I could feel nasal prongs in my nose. Oxygen.

"Am I fixed? I've got work to do."

"This is medicine, not magic." His voice grated in an unusual way. "Your lung is recovering. Deep breaths, rest, and oxygen will help."

"Okay. Do I have a chest tube?"

"No, it's a partial collapse. It will heal by itself."

"Okay."

"Noticed that you can breathe a bit better now?"

"Yes." My throat was scratchy.

"Slow, steady, deep breaths. You've been out for over an hour." He adjusted the bed so I was semi-sitting.

"Where'd I go? Did I have fun?"

Right then I saw a flash of actual anger in his eyes.

"You know what? I can't … Mitch can do this."

And he walked away. I don't ever remember Kurt walking away from me before. It did occur to me that I'd never done anything quite this stupid before. Then I saw Mitch. He approached the bed. No smile. No frown. I couldn't read his expression. It wasn't something I'd seen before.

"Are you all right?" His voice was low, deliberate and tinged with anger and disappointment.

That was the look.

"Yes."

"What the hell were you thinking? Were you thinking?" He exhibited great control. I would've preferred him to raise his voice, even yell at me, anything that didn't hold so much disappointment and controlled anger.

"I was doing my job."

His head shook slightly. "Don't. Don't pull that. You need to take better care of yourself. You knowingly put yourself at risk."

I wanted to repeat that I was doing my job. I put myself at risk every day. But that wouldn't help, nor was it what he wanted or needed to hear. Instead, I sucked it up and accepted I did a stupid thing.

I mustered as much contrition as I possibly could. "I'm sorry."

"Sorry for?"

He wasn't going to let me off without an explanation. Damn.

"For not taking better care, for acting without regard to my health and wellbeing. For being fucking stupid. But mostly, mostly, for worrying you."

"I need to understand why you thought you could do what you did. Why do it? Why not let Lee?" Mitch leaned against the wall. "What was wrong with him that he let you?"

I held up my hand. "Stop. This is not about Lee. He had no choice. I am his SSA. It was my decision not his. I did it knowingly. My responsibility, Mitch."

"So explain it to me. Talk to me."

"How angry are you?"

"Very. I need to hear your explanation."

"It won't make a difference ... the outcome doesn't change, the bad decision still stands."

"For me. I need to make sense of this." A small smile. "Yes, it is all about me."

"Okay." I took some slow, steady breaths. "I was only going into the house to plant some bugs. In and out. No problem." More slow deep breaths. "We all have our strengths. I'm good at picking locks. I'm smaller than the guys and can hide easier. Lee is kinda like a battering ram. Not so subtle at times. It was a subtle situation." More breaths. "When Kennedy arrived home, I hid in his closet. It was so close. Close but I was okay. He would've sprung Lee within seconds. I did the job." Slow breaths. "But Kennedy didn't leave right away and I couldn't use the front door, it was too dangerous to stay in case he came back in."

"So up until it all went pear-shaped, everything was fine?"

"Yeah, not really. He stirred up dust while I was in the closest ... that was the beginning of the end really. Jeez, sneezing hurt."

"Did you plant the bugs?"

I smiled. "Of course."

Mitch smiled.

"Next time ... can there not be a next time, please?"

I shook my head. "I want to promise I won't do anything that stupid again but I can't make a promise I may not be able to keep." I looked at him. His eyes never left mine. "But, I will promise to always talk to you."

"If you could manage that before an act of sheer stupidity ..."

"I can try."

He pushed himself off the wall and sat on the bed.

"You scared me."

"I know. It wasn't my intention. I didn't think—"

"That was obvious." Mitch's expression softened. "I've only just found you and I'm not ready to lose you. Take better care." He whispered, "I'm not leaving you again, not until you're well."

Chapter Thirty-two.

Breaking the Law

Kurt kept me in hospital for three hours. Three hours lying on my good side while my lung re-inflated, breathing as deeply as I could. I was lucky there was no chest tube, I knew that. A chest tube would really slow me down. I sent Lee and Sam to find Danni. They reported that she was not at the hotel. My phone app showed her at Fair Oaks Mall. They searched the mall. Nothing. No Danni. Getting annoyed over losing my surveillance team wasn't going to help anyone.

Once I was allowed up, Mitch and I headed for the field office with Kurt. Lee and Sam were on their way to the hotel the women were staying in to see if Danni was back there. I wanted to see Caine and Sandra, and see what came back from the tag number of the car I was still sure I saw Danni Lane driving.

I'd gone from having little yellow ducks in a neat little row to random quackers all over the show.

Sandra ran the registration tag and we hung around for the results. Turned out the car was registered to Danni Lane, a thirty-year-old female with an Oakton Virginia address. Unmarried. Gainfully employed at the Hard Rock Café on 10th Street as a barista. None of which made much sense. The photo on her driver's license was the same Danni Lane. How could she be traveling on a

New Zealand passport and, according to ICE, have arrived in the USA with her traveling companions from Canada two weeks ago and living in Oakton, Virginia? I thought about what I'd learned from the Secret Service. Caroline Clancy visited the White House. She was a resident of Virginia. Caroline Clancy and Caro Clancy were the same person. They were both Danni Lane.

Sense? None.

No criminal record, not even a speeding or parking ticket. Nice. No reason for her to be where I saw her.

The little yellow duck waddled across the floor and quacked furiously. Lost? Hell, yes.

"Okay, again we have something that makes no sense," I muttered. "First, the other women appeared to have secret lives and now Danni is three people." My mind spun for a moment but got nowhere. "Sandra, Danni Lane is also Caro Clancy and Caroline Clancy. Caroline Clancy is a resident of Virginia. Whoever is behind this is really having some fun."

"Okay, I'll get as much background on all of Danni's identities," Sandra said.

Kurt nodded. "But what was she doing in that car? You saw her, yes, Conway?"

"I did."

"So it's her car." Kurt said.

Sandra joined in. "Just working on Danni right now. There is no record of her leaving the country, only entering. Yet, according to our searches, there is a record of her living here."

"She holds a Virginia driver's license, has an address, a job, a social security number, a car ..." Kurt said.

I struggled as much as Kurt to make sense of what was happening.

"Yes. According to us, Danni Lane was born here and according to New Zealand she was born there," Sandra said. "This is an interesting situation. Do you want me to pursue the Caroline Clancy link? Because I'm seeing a Secret Service flag on her. They're investigating that angle."

"Leave that to them," I replied. It'll make them feel useful.

"We need to find her. We also need to go to the Hard Rock and talk to management," Kurt said. "Field trip, boys and girls."

"I need to see Caine first," I said. "I think Misha is in town and he might know what's up with Kennedy. I'm looking at the bug read-out and that man is all over D.C. He's looking for someone. I want to know who."

Sucking up pain and pretending it didn't hurt like a sonofabitch to move was my new thing. I dropped into the temporary Delta bullpen. Empty. Next stop, Caine's office. I rapped lightly on his half-open door. Mitch and Kurt hung back.

"Caine?"

"Ellie?" he replied, beckoning me in.

I sidled through the door and over to his desk. "Have you heard from Misha?"

"Yes, he flew in last night."

"Uh huh." As I thought. But why was he here now? This week? With Kennedy in town? "Don't make this harder than it needs to be, Caine. Just tell me what's going on with Misha."

The corner of Caine's mouth twitched twice. "This is to do with the explosive cards."

"Oh, you mean the card Doug told me about?"

"Yes." He narrowed his eyes at me. "I don't want you looking into the cards. You received two, or you and Delta did. You're off the bombings."

"Fucking what?"

Caine's eyes opened wider. "Language!"

"You can't take us off the bombings. That's ours."

"Not now. You and Delta A have the Czech woman and the three New Zealanders. The D.C. bombings are Delta B and C."

"Why?" I was not impressed.

"The Chief, assistant Directors and Director O'Hare and I are of the opinion that you were right and that Delta A is a target and you in particular."

"Did O'Hare pull us?"

"It was a combined decision."

"See that wasn't so hard, was it?" I muttered.

"The bombings are nothing to do with you. You got that, right?" Caine reiterated his position and ours. "I want you to hand over everything you have regarding the terror attacks to the other teams."

"Absolutely." Sure. I'm just a target. I have nothing they haven't seen except Alexandra and no one is getting her. Related? Not proven. My gut says yes but that could be wrong.

A duck quacked and another one joined it. Maybe not wrong then.

"I have nothing that they don't already know."

Caine's lip twitched. "I find that hard to believe."

"Believe it or not, your choice. I've been in hospital, what I could I possibly know?"

He shook his head a little. "I don't know, but I know you."

Time to leave.

"I'll see you later." I rejoined Kurt and Mitch.

Lee rang my cell. "I found Danni. I just saw her talking to Misha Praskovya."

"She's what now?"

"With Misha at Fair Oaks Mall."

"This is driving me crazy."

"Tell me about it."

We hung up. Mitch and Kurt both heard the conversation.

"What does it mean?" Mitch asked.

"That she's definitely not who she says she is. I'm starting to get why Trudi and Susan are so protective. They could be a freaking protection detail. Danni is somebody."

The scene I saw when I first heard about the New Zealand case slid across my internal screen. I'd seen both Alexandra and Anastazia - or at least I thought I did - two young women who looked very much alike. Armed men. But no explosives. The younger woman was forced to sign something; that couldn't be good.

"I need to talk to Alexandra again. I remember something I saw."

"She's still here. It's too dangerous for her anywhere else," Kurt said. "Although this isn't terribly comfortable. We should look at getting her moved to a hotel."

We walked down the hallway to the interview room where Maryann still kept Alexandra company.

"Stay," I said to Maryann. "I have one question for Alexandra."

"The men who held you captive, they forced your sister to sign a piece of paper. What was the paper?"

She took a deep breath, anger flashing in her eyes.

"It said she was a virgin."

As I thought, not good.

I placed my hand on Alexandra's shoulder. "I'm going to find her."

I left the room and made a call to Caine. I asked him to check her into the Marriott at Metro. Alexandra would be comfortable there. I also requested that Maryann and two other female agents stay with her, with no one stationed outside the door. It wasn't in anyone's best interests to arouse hotel guests' curiosity.

The phone in my hand gave me an idea. Sure I'd technically need a warrant to carry out my sneaky idea *if* Kennedy were a suspect and *if* I was intending to use anything I found to make a case against him. Aware I was walking a fine line I scrolled through some apps on my phone until I found one that I could use. Kennedy was here for a reason and I wanted to know what that reason was. I opened the app and added the phone number I found on the box at Kennedy's home. The number turned from red to blue. It was current and in use. On the next screen I tapped an icon that looked like an envelope in a fishing net. A smile found my lips.

Two taps later, installation of a cunning little program on what I hoped was Kennedy's phone was complete. I could now download copies of any incoming and outgoing email. I closed the email app.

"Okay?" Kurt asked.

"Yeah. I am," I replied with a smile.

My phone chirped. The GPS tracker told me Kennedy was moving again. I wanted eyes on him. He wasn't far away.

"Let's see if we can get close to Kennedy and find out what he's doing. Bug says he's nearby."

"Where?" Kurt asked.

"By the carousel in the Mall."

"You're not walking. We'll take the car."

"Okay." As long as we go. I don't care how we get there. Although maybe I'd think twice about a helicopter trip.

Lee and Sam had eyes on Danni while she met with Misha. That didn't thrill me but as long as I knew where she was, I wasn't about to worry about her, feeling she could take care of herself.

Kennedy, however, was a different kettle of fish; my

curiosity now piqued and knowing where he was did nothing to allay my fears that he had something to do with the current climate in Washington. What was he up to?

Kurt parked as close as he could to where we needed to be.

"Mitch and I can get closer than you and I can," I said to Kurt.

"True. Especially if you're acting like lovers," Kurt replied.

"That's the plan," Mitch said. "Think I can handle this job."

We climbed out of the car. Such a simple thing that I'd never take for granted again. Pain coursed freely for a few seconds as I caught my breath.

"Take it easy, Conway," Kurt said as Mitch closed the door. We walked slowly, arm in arm toward the silent carousel. No children having rides today. Washington was no place for children at the moment. I could see Kennedy. He wasn't alone. Mitch and I walked parallel to the carousel and Jefferson Drive. I recognized the men with Kennedy, confirming my suspicions: definitely the Quasi-UN. Tim Jones, Colin Holmes and Seamus Kennedy.

I wanted to know why an Irishman, an Englishman, and an American met in a park.

As I walked scenarios popped into, my mind but they all sounded like those dreadful old jokes. Before I knew it, there was a joke.

An Englishman, American, and Irishman, all walk into a bar and order a beer. The bartender hands them their beers. However, there are flies in each mug of beer.

The Englishman pushes the beer aside and says, "That's disgusting."

The American pulls the fly out and starts drinking the beer.

The Irishman pulls the fly out, sets it on the counter and shouts, "Spit it out, you bastard."

I doubted the reason they were in D.C. was amusing or in the least bit funny. There was no way around it, the whole meeting in the park thing was enthralling. Meeting in the open. Probably didn't want to be overheard. That was working well for them.

I opened the app and listened.

"They're talking in code," I muttered. "I don't have time to crack their codes."

Plan B. I turned around, Mitch stayed with me.

"What are you doing?"

"Confronting the dragon."

As we approached, Holmes made eye contact. They scattered and there was no way I was running anywhere.

Crap.

"They're definitely up to something," I grumbled. "And now they know I'm onto them."

Well, they'll think I am.

I so wasn't. I had no idea what they were doing in D.C. at the worst possible time. My thoughts turned to Misha and the mysterious Danni Lane.

If Misha knew Danni, then they probably did too, I needed to know why and how Danni was involved with whatever they were here for.

I called Sam. "You still got eyes on Danni?"

"Yes, Chicky Babe."

"I'm coming."

We walked back to the car and Kurt. Mitch opened the front passenger door for me.

"Thank you."

"You're welcome." He closed it firmly after passing the seatbelt to me. Twisting wasn't good.

"What happened?" Kurt asked.

"They scattered. They were talking in code. I went over. They took off. I couldn't pursue anyone."

A smile crossed his lips. "Very restrained of you. Now what?"

"Danni?"

"Yep."

I leaned back. "Change of plan. Let's not go talk to Danni. Let's let her think we don't know anything about her. I want to do some digging."

"You all right?"

"Uh huh."

"I'm taking you home. You can pack a bag and we'll all check into a hotel in the city until this is over."

Yeah, sure, let's all stay in the same place and make it easy for the bomber.

"Really?"

"Yes. We need to be central. Come on, Conway, you

know this."

I knew that. I also knew we'd be checking into the Marriott at the Metro until this was over. Central we would be. Also felt like we should be close to Alexandra.

"Home then. Do you need to go home?" I asked Kurt.

"No, have my go-bag, I'm set."

"Rachel?"

"I sent her and Olivia out state to her parents until this is over."

Good.

"Mitch do you need to go home?" Kurt asked.

"Nope. Everything I need is at Ellie's."

***

The last rays of evening sun streamed through the window, catching the prisms and sending rainbows beaming onto the living room walls. I stood in the middle of the room and tried to remember what I was doing. Packing. Didn't explain what I was doing in the living room.

A rainbow captured my attention as it played over the bullet hole in the wall. Maybe it was time to fix that.

"All right?" Mitch asked from the doorway.

"Yep, can't remember why I came in here."

He laughed. "Your phone charger, it's on the coffee table."

"Ah." That'll be it.

"You packed?"

"I think so," I replied, bending down and picking up the charger. Straightening up hurt.

"Got your laptop?"

I shook my head. My brain sloshed. That wasn't good. "It's where ever you left it."

He smiled. "I'll get it. It's in your home office."

I watched the rainbow dance across the wall. It smudged, like a watercolor pencil drawing. I turned around. The room flattened. Edges sharpened. Black lines appeared. I held my breath. Chance sauntered through the open door.

"Hey, Ellie. How's it going?"

"Not awesome."

"Yeah, I can tell. Nice toy," he said, tapping the pulse oximeter on my wrist. "Feeling better?"

"Yeah." I'm great. "You're here why?"

"Like being around you ..."

I laughed. "Not likely. Waiting ..."

"The author. She is actually an author, and her main character is the fictional image of you, but she's also Interpol. Check it out."

If she was Interpol that might explain how she knows so much about the FBI and it sure would be helpful research-wise to be Interpol. It's possible that she could also get information about me via contacts in Interpol. Could also explain the other identities.

"Interpol. Why wouldn't we be notified that an Interpol agent is here?"

"She might not be here officially."

"And if she was here unofficially, what would that be about?"

"The smart money is on something to do with Justin Troy and Senator Robinson," Chance replied with a wink.

"You think Troy knows Robinson?"

"It's D.C. Who doesn't know a senator or two?"

True. But not much help.

"A straight answer, Chance."

"Troy knows Robinson. Robinson is not a nice guy."

"Is Robinson the guy my CI was trying to tell me about?"

"What do you think?" Chance replied, leaning closer. "It's a helluva coincidence, wouldn't you say?"

Yes. And Chance knew how I felt about coincidences.

One more question. "Is this about the Czech girls?"

"Yes."

"Thank you."

"Don't thank me. You have to prove the link between Troy and Robinson and dig into his world. I wouldn't thank me." Chance looked disgusted. That didn't thrill me. I had a feeling Robinson's world was not somewhere I wanted to be.

I watched as a pencil drew a can of worms. Worms wriggled and slid out of the can onto the floor. A little yellow duck waddled over and ate the worms. The duck quacked.

"Now I know where to look. So thank you."

A big fluffy gray cloud blocked out the rainbow. There was a cloud in my living room. Rain poured from the cloud, washing the drawings away.

Chance grinned and waved as he ran for the door. He

just got through before the door melted into a puddle.

My head reeled. Cold rain stung my face. I wiped my hand over my face. It wasn't wet. Odd.

A voice penetrated my brain. "You all right?"

Mitch.

"I think so."

"Let's get going. Kurt is waiting in the car."

I looked at Mitch. He was real. He had my bag, his bag and my laptop case and still held a hand out to me. In my hand was my phone charger. Mitch took it and slipped it into the laptop case.

Chapter Thirty-three.
Pull Me Under

From the car, I called Sam. "Marriott at the Metro. I'll reserve rooms for all of us."

"We'll see you there."

I hung up.

"I need to talk to those women," I said.

"Not now," Kurt replied. "They're in custody. You need to rest first. Then you can talk to them."

"It's important."

"Yes, I know. Rest. Then talk."

He wasn't going to be swayed.

"What if Danni is Interpol?"

"What?"

"You heard."

"Left field!"

"Not at all. Remember how I said Chance is back … what if she's Interpol?"

"Then this is more gripping than the storyline of a daytime soap." He glanced at me.

I rolled with the crazy. "And what if Senator Robinson is the Rob Arnie tried to tell us about?"

"Then this is going to get very very messy," Kurt replied. "It's hard to believe the only thing on your head CT was a skull fracture."

"What no brain?" I smiled.

"Most certainly a brain. But I half expected to see a mini movie with a colorful supporting cast."

"Disappointed?"

"Maybe a little bit."

Mitch laughed. Probably because a lot of the time he could see the mini movie. He just hadn't seen Chance yet.

"I'm tired," I said, without meaning it to be audible.

Kurt looked over at me. "You will be tired for a while. That's why I want you to rest. Need to avoid physical and mental exertion for several days after a brain injury. Never mind the rest of the trauma you suffered."

"You're not very good at resting, El," Mitch said. His hand touched my shoulder. "We're almost at the hotel."

I'm not very good at resting. Seems like waste of time. Bon Jovi's 'I'll sleep when I'm dead' filled the car. My eyes flicked to the radio. It was off. Just for me then.

Mitch tapped on the armrest in time to the music in my head. Then he said, "If you don't learn to rest, you will rest in peace."

I smiled. "You can hear it?"

"Oh yeah," he replied.

"Hear what?" Kurt asked.

"Bon Jovi," Mitch replied.

"You two are perfectly normal." Kurt replied, shaking his head. "Check-in time."

Half an hour later, we walked down the hallway to our rooms. I had a preference when it came to rooms. Not the one I'd stayed in with Mac and subsequently with Carla. Not that one. Not that floor. Kurt took the first room, with Mitch and I opposite. Sam and Lee could choose either the room next to ours or one next to Kurt's.

Kurt waited until our door was open.

"Conway, sleep. Give it a couple of hours and we'll go back to work. Okay?"

"Okay."

"Do not take off that oximeter," he cautioned. "You're not out of the woods yet."

"I know."

I went into the room. The bed looked good. Couldn't deny it. I was tired. Really tired. I could hear Mitch and Kurt talking at the door. I lay on the bed. My feet still on the floor. Still wearing my boots. I had no memory of ever being this tired before. All noise faded into the dark.

Eventually the dark gave way to gray and the gray to light. I live a wondrous, strange life. Peppered with gunfire, explosions, blood, death and music. I didn't remember getting into bed but I was. I didn't remember taking off my boots but they had gone. Ditto my jeans and jacket. Interesting. My side hurt a bit. Ribs. I tried a deep breath, remembering that Kurt said I needed to breathe deeper to help my lung heal.

My head hurt. It took a bit of time before I could figure out whether it was the concussion and skull fracture, a dehydration headache, or the beginning of something bad. A migraine now would be bad. I stopped taking narcotics to deal with migraines when I discovered an aromatherapy synergy in New Zealand. Using the synergy early enough can stop them dead. Pain jabbed me in the right side of my brain. I needed the synergy. Think. Where was it? In my desk. My desk is in pieces all over 10th Street under a couple of tons of concrete. Not helpful.

What did I have with me? The pain stabbed again. Physical pain was controllable. My right eye closed. Kurt carried pain relief. Just in case. Did I need it? Slow deep breaths.

"Ellie, you okay?" The bed moved. Mitch was lying next to me. He rolled toward me, supporting himself on one elbow. "Okay?"

"Jury's still out."

"What do you need?"

"Not sure. Might have a migraine."

Mitch moved. He came back a few seconds later. "Hold out your hands."

He dripped a familiar smelling oil into my palm. Synergy. I rubbed my hands together then cupped them over my mouth and nose and breathed deeply. The warm aroma soothed almost instantly.

"Thank you," I said. Breathing in deeply.

"You're welcome." His fingers felt cool on my forehead as he brushed my bangs aside. "Where'd you get the scar?"

"Bullet graze, a long time ago." To me my voice sounded remote, as if I were standing at the end of a tunnel trying to hear someone at the other end, as I talked into my cupped hands and the pain in my head faded to a slow, dull drilling.

Mitch's voice undulated - I knew he was talking but it was so soft I couldn't make out the words, just rhythm. He was singing. A familiar song, a song I loved. 'Beneath Your Beautiful.' My mind drifted with the melody of his music. Danni's face twisted, distorted, and spiraled into the ground pushed further and further down by Kennedy and his two cohorts. Suddenly, she popped back up right in front of me.

Smiling.

A gun in her hand. I stepped in front of Mitch. Her smiled widened. Two birds flew from a bush. I staggered then heard a loud crack. Staggering became falling. Another crack. I turned my head and saw a man in black with a gun. A thin plume of smoke rose. Danni fell bleeding. People screamed. I looked sideways as a massive explosion rocked the area.

One eye opened, the images disappeared. I couldn't see him.

"Mitch?"

"Here, okay?"

"Bad dream."

I felt him move next to me. His hand touched my head. "How's the head?"

"Okay."

"Sleep, dreams can't hurt."

I closed my eyes again. When I next checked the clock, it was midnight. I had a moderate headache nagging on the right side of my head but it wasn't a migraine, which was a win. My ribs hurt. Deep breathing was good for my lungs not so much my ribs. I needed to get a handle on the pain.

"Mitch, do we have Tylenol and codeine?"

"Yes." He got up. When he came back, he dropped four white pills into my hand and gave me a glass of water.

Twenty minutes later, everything was more manageable.

"Shower?" I asked, as Mitch lay next to me flicking channels on the TV. I knew he was looking for news. Something that would tell us what was happening outside.

"Invitation?"

I smiled. "Yes."

"I'm there."

Kurt called. "Kennedy is on the move. How you doing?"

There's always someone ready to ruin a damn fine shower moment. I stifled a sigh.

"Okay. About to have a shower, give us ten minutes?"

"Meet you out front in fifteen."

"Okay."

Chapter Thirty-four.

The Four Horsemen

Kurt was in the car when Mitch and I walked out the front entrance of the hotel, with Lee and Sam parked behind him. A Delta outing. Nice. Kennedy was in a bar with Holmes and Jones, one that was not one of my favorites. It sucked and so did the clientele. Creeps and morons. The deep discussion part of their meeting lasted exactly fifteen minutes; I listened to the conversation via the app on my phone. That was the longest fifteen minutes I'd ever spent while fending off five butt-ugly men with severe and repellent personality disorders, as each one tried to persuade me to go home with them. Rude, not like I was alone. Mitch was right there. Kurt was at the other end of the bar. Sam was by the door and Lee was outside.

I knew Lee would catch up to a few of the losers outside, and explain in his special way why no one would ever date them and how no one would find their bodies if he ever saw them around again.

The meeting between Kennedy and his buddies was confusing. I was none the wiser as to their plans. They said nothing that was even remotely troubling in a national security kind of way. Still talking in code. I observed their body language. They were on edge but not paying any attention to their surroundings, which was out of character but good for me. I considered that the bar might be somewhere they felt secure but couldn't fathom why. Maybe because they were big tough men?

How did they know Trudi and Susan? Did they know Trudi and Susan? Did they know Danni? I knew Misha knew her but did Kennedy?

I turned to Mitch and whispered, "I'm going to go join them. Hang back, okay?"

I angled my body toward Sam and flashed two hand signals, really fast. He nodded. No one was leaving through the front door. I did the same to Kurt. He nodded. With utmost confidence, I approached the table in the corner of the room, grabbed a chair from a nearby table and joined the throng.

"Morning," I said. They started to move. "Look around."

Sam and Kurt nodded at the table.

"Conway, you don't need to be in the middle of this," Kennedy said, his Irish accent warming his voice.

"Why don't you let me be the judge of that?" I replied. "Whatever you're up to has encroached on my case. You're here, Praskovya is here, Washington is exploding, and someone shot down the helicopter I was in." I leveled a stare at Kennedy. "And again, you're here."

"Wasn't us," he said with a smile. "I made you a promise that I wouldn't shoot at you again."

That's what they all say, and yet the bullets keep flying.

"You can see why I asked. You turn up and I get shot out the sky."

Kennedy nodded. "I get that a lot."

I just bet he did.

"Do you know who did kill my pilot?"

"No."

"You're here why?" I asked. "I'm not one for coincidences and I seem to have a few in front of me."

"We're looking for someone."

Colin and Tim sat listening but had nothing to offer.

"What's it got to do with Interpol?" Throwing it out there, hadn't even checked it, just went with what Chance told me. Plus I knew Danni met with Misha. I fully expected that these three knew her as well.

Kennedy's eyes narrowed. "You're a fecking smartass, Conway."

That wasn't denial.

"Then you'll love this. I am holding a young woman by the name of Alexandra Dobrovolný."

"Feck," he half-whispered. "You don't want to be in this, Conway."

Funnily enough, I'd heard those very words from Seamus Kennedy before, when he was in Washington trying to find a girl and a pedophile.

"Probably not but someone wanted me in. I got the tip-off from a trusted CI. I found her. My CI was killed before he could tell me where he got his information. The girl became a bomb and was in the same hospital as I was." I still thought someone got that wrong because there was no way for her to get close to me. Unless the person behind this thought I was well enough to want to interview her myself? That wasn't a good thought.

"Jesus. She all right?"

"She's safe. She's traumatized. We are taking care of her." I leaned forward, resting on my elbows. "And you know her?"

"I know of her," he replied. His mouth set in a thin line. He wasn't anywhere near as chatty as I needed him to be.

"Anything else to add?"

His head shook. "She's safe?"

"Yes."

I watched the three of them exchange looks. Yeah, she had something to do with the reason they were in town.

"Can you keep her safe?"

"Yes. Can you tell me what the hell is going on?"

"No. Not yet. Patience, Conway, this is fecking messy."

"No kidding."

"Get some sleep, you look like you need it," Kennedy said. "How badly hurt are you?"

I dismissed his comment. "I'm fine."

He tossed a fast smile at me. "You're not, but that's okay. We can watch your back too." Kennedy's smile vanished as quickly as it came. His mouth set in a straight line. "You're playing with fire, Conway."

"Maybe, but someone invited me in. For whatever reason. I'm beginning to think the reason is to cause me and Delta A harm."

He nodded. "I thought that might happen."

"And yet no friendly heads-up?"

"I was hoping we could make this disappear before anything bad happened."

It was possible that his definition of bad may differ from mine.

"Initially, I thought this was about Renegade," I said.

He leaned forward and so did the other men. Tim whispered, "The President. Crap. What made you think that?"

That gave me the impression they hadn't thought of that. Fascinating. Was I way off base? I thought I'd seen Air Force One being shot down but that was before I was shot out of the sky. Perhaps I saw my own crash and not the President in danger at all.

How to explain my random hallucinations without giving the impression I was insane?

"A gut feeling I had around about the time the Navy Yard exploded," I said with a small smile.

"You may not be wrong, Conway," Tim said. "Whoever is behind the current situation has more irons in the fire and more reasons for these actions than we have been able to fathom."

"Not long ago I considered that the Unsub wanted me to think Renegade was a target so I'd have him moved. I was nervy about ground-to-air missiles."

"Maybe not unduly," Kennedy said. "Something shot you out of the air."

"Which makes me think that my gut was warning me about that and not Renegade at all."

"Best to err on the side of caution," Kennedy said.

"Next issue, I've been pulled off the bombings."

Tim frowned.

Colin who'd remained quiet found his voice. "Everything intersects. Taking you off the bombings is neither here nor there."

"That's what I thought. Officially, I'm not investigating bombings. I am concentrating my efforts on Alexandra and her sister, and the three kiwi women."

All three men exchanged quick glances. I felt them close down. It was the first time I'd said anything about Alexandra's sister and I hit a nerve.

"Good luck, Conway," Kennedy said. "We'll keep an eye on you as well as we can."

"Worry about your own backs. I've got Delta."

"We'll talk soon."

I stood up and said goodbye to the three of them. As I walked away, I wondered why I didn't mention Senator Robinson. No reason that I could come up with, except I didn't want him tipped off. The fewer people who knew, the better.

Chapter Thirty-five.

Symphony of Destruction

Our next stop promised a certain level of interest.

The two women were in separate interview rooms at two in the morning. They looked tired. Probably wanted to go to sleep. They'd been in the rooms for three hours; before that they were in separate holding cells and more than likely asleep. We'd said the magic word. Terrorism. Even though I didn't for one minute think they were responsible for any of the explosions, or indeed had any knowledge of any of it.

But the word was said and all bets were off. One whiff of terrorism and their rights started to magically disappear as Guantanamo Bay was considered a suitable place to hold them.

Walking the corridors of the Washington field office felt peculiar in the middle of the night. Empty. Hollow. Little bit spooky.

I slipped into the viewing room attached to the interview room Sam and Lee occupied. Trudi sat between them. Not an unattractive woman. About five foot six inches tall, blonde shoulder length hair, average build.

I turned up the speaker and listened.

She couldn't very well deny knowing Danni Lane or working with her. What we needed to know was how much she knew and in what context she was working with her. Friends. Quite possibly but it was more than that. Her face looked familiar. Where had I seen her? My head ached and refused to place her in context. How could I have seen her before this case? I closed my eyes and listened to her talking. Accent. Predominately a New Zealand accent but there was a hint of something familiar. A hint of Pennsylvania?

With a flourish, someone interrupted the interview. A tall man dumped his briefcase on the table and announced his client had nothing to say.

He too seemed familiar but in a more general slimeball way. I tried picturing the lawyer in other settings. None fitted.

Sam joined me.

"She's more than just a friend of Danni's. I think she was hired by someone to travel with her. We're dumping the contents of her cell phone. Hope we get some recurrent numbers and a lead or two."

"I hope you do too. You see him before?" I pointed at the lawyer.

He nodded. "Can't place him though. He's forgettable."

Simon and Garfunkel peeked around the corner of my mind, bathed in Kodak color, and led immediately into Mrs. Robinson. I smiled.

"What?" Sam asked.

"Senator Robinson, New Jersey. That's where I've seen him – with Robinson."

"Now that's unsettling. You spend much time with senators?"

"Not so much." I'd never met Robinson but I knew him to look at and I'd seen him with the lawyer in a coffee shop a few weeks back.

"Wanna tell me how you pulled Robinson out of thin air just now?"

"Simon and Garfunkel," I replied casually. And a little something Chance told me. "Also, he got an exploding card too, like me and Misha. Caine told me."

"That's interesting."

"That's what Kurt and I thought too."

We moved onto to interview room number two. I slipped into the second interview viewing room. Susan was about five foot five, blonde, pretty. No lawyer in sight.

Lee chatted with the woman. I listened to her accent. Again, I heard a hint of something else under the distinct kiwi twang. Moments later a sharp-faced, almost rat-featured woman barged into the room. "My client has nothing to say."

"Know her?" I asked Sam.

"Yeah, her I know. She used to be a prosecutor."

"And now?"

"Defender of scumbags, private practice."

"Find out if she's on Robinson's payroll."

"Will do."

I called Lee's cell phone. "Let's leave the lawyer to it."

He looked over the top of the lawyer and pulled a face in the mirror.

We all met outside the interview room.

"They got lawyers at three in the morning. How?" I asked.

"Good question," Lee replied. "We had them put in the rooms hours ago. No phones."

"Well, someone made a call for them when we turned up." And we needed to know who and then why. "Who's in the building?"

"Search?"

"Yes. Now."

We divided up the building. Sam and Lee worked together. Kurt and I had Mitch with us. At three in the morning, I'd expect the place to be quiet. I headed for the front desk and the agent who sat there watching monitors and the door. I recognized him.

"Caldwell?"

"Yeah, how you doing, Conway. Haven't seen you since ... Quantico."

"Who is in at this time of the morning?"

"Your team. I've logged in two of Delta C and one Delta B in the last four hours."

"Anyone else?"

He scrolled through the screen in front of him then stopped. "Had some young guy at the desk at twenty-two thirty. Justin Troy. Said he was attached to Delta A."

I swallowed. "And?"

"You revoked his clearance and suspended him according to Sentinel. He didn't get in."

"Any idea what he wanted?"

"Nope. Didn't say."

"Was that before or after Delta B brought the two women in?"

"Exactly eleven minutes after."

"Eleven minutes."

"Got any video footage of him coming in and leaving?"

"Of course. Come around here." Caldwell moved his chair enabling me to get in beside him. I leaned on the desk and watched as he found the right time stamps and ran the video. That was him. He came in, had a conversation with Caldwell and left. He didn't look happy.

"He didn't come back?"

"No."

I called Lee's cell.

"You find anyone who shouldn't be here?"

"No. There are only seven other people in the building. They all check out."

That's what I figured.

"Troy was here."

"Not looking good for him," Lee commented. "You're on speaker, Chicky. Sam is here."

"No, it's not looking good for Troy."

"What do you want to do?" Sam asked.

"Get the little fucker in here." I wanted to know why he was trying to get into the building and what he had to do with the lawyer situation. My gut said he made the calls and had been tailing us.

I called Transit and asked for the commanding officer.

"It's SSA Conway. The surveillance job I handed over

to Transit, are you familiar with it?"

"Yes. Yes, I am. We had two teams on the target until yesterday."

"Excuse me, until yesterday?"

"You revoked the surveillance. I have the paperwork in front of me now. About to review it."

He's reviewing orders in the middle of the night? Dedicated.

"Can you bring that paperwork to the Washington field office, please?"

"I'll fax it?"

"No, I need the original documents."

"Is there a problem agent?"

"Yes. I didn't ask for surveillance to stop."

"I'll be right over."

"Thank you." I pocketed my phone.

Caldwell, Kurt and Mitch watched and waited. "We need coffee. Well, I need coffee," I said.

Caldwell smiled. "There is an office with a kitchen through that door behind me. Coffee is on and fairly fresh."

"Thanks," Kurt replied. "You got monitors in there?"

"Absolutely."

"Then join us," I said with a smile.

Two cups of coffee later, I felt wide-awake. Caldwell pointed out a man in uniform walking in the front door.

"He looks like Transit," he said.

"I'll go see," I replied, opening the door and greeting the man at the desk. Mitch followed me out.

"Agent Conway?"

"Yes." We shook. "And you are?"

"Commander Terry Simons."

He handed me a manila envelope. "The orders."

"How many people handled this paperwork?"

"Just me. The envelope was addressed to me and I opened it."

I nodded. "That's helpful. We can rule out your prints and hopefully find some belonging to whoever signed this." I pulled latex gloves from a box under Caldwell's desk and put them on.   The FBI seal was in the upper left corner of the envelope. The paperwork bore the FBI and Delta A header. I read the orders and paid special attention to the signature. Looked like mine. It wasn't, I knew that, but at first glance it looked like mine. Clever.

Mitch looked over my shoulder. "The 'a' in Conway is slightly off."

I smiled. "Yes, it is."

"Do you want us to put surveillance back on Justin Troy?" Commander Simons asked.

"No, thanks. We're bringing him in now. Can you email me your report?"

"Sure," he replied.

Mitch handed him one of my cards.

"Thanks for this, Commander. I appreciate your help. Once this case is over, there will be an open bar at O'Malley's for all the LEOs involved."

"That'll set you back a bit, Agent," he said with a grin.

"Usually does, but it's well worth it."

"Let me know when and I'll be there."

We watched him leave. I slid the envelope and paperwork into an evidence bag I found under Caldwell's desk. Then addressed it to the Questioned Documents Lab. Caldwell came through the door to the back room.

"I'll get the courier in for that, Conway," he said, taking the bag and signing the chain of custody panel on the back.

"Cheers," I replied.

Kurt appeared.

"Sam and Lee just came in the back entrance with Troy."

Chapter Thirty-six.

Balls to the Wall

Sam and Lee dumped Troy in an interview room, took his cell phone off him, and left him there. Caldwell rang my cell and told me the courier had picked up the documents. Great. Could get something by the end of the day, depending on backlogs. I did have an advantage this time though. This was a priority case and linked to possible terrorism, which would work in my favor. Nice that something did for a change.

We all sat in the adjacent viewing room and had coffee, watching him through the one-way mirror.

"Don't you think he's looking a bit too calm?" Lee said.

"Bet we can shake him up," Sam replied.

Kurt smiled. "I bet we can too."

I handed Kurt paperwork from Troy's file. "Have a look at what his instructors had to say about him while he was at Quantico."

I'd seen his file when Troy was assigned to me. There was nothing remarkable about it but now I looked with new eyes.

He flipped through the pages, reading comments and grumbling to himself. He passed the papers to Mitch. "Sycophant and labeled as such."

"That explains why he was so eager to get my approval," I said with a small laugh.

"And why he was keen to be around you when O'Hare was mentioned."

I hadn't noticed. Oblivious. I thought about it for a second. No, not oblivious. It just wasn't important. My focus was on his ability to learn and to learn fast, not how brown his nose was. Although in light of recent events anything that indicated he was super attentive at the mention of O'Hare was of interest.

"Okay, Lee, you're up," I said. "Don't make him cry yet ..."

"I'll do my best," Lee replied and left the room.

We watched as Lee opened the interview room door and walked in. I was interested in how Troy reacted or didn't react. And he didn't react. He remained calm, as though he thought he had a 'get out of jail free' card. I just bet that card was in the form of Senator Robinson or his minions. Couldn't wait to see when he tried to play it.

Lee jumped in with a question about Senator Robinson.

"I don't know Robinson," he announced, rubbing his nose. A lie.

This was going to be fun. I wished I was less beat up so I could fully enjoy the show.

"Who *do* you know?" Lee asked, laying a closed manila folder on the table in front of him.

Troy folded his hands on the table.

"How about I fire out some names and see if any stick?"

"If you want," Troy replied. The hint of smugness in

his voice didn't impress me much.

It was too late to stop the video clip from playing in my head, Shania Twain 'That Don't Impress Me Much'. I blinked to stop the clip and focus on the scene beyond the one-way glass.

Mitch nudged my arm. "All right?"

"Yeah, why?"

"Oh, I don't know, Shania Twain?"

"Little bit out there ... it's him, he doesn't impress me much."

Mitch laughed. "I gathered that."

I leaned forward and turned up the volume in the room. Lee reeled off names. Kurt and Sam waited for responses from Troy. I wanted to hear his voice and see any visual clues.

"Misha Praskovya," Lee said.

Troy stared straight ahead. "Don't know the name," he said. I detected an almost imperceptible rise in his voice on the last word. He had heard Misha's name before.

"Seamus Kennedy."

He blinked and shook his head. "No. Don't know him."

"Trudi Welsh."

"I don't know her."

"Danni Lane?"

He fixed his stare on the wall beyond Lee. "Don't know that name." Same slight rise at the end of the sentence. Another lie.

"Alexandra Dobrovolný."

His jaw clenched. He shook his head but didn't speak.

He knew of her.

I rang Lee's cell. "Push the Dobrovolný thing. He knows something."

Lee hung up without speaking to me.

"How do you know Alexandra?" Lee asked.

Troy's eyes widened for a second. I could see him struggling to remain composed.

"I don't," he said. No longer fixed on a spot on the wall now, he'd cast his eyes downward.

"Yeah, you do. We can play this game all night, but eventually you're going to get tired and you're going to talk. Why not do it now and save all the nastiness that will soon follow."

His eyes flashed at Lee then back to the table.

"I have a lawyer. You can't hold me here."

His modicum of bravery and defiance made me smile. It wouldn't last long.

"With what you did at the Hoover Building, you're lucky you were walking free to start with," Lee replied. "Now, tell me about Alexandra Dobrovolný. What is your relationship with her?"

"I don't have a relationship with her," he replied. "I don't know her."

"Yeah, you do. But that's okay, you carry on being uncooperative, you little shit, that's your choice."

"I don't know her."

"You know of her. You know something. And it's time you shared that knowledge." Lee remained calm, obviously enjoying himself. It was amusing to watch.

Small beads of sweat gathered on Troy's brow.

Sam spoke from beside me. "Look at this, Chicky."

He passed me Troy's phone, with an email open on the screen.

"Hmmm, what does it mean?"

"I have no idea. Looks like a code. You're good with codes."

Nice that he had faith in my code cracking ability. I'm good at seeing patterns.

"Okay." I sat down with the phone. It wasn't an immediately recognizable code. "I'll forward that email to my work account ... screen on the phone is too small for me to get a good bead on it."

"Good thinking," Sam replied.

I forwarded the message and then handed it back to Sam. "Carry on. I'll be back when I have something."

Mitch was right behind me as I headed for the door; his hand reached past me to the door handle. I stepped aside and let him open the door.

"Thank you," I said.

"You're welcome," he replied with a smile. "Where are we going?"

"The bullpen."

A few minutes later, I sat at my temporary desk, reading the email on a much bigger screen.

I flipped my hair back off my face, irritated. It slid forward again. There were no hair ties around my wrist. There were always hair ties around my wrist. I sighed and pushed my hair behind my shoulders again and gave it a twist, hoping it would hold it for a bit.

Mitch handed me a rubber band. "Will this help?"

"Yeah. Thanks." I pulled my hair into a loose ponytail. My fingers touched what was probably a massive bruise on the side of my head. I made a mental note not to touch it again.

"That's not what that sigh was about."

"You're right. It's this email. And my hair was annoying me."

I turned my attention back to the screen and the email. "I don't know what the key is."

"Try closing your eyes."

I closed my eyes.

"Now open them. What do you see?"

"Numbers, I think it's a price list."

"For?"

"I don't know."

The Crystals 'Da doo ron ron' broke into my thoughts. They were quite adamant when they told me that his name was Bill.

Bill.

"Ellie? Did you just hear 'Da doo ron ron'?"

"I did." There was a smile in my voice. "It's got something to do with Sunday and a man called Bill."

"That's what you got from the song?" Mitch asked with a hefty dose of bemusement.

"Yeah, what'd you get?"

"I just heard a song. My powers of deduction work better on people than music."

I called Lee. "Something is going to happen on Sunday and we need to know who Bill is." I took a breath. "Also, I think an email on his phone is a price list but it's in code. See what you can do?"

He listened then replied, "I'm on it, SSA." Lee hung up. I knew he would dig up something armed with a possible name.

As Lee attempted to crack Troy's pseudo tough-guy façade, I called Kurt from the phone on the desk and told him Mitch and I would head back to the hotel soon.

Bits and pieces of songs and conversations milled about in my head, stirred by a giant wooden spoon with the word revenge in red letters on the handle. A long sigh forced its way between my teeth and out into the office. It wasn't helping.

"Okay?" Mitch asked.

"Sure, why not."

"That's not an answer," he probed. His voice was gentle and smooth.

"My head hurts. I'm not getting anywhere with this case. So, 'okay' is stretching the truth somewhat."

We went back to the viewing room and watched a few more minutes of the live entertainment, all the while wishing waterboarding was legal.

I pulled out my cell phone and made a call to Iain Campbell. He answered on the fourth ring. "Asleep?"

"Nope, working. What do you need, Ellie?"

"Danni Lane. Who is she? I've heard she's Interpol."

Keys tapped. "New Zealand citizen. Born in

Christchurch, New Zealand. An author. Hold up, I'm plugging her picture into our system." More tapping. "Now we wait. You think she's any good as a writer?"

"No idea. Kurt thinks so. He was all fan-boy when we met her."

Kurt rolled his eyes. It was true. I was there.

"Her photo has pinged up a classified file. One moment. Let me get this thing open."

The line sounded hollow. Iain had left his desk. I watched the floor show through the viewing room window until he came back.

"Back. File is open. Danni Lane is an alias. She is an author. She is a kiwi. She is also Danielle Marie Malevich. She's worked as an Interpol agent for ten years, living in New Zealand but working cases globally. She uses research trips as part of her cover. Currently assigned to an abduction case."

"Abduction? Got details?"

"No. Not even I can get the details for this case. Just that it's an abduction. No details on the victim or where the person was taken, not so much as an operation case name."

That's bad. If the case is so tightly locked down Iain can't access it, then there is a reason.

"Not good news," I said.

"Not at all. How did you know she was Interpol?"

"Gut feeling," I replied without hesitation.

"If only we could bottle your gut feelings and sell them," Iain said with a laugh.

"Make life easier, huh?"

"Sure would." Iain paused. The silence on the end of the phone filled with the sound of papers being moved around. "You wouldn't happen to know why some mutual friends of ours are in town would you?"

"If you're referring to the Quasi-UN who shot up my house a while back and then found that kiddie fiddler for us ... no."

"Yep, that's them."

"I know they're here. I know Praskovya is here too. The whole gang is in town. Also, Praskovya had coffee with Danni Lane."

"She's working an abduction and they're in town. They have to be together," Iain muttered.

"That's my feeling too." Especially because when we met them the first time, they were in town to rescue a kid.

"And you think this has something to do with Alexandra?"

"I do."

I think they're here to find both women.

"Take care, Ellie. Let me know if you need anything else."

"Will do. Thanks, Iain." I hung up and pocketed my phone.

"Danni Lane is Interpol. She's on an uber-secret assignment." I leaned on the wall. "I'm not happy about the secrecy. It points to a worrying situation with people who should not be involved in anything bad at all."

Kurt frowned. "What are you rambling about,

Conway?"

"The level of secrecy surrounding Danni Lane."

"Ah, I see, yes. Bad. People high up the food chain probably involved?"

"How high, that's the question," I replied.

"Have a feeling we'll find out," Kurt responded with a grin. "I know you and secrets. Like a dog with a bone."

As long as he meant that in a good way.

"I'm going to the bathroom then I need to rest a bit and figure things out. Hotel time. I'll meet you out front?" I said to Mitch, quietly pleased with how I recognized that I needed to rest and being so grown up about it.

"I'll wait for you."

Kurt handed Mitch the keys to his car. "Or you can pull the car around," he said.

"See you out front."

We went in different directions.

Chapter Thirty-seven.
Into the Void

I sat up slowly, unsure of my whereabouts. Swirling gray fog clouded my vision. My head hurt. It wasn't an ache like a headache. It hurt. I avoided the bruised area and tentatively touched the fresh sore area at the back of my head. Wet. Sticky. My fingers caught in matted sticky hair.

"Ouch," I muttered as I pulled my hand away from my head and saw strands of bloody hair wrapped around my fingers. "Not good."

Blood.

Confusing. The last thing I remembered was walking out of the viewing room with Mitch. I moved my head with care and looked at my surroundings. Half-expecting to be on the ground amongst a pile of rubble. But I wasn't.

I was in a room, a small clean windowless room. Clean. A faint but familiar smell lingered. Disinfectant. The air felt fresh yet there were no windows. I held up my hand and felt the airflow. Looking up hurt but I did it anyway. There was a vent high on the wall where cool air blew in. I shivered. No jacket.

Never mind no jacket. No boots, socks, jeans, or shirt. No holster, no gun, no cuffs.

Sitting on a floor, bleeding from a head wound,

wearing only my underwear. There was no good explanation for that.

The floor felt odd under me. I pressed my hand onto it. Almost bouncy. Rubber? A rubber floor. Behind me was a bed. I reached out and levered myself up using the bed. Once upright, I noticed my phone sitting on a gray woolen blanket that covered the bed. I shivered again, picked up my phone and pulled the blanket off the bed, wrapping it around me. It felt prickly and itchy but it was better than freezing. Then I noticed I still had the pulse oximeter on my wrist and the sensor on my index finger. Someone took my clothes off but left that on me, or put it back on me. To what end? Someone left me my phone. That didn't fit either.

The bed faced a door, about six feet away. No door handle on the inside and it looked odd, not wood or metal. I walked carefully to the door and touched it. A firm surface but like the floor, it felt rubbery. My hand reached out to the wall by the door. It was the same. A rubber room. A windowless, well-lit rubber room that lacked door handles. I noted the recessed lights in the ceiling. No light switches on the walls. I was in a cell. A special kind of cell. Purpose designed. Turning around, I saw metal rings in the wall on my right. Four metal rings. On closer inspection, I wished I hadn't seen them. I didn't want anything to do with their function. I staggered back to the bed and sat down. I had my phone. I pressed the button on the top and turned the screen on, then swiped my finger up the screen to unlock it. Scrolled left once and tapped Mitch's image; a few seconds later, I heard Mitch's voice.

"Where are you?"

"I don't know," I replied. "Please ..." The word hung in the air before shattering and falling like snowflakes to the ground. "Something bad is going to happen."

"El?"

"Please, Mitch ... find me."

"We're working on it. Sandra is tracing your phone. I'll be there soon. Keep your phone on."

"I'll try."

"There is no try. There is do or do not."

"Mitch ..."

I leaned on the wall behind me. I had no idea how I got there or where I was. Having my phone but no clothing was alarming. I looked at Mitch's picture on the screen. Cold clawed at my insides.

"Mitch ... it's a trap."

"That's being considered, El."

"Someone wants Delta A all fucked up."

"It sure looks that way. Sit tight." He paused. I knew what was coming. "Are you hurt?"

"Honestly, it's hard for me to tell with much accuracy." I didn't want to say I was bleeding and almost naked. "I still have the pulse oximeter on. Kurt can monitor me."

"He is. How do you feel?"

Vulnerable.

"Okay. I think. Bit of a headache." I lay down. My words floated in the air all white and shiny. What's that all about?

"We have a fix on your location, Sandra tracked the GPS on your phone," Mitch said. "Anything we need to know?"

"I'm in a windowless room. It's like a padded cell." Or torture chamber. I just bet the room could be easily hosed out. Maybe that accounted for the smell of disinfectant.

Mitch talked to someone. A car started.

"We're bringing SWAT," Kurt said. He must've taken the phone from Mitch.

"Good. Where am I?"

"The abandoned factory," Kurt said. "Where we found Alexandra."

My eyes searched the room for something that said abandoned, dank, wet, cruddy factory. It didn't fit with what I saw.

"This isn't the old factory," I replied.

"GPS puts you in the center of the factory," Kurt said. "Could you be in the center of a building?"

Panic rose. I didn't need the gadget on my wrist to tell me my pulse rate was climbing.

"I could be."

"Breathe. We're coming."

It was all wrong.

"Not the factory. I'm sure this is not the factory."

"Conway, calm down. We're almost there."

"Give me Mitch."

I closed my eyes and recreated the room in my head, complete with metal rings in the wall and me almost naked. While I concentrated on the scene in my mind, I said, "Mitch, can you see it?"

"God, yes." His voice cracked a little. "A padded cell. What's with the rings in the wall? Where are your clothes?"

"I don't know."

I listened as he tried to tell Kurt they were at the wrong place. They weren't in the car anymore, there was too much atmospheric noise. I couldn't hear exactly what was happening. A cacophony of raised voices let loose. I held the phone in front of me and flipped it over then back, activating the speaker. A loud explosion took me by surprise. I almost dropped the phone.

"Mitch?" I said to the phone.

"I'm here."

"What happened?"

"SWAT breached the outer doors. There was an explosion. Did you hear anything where you are?"

"No." With more determination I said, "I'm not in the factory. Injuries?"

"Four men down," Mitch replied. He paused. I could sense his mind working. "If you're not here then where are you?"

"I don't know."

He was walking, I could tell by his voice. "Trudi and Susan's phones had bugs or viruses in them, yes?"

"Yeah." I almost nodded before reminding myself not to.

"Same thing could have happened to yours. Anything

updated recently?"

"I think Instagram and Voxer updated over the last day or so," I replied. "I'm taking the battery out now. I hope you can find me."

"I will find you. I'm coming." A car door shut and an engine started.

It was possible that whoever added the program to Trudi and Susan's phones altering their GPS location could've done the same to mine. My cell number was on my cards. Lots of people had it.

Knowing Mitch was trying to find me made me feel a little better. Hoping he did know where to look, not so much. Hope and faith went together. I was all out of faith in any kind of Supreme Being. Mitch's voice broke into my thoughts. "Have faith in me."

I swiped the phone screen and held my finger on the Voxer icon until all the icons wobbled. A small cross appeared next to the icons. I touched the cross on the Voxer app and deleted it then did the same with Instagram and Facebook, just in case. I turned the phone off, then on again. As it started up a list of available WiFi connections appeared. I scanned the list. They were all locked. The fourth one on the list interested me. The signal was weak but it gave me a general vicinity.

I rang Mitch back.

"I'm somewhere near Inova Fairfax."

"El, how close?"

"Close enough that I can see the Emergency Department WiFi signal, it's weak but it's visible."

"I'm coming."

I hung up and removed the back of my phone and took out the battery. Deleting the apps I thought were sending coordinates wasn't enough, I had to be sure nothing else was sent from my phone. All I could do was hope I'd removed the battery before another set of coordinates could be sent. It occurred to me that if that were the bomber's game, then it would go on until he or she won. I was the bait and under no illusion what my fate entailed. Someone would not go to this much trouble to kill Delta A and let me walk away. I set it on the mattress then snapped the back on the phone again. It felt very lonely without a functional phone.

Whoever did this genuinely wanted us dead but didn't want to confront any of us in the process. Coward? Or was it all part of an end game we didn't know about yet? I heard Mitch's voice in my head again. He told me he'd be there soon.

On his own? I didn't know.

Who from SWAT was injured?

No idea.

Was there a trap here?

No idea.

I needed to concentrate on what I did know. I was alive. That I knew. I was still dangerous despite my lack of clothing and weapon. Something felt odd, inside me. Why would there be anything inside me? Nausea washed through me. Oh my God. That's what felt wrong. A badly positioned tampon. God no!

Not wanting to know but needing to know, I felt inside my panties and sure enough, I found a string. With care, I felt for the end of the tampon; it wasn't fully inserted which was why I could feel it. I grasped the tampon with my fingers and extracted it. Holding it carefully, I examined it. It looked perfectly normal. Using my fingernails, I dug into the cotton and found an orange core. Semtex?

A noise outside the door. I stuffed the tampon down between the wall and the mattress.

My innards froze. It wasn't Mitch's voice. Two men. I steadied my breathing and closed my eyes.

Focus. I needed my hands. One of them had the bloody annoying sensor on it. Knowing I should keep it on didn't worry me as much as not being able to fully use my hands. I undid the sensor and dropped it on the bed.

The voices were close to the door. I dropped the blanket onto the bed and moved to the right side of the door, with no idea if it was the hinge side or not – hard to tell without a door handle. If it were a cell, the door would open outward not inward.

My ribs hurt and so did my head; hair stuck to my back.

The door moved. I knew straight away that I was on the handle side. Whoever it was would be within my reach. I took a deep breath. A shadow fell across the floor before a shoe came into view. Male. He walked in, his head turned away from me, talking to the other male behind him and carrying a shallow box. I kicked his kneecap backward while I lashed out with my arm, chopping him across the larynx with the side of my hand. He tumbled. The box and its contents flew across the floor. Surprised, the man clutched his throat and made weird noises. The other male pushed him out of the way and made a grab for me. I ducked, kicked the first male in the throat with my heel, then jumped over him, glancing at his face. Gasping and gurgling, he didn't sound as if he would be much of a problem. The second, bigger, male lunged. Over reached ... and staggered. I elbowed him in the side of the head. He reeled but came back.

"A fighter," he growled and shook his head. "This will be fun."

"Not feeling in a fun mood." I sucked up all the pain I felt and turned it into an escape plan.

"You're hurt," he countered.

"Yep, but you're dead," I replied.

I saw a knife in a sheath on his belt. He swung at me with a closed fist. I stepped into the swing, diminishing the power of the punch. He connected with my shoulder, I staggered a bit but now I was inside his reach. I ducked and slid around him. He didn't expect that. While he tried to grab hold of me, I pulled the knife from the sheath. Before he could react, from behind I shoved the blade in between his ribs, through his heart, and twisted. It hurt my arm but fuck him. I pulled the knife out of his back and jammed it in again. Blood cascaded onto the floor. I shoved my knee in his back and pushed. He fell forward with the blade stuck in his back.

Good thing the room was washable.

The other guy gurgled on the floor holding his throat. I doubted that would help. I could see it swelling.

The sound of footsteps echoed in the corridor, running feet moving toward the room, then they stopped, and went back. The door was still open. I stepped carefully around the dead and the dying to grab my cell phone and the blanket. I saw what was in the box scattered on the floor. Tampons still inside the cellophane wrappers. Maybe they didn't know I was already wearing one. Four sets of handcuffs. Several different types of knives. Wrapping the blanket around me, I put the battery back in the phone and called Mitch.

I listened by the door for the familiar sound of his phone. All I heard were footsteps walking away. "Where are you?"

"In a corridor, the west wing of an old psychiatric hospital within a half mile of Inova."

That felt too far away. Could I pick up a WiFi signal from a half mile away? Maybe.

"I don't know if that's where I am, there are other people here. I can hear footsteps. I just killed one guy and another is dying. I'm leaving this room now."

"I'd like you to wait for me?"

"I know, but I'm a sitting duck here."

A little yellow duck popped out from under the dead body and shook bright red blood off its feathers then sat down.

"I'm trying to find you."

"I know. I have to go. I'll find a way out. Don't be in here. Let me come to you." I didn't even know if we were both in the same place. But an old hospital might be about right. Except the room I was in didn't look old.

"Three little words."

"Me too."

The call ended and I tucked the phone into my bra.

I needed to move before the footsteps came back this way. I searched the almost dead guy. He had a pistol. A SIG p226. I clicked the safety off and held it inside the blanket in my right hand.

I peered out the door, looking right then around the open door to the left. No one around. I opted to move in the same direction as I'd heard the footsteps, which had come and gone the same way. As I walked down the dimly lit corridor, I passed more doors. Numbered. The numbers decreased as I walked. I hoped that meant I was going toward an exit of some kind.

Being out in the open concerned me but less so than what could've happened to me back in the room. Those men weren't there for the good of my health. Or apparently theirs. The thought made me smile. Will people ever learn to stop fucking with me?

Nope.

A door closed somewhere ahead of me. A little yellow duck quacked and sat down by my feet. I leaned my back against the wall and waited for a moment. Footsteps. I held my breath. The steps faltered. Paused. Turned. Moved away. The duck vanished.

Relieved, I let out a sigh and continued. Around the corner was a double glass door. Through it, I saw an exit sign and elevators. The number, clearly visible on the floor display next to the down arrow, dropped to three and the doors opened.

Crap.

The man didn't look straight ahead. He looked left as if he was expecting someone to be there. I darted back around the corner and waited.

My heart pounded, it was hard to breathe. I wondered if maybe I should have left the oximeter on but it wouldn't do me any good watching my stats fall. I couldn't fix whatever was wrong. I had to get out of wherever I was. I looked around the corner. The man had gone.

I pulled one glass door open and looked into the new corridor. No one.

Decision time. Elevator or stairs?

Stairs. I didn't know who might be waiting at the bottom of the elevator. At least with the stairs I could maybe make it back to another floor if I had to. I knew by the elevator display that I was on the third floor. I drew in a breath. Disinfectant. Hospital smells. Not disused, abandoned hospital smells but current ones.

What if it was an operational hospital? A private facility?

In the stairwell, I called Mitch back. I carefully walked down the stairs.

"Mitch, this isn't an old disused hospital. The elevators

are working and modern. The place is not falling apart. It's still operational. I could be in a private hospital … ask Kurt about private facilities that care for mentally ill patients near Inova."

"I'll get back to you. You all right?"

"Just trying to find a way out."

Not all right but I will be, as soon as I get out of here.

I put the phone back in my bra. I passed the second floor landing and kept on going. Even with dodgy breathing, I reached the first floor landing in record time and then the ground floor. I listened for any noise beyond the door.

Steeling myself, I gave the door, a fire door, a good shove and peered out the gap. No one around. I opened the door further. There were large potted plants by a big plate-glass window. The gray-tinged sky beyond told me it was early morning. I could see a main door. To the right of the door was a reception desk. No one there. I needed to get out the main doors. Unsure if I could run, I heard Mitch in my head telling me I could run. I ran all the time. We both did. We ran three times a week if not more, when time and jobs allowed. All I had to do now was run to the door, open it and run across the parking lot of whatever was out there.

Somewhere beside me, an elevator dinged.

It's now or never.

I didn't look toward the elevator as I ran. I just gathered the blanket closer and kept on going, shoving the door wide as I plowed through. My ribs and lungs complained loudly. I growled at them. No time for collapsing lungs now.

One foot in front of the other, that's all. Just one foot in front of the other.

I ran across the black top, across grass, across a six-lane road to a wire fence, jumped over the fence and walked into the woods wrapping the blanket tighter against the morning chill. Once in the woods I stopped. Looking back at the road, I knew where I was: Gallows Road. I pulled my phone and called Mitch.

It was harder to talk than I realized and took several attempts before my voice broke free. "Meet me at Exxon Mobil on Gallows Road. I'll be by the front entrance to the main building. Drive in."

"On my way," he replied. "Kurt is with me."

"Good." I hung up, this time I kept my phone in my hand and continued through the woods.

Mobil on Gallows was right across the road from Inova Fairfax, so I was right about being close to the hospital. Wherever I was held was further along the road and it took a while for me to walk through the woods and find the path that led to Exxon Mobil.

Chapter Thirty-eight.
Over the Wall

The quiet by the Exxon Mobil building was deafening: very few cars in the parking lot, but lights on in the building. I tried the door. Locked. I checked the time on my phone. Too early for more than a handful of dedicated souls to be at work. I waited near the main entrance wrapped in the blanket, clutching the gun. Cold bit into my bare feet and curled up my legs. It felt like I'd been standing on the cold concrete for hours but it was probably minutes. Sitting was not an attractive alternative but I considered I could curl up on the blanket and still have it around me. Might be warmer.

As soon as I sat down, I knew I wasn't getting up again under my own steam. I was done. Exhausted. Hurting. Shaky. Cold and really thirsty. Hungry not so much.

A squirrel scampered across the road from the woods and ran up a cherry tree nearby. At least it wasn't a duck.

I heard a car coming. My hand adjusted on the grip of the SIG. My index finger moving against the edge of the barrel felt comforting. A black Ford Explorer came into view; I didn't breathe out until I saw the tag number. Kurt's car. The car pulled up. Mitch dove out the driver's door and slid around the hood.

"El?" He crouched in front of me.

I managed a smile. "Yep."

"Want a hug?"

"Yes."

His eyes gleamed in the new day as he smiled. "Standing or here?"

"Here."

I can't stand.

He wrapped his arms around me then leaned back, a questioning look in his eyes. "Tell me that's a gun?"

"It's a gun."

I placed the SIG on the ground and slid my arms inside Mitch's jacket. The warmth from his body helped. Kurt knelt next to us. I felt him touch my head and winced. Mitch's arms tightened around me.

"You scared me," he whispered in my ear.

Kurt inspected the wound in my head. I held onto Mitch. He talked. Soft words flowed. Lulling me into a sense of security. The rhythm of his heart matched mine.

I turned my head a little to see Kurt.

"Conway, where were you being held?" Kurt asked.

"A building near the hospital."

"Were you on Gallows?"

I nodded.

"Is that where you were held?"

I nodded again.

Words in my head tumbled around as I tried to get them out in some semblance of order. "Need SWAT. Two bodies." There was the tampon too. No blocking that out. "Kurt. Tampon by the bed."

Mitch's arms tightened around me. "They're not

words, baby," he whispered in my ear.

What was he talking about? Of course they're words. I just told them where I was held and what they'd find there.

Kurt took out his phone and made a call. Moments later he said, "You need to be in hospital."

"No, I don't. Get whatever you need to patch me up. We're going to the hotel. No hospitals."

At least they were the words in my head. Judging by the look on Kurt's face, I didn't say anything like that.

"That garble is worrying," Kurt said.

I tried again.

"No."

"No?" Kurt queried.

"No ... hospital."

"Conway, you need medical care."

Medical care? I needed the bomb squad. I had a horrible feeling there were two tampons which is why I could remove one so easily: it wasn't inserted correctly and there wasn't enough room for the second one. The tampon I'd removed was longer than the normal non-explosive type.

A duck quacked and flapped its little wings as it half flew, sort of jumped to Kurt's head.

"No." My agitation rose.

"Shhh," Mitch said holding me tighter. He spoke to Kurt, "Is the hospital absolutely necessary?"

"She has another head injury. I think so."

"No!" I struggled against Mitch trying to break free

and stand. Fuck this. I'm going to call the bomb squad myself. Keeping the whole tampon thing at a distance was working for me. The minute my mind tried to wander into the dangerous space labeled 'who violated Ellie?' I shut it down. Don't go there.

"Shhh," Mitch soothed. "I'll help you stand." He did. His hands wrapped the blanket around me and drew me close. Mitch's voice slipped sideways.

"Bomb." I saw the words grow feathers and fly away. As they flew, they pulled a thread in the sky, unraveling the gray-blue, leaving inky black.

I fell through the black, toppling head first into nothing.

Eventually the nothing became a steady beep, beep, beep.

The beep led to light.

At first, it was dim and soft-focused. After a while, it sharpened and the world was back. I was alive.

"Hey, you," Mitch said from a chair by my bed. "How you doing?"

My mouth turned up at the corners. I'm okay.

"Okay."

"You took a nap," Mitch replied, pressing something near my hand but on the bed. I heard a buzz. My eyes closed again. I was warm. Mitch was with me. Sleep beckoned.

Chapter Thirty-nine.

Rainbow in the Dark/Mitch.

"She's gone again," I said as Kurt hurried into the room.

"To be expected," he replied checking the equipment. "Leon will be in soon. I need another opinion."

"Did you find where she was held?"

"We think so. No evidence at all apart from the tampon. Whoever cleaned the cell missed that. No bodies. No one saw Conway."

"Her clothes etcetera?"

"Clothes, boots, gun and holster, wallet and badge, all found in a neat stack outside the Washington Field Office."

"Isn't that a little weird?"

"Yes. Bit odd that the only prints on anything were yours and Conway's."

"My prints on her stuff isn't odd."

"Well, no, but what is odd is that there were no other prints, not even mine. And I had her gun in my possession a few times over the last week. My prints should have been on it as well as her holster and her belt."

"Now that is odd."

"I'm thinking someone cleaned everything and added back your prints and Conway's. But how would someone get prints?"

"Same way someone took her from outside the field office? We're being watched from the inside?"

Kurt nodded. "That's what I'm thinking. CCTV operates in the hallways, stairwells, entrance and exits."

"Someone didn't necessarily need to be in the building then, they just needed to be able to access the feed?"

Kurt nodded. "That's right."

"Anyone watching that feed would've seen us go in different directions."

"If that's what happened, then yes, they would've seen their window of opportunity to grab Ellie."

I let that roll around in my mind for a moment. "How did anyone manage that?"

"It would've taken more than one person and judging by the wound in her scalp she was hit with something, pistol-whipped maybe."

She wouldn't have left willingly and it had to be quick. That made sense to me. My attention returned to the fingerprint thing. "We both had drinks while in the building, we left coffee cups in the break room."

"That is not comforting, Mitch." Kurt replied, grim-faced. I was used to seeing him serious but with a bit of light in his eyes. No light now, just dark.

"Surveillance video from the private hospital?"

"Erased."

"Surveillance from the field office cameras, there are cameras overlooking the street?"

"Erased. Sandra's working on trying to recover any hidden temporary files. She's good, so if there is anything at all, even a shadow of the erased timestamps, she'll find it."

I settled back into the chair. My eyes fixed on Ellie. She slept. Seemed good that she slept, as long as she woke up again. My mind wandered. Images from the night before crowded in, I scanned them for anything that might lead to a person: someone was responsible - and someone knew who.

Kurt pulled up a chair and sat on the other side of Ellie, near the monitors.

"The women?" I asked. Not entirely sure what my question was.

"The lawyers are trying to secure their release. I've turned it over to legal, they can deal with it."

"Are they being held on any charges? Don't you have a limit for how long you can hold someone without charging them?"

"Yes, we do and then the Patriot Act kicks in and all bets are off."

"Are they being charged?"

"Not at this stage. Legal are talking conspiracy to commit terrorism. That should keep them in custody for a bit longer."

"Are they involved?"

"No, I don't believe so. They're being used."

"And you're holding them why?"

"To make it hard for the puppeteer to carry on."

"Puppeteer," I repeated. Good description.

"We're holding the two women for the same reason

Conway took the battery out of her phone."

I nodded. "Why is this happening?"

"I don't know," Kurt replied. "The only one who might have a shot at figuring it out is Conway. Her brain works differently from the rest of us. She sees things we don't."

"She's not seeing much right now," I said, holding her hand in mine.

"Don't be so sure. I've known her to wake up with amazing insight. I don't know where she goes but she comes back with things that boggle my brain."

"I hope you're right."

"Trust me," Kurt replied. He regarded me for a moment then spoke again. "You operate a little like she does."

"A little. I see what she lets me see. I saw the room where she was held."

"But not where she was, correct?"

"Correct. She didn't know, so she couldn't share it."

"Try seeing what's happening in her head now. I need to make some calls and make sure everything's moving forward."

"I'll try."

Kurt stood up and leaned over Ellie. "Wake up, Conway. Washington is burning and you're the only one who can figure this out." He waited for a few seconds. No response. "I'll be back soon. If Leon comes in while I'm gone, give me a call."

"Sure." I had Ellie's phone in my pocket. I patted my jean pockets just to make sure.

Kurt slid the glass door open then closed it behind him. He walked away, leaving us alone. The quiet punctuated only by the steady beep from the monitor on the other side of the bed. Her breathing so soundless, if it weren't for the monitor I'd have to check every few minutes to make sure she was breathing.

I closed my eyes and leaned back in the chair, focusing on Ellie. Positive, healing, happy thoughts about what we'd do when she recovered. Vacation. Yes, a vacation. Just us. Somewhere warm and anonymous. Somewhere by the sea. Fishing. We would go fishing. Yes, fishing.

Sometime later Kurt entered the room again. "Everything all right?"

"I think so," I replied. I had questions but every so often with questions, I've found I don't really want to know the answers. Did I really want to know the answers this time? I couldn't be sure.

Before I could stop myself, the first question was upon me and directed at Kurt. "Will she remember what happened?"

"I don't know," Kurt replied. "Depends on the head injury, depends if she lost consciousness at all while she was gone, and it sounds like she did. It also depends on whether she was drugged. I suspect she was given something to keep her unconscious, maybe even Ketamine."

"And that is?"

"A pain killer, anesthetic, memory eraser ..."

"And you think she was given that drug?"

"Yes. I'm waiting on toxicology to confirm or otherwise the presence of drugs in her system."

"Do you know what happened to her?"

"Not really. Not much more than what Conway told you on the phone."

Not much more. So they did know more.

There was a question sitting there. Ominous. Unasked and unanswered. This could be one of those times that I don't want to hear the answer. If El had no memory, did I need to know?

"Should I ask?" I whispered to Ellie, as she lay pale and silent. Uncharacteristically still.

"She can't answer you, Mitch. And I can't answer for her," Kurt replied.

Another thought barreled into my consciousness. DNA. Swimmers to be precise. It wasn't a great thought. Telling Kurt that our relationship was physical wasn't my idea of a good time. Also, if I asked him about DNA, then I'd have half an answer regarding my unspoken question. I'd know he did a rape kit. I swallowed hard. Maybe not. He did say the ultrasound showed another tampon, which he removed. DNA could be on that. Another explosive-filled tampon. She obviously didn't know there were two. Even if she had, there was no way she could have removed the second one without using the cord. Kurt used forceps.

"DNA?"

"Will it be yours?"

"Yes." And hopefully no one else's.

"Then I need a sample of your DNA. Unless it's on file?"

"It's not. My fingerprints are. Where did you find the DNA?" Feeling brave, asking the hard questions.

"On the tampons."

I nodded.

"I'll be right back," Kurt said. I saw his mouth curve upward as he turned away and left the room. I was surprised and relieved that he didn't have a comment to make.

Kurt returned with a long cylinder in his hand. From the cylinder, he took a cotton swab. It looked like a giant cotton bud and handed it to me.

"You can do this yourself. Rub the swab over the inside of your cheeks."

I did as he instructed and then handed it back. Kurt sealed the swab into the cylinder and wrote on the outside.

"Be right back." He had his phone in his hand and made a call as he left the room.

I settled back and watched El breathe, still holding her hand and not wanting to let it go in case she didn't know I was there. I concentrated on sending as much positive energy to her as I could. I had a lot, plenty for her and me, until she woke up and bounced back. Her eyes flickered every now and then. Hope. That's what the flickers were. Hope that she'd wake up and not remember anything bad that may have happened to her.

I didn't want her to carry anything that ate away at her

sense of security or sense of who she was. I knew that wasn't up to me, but if it were, I'd carry it all and never let her know what transpired. A soft moan came from the bed.

"El?"

Chapter Forty.

Guardian

"Mmmmitch?"

"Right here." He held a straw to my lips. "Drink?"

That was exactly what I needed. Cool water felt good.

"Am I okay?"

"Yes."

"Good." I sighed without meaning to. "Hospital again?"

"Yes. Before you get cranky and want to leave, you had to be here."

I considered his words as the events that led to me passing out in his arms outside Exxon Mobil came back in glorious Technicolor. Deep breath. No real pain. That was a plus.

Bits and pieces, images, feelings, random thoughts all jumbled together. There were two tampons. That was why the one I removed wasn't inserted properly. No room in the inn.

"Did Kurt find the other tampon?" I looked Mitch in the eye. "This is where you say 'yes.'"

He smiled. "He did."

"Did they find where I was held?"

"Yes. But apart from the tampon there was no evidence that you'd been there."

"Good thing I hid it then." My throat was dry. Mitch

held the straw to my lips again. Nice.

"I'm glad you're awake," Mitch said putting down the glass. He leaned over and kissed me. Slow warm kisses that reminded me how good life could be.

"Me too." I smiled. A real smile. An 'everything will be okay' smile. I had nothing to base my feeling on but I didn't need anything. I knew deep down it would be okay. "Now I'm awake, let's get back to work. Got a perverted piece of terrorist shite to find."

"Not so fast, Grasshopper. Patience. You have another head injury. We're waiting for your neurologist for the second time this week."

"Really? I thought it was a flesh wound?"

"Yeah, you would. Let's let the doctors decide, shall we?"

"You sure? Because I feel pretty good."

I wasn't lying. I did. All things considered. Helicopter being shot down. Getting into a fight with broken ribs. Having two head injuries and a recent brush with a partially deflated lung. I was, all things considered, feeling as okay as humanly possible. And happy for no fathomable reason other than Mitch was right there. Maybe that's all I needed. Maybe he's all I've ever needed. Timing. It's all in the timing.

I fumbled for the bed controls. Sitting up seemed like a good place to start on my quest for release.

Chapter Forty-one.

Elimination

Looking out the window while I waited in my hospital room for Mitch to do whatever he needed to do, I noticed a car I'd seen before. Danni. I wondered how she gave her surveillance team the slip.

Feeling the love. Everything in my world was where it should be. Odd thought to have. I pondered on it for a moment. It was almost as if Danni had become a stalker. The woman wrote books and her main character or protagonist, or whatever the term was, was me? But she was also Interpol? Did we ever get verification of that? I scoured my memory looking for something that identified her as Interpol and remembered the conversation I had with Iain Campbell. Yes, verification. She was Interpol and here on some special assignment.

I turned around in time to see Mitch walking towards me, hands shoved deep in his jacket pockets. A generous smile plastered his face when he reached me. His arm slipped around my waist. "Your chariot awaits, shall we?"

"Yes, please," I leaned close. "We have an audience. White car in the Gray parking area."

Mitch peered out the window.

"Game time. On three, we wave," he replied. "Smile. One, two, three."

We waved. Disappointingly, she didn't wave back.

Chances are she couldn't see us behind the reflective glass on the fourth floor.

Feeling a certain amount of relief as I got into the car, a yawn escaped. My head leaned back on the headrest. Wrong thing to do. I sat up straighter.

"All right?"

"Yeah, my head doesn't like being leaned on right now."

"Fair enough."

I glanced toward the Gray parking area as we left the hospital grounds. Danni was still there.

"Want me to pull some secret squirrel evasive driving technique?" Mitch asked.

"Nah, don't worry about it."

The whole thought of that made me feel sick. It did make me smile that he'd suggest it. I knew he'd taken a class in evasion and defensive driving. It was one of the mandatory training exercises for people dealing with big Government defense contracts. The point of it was to help people avoid taking unnecessary risks and to make it harder to abduct them by learning how to avoid being an easy target. In my view, everyone should take such practical classes and make my job easier.

We had an uneventful drive to the hotel. Six cars back I saw Danni's tailing us and wondered why but that's as far as I took the thought. She wasn't after me. She may well be after the same people I was though. That thought didn't please me. I did not want someone swooping in at the last second and stealing my arrest from under my nose. American soil. My arrest.

A gravelly voice in my head said, "Let's not get too giggly too quick, we don't know for sure she's after the same person." The voice sounded a lot like Sam Elliot. That was new and unexpected. Definitely not unpleasant, just surprising.

I love my life.

***

I lay down for half an hour but rest was elusive so I got up and sat at the small desk in our room. Mitch lay stretched out napping on the sofa. The temptation to crawl up next to him was high. I resisted. Catch the bomber first.

I started going over the surveillance my phone had captured. The bugs I'd planted on Kennedy and the GPS tracking used on Danni.

Did they intersect?

Yes. Yes, they did.

Where else was Danni? She was at the hospital a lot. She was near the field office when we were. I plotted her movements when surveillance was on her and when she was alone. She didn't deviate. But the pattern was what interested me.

She was where I was. I wrote it all down with time stamps. She at the private hospital when I was there. She was outside the field office at approximately the same time I was abducted.

Danni Lane irked me. She was coming off as a stalker. I was stalking the stalker and it made me smile. What didn't make me smile was her turning up everywhere I went. I checked the rest of the locations she was in with the times I knew I'd been in certain places. By the time I finished, I wished she'd been bugged a helluva lot sooner, like on entry to the USA. Yep, that soon. Her ability to be everywhere creeped me out. Knowing she was Interpol and that she was everywhere I was? Now that felt hinky. She wasn't after me. It was starting to look like she knew from the outset what was going on. If so a warning would've been the polite thing.

Maybe Danni and I need to chat about interagency cooperation?

She wouldn't be invited to O'Malley's bar when this was over for my traditional LEO end-of-case-drinks. My shout. Not for her. Oh no. She can buy her own drinks.

Lee burst in the door nearly knocking it off the hinges. I jumped. The door slammed behind him. Mitch woke with a start.

"Jeez, Lee, the door okay?" I asked as he crossed the room to the desk.

"Kennedy!" he said, thrusting his camera at me.

"Kennedy?" I replied, taking the camera and removing the memory card. I plugged it into the slot on my laptop.

"Yeah. Just saw him meet with someone we know."

I heard music. It took me a minute to realize it was in my head. I expected the person we knew to be Misha. Bon Jovi powered through with 'Always.' I just bet Danni was there somewhere. Something about 'Always' and the reference to pictures left behind spoke volumes. It didn't mention erased pictures though, might have been handy if it had.

"Misha?"

"Yeah," Lee replied. He didn't bat an eyelid, well used to my odd ways of getting information. "Caught the meeting in the back of a coffee shop."

"Guess no one was supposed to see them," I said.

"That was what I thought too," Lee agreed.

Twenty new pictures popped up on my screen. Most of them from the bar, and five from the coffee shop.

"You spotted them in a mirror?"

"Yeah, super sleuth powers at work," Lee said with a grin.

"Way to go, Special Agent Ridiculously Good-looking."

I inspected the photographs. "Well, shit," I exclaimed. Bon Jovi stopped singing. "Look at that!"

The picture was of a woman sitting at a table in a coffee shop, staring intently at Seamus Kennedy and Misha Praskovya sitting a few tables over. There were two different pictures with the same intent look and she watched Kennedy and Praskovya in both.

"Oh, no, that ain't good, Chicky," Lee drawled.

"No, it ain't."

"What the fuck is Danni doing watching Misha and Kennedy?" Lee asked. "If she's part of what they're doing here, then why isn't she at the table with them?"

"I don't know. But she followed us to the hotel. She was waiting outside the hospital. And look at this ..." I showed him the spreadsheet I'd been working on. Time and places, my movements versus Danni's. I used verified sightings, information from the bug we planted on her phone and from Voxer. None of our surveillance measures lined up since the Newseum explosion. My ducks were all over the place like a mad woman's knitting. Danni Lane was everywhere all at once and I couldn't explain it. The only thing I felt I could trust were actual sightings of her but it would be foolish to discount the other information completely.

"If she's Interpol, then why the hell is she following you?"

"I don't know." My skin crawled and a rush of cold shot up my spine.

"I don't like this, Chicky. Not one little bit. Especially that." He pointed to the time stamp that was the helicopter crash and the time stamp that put Danni in the vicinity of the Mall according to our bug. "She could've shot that chopper down."

I hoped that wasn't the case. Lee was right. It didn't look good.

Between Trudi, Susan, and Danni, none of it looked good. I needed to dig myself out of the ton of manure that had built up around this case.

When the surveillance was on them, she still managed to be in places near me. Albeit not as close as without surveillance. I wondered if she knew Troy.

Odd that I thought of him.

"What irks me is that she was at that private hospital too, how hard would it have been for her to make a fucking call?" I grumbled. "Unless she was there because she was the one who took me there?"

Mitch and Lee froze. They looked at me like I'd grown horns. Nothing new there then.

"I'm serious," I said.

"I know," Mitch replied. "That's what worries me."

"She's Interpol. We're supposed to be able to trust fellow LEOs," Lee replied.

"I know." But it's been my experience that there are bad and good people everywhere. Holding a badge doesn't instantly make someone a good person. In a perfect world, it would. But this is our world and it's far from perfect most of the time. "I think we should be ready for that possibility."

Lee nodded. "Not happy about it but I understand where you're coming from. I can see the pattern in this spreadsheet."

"Good enough," I replied.

Until I wrote all that out, I'd had no idea how close she'd gotten to our operation or to me. The only people closer were Delta A and Mitch.

"Nice that Misha is having coffee with his old friend, don't you think?" I said, pointing at him and Kennedy deep in conversation.

"Caine know anything about Misha being here?" Lee asked.

"He knows something but didn't elaborate."

No one was keen on talking. Really, communication was the key. If we all talked and shared information, we might have a shot at stopping whatever the hell is going on here. I could see the irony. Me grumbling about a lack of communication. Pots and kettles.

"We need to call a pow-wow, and sit the hell down and get everyone talking," Lee said.

"Now that's the best idea I've heard all week."

Great idea but it wasn't going to happen. Everyone was running around like headless chickens.

Lee nodded sagely. "There are some big questions here and we're not getting to them fast enough."

"You didn't go to the Hard Rock Café did you?" Would be weird if he had.

He shook his head. "No."

"Well, it wasn't the Café Danni supposedly worked at then," I muttered and hauled my jacket off the back of the chair and headed for the door.

"Whoa, where you headed, little lady?" Mitch said, crossing the room in four long strides.

"I've got a stalker to see about stalking a spook."

"Not alone you ain't," Lee said, joining Mitch and me by the door.

"I'm not alone. I have Mr. Glock 17 right here on my hip."

"Nah, not happening," Mitch replied, his hand flat on the door. I didn't have the strength to pull it open with him leaning on it. Not with fractured ribs and so forth. He knew that.

I twisted the door handle and pulled. Nothing happened.

"Really, Mitch?"

"Yes. Really. You'll hurt yourself trying to open the door. Just hear us out," Mitch said. "We'll come. You aren't supposed to be alone. We aren't supposed to be alone."

Lee agreed. "Plus, I don't like the way you said stalker. You could be right. She could be a stalker."

"I was kinda joking, Lee. Stalker? Really? She's Interpol and an author and works in a coffee shop and a New Zealander and an American, how on earth does she have time to be a stalker?"

She was an enigma wrapped in a riddle and I didn't like it one little bit.

Lee nodded. "Still don't like it. You go, we all go."

"Okay."

Mitch stood straighter and let the door go. I turned the handle and pulled, he caught the edge of the door with his fingers and pulled it open the full way.

There outside the door with a tray of take-out coffee cups was Misha Praskovya.

I looked over my shoulder at Lee and said, "I think you were snapped."

He poked his head around the door above mine.

"Howdy, stranger," I said to Misha. "What brings you down to my comfortable hotel room?"

"I am wanting to talk with you."

What a coincidence. I am wanting the same thing. I noted he had four coffees. Disconcerting.

"Come in, bring the coffee," I said, going back inside.

All four of us sat at the small square table. It amused me that the men all sat sideways; no one's legs fitted under the table. Misha passed the cups around. He smiled at Mitch.

"Mochachino for you?"

"Yes, thanks."

"How did you know that?" I asked. I hate being watched and obviously we were, but by whom and why?

"I have my ways," Misha replied.

"Misha, not cool. We should not be under surveillance."

"I am not sure I understand. I am just a friend bringing coffee."

"Nah, no, not buying the 'my English isn't very good' line," I said shaking my head ever so slightly. Not wanting to wake the dragon that slept in my skull. "I've known you too long for that."

Misha looked at Mitch. "He looks like a mochachino man."

"You talk so much crap, Misha, bet you have to wash your mouth out a lot."

Misha grinned. His bluer than blue eyes sparkled against his olive skin. He still looked like he should be on the cover of a Mills and Boon novel.

I let the coffee thing go. I began: seemed fair, he was the one caught chatting with my target.

"Caine told me ..." I considered that before saying it, and it was a warning, "...you were here on a case or regarding something that was nothing to do with me. I found you talking to someone who is a target of ours."

"Your target?" He seemed genuinely surprised.

Imagine that.

"Yes, my target."

"Who is this target?"

Lee stood up and reached for the laptop. He passed it to me. I pulled a photo up on the screen and spun it to face Misha. "Who is she? The woman you're talking to."

Without hesitation. "Danni Lane."

"And she is?"

"A novelist. I love her books."

I bet.

I pulled up the other photo of him and Kennedy.

"And?"

"I know Seamus many years. He is old friend. I see him purchasing coffee and stop to say hello." Misha looked at me. "You know him. We are old friends. We are all old friends." Misha flipped his index finger between himself and me.

"Oh, I know Seamus. I've spoken to him. He sent you here? To dig around and find out how much we know about whatever the three musketeers are up to?"

"Of course not. I came for coffee with old friends. I am in town, it is polite to look up old friends."

"Look, Misha. I love seeing you. And this is good coffee. But I need straight answers. I need to know what the hell is going on in Washington and why people keep trying to blow me the fuck up!" I leaned forward and glared at him. "I'm in a fucking hotel. Someone shot down my helicopter, and you knew what type of coffee Mitch drinks. I think we have a rogue agent. Something screwy is up with a senator. The Navy Yard, Newseum, and Hoover building fucking exploded." I paused for a second to catch my breath. "Kennedy, Holmes and Jones are in town along with you. We rescued a Czech woman from god knows who and someone inserted a fucking exploding tampon into her vagina and had her sent to the hospital I was in." Anger came in waves now, almost impossible to control. "Someone called off my surveillance and forged my signature. I need to know what the hell Senator Robinson is involved in. And where Anastazia Dobrovolný is. And what the connection is between you, me and Robinson. Why did someone send the three of us exploding cards?" I stopped and made eye contact with Misha. "I'm really sorry about your assistant."

He nodded and opened his mouth to speak. I held up my hand.

"I'm not done yet. Someone abducted me from outside the Washington field office to a private medical facility."

"I heard."

"How did you hear?"

"Kennedy told me."

I had no idea how he knew. And if he knew where I was, why didn't he come in and get me?

"Did you also know that someone inserted explosive tampons into me?"

He shook his head.

"Well, they fucking did. I don't know what else was done. I was unconscious. I did kill two men, but we haven't found their bodies yet." I leaned back in my chair. "I'm looking for answers, Misha. I need answers."

I pulled up a picture of Danni Lane.

"Talk to me about her?"

He shook his head. "I cannot."

Lee spoke, "Good. Maybe this is a coincidence after all, all these things just happened to coincide with y'all being in town."

We both laughed. Coincidence wasn't something either of us put any stock in.

"Okay," I said switching gears, becoming more jovial. "What did you want to see me about Misha?" I didn't want to make it look like I was interrogating him.

"The reason Kennedy is in town is none of your business."

"And yet?"

"You have a connection."

"Well, I could have told you that. But I don't know what the connection is. Do you?"

He looked a little uncomfortable then took a long sip of his coffee. He set the cup down on the table, his fingers playing around the edge of the plastic lid.

"Let me help," I said, sipping my own coffee. "Delta found Alexandra. We were also expected to leave D.C. and go to New Zealand to help with a case involving heads."

Misha frowned and shook his head. "I don't know

this."

"Seems you don't know everything then, do you?" I replied. "We were requested in Wellington. A box of heads showed up on a ship that arrived from Indonesia. They were American."

"What has this to do with Alexandra?"

"That's what we don't know, but it has something to do with her. We were supposed to chase the heads. Plans changed. Agent Troy came to me with a surveillance video of three women. Danni was one of them. Lee and Sam went to New Zealand. Kurt and I stayed home."

"You think you were all supposed to go?"

"Yes. The head thing was a non-event, easily sorted," Lee replied. "The interesting thing was that the two women with Danni were implicated in the placement of the heads on the ship. But neither of them were ever in Indonesia. Someone fabricated their part in this. To what end? We don't know."

Misha frowned again. "I was not aware of any of that."

"One of the envelopes addressed to me came from New Zealand. It was given to Sam and Lee to bring home."

Misha nodded. "The chances of all of you being in the same room when you opened it were high."

"Yes."

"If you had all gone, then maybe none of you would be coming back," Misha said quietly.

My phone beeped. I looked at the screen: the app I was using to track Danni. She was on the move again. I swept my finger over the screen and tapped the app icon.

She was in the hotel.

"Danni is in here somewhere."

"So is Alexandra," Lee muttered. "Let's go. We need to get hold of Danni and get some answers."

Chapter Forty-two.

Killers

A thought rampaged through my mind: Danni might not be here officially, because she isn't trying to reunite Alexandra and Anastazia but working for whoever abducted them in the first place. Cold clawed within my gut.

I walked up to the security guard by the entrance to the hotel and flashed her picture.

"Seen her recently?"

"No, ma'am."

"Anyone come through that door in the last half hour?"

He nodded. "Half the hotel guests, ma'am, there is a conference on."

Crap.

Mitch and I did a quick search of the bathrooms, bar, restaurants, stores, lobby. There was no sign of her. Lee and Misha talked to hotel staff and went through the kitchens. No luck.

Faced with a floor-by-floor search, my determination waned. Cleverly, I knew of another way to locate her. I smiled sweetly at the concierge and asked to be shown to the security room. A couple of minutes later, I showed her picture to the person responsible for monitoring the many CCTV cameras in the hotel. He ran back a tape from a few minutes earlier showing someone who looked like Danni exiting the elevator on our floor. As I watched the screen, she walked down the hall and stopped near the door to my room. Then entered my room.

Now how did she know which floor we were on? How'd she get in?

Giving him my number I asked him to call me if she reappeared and on one screen I noted the concierge walking down a long hallway, nowhere near the front desk. The security guard was otherwise occupied as well, surrounded by a gaggle of women.

Then thanking the man in the security room, I went back to the front desk; I had something I wanted to check.

"Concierge, please," I said to an older woman manning the desk. She went to fetch him for me.

While she did that, I slipped around the desk and checked the computer screen in front of her. It took me under two seconds to bring up a guest list. All Danni had to do was send the woman on a wild goose chase and then she had computer access. But how did she know the names. Because in the guest book we used Priscilla and Elvis but on the computer you can access billing information. A little yellow duck quacked at me from the floor. I glanced at it. It quacked again. From behind the desk, there was also access to master keycards – such as housekeeping used. She could get into any room with one of those.

"Mitch, let's go back to our room. I think she's still there."

I walked as quickly as I could to the elevator. Slowest elevator ride ever. Or maybe it just seemed that way. Lee and Misha took the stairs, just in case she left that way. My heart thumped. I wiped my hands down my jeans. With a deep breath, I swiped my key card and swung the door wide open.

"Hello! Housekeeping!" I called.

To my astonishment, a female voice answered, "Can you come back later, please? Thank you."

Her voice came from the bedroom.

"Yes, ma'am," I replied, signaling to Mitch to stay put outside the door. He shook his head. I gave him a look. No time for this. He stepped in and I shut the door. I drew my gun, adjusted my grip and crept to the bedroom with Mitch right behind me.

I pushed the door open.

Danni Lane was rifling through the clothing in my bags with a camera around her neck.

I coughed.

She jumped.

Could've been the gun pointed at her.

"Hello. Can I help you?" I tried the calm syrupy voice I'd used on mentally challenged people to great effect.

Flustered she replied, "I ... um ... I ... ah ..."

"Need something to wear?" I offered, indicating my black shirts strewn over the floor. I lowered my weapon slightly.

She moved a hand. My gun swung back to her head. Yeah, I'm not keen on being shot again.

"I was just ..." She appeared lost for words. I struggled to believe she was some kind of wonder agent with Interpol.

"Breaking and entering. Doing a touch of burglary?" I tut-tutted softly. "This is no way for a lady to behave."

Something snapped. Her eyes hardened. "You are making a mistake."

Her right hand reached for something. My aim adjusted to her shoulder. My finger squeezed the trigger. She squawked like an injured bird and staggered backwards. Bit dramatic. I had the urge to roll my eyes. At least she didn't crumple into a heap; for that I was grateful. Something black fell at her feet.

I saw the same gun I'd seen in my dream.

"Kick that over here," I instructed.

She pathetically kicked at the gun. On the fourth kick, it made it to my feet.

"You shot me," she lamented.

"You had a gun. You broke into my room. You've been following me."

I kicked my smallest bag closer to the bed, and then hoisted it up, picking the gun up at the same time. Two feet away from me, dripping blood on the carpet from one hanging arm, stood Danni.

I forced her to her knees, searched her, took the flash drive from her wrist and then removed handcuffs from my bag. She screeched as I pulled her right hand behind her back. Guess it hurt her shoulder. Shouldn't point a gun at me.

"You brought this on yourself," I said, reaching for her other arm and snapping the cuffs on tightly. "We need to have a chat in a minute." I took a small towel from the bathroom and some duct tape from my bag then wadded up the towel and taped it to her shoulder.

I found her bag and rifled through it until I came up with her notebook.

"Bet this makes exciting reading," I said.

"They're my notes for my next book. Nothing to do with you," she muttered.

"I have a feeling they might have more to do with me than anyone realizes."

There was a knock at the door and Mitch opened it. I heard Lee and Misha enter.

"Ellie?" Lee said from behind me, then stepped up beside me and surveyed the bedroom. "Not like you to have a messy room."

"I didn't do it."

"You okay?"

"Yep. Our friend here needs an ambulance but not yet."

"I heard a shot," Misha said from somewhere back near the door. "You are okay, Ellie?"

I nodded.

I pushed Danni into a seated position on the edge of the bed.

"You are going to talk to us. If I don't like your answers, or if I think you are holding back, it will go very badly for you," I said.

She stared straight ahead. Not making eye contact with anyone.

Mitch moved. I caught him in the corner of my eye. "You don't have to be here," I said with a smile.

"I know. I want to be."

"Okay."

No secrets. I liked that. I liked that a lot. Made it easier to be me.

I looked at the pictures on her camera. They were all me, even shots when I knew some of my team were right next to me at the time. She'd cropped the pictures on the camera, taking everyone else out. Weird. The contents of her camera made me feel a little sick. I looked at her.

"Why are there so many of photos of me?" I scrolled through the photos. That was when I spotted a picture of what could've been Gallows Road. I took a closer look. A blanketed figure in motion. Me. Crossing the road after I escaped. "If you knew where I was, why didn't you get help?"

I dropped the camera in disgust. Misha caught it.

"What are you talking about? It was a hospital. You were obviously ill."

"Then why the escape, wrapped in a blanket?" I turned away, bile rising. Her peculiar detached smil made me feel ill.

She smiled, wide-eyed, a tad freaky looking. "You're amazing. I met you once at a book signing. That moment changed my life," she beamed. "I knew as soon as I saw you, I knew that we were meant to be more than friends."

What?

"How so?"

"We have a connection. You know that. That's why you stopped coming to my café. You're denying the truth."

I wracked my mind but could not remember ever seeing her in a café.

"You're strangely talkative for someone who has a hole in their shoulder." Very talkative.

"You're my hero," she said with a delighted grin.

What now?

"You're Interpol and I'm nobody's hero."

She frowned for a split second then the crazy grin returned.

I spoke again, "We know who you are. You can drop the café-worker routine."

She looked blank for a second then her mind rolled back, I could see it happen, weird. "I'm what?"

"Interpol."

Misha stepped in. "Danni, you remember me, yes?"

Blank again.

What the hell? Something was wrong.

I looked into her eyes. Fuc'n hell.

I turned to Mitch. "Mitch, you gave me codeine when I had a migraine, where's the bottle?"

"Bathroom, on the counter with the Tylenol and Advil."

I left her where she was and hurried back to the bathroom. I turned as Lee threw me a balled up pair of latex gloves. "Thanks."

I pulled on the gloves and carefully picked up the codeine prescription from the bathroom counter. I tipped the pills into my hand and counted them quickly. The bottle said fifty, thirty milligram tablets. Mitch gave me two. I hadn't used any prior to that. There were ten missing. Well fuck, that sucked out loud and gave change.

I could hear Danni still talking in the other room. Still declaring we had a connection. The only connection we had was the tentative one that came from my bullet hitting her shoulder.

"Lee, call paramedics and tell them she has a shoulder wound and that she's taken ten thirty-milligram codeine tablets and I don't know what else."

"Wonderful," he growled.

I went back to Danni. "What else did you take?"

Her reactions had slowed. "Just some valium before I came. I was nervous."

"Did you hear that, Lee?"

"Yep, she's an idiot. Still think she's Interpol?" Lee asked, pocketing his phone.

"According to Interpol she is," Misha replied. "Danni, do you remember me?"

She smiled at Misha and nodded. "You know Seamus."

She was getting chatty. Excellent.

"Danni, what are you doing in Washington?" I asked. "Why are you following me?"

"They're two different things," she said. "I got lucky with you."

"Great, now go back to why you are here."

"The Dobrovolný girls. They were abducted from Prague. Their father wanted them found. I traced them to Northern Virginia. Then one turned up at that old factory and you found her."

"Okay, who turned her into a bomb?"

"Not us. Someone got to her while she was in ICE's care. Before we could. That's why Kennedy is here now."

Chatty. I like chatty.

"Who sent letter bombs to me and Misha?" Grasping at straws. A duck quacked. I looked at it on the floor by the edge of the bed. The duck didn't think I was grasping at straws.

Danni smiled vacantly.

"Hey, you with me? Letter bombs, who sent them?"

She shook her head. "I don't know about letter bombs." Her eyes darted sideways. "I know about Alexandra and you."

"What do you know about me?"

"You are the best main character ever."

"I'm not fictional. I am real." I sighed. She was losing it. "What about Alexandra?"

"She was taken from Prague. I don't know who took her, but her sister might be for sale."

"For sale?"

The code. The price list.

"I think so," she replied. Her voice became lazier as she spoke.

"Do you know anything about the sale?"

"No, not yet."

Okay, moving on.

"Tell me what you were doing with my clothes," I said, curiosity brimming.

"I wanted to buy you something pretty. I needed your size. Your wardrobe is so dark."

"I'm FBI, Danni. It's a dark job." Some days darker than others.

Someone knocked. I called out for them to come in. Two paramedics bustled into the room. I spoke to the paramedics. "Danni Lane, thirty-year-old female. Has taken ten thirty-milligram codeine tablets and unknown valium quantity. She also has a shoulder wound, it's a through and through. The slug is in the wall over there."

The paramedics went to work. Lee got to work as well. He took her gun into evidence.

"She's interesting, huh?"

"You believing her story?" Lee asked.

"Parts of it, only because she's so whacked out, I don't think she could lie right now ... but I think she's still withholding information." I didn't want to tell him that I was right about the stalker thing. I had a feeling that would get me razzed for years to come. I think he detected my reluctance.

"Ellie?"

"She's stalking me, because *we have a connection*." I still thought it was more than that. That wasn't enough, not in my book anyway.

Book? Where was her notebook? I looked at the bed, there it was. The notebook and the flash drive. I must've put them down without noticing. I scooped them up. They needed looking at.

Lee's face cracked with a huge grin. "I thought we'd seen the last of the crazy fanatical types when you ditched Grange. Seems Ellie fans are just as nuts. Ya think the gay Ellie fans will beat Grange fans to a pulp?"

"Shut up. We're never going to find out." I leaned on the wall. "How did she pass the psych testing or isn't Interpol as rigorous as the FBI?"

"No idea. Maybe she was perfectly normal until she clapped eyes on you …" Lee laughed. His laughter bounced off the surfaces in our room and pinged out the door.

"Laugh it up, chuckles."

"Write your statement, Ellie. I'll take it then I'll travel with the loopy woman to hospital and be in touch if she imparts any more tidbits or maybe a sonnet or a love poem all about you."

"You think you are so freaking funny," I grumbled. "I need your room key." He handed it over.

I wrote fast, making sure to note the concierge, woman at the desk and lapse in security that made accessing keys and patron information so easy. Then wrote about the CCTV, the security guard and my version of the events from when I entered my room. I signed it and handed it to Lee. Mitch did the same and so did Misha. I didn't want anything left unsaid or unwritten. Document everything, especially when dealing with lunatics.

Lee called the crime scene unit to my room. It would

be half an hour before they arrived and an hour at least until they left. I sighed heavily. Lee's room was the obvious choice for a temporary base.

I'd lost my codeine too, because the silly bitch took my pills. I had a receipt for them so I could get a replacement script from my doctor or Kurt without being treated like a prescription pill-munching junkie. I thought about that for a second. Maybe I wouldn't replace them and hope I don't need them.

Chapter Forty-three.

Tornado of Souls

We took our gathering to Lee's room and assembled the rest of the team. Lee opted to stay, not go with Danni. He sent a uniformed officer instead.

Sam and Lee grinned at me.

"You really do attract aberrations, Chicky Babe," Sam said, letting loose a low whistle.

"No denying it," I replied, settling with care on the couch, cautious of leaning my head on the high-backed couch.

"Now what?" Sam asked.

"I have this notebook and a flash drive," I said. "Let's find out what Ms. Lane has been writing, shall we?"

I opened the notebook at the first page to a title. Her next book. *IED*. Ominous.

The next page had the beginning of an outline.

"What's it say?" Kurt asked sitting in an armchair opposite me.

"Her next book is called IED," I said. "Are her books first-person?"

"Yes, they are," he said.

"Gimme me a minute or two to read this."

The outline talked about terror attacks in Washington D.C. IEDs. I skimmed over the next six pages of outline. The pages that followed held detailed descriptions of all the places they'd visited and the security. Turning another page, I found a name and phone number. The phone number was a DC one. The name a codename. Not many people are called X in real life. I picked up my phone and called the number: State Department.

"Oh, crap," I muttered hanging up. Seconds later I called Iain Campbell.

"Hey, I just made a call to a number at the State Department. You might want to check it out. This person's number was in a notebook belonging to one of the women from the Navy Yard surveillance job."

"Do you know who she called?"

"Yeah, a guy calling himself X, turns out his real name is on his phone. David Krauss."

"I'll have a chat with him."

"Thanks."

I hung up and delved back to the notebook. By the time I ran out of pages to read, my head spun.

"Share, Conway," Kurt said, frowning at me.

"There a lot of details here of possible scenarios and how her main character will or does react to them."

"She's a writer so that would be normal?" Sam said.

I shook my head and regretted it. "Every scenario is one I've been in recently. Her main character's name changes back and forth between my name and her character's."

Sam struggled to hide his smile. "She likes you, Chicky Babe."

"It's worse than that, Sam. She knew where the

explosives were placed. There are sketches showing the placement of explosives in the buildings that exploded, and as far as I know, they're correct."

"What are you saying?" Kurt said, leaning forward.

"She's a little bit too hands on with her research."

Kurt leaned back again. "Anything that actually says she planted the bombs?"

"No."

"Then we have nothing," Lee said.

"It's enough to hold her. We have reason to hold her on suspicion of terrorism," Sam said.

Yeah, it is. "Except she's Interpol and has a connection in our State Department, and could easily make this go away." I threw Lee the flash drive. "Have a look, if the notebook matches a manuscript and we've got dates, it might be more useful."

He plugged it into his laptop. Ten minutes later he'd copied then checked all the files.

"There is a file called IED, created three months ago. Last updated yesterday and looks to be the book based on the notebook."

"And?"

"It looks like she wrote the bulk of this manuscript before the explosions."

I sighed. "Any way of knowing what was written after?"

"No, she could've added stuff to any chapter at any time."

Fuck! Nothing then.

I growled. "Okay, moving on. Let's hope Iain finds something when he talks to the State Department guy."

"Next?" Lee said.

"Danni Lane is out of commission. She's no use to Kennedy's team." I wondered if she was ever any use. "I have a fancy wee program downloading all Kennedy's emails. Well, copies of them."

"Why?"

"Because I bugged him and we've seen him. They haven't talked or met with anyone else apart from Danni. They must have a way of communicating with their employer and possibly the people who have the girl. Or at least of getting information that could lead to the people who have the girl. You know Kennedy. Whoever that idiot is, they're not walking away from this."

"Good thinking, Chicky."

"Yeah. Think we all know information didn't come from Danni Loopy Lane."

Sam looked around the room.

"Where's Misha? I haven't seen him yet."

He was right there with us earlier. Jeez. Freaking phantom in a long black leather coat.

"Gone with the wind," I replied. "I imagine he's gone to fill Kennedy in on the situation with Danni." I looked at Kurt. "And you reckon she's a good author?"

"One of the best thriller writers I've read—"

"Maybe it takes a special kind of insanity to write thrillers?"

"Maybe," Kurt said. "We now know how she knew so

much about you. Interpol is a handy organization when you want to stalk someone."

The four of them barely contained their collective amusement.

"I still don't remember meeting her," I said.

"Sad. You made such an impression," Kurt said. "She started writing about her FBI agent a few years back. Before your poetry book came out."

"We must've met after that. She said a book signing. I didn't know about her so it wasn't hers." The penny dropped. "What do ya bet she was on the guest list for our launch? It was extensive. Wonder if we can check?"

"Simon might still have records," Mitch said.

"Does it matter?" Kurt asked.

"To me, yes," I replied. "I like to know where I met these lunatics."

Kurt's merriment bubbled over. "I think she invented her character then fine-tuned her to be more like you, once she'd met you and started stalking in earnest."

"Anyone else want to say stalking before we move on?"

Lee clamped his hand over his mouth and shook his head. Yeah, right. I saw Mitch shake with silent laughter.

"Moving on ..." Kurt said. "Questioned Documents pulled two sets of prints off the surveillance order. Yours and Mitch's."

"That's not even possible," I said with a sigh.

"Also they confirmed your signature was forged."

"Good. That's something."

Mitch spoke, "So our prints were on Ellie's clothes,

gun, etcetera and the paper. To what end?"

"We don't know yet," Kurt replied.

"Discounting everything to do with Danni." I hated saying her name. "Someone has gone to a lot of trouble and effort to accomplish what?"

"The destruction of Delta A," Mitch said.

"That's what it looks like," Sam agreed.

"Is this related to the missing Czech?" Lee asked. "Or overlapping by coincidence?"

"Really? You're going to say the word coincidence around me?"

An eyebrow arched. "Could it be?"

"I dunno. See any flying pigs lately?"

From under the bed, I heard a weird noise. A muffled quack. Two little ducks popped out, shaking their feathers, water droplets flew around the room. A third duck followed. They lined up. Imagine that? Coincidence? The three ducks quacked.

"Okay I'll bite. Imagine for a minute that the ducks are right and it's a coincidence."

The room froze.

Kurt leaned forward. "What ducks?"

Crap.

"Did I say ducks? Slip of the tongue." I smiled. "No ducks."

They quacked again. Dammit someone was going to hear them if they kept up that racket. Ducks shuffled all over the floor, dodging legs and quacking. Three were in a line. Just three. I took a stab at which three they were.

"With the women, Danni, and Troy in custody, we've narrowed the playing field," I said. The three ducks quacked with joy.

"Yes, we have," Kurt agreed. "Time to concentrate our efforts and find Anastazia."

"That's our brief," I replied. "Well, our brief is not the explosions, so let's take Anastazia."

I leaned forward and ran my finger over the touchpad of my laptop, clearing the screensaver.

My sneaky little program was hard at work downloading copies of all Kennedy's emails. It's just not that hard deploying viruses onto specific laptops and phones. Kennedy checked his email on his phone. I loved him for that. My toys of choice lately have been programs to do my bidding, disguised as updates for various apps. My computer beeped. The latest email was ready for me to read.

I started with the most recent, working backward. The first four I came to were spam. The fifth contained a link but no information. I followed the link and discovered what appeared to be a live streaming video.

My hand reached out and beckoned the team. My eyes never left the screen.

"Who else has a laptop?"

"Me and Lee," Kurt said, picking his up from the floor.

"Sending you both this link."

"Lee, can you run a ping and trace on a website?"

"Sure, link me, Chicky." An instant messenger window opened on my screen with Lee's name at the top of it. I dropped the link into it. Kurt followed suit.

As I watched the images on my screen, a woman struggled with a much larger man. He succeeded in handcuffing one of her wrists to an upright metal frame. She kicked out. He caught her ankle and cuffed it to the bottom corner. Screaming, she thrashed around. I could see the metal handcuffs biting into her. She smacked him with her free elbow, connecting with his jaw. He yelped and stepped back. His hand reached for a dark object. Her body jerked and head dropped. Guess he'd zapped her with a stun gun. He used the opportunity to secure her free hand and foot. Now splayed on the metal frame and at his mercy, he laughed. A printer sitting on a nearby desk spewed forth a piece of paper. He picked it up and read it. As the woman regained consciousness he said, "Knife."

He took a small knife from a drawer and ran the tip of the blade up the woman's exposed thigh. She sobbed as he traced the blade around the leg of her panties and began cutting the side seam in tiny increments.

I minimized the screen. "Jesus, Lee. This is real time. We need an address."

Mitch breathed out long and slow behind me. "Don't look. You can't ever unsee this, so don't look," I whispered.

I felt him turn away. Sam handed him an iPad and in-ear phones. "Watch something on this, turn up the volume. Trust me, Ellie's right. You don't want to carry this shit."

"Thanks," Mitch said. I felt him put in the earbuds and thought, Bye, Mitch. His voice echoed in my head then was gone. I closed the figurative door.

Lee spoke, "I'm trying for an address. Can you see anything in the picture that gives us any clues?"

I pulled the screen back up, not looking at the woman or the man, but instead searching for something identifiable. A window. I snapped a screenshot and zoomed in on the window and discovered a green lawn and high stone fence. Nothing remarkable. My hopes of a street sign and house number disintegrated. From my speakers, I heard screams. I flicked back to the room.

The camera angle had changed. The knife moved across her belly leaving small bleeding cuts. The woman's expression changed from terror to defiance. She had some inner strength she tapped into. I hoped she could hang on until we found her.

"It's not a stationary camera, it moved."

"Great, some other pervert is in the room."

"Oh, for a glimpse in a window." The idea hit like Christmas. I flicked back to my picture and zoomed out.

"Here, do something techy and show me the camera man in the windowpane."

Lee took my laptop. He took another screen shot then twiddled with things within a program I never knew I had, bringing up a faded image of a male holding a camera. Oh, the joy of living in a digital age. He held the camera at chest height. We could see his ghostly face.

"Can you make that any clearer?"

"No, but I know someone who can."

"Yeah, I used to as well. Bit hard to contact him these days."

Lee clapped a large paw on my shoulder. "It really is but Sean is as good, maybe better than Mac was at this stuff."

He dropped the pictures onto a flash drive.

"While the ping is running, I'll see what I can do with this." He stuck the drive in his pocket.

"I'll be semi-watching this asshole and see if I can snap some more pics of the girl, and the men."

"How much other email is there?" Lee asked from the doorway.

"I kinda stopped looking when I found this."

"This is something I almost don't want to ask, how'd you get his email address and get that app installed?"

"A little program Sean once gave me. I just sent it to Kennedy's cell phone. It sends copies of every email at a specified email address to one of my anonymous accounts." I saw the amused look on Lee's face. "I'm becoming a geek, huh?"

Lee smiled and left. There was nothing to say. Back on my screen, the girl's head lolled about as the man slapped her then tossed water in her face.

He held a piece of paper in his hand. He read it and said, "Not yet, be patient."

He slapped her again. I felt sick. The urge to shoot the screen grew exponentially with each slap.

I got as many good pictures of her face as I could

before the swelling disfigured her too much. Her bone structure and eyes looked familiar. As I studied the pictures carefully, a horrendous scream ripped through my speakers. My little finger hit the mute button on my keyboard. I pulled the video screen back up to view the live feed. The man was working something into her vagina. I couldn't make out what it was in his hand. On one breath, I minimized the screen and unclipped my gun from my holster; it just felt better to have it on my lap.

"Kurt, is it her?"

He checked photos on his phone. He nodded. "Could be. If not, it's someone similar."

My left hand snatched up my phone from the floor while my right toyed with the grip of my pistol.

I called Kennedy.

"Kennedy, did you get your email?"

He replied calmly, "What business is it of yours?"

"You didn't strike me as the torture or snuff type. We need to talk now."

"You are?"

Your worst fuc'n nightmare if I find you are involved in this.

"You know who I am. We don't have time for games."

"Do I?" he replied coldly.

"Listen up, Kennedy, you need me. Your place or my temporary hotel home?"

I heard the email alert telling me Kennedy had more mail when I opened the screen I discovered a coded email. I'd seen the code before. Troy had an email just like it. Ah, crap! He was involved somehow. A participant? I ignored Kennedy on the phone for a moment.

"Sam, what do you think this is?" I spun my laptop to face him.

"A list of prices," he said. "Down the side is probably a list of things the various amounts buy."

I felt sick. It was a long list. "Can you have a go at cracking this code, please?"

"Sure, send it to Lee's laptop. I'll work on that."

Another email arrived. It was a follow-up email regarding bidding. It wasn't a fixed price thing. That suggested the girl would be alive for a while yet; they'd want to get as much money as possible.

Kennedy had a sudden change of heart and even remembered my name. I guessed he read the email too. "Conway, whoever is sending these could be watching me."

I didn't want to tell him I hadn't picked up any other surveillance – didn't want to spoil the surprise of my operation. Even so, I didn't want him at the hotel. We needed middle ground. Ruby Tuesday's would work.

"Meet at Ruby Tuesday's in D.C. A-sap. I'll make the booking now. Ask for the Iverson party." I used Mitch's name because it was not connected to anything we'd ever done.

"I'll be there."

My next call was to the restaurant reserving Mac's

favorite table in the far corner facing the door. Just like old times.

But unlike old times I wouldn't be spending an hour in the nearby Bed, Bath & Beyond store first. Sometimes I hated the way everything twisted to remind me of Mac. The memory faded. New memories surfaced. Happy life-affirming memories.

In my mind's eye, I saw me and Mitch going out for coffee, which inevitably led to wine. He loved going out even for something as simple as coffee. Hence, we didn't spend a lot of time at home, which suited me.

Another email alert sounded. Notification of other bids.

"You've got mail, Chicky Babe," Sam said. The chime sounded again. "That code wasn't too hard once I got into it."

"Thanks, Sam."

I sent the email from Sam to my phone. He was right. It was a price list. It would take a lot of cash to keep her alive until we found her. Quarter of million dollars gave a bidder the right to choose her manner of death. Before that, varying increments of cash were required to bid on various forms of torture. Each and every option made me want to vomit. I called Caine.

"What have you got?" he asked without bothering with pleasantries.

"A streaming video of a young woman being tortured. I need authorization to bid to try to keep her alive while we find her."

"Who is she?"

"Wait one ..." I looked at Kurt. He glanced up. "Is it her, for sure?" I asked.

"Yes."

"Anastazia Dobrovolný. We believe she was abducted along with her sister Alexandra from Prague."

"Do what you have to do."

"I may have to bid over a quarter of a million."

"Don't lose that money ... if you bid it, you better be sure of catching the freaks responsible and getting the money back."

"I'll do my best."

Caine grumbled and the line went dead.

Kurt was watching me. "Okay?"

"Yeah. He doesn't want me to lose the money."

"Hard ask."

I smiled. "Nah. This is why they pay us the big money."

Sam and Kurt laughed. "You're a smartass, Conway."

With a painful shrug and half a smile, I said, "Time we put in for a substantial pay rise."

I closed the link on my laptop. I had somewhere to be.

Time for a quick call to Lee. "We're running out of time, the final decision on this girl's life rests with the highest bidder." I checked my watch with the computer clock. They were the same. "I want to make sure *we* are the highest bidder."

"I'm working on it, Chicky. How's the ping?" Lee replied.

A look at his laptop told me it was running, routing all

415

over the world and giving us nothing. "Nothing much going on, we're not getting any closer."

We needed more powerful software or a specialist who could get the most out of ours.

"Not good. I'll be back soon, hopefully with something we can use."

"I'm meeting the United Nations at Ruby's. Call me as soon as you have something."

"Message understood."

I set the timer on my phone at eighty-two minutes and made sure it was visible on the lock screen.

I looked at Kurt and pointed. "We have eighty-two minutes to stop a death. You're with me. Sam and Mitch stay here."

Mitch glanced up as I stood and moved past his legs. His hand touched mine. "All right?"

I pointed to the earbuds he was wearing. He took one out. "Kurt and I are going to meet some people. Sam is staying with you and working on something here."

Kurt stopped me before I got to the door. From his medical backpack, he took another pulse oximeter.

"Again?" I asked.

"Humor me. Don't lose this one, they're not cheap."

"I didn't lose it. I took it off ... and never picked it back up."

"Don't do that either."

Kurt and I left to meet the UN team. On our way down the stairs, I called Sean O'Hare.

"It's me. I need you to do everything you can to help

Lee and also, set us up so we can bid on the girl?"

"Lee's right here with me. I'll set it up. We're working as fast as we can."

"Can you send me a tech to monitor what's happening here while we go meet some mutual friends?"

"Sure, where do you want him?"

"Lee's room at the Marriott. He'll give you the details. Sam and Mitch are there. We need to find that address before the girl dies." There was a chance we wouldn't be the highest bidders.

"I'll get someone to you – you there?"

"No, Kurt and I are meeting someone else to see if we can keep this woman alive. I'll need Lee back A-sap."

I hung up, checked the timer, noted it said seventy-five minutes and shoved my phone into my bag.

When I turned the corner, I spotted my favorite stalker, lurking by a newspaper stand. Kurt grabbed my arm. "How?"

"I have no idea!"

I made a call Caine.

"We placed Danni Lane under arrest, she was sent to hospital with a uniformed agent. I'm looking at her on the freaking corner not far from our damn hotel."

"I'll look into it."

"I got a feeling we'll find another rescinded order with my signature on it."

"I'll find out."

He hung up. Danni's arm was in a sling; I felt no satisfaction in knowing I'd caused her injury. I was surprised she was out of hospital so fast, especially considering her stupidity in swallowing pills.

She watched me but didn't move. Kurt was on his phone. He called the Delta B SSA and asked for backup. There was no time for her nonsense; I needed to meet the International Rescue Squad or quasi-UN; it depended how generous I was feeling as to what I called them. The whole International Rescue Squad thing reminded me of the *Thunderbirds*. It didn't please me to know I was heading into television shows that weren't even real people. Walking briskly, we were soon out of her sight, then we took short cuts through stores and alleys, making following us, even from a distance, very difficult.

Inside Ruby Tuesday's, I asked for Mr. Iverson's table. The girl on the desk smiled and said it was ready.

"Will Mr. Iverson be joining you?" she asked pleasantly.

"Not today," I replied. "I am expecting company though."

The United fucking Nations.

I sat in the corner facing the door, ordered a long black, Kurt sat next to me.

My guests were prompt. Kennedy approached the table and with a nod, he slid into the seat directly opposite me. My fellow countryman, Timothy Jones sat next to Kurt, who was beside me and the British man, Colin Holmes, opposite him.

"Supervisory Special Agent Conway?"

"Lieutenant Colonel Kennedy."

He gave a small smile and said, "Kennedy will do fine."

I checked my watch which I now wore on my right wrist. Bit of a false start as my eyes glanced at the pulse oximeter first.

"Unusual jewelry," Kennedy commented pointing at the oximeter. "Should you be in hospital?"

"No, I'm good. Henderson is a doctor, remember?"

"I do," he replied nodding at Kurt.

"Let's get to it," I said.

"That'd be a fine idea, wouldn't it now."

"We now have sixty-five minutes before the bidding closes," I said. "If I'm right."

The other two waited.

"Sounds about right to me," Kennedy said. "What do you think, boys?"

Holmes and Jones nodded.

"Good to know."

"Conway, I don't think that video link is a live feed. I suspect that it's pre-recorded and running on a loop," Kennedy said. He showed me the video running on his phone.

I recognized the sequence of events and looked away before the scream. He fiddled with the packets of sugar in a bowl on the table. Flicking them over, then standing them up again.

My stomach churned. I wanted to find her.

"Is she alive?"

"The bidding would indicate so, although its upfront payment could be a scam. Even if they get half – that's more than they had to start with."

Everyone nodded.

"Do you know where the place is?" I asked.

"Not yet," Kennedy replied. "Danni Lane was supposed to be working with us, but her information was rubbish."

"Yeah," I replied but didn't elaborate. What was the point? "So far we know there were two men. We have a clear picture of the camera man." I slid my finger across my phone and showed him the picture. "Recognize him?"

"Not at all." He handed the phone to the other men. No one knew him. "And the other man, the one who was handy with his fists?"

I produced a second picture. Again, no one recognized him.

"He's considerably older than the camera man, is he not?" Kennedy asked.

"Also there is some resemblance. I'm thinking father and son," I said, pushing the photographs together on my screen and showing him again.

When the waitress approached, I dropped my phone into my lap. They all ordered drinks, all coffee and all NATO. White with two sugars. It amused me that my little UN gathering ordered NATO coffee. Curbing my sense of humor by the time coffee arrived was easy: there was a young woman being tortured to order somewhere, and we needed to find her. The curling twisting cold daggers in my gut made it impossible for me to see past the situation in front of me.

"Kurt is sure she is Anastazia," I said. "We have

Alexandra in a safe place. What I want to know is why these young women were taken."

"Alexandra. The older daughter of Eduard Dobrovolný," Kennedy replied.

"I know that much," I whispered into my cup. "What is it that makes these two such high-value targets?"

Kennedy leaned onto his elbows and regarded me. "Eduard and Alena Dobrovolný are physicists. Eduard is a medical physicist and Alena is a condensed matter physicist. Their research in the field of nanotechnology is the best in the world."

"Alexandra told me the mother is a teacher and the father works for the government in Prague."

He smiled. "She's not wrong. She may not know the whole truth. The mother does teach at University level and the father does work for the government."

"So this is about some kind of nanotechnology?"

"Yes. And before you ask, we didn't need to know. We just need to get the girls back."

Okay. I can see that.

"I have the best tech guy imaginable trying to negotiate the many proxy servers and narrow down the original location of that video feed. Tracking a source in that mess is like trying to find a needle in a haystack." My fingers crossed and I hoped like hell we did have a tech wizard working on the trace.

Holmes spoke, "Why is the video looping? I haven't seen the emails."

I pulled up a copy of the email on my phone and gave

it to him. His face blanched a deeper shade of cream as he read the list of auction instructions and what the money would buy.

"Oh my God." He gave the phone to Tim Jones. "You seen this?"

I watched his tanned face bleach to a yellowish green.

"Kennedy, you didn't show us this. I have been operating on the assumption she's dead."

Kennedy's face broke into a wry grin. "You know never to assume."

I smiled. Oh yeah, I sure did.

"All I know for sure is I have her sister," I told them. "But without a location on Anastazia, anything's possible." I looked at Kennedy. "You need to start talking. How did this scumbag happen to get your email address and include you in this bidding war?"

"That won't help you find the girl," he murmured. "Lucky man that I am, I cannot say."

"You can, and will. If you want the help I can provide."

He smiled widely. "I joined a mailing list a few days ago. You've read my email. You must've seen the confirmation from the lists."

"Luckily for me, I've only just downloaded your email – I haven't yet traveled back. I started with today. Tell me about the list." I'm not sure if that was lucky or not.

"It offers young girls to the highest bidder and provides kinky voyeuristic streaming, live porn and S & M."

"Which begs the question why?"

"Because the world has a lot of sick perverts in it and what better way to get a father to cough up a few million or some trade secrets?"

That sounded plausible. They weren't just here for the girls; if they found the place where Anastazia was being held it would be war. Can't say I'd be upset about these three letting loose on some evil bastards.

"Let's get bidding. We need to try to find a way to get to her, not just to send her to her death."

Kennedy pulled a laptop from the satchel he carried diagonally over his shoulders. I called Lee.

"I need to know how close we are," I said.

"We are real close." I heard him walking and a door shut. "NSA? You got some crack cyber guy from NSA to track this sick bastard. How the hell did you do that?"

"Oh, that's where he's from, groovy. I just asked O'Hare for the best." Imagine that. I got it.

"He's fuc'n awesome. He's through several of the proxies and honing in on the source now."

Magic is real and unicorns poop rainbows.

"We're bidding. As soon as you get a location – send SWAT. Don't fuck around. There's no guarantee we'll win. And find Praskovya A-sap, he's not here with the UN."

"Will do, Ellie."

I hung up and saw all eyes were on me. I smiled sweetly.

"Yes?" I used my very best, can-I-help-you voice.

"UN?" Jones queried.

"You seen yourselves? And by the way, where the hell is Praskovya?"

Tim Jones smiled. "I don't know where Misha is."

Holmes piped up, "O'Hare. I know that name?"

Kennedy spoke but his eyes never left his email. "We met Sean O'Hare the first time we met Conway and Henderson."

"Ah, that's right." I could see it falling into place for him. "Sean O'Hare is related to your Director.   I remember now."

A small smile crossed Tim Jones' full lips. "I never made the connection last time, Conway. But a Special Agent Conway was in MTAC during the final phase of Operation Hoboken. That would be you?"

"Indeed that would."

He said nothing else. We watched in silence as Kennedy placed another bid.

"How well bankrolled are you?" I asked him.

"I can cover this."

"Okay. Let me know if it goes too high. I can cover the rest." I crossed my fingers. I hoped we could cover it.

Two others were bidding. Or that's what the emails told us. I checked my watch. Time ticked on. Willing the NSA guy and his magic fingers to hurry up wasn't working as well as I wished. Crazy excerpts of songs peppered my mind. TV shows mingled with the songs. Everything had become a *Without a Trace* episode, complete with a pretty convincing Jack Malone lookalike in the form of Colin Holmes. Quiet delight enveloped me, he did look like Jack Malone. Something about gruff, well-meaning older men made me feel all warm and fuzzy inside. Thoughts whipped around like a mini tornado. I needed to get this young woman before it became a *Cold Case*. I needed to stop the craziness. Blonde I may be but my name is not Lily.

My phone rang just as Kennedy bid two-hundred-thousand dollars.

"Yep, Lee."

"I've dispatched SWAT to a property in Clifton, Virginia."

All eyes were on me again. I nodded at them.

"Pick me and Kurt up."

"And your guests?"

"I'm expecting them to tag along. So, I guess I'm bringing the United Nations with me. Did you find Misha? I want him with us."

"Misha is here." That brought a smile to my face. Where else would he be? The sheep are all back in the fold.

"Bring him. Sam stays with Mitch. Can you ask the NSA guy to hang around in case we need him, the more information he can get the better?"

"Done."

I hung up. "You guys got a car handy?"

Jones spoke, "Yes."

"Kennedy, do you need to be in our car, and feed off our satellite internet?"

"That'd be a fine idea."

Chapter Forty-four.

Divine Wings of Tragedy

Fifteen minutes later a car tooted outside. I dropped a bunch of bills on the table and headed for the door with Kurt and Kennedy and his laptop in hot pursuit. Misha opened the door as we got to it.

The men acknowledged each other with nods as we hurried to Lee's Explorer.

"Kurt, take the front, I'll sit with Kennedy," I said. Opening the driver's side passenger door and angling into the car, I avoided touching the headrest and sat twisted to half lean on the door and face Kennedy. As we peeled away from the curb, I saw Misha and the other two run up the street toward a parked dark blue Subaru Outback. One of the men pressed a remote control on the keys in his hand, the lights flashed as the alarm deactivated.

Kennedy settled himself in the back. I handed him a piece of paper with a code on it.

"That'll let you hook into our satellite feed. You should be able to check your mail. The plus side being, if they're running ping and trace software – we've just eluded them. With a bit of luck they'll think you're still sitting in Ruby Tuesday's in the District."

He made another bid.

"How long before we're there?" he asked. "This is getting very high."

"Forty-five minutes or less, SWAT will be there within twenty minutes." Lee replied, putting his foot down. "Buckle up, we gotta get out of the city."

The grill lights flashed on the wet road surface ahead of us. Our siren wailed. Lee hit the bridge like a battering ram. Cars pulled over as fast as they could. We clipped one with the front edge of our bull bars. The jolt hurt. My breath caught in my throat. In the wing mirror, I saw the car spin and stop, facing the wrong way.

We weren't stopping for anything.

The stunt driving didn't do wonders for my already battered body. I felt like a rag doll by the time we hit the smooth highway.

"Can you do anything to slow the bidding?" I asked Kennedy.

"I'll do my best."

"Maybe a few questions between bids. Get some dialog flowing?"

My watch seemed to burn into the skin on my wrist. I willed SWAT to get to the woman.

The GPS system was going berserk on the dash. I watched Kurt's hand re-entering our destination as the unit rapidly fired out changes to the route. Then it flashed up with heavy traffic delays.

"This is not a good time to be stuck in traffic." Kurt grabbed the radio sitting on the dash and pressed the talk button. "Supervisory Special Agent Henderson requesting assistance." He let the button go. Seconds later crackling offers of help came back.

"Our location is southbound highway I-66 west heading for Lonesome Dove Lane, out of Clifton, VA. We need a path A-sap, no obstructions."

"Henderson – Fairfax County police here. That's at least an hour and a half trip, we have some massive road works going on today with hefty delays, and how much time do you have?"

"We need to be there yesterday."

Another voice broke in.

"Agent, I'm Commander Frederick. Our helicopter is standing by. Tell us where to meet you."

"Thank you, Commander, I appreciate it. Can you have the chopper meet us at the I-66 Braddock Road exit?"

"We'll be waiting, sir."

"There is another car following us."

"I'll send cars to provide an escort. We can take them around the worst areas as fast as we can."

"Thank you very much."

"You're always welcome, Agent Henderson. I take it Agent Conway is with you."

"Yes, sir, she is."

"Always happy to help Delta A." He hung up.

Lee grinned but never took his eyes off the road. "Those Virginian cops are fuc'n excellent."

Agreed. They've helped us out before, often.

Kennedy grinned at me. "You have everyone falling all over to help you. I think I want to know more about you and Delta A, Ms. Conway."

Seemed best to ignore his comment. What's to know?

I called Misha in the car following us and let him know to keep on us and that police would provide an escort from Braddock Road and get them around any road disruptions.

Lee pulled over on the edge of a large barren piece of land to the left of the turn to Braddock Road from I-66, where a helicopter waited, rotors turning.

A police officer leaped out and ran to meet us. Shouting to be heard he said, "I'll drive your car. Where to?"

"Lonesome Dove Lane, Clifton," I replied. Lee dropped the keys into his hand.

We clambered aboard the helicopter, a wave of cold dread smashing into me as I pulled the harness on. Even though I couldn't remember the crash, I didn't want to be in a helicopter again so soon. Another police car pulled up behind our car. Misha's car followed. I waved. Misha waved back.

"You okay, Ellie?" Kurt asked. He sat next to me. His hand took mine.

"Not sure."

"Breathe. You see how many cops are out there? No one is going to shoot at us," he replied, he gave my hand a light squeeze then let go.

Lee gave the pilot directions and we lifted off easily, turning slowly. I checked my weapon twice during the short flight. Seamus announced the bidding was about to close. His Irish brogue made the bad news sound like a stroll in a leafy park. I resisted the urge to ask him to say 'third'. The stern voice in my head cautioned me – this was no time for games. A life hung in the balance.

The pilot spoke, "I'll set down in thirty seconds. SWAT have cordoned off the road. They asked for no air traffic. A marked car will take you the last mile."

"Thank you," I replied, everything sounded muffled and hollow through the headsets we wore. "We truly appreciate the support."

"Aye, that we do," Seamus chimed. Then to me he said, "We're leading the bid."

The helicopter set down in the middle of a road between two State police cars.

"Throw as much as you can in the last bid and let's hope we win. We gotta go."

Seamus pushed the bid higher and closed the laptop.

We hauled our asses from the helicopter, dropping the headsets on the seats. A police officer waved us over. Moments later the four of us climbed out of a police car beside a mobile SWAT command post. Lee, Kurt and I introduced ourselves to the Special Agent from Manassas who was in charge of the SWAT team.

"Conway, do you want to go in with SWAT?" he asked in an unemotional tone, as if asking if I wanted sugar with my coffee.

Lee and Kurt shook their heads. I smiled to myself.

I replied to the agent, "Thanks for the offer, Agent Drummond, I'll pass."

He nodded sagely and gave the 'go' order. I watched as

men clad in green combat gear scaled the high walls. Others forced the large iron gates. The gates swung open. Men hurried through, disappearing into the shrubbery and other cover as they made their way to the house. It was tense. My breath came in shallow bursts, mimicking what it would be like being inside the walls with them. I checked the monitor on my wrist. Oxygen levels, ninety-nine per cent, heart rate climbing. Kurt appeared at my elbow; he took my left wrist and checked the display.

"I just did that," I said.

"And now I'm doing it. You're doing well," he said with a small smile. "Bit of adrenaline in your system?"

"Little bit."

"Me too."

Gunfire erupted, sounding some distance away.

Two agents reported several large freestanding structures on the property. Stables or barns. Another squad moved in to secure and search outer buildings. Anxious minutes ticked by in silence.

Seamus leaned back on a car door and watched the driveway with interest. Lee spoke quietly with the lead agent from Manassas field office. I looked around, feeling as though something was missing. A yellow duck waddled out from under a police cruiser and quacked.

My phone rang and Misha's name lit up the display. "Is she there?" he said. His voice sounded strained.

"No word yet. SWAT are inside."

"Not you?"

"No."

"Good."

I had a sudden urge to draw my gun and charge headlong into the fray. To prove I could.

Two men in green walked a male toward us.

Lee snarled, "Looks like junior ... where's the old man?"

He and Kurt strode forward to meet them, with me almost running to keep up.

"The woman?" I asked, ignoring junior's smarmy grin.

"Ma'am, there are three women in various conditions. Still searching the buildings."

One of the agents looked directly at me. "Ma'am, you can go in. We're sending in the paramedics. Walk toward the main house and the front door."

An ambulance crept up behind us. We stepped aside. The agents dragged junior to the nearest police car. Lee and I hurried up the driveway. I beckoned Seamus to come with us. The last thing I wanted was him killing junior while we were gone. No doubt, he could make it look like an accident and no one would be any the wiser, but I wanted junior alive, for now.

I called over my shoulder to the escorting agents. "See if you can persuade him to tell you where the old man went."

Someone had answered the emails up until ten minutes ago, dealing with the business end. I doubted it was the junior cameraman. Something about his smile suggested he was one sandwich short of a picnic.

Good thing there was a family business for him to

inherit.

Sam called. "Your NSA guy here found more email and links. He also found what looks like homework assignments. There could be a kid somewhere. NSA thinks the perpetrator or pervert if you like, has a kid, a girl by the tone of the email and the name that keeps showing up. Lily-Ann."

"How old?"

"Guessing about fourteen."

"Okay, thanks."

Great a kid. I told Lee, Kurt and Seamus as we reached the front door. Lee scowled. Seamus squared his jaw. Kurt shook his head.

"How old, Conway?"

"Fourteen."

"Stick close to me," he said.

"You think the kid is related to the old guy? Or some poor unfortunate he kidnapped earlier?" Lee asked.

"We won't know until we find her," I replied. But I suspected she was his daughter, this is a family business. Daughter was probably being pimped over the internet from toddlerhood. This family was taking dysfunctional to the max. It was fast turning into one of those days that made me hate my job.

An agent carrying a rifle greeted us and pointed the way.

"The porn business is lucrative, I see," I commented. The interior of the home was expensively and very tastefully decorated and furnished. Like a country estate of the rich and famous. I got the feeling the owner hired an interior decorator.

Lee agreed the house was like something from *House and Garden* magazine rather than a family home or torture chamber. Paramedics followed us closely. Not knowing where the older man was, made me jumpy. My hand rested on the butt of my gun. Security.

I noted bullet holes in a wall ahead of us and pointed them out.

An agent replied, "Junior tried to shoot his way out."

He wasn't wounded, lucky him. I raised an eyebrow. The agent smiled. "He emptied his revolver, then Lenny tackled him from behind."

I was right, not a smart boy.

Another armed battledressed agent stood guard by an open door. Our accompanying agent said, "The first victim is in here."

I entered the room. A blonde girl lay on a bed, wearing short shorts and a tank top. She looked at me. Her face was a mess, one eye swollen shut and covered in a deep blue bruise. Dried blood around her mouth. Bruises and cuts tracked up her arms. I noted ligature marks around her neck, wrists, and ankles. It wasn't Anastazia.

"I'm Agent Conway. These two people here are paramedics. You're safe."

A tear trickled down her face.

The paramedics sprang into action. Leaving the guard on the door, we moved on. In the next room sat another woman, her body battered and swollen. She wore only underpants and a small tee shirt. Again, I introduced myself.

She said nothing but looked away. We left the next two paramedics with her.

I took a deep breath.

"You okay?" Kurt asked, checking the oximeter. "No, you're not. Deep breaths, Conway."

I breathed. Ninety-seven became ninety-eight. My heart rate dropped. A few more deep breaths and Kurt said we could carry on.

Around the corner and down a longer hallway, past more expensive paintings and vases on antique tables we found another guard. I stepped into the room and there she was. Naked. Beaten. Tragic.

"Anastazia?"

Surprise registered on her face. She nodded. Tears cascaded over purple and blue bruises and dried bloody cuts. I pulled off my jacket and wrapped it around her. She gripped my hand tightly.

"I am Special Agent Ellie Conway. Before we say anything else, your sister is safe."

The young woman sobbed, she pulled on my hand to stand up. I caught her as she propelled herself forward. "Wait," I said as she tried to walk. Lee pulled a thermal blanket from a paramedic's bag, ripped the package open and wrapped the silver sheet around her beaten body. Kurt ushered everyone from the room. I tried to stay but he told Lee take me out.

"Kurt?" I asked.

"I saw a string," he replied. "Go."

"What?" I wasn't sure I heard him correctly.

"Conway, there's a *string*. Get out of here."

Kennedy slung his arm around my shoulder and marched me out of the room. "Come with me."

Kurt's voice followed me, "Breathe, Conway, I can't be in two places at once."

Kennedy walked me about six feet back down the hall.

"What about the other girls?" I said.

"Oh, God," Lee muttered. "How do the tampons explode?"

"Pulling the string," I replied.

He ran back where we had come from.

Kennedy stood in front of me. "You okay?"

"Yes." I took several deep breaths and leaned a shoulder on the wall. I heard Lee running back toward us.

"You were right. I need Kurt," he said as he stopped in front of me.

Kurt opened the door and poked his head out. He looked right then left and saw us.

"All clear," he called.

"Good," Lee called back. "You've got two more to remove."

Kurt nodded. "Conway, you and Lee in here and look after Anastazia."

We walked back to the room. Kurt took his backpack and ran down the hallway. Kennedy stayed outside the door while we went in.

"We're going to take you out," I said to the messed-up

young woman sitting wrapped in the silver blanket on the edge of the bed. She struggled to her feet.

"Lee will carry you."

She tried to argue but didn't have the strength. My guess was it took everything she had to hang onto life to reach this point.

With a nod, he scooped her up into his massive arms.

Seamus pulled his cell phone and made a call. Twenty seconds later, he held the phone to her ear and said, "Your father."

We all pretended not to hear the conversation. The language was not familiar but the tone and the fear we knew well. I heard my name. Anastazia passed me the phone.

"Hello," I said, walking ahead so the conversation would not be overheard.

"Is she hurt?" he asked.

"Beaten as far as we know. We don't know the full extent of any injuries yet, sir."

"I am Eduard," he replied. "Thank you, Agent."

"I did my job."

"I am very grateful."

"Pleased we could help," I said. I'm a sucker for a happy ending.

"I will be in touch. May I speak with Seamus again?"

I handed Kennedy the phone. They spoke at length and were still speaking when Lee handed Anastazia over to the ambulance personnel. I moved to Misha, who waited with Holmes and Jones. "We have her."

"I know," he replied. "I saw."

"The old man and we think a younger teenage girl are missing," I said.

"It would be best if they were found," he replied.

"Yeah. I'm going back in to search. A picture of him and his kids would be helpful."

"Where do you want me?"

"With the girl. Keep the UN together. Alexandra and Anastazia will be reunited in the hospital. I don't have spare personnel, keep them safe?"

"*Da.*"

Chapter Forty-five.
Children of the Grave

I signaled Lee to accompany me. Together we went on a scavenger hunt. Both family photos and trophies were our objective. It felt a bit like we were contestants on *The Amazing Race*. I expected Phil Keoghan to be waiting in the next doorway and hand us an envelope or dismiss us outright for tardiness.

Our hunt netted plenty of family photos. In some, the incredibly dysfunctional family even looked happy.

The bedrooms held more treasures.

Daddy's little girl had a pretty Barbie pink room. Books filled a large pink bookcase, with more books piled on a matching nightstand. There were photos of her in a drawer. Each photo was of her and one other girl. Each photo contained a different girl. The backdrops appeared similar, if not the same. A park maybe. As I thumbed through the photographs, I came across Anastazia. There were thirty-seven different girls aged between twelve and eighteen or nineteen.

Lee called out from across the hallway. The father's room netted more photographs but only of his family. Framed photos sat dust free. I noted the en suite bathrooms were spotless. Beds were made.

I ducked back into the girl's room. A clean and tidy teenager's room? No glasses sitting half full of soda. No junk food wrappers. Even the waste paper bin was empty. Toilet paper folded to a point. I pulled a drawer open. Clothes meticulously folded sat in piles.

"Lee, there's no wife or mother?"

"Not that I've found."

"Then where's the housekeeper? She's someone we need to talk to."

"This place is kept like a show home."

I agreed. It truly was.

The daughter's room was like no teenagers room I'd ever seen. Where were the signs of life? The magazines strewn over the floor. Posters stuck to walls. Stickers on mirrors. Piles of unwashed clothing on the floors. The unmade bed. Dog-eared homework and required reading? No school bag or textbooks anywhere.

"Shouldn't there be signs of life in here," Lee said.

"Yeah, and a school bag and signs of school life."

I waved my arm around the walls. "No pennants, no corkboard filled with pictures of friends."

"Home schooled?" Lee offered.

"Maybe but even home-schooled kids have friends and school books."

"All right. It's weird."

I picked up one of the books from the nightstand. The spine creaked as I opened it.

"A book that's never been opened."

I pulled one from a bookcase and again, brand new and never been opened. Looking at the back I saw the bookstore label.

"We got something, Lee. Look at this." I handed him the book and pointed to the label. Then pulled out more books at random. They all had the same label. Danni Lane's name on the spine of three books turned my blood to jagged ice crystals. I stopped breathing and just stared. I don't believe in coincidence. I don't. Staring, but unable to reach my hand out and take one of the books. Lee's voice jolted through me.

"Hey!"

"What?" Startled, I spun around.

"What were you looking at?"

My hand rose and pointed. He hooked the books from the shelf.

"These?"

"Yep."

"What do we make of it? Bearing in mind neither of us are fond of coincidence."

"I don't know." From the corner of my eye, four little ducks wriggled out from under the bed and headed for the door. Each one quacked. Four ducks now. "She's part of this. She wasn't helping Kennedy and his men. She was playing both ends."

"Jeez. You sure?"

"Yep."

Any sane person would draw the same conclusion from four little yellow ducks.

"Let's make sure Delta B picked her up," Lee said making the call. Two minutes later he gave me a thumbs up.

441

Okay, good.

"Why buy so many books and not read them?" I asked.

"No idea. But I'll call Holly's store she might have something," Lee replied.

I listened to his side of the conversation.

"Holly, this is Special Agent Davenport. I have a few questions about a customer."

I tapped his arm and mouthed, "We need to go see her."

All the books came from Holly's bookstore. She would have the till receipts plus there was an added advantage; my sister-in-law slash best friend, Holly, made the best coffee ever.

I took the phone from Lee. "We're coming over, Holly, put the coffee on."

"Davenport, that was Lee, yes?"

"Yes."

"So formal."

"Big case. See you soon."

I handed his phone back.

"You ready for some decent coffee?" I asked.

"Are we done here?"

I walked to the door. "I think so. Manassas can handle the scene and keep searching for the father and daughter. We'll come back once we've spoken to Holly."

We hurried from the house. I had a suspicion there was another house, somewhere they lived and it wasn't here. This was the show home. The place where they produced the sick videos for the highest bidders and pretended to live. If there was another house, Holly might have the address.

While Lee found the officer who drove our car to get the keys, I considered the book titles I'd seen. They were all books I'd seen before. I'd seen them in other kid's bedrooms, and in bookstores. Teenagers liked them. Chances are this missing teenager liked them too and had copies she actually read. Seemed possible. This was an uncharacteristic case. A lot of deception carried out on a grand scale. Money spent to uphold an image. Yet no one really lived there. Seemed crazier than me.

That was plenty crazy.

The song I heard the loudest as we walked away was one I loved and couldn't fathom why I was hearing it now. 'Beneath Your Beautiful.'

Chapter Forty-six.

Eyes of a Stranger

I opened the door to Holly's bookstore. The old fashioned, probably antique, brass bell above the door rang gently. A simple and musical ding-a-ling. Lee followed me in, casting a deep shadow over me, and the books on the first display. I took a book-filled breath. Loving the smell of books can be a handicap and an expensive hobby.

Holly called out from the back room.

"Coffee is on, Ellie. Hi, Lee."

Lee replied first, "Yo, Holly, how goes it?"

We strode through the store. I tried not to look at the pretty books and shiny covers as I passed by. The temptation to stop and browse was enormous.

"It goes very well, Lee," Holly said as we entered the backroom which doubled as a kitchenette and storeroom. She placed steaming mugs of coffee on the square kitchen table. "Have a seat."

Holly hugged me briefly. I tried not to wince and slid into the nearest chair.

"What's that?" she asked pointing at my wrist.

"New jewelry from Kurt," I replied, trying to sound blasé about it.

She shook her head. "Aidan said you were badly hurt in the crash. When I got to the hospital, they weren't allowing visitors and then you'd gone."

"Aidan never came," I said, no accusation just fact. "We're here on business."

"Right, tell me what you need," Holly replied. She knew better than to try to defend my brother's actions. We'd work it out our way. I could still make him cry if I felt like it. A duck popped its head around the edge of the fridge, its beak bobbed up and down then it waddled away quacking.

"We found a customer of yours, and believe he might have two residences," I said. It was best to get right to it with Holly. My hand pulled my notebook from my jacket pocket. I opened it to the relevant page and handed it to her. "That's the address we were at ... the home of Keith, Keith Jnr and Lily-Ann Blackwell."

Holly gave it back. "I deliver to Keith senior, regularly. He orders books for his daughter and I deliver them to that address."

My blood thickened and seemed to slow in my veins. Holly was a regular at that house. I shuddered and winced. She caught the shudder.

"Give."

I shot her a look that said, not yet. "Did you deliver them anywhere else?"

"No. But ..." she hoisted herself from a chair and disappeared into her adjacent office, calling, "I'll be right back."

Lee sipped his coffee. He leaned back in the chair until it balanced on two legs. I frowned at him. "You'll fall."

He smiled. "I doubt it."

The temptation to tap one of the precariously balanced chair legs was hard to resist.

"It's all fun and games until someone loses an eye," I cautioned.

Laughter erupted. "I'm not going to lose an eye by tipping on a chair."

"They sound like famous last words."

Holly called out from the office. "Lee, do as you're told!"

He laughed. "Yes, mom."

Holly returned clutching several bank-card receipts.

"These might help." She handed them to me. "He always pays by credit card. I went through the receipts and he occasionally uses a different card, same name but MasterCard not Visa. And sometimes he picks up the books. I can't remember if the times he picks them up coincide with him using a different card though."

I looked over the receipts, different banks too.

"Thanks, Holly. I'll check the addresses the banks have on file."

"So what's all this about? He seems like a nice man and a devoted father."

I just bet he did. "What's the daughter like? Lily-Ann?"

"Yeah, that's right. She's bright, bubbly, always pleased to get new books."

"Does she read them all?"

"As far as I can tell, she sure talks about them when I bring new ones."

"Her favorite this year?"

"That would be anything at all by A.S. King."

"Did she talk about those books?"

"Yes, she did, in depth. Her favorite was *Dust of a Hundred Dogs*. She loved the main character and the whole pirate thing."

I remembered seeing that book in her room. It stood out with its black, white and red cover. I'd opened it and was pretty sure it had never been read.

"Did her father order multiple copies of any books?"

Lee had the receipts, studying them intently.

He and Holly spoke at the same time, "He did."

Lee continued, "Almost everything was bought twice but in separate transactions and using different cards."

"I thought he was buying them as gifts for a niece or Lily-Ann's friends. It seemed the sort of thing he'd do," Holly replied. "He didn't, did he?"

"We don't think so."

"What's he done?"

"Nothing good, Holly. Nothing good," Lee replied. "You don't want to ask that question again."

"Seriously? He seemed so nice."

Reports on the six o'clock news also tell of how quiet people were and what good neighbors they were when mass graves were discovered in suburban backyards. No one knows what goes on behind closed doors.

"What's that they say ... never judge a book by its cover?" I added. "Any idea where Lily-Ann likes to hang out?"

"None, sorry."

"Has she ever mentioned any school friends?"

"I don't think so." She thought about it for a minute. "She did once mention someone called Terry. I don't know if that's male or female or a school friend or what."

While Lee wrote everything down, I watched Holly looking for signs that she remembered anything else.

"How long ago did she mention this Terry person?" I asked. Terry sounded awful like Troy as it bounced through my head.

"Last week."

Damn, she was there that recently.

"When you go to the house, do you go inside?"

Holly nodded. "I usually stop in for a coffee."

My heart wanted to stop. It thumped slowly then faltered. I waited. It gave an almighty bang and resumed normal rhythm. I looked over at Lee. His head nodded ever so slightly. I knew he was about to take over the questions.

"How long do you stay?" he asked keeping his voice light as the situation allowed.

"About a half hour, sometimes three-quarters of an hour, it all depends how many deliveries I'm making and the order in which I do them. We often have a chat and a coffee. Lily-Ann gets her books. Then I leave."

"You ever seen anyone else there?"

"Just Lily-Ann and the son. They just call him Junior." Her eyes narrowed suspiciously. "What is this all about?"

"Remember earlier when I said you don't want to ask

that question?"

"Uh huh."

He moved to the next question. "Did you ever see any cars parked out front, ones you didn't recognize as belonging to the household?"

Holly faltered. I watched as she backed up her thoughts. "Yes, I did. On three occasions, I think it was three. Different cars were in the driveway. I never saw anyone else in the house though."

"You're doing great, Holly. It's never easy trying to remember things that didn't make an impression to start with," Lee said, reassuring her. "Let's think about noises." He paused a moment. "Noises, did you ever hear anything on the property or in the house that required some explanation?"

Holly frowned. "Like?"

"Like any noise that would seem out of place?" I intervened. "Just something you didn't expect to hear."

I watched her thinking. It was quite entertaining. Her lips moved. Her eyebrows knitted. She tapped her hand against her knee. Her foot tapped against the table leg. Tempted though I was to ask outright if she ever heard any females screaming, the words in my head reminded me not to lead the witness. Let her answer the questions she wants to, the way she wants to. I sat on my hands. To prevent myself reaching out and shaking her. Hurry up, dammit. How hard is it? Did anyone ever scream or not?

She stopped fidgeting. "There was this one time ..."

Before I could stop the association my mind jumped to

American Pie and finished Holly's sentence. "At band camp." I looked up to see Holly staring at me like I'd sprouted horns. "Oh, crap. I said that out loud, huh?"

She grinned. "We should watch *American Pie* again."

"No, we really shouldn't."

Lee coughed.

Holly rephrased her opening. "There was this one ... once ... while I was there, Lily-Ann wasn't around. I heard something that sounded like a terrified scream."

"His response?" Lee asked.

"He sent the son to check it out, saying it was probably a spider that scared Lily. She was apparently in her room. Was the first time she hadn't met me at the door."

"How long ago would you say that was?"

"Three weeks. Lily-Ann met me last time."

"Thanks, Holly," Lee said.

Holly smiled. She picked up the coffee pot from the counter top and refilled our cups. It was time to change the subject.

"What's Aidan up to?" Some chitchat about my brother, her husband, should be enough of a subject change. I could talk about his work without feeling like throttling him. Progress.

"He's spending less time on the road these days. It's been nice. More and more he's dealing with assessing insurance claims closer to home."

"Good."

"Are you still active on the Foundation forums?"

"Sporadic at best these days. I keep an eye on things

but haven't been posting a lot. Still getting tons of emails from the kids on there though." What I didn't say was, it gets filtered by my mail program and sent to my dad to handle. I don't answer their emails. Not since Carla.

"Aidan mentioned he hadn't seen you much lately." She smiled. "Before your crash. He mentioned he hadn't seen much of you." It was a knowing, almost cunning smile. "How's Mitch?"

And there it was. The reason for the smile.

"He's fine."

"Anything to report?"

"Nope, not a thing."

Lee stood up. Damn he was good. He tapped his phone. "We should get going, Ellie. Before traffic gets heavy."

"Absolutely."

A lucky escape executed before Holly could ask more Mitch questions.

Chapter Forty-seven.

Screaming for Vengeance

We stood on the street not far from rubble and remnants of chaos.

"Great, the whole gang's here," I said. The circle closed in. Last time we stood like that, all hell had broken loose and nothing was ever the same again. Sun warmed my back. The breeze chased long strands of hair across my face. I dragged a hair tie off my wrist and tied my hair back into a no-nonsense ponytail.

I looked around. This time there were more of us. This time I had an assortment of people that no one fucks with.

Breathe.

Words fell without checking. I took two virtual steps away from the chaos that enveloped me.

"Right, let's break this down. You listening?" I nudged Sam. His gaze was fixed over my head and at something on the street. I turned to see what was so captivating. What was left of NCIS had arrived. They stopped and didn't approach our huddle. I guessed they were waiting for word from the boss. That's when it occurred to me, the boss was me.

"Listening, Chicky Babe," Sam said.

I waved them over. "Introduce yourselves, please. Go left around the circle."

I waited for everyone to get acquainted.

"Take notes boys and girls, this is about to get messy." I shuffled all my ducks in a row. They quacked but obliged. "Danni Lane, our happy little author, stalker, Interpol agent, is working both ends. News to some of you, I'm sure. My cyber guy has been working his ass off and we have names, dates and places." I looked at Kennedy. "This next phase, you three are sitting it out. You have no jurisdiction here.

"From the search of the Blackwell residence we can now confirm that both Special Agent Justin Troy and Senator Robinson are linked to the trafficking and torture of thirty-five girls aged between twelve and nineteen."

Blackwell kept detailed ledgers. It hadn't taken long to unravel his code and work out who Juliet and Sierra were. Blackwell was a lot of things but he wasn't the sharpest pencil when it came to codes. "This case has tried the hell out of us. Failure is not an option. We will get these pricks."

No one said anything. Frowns greeted me as I glanced around the circle.

"None of this goes any further. Someone within the FBI has altered orders I've given. It's not Justin Troy, although he's probably passing information to this person." I paused again. "The second Blackwell residence netted a ton of evidence. Delta B are processing that now. We confirmed the kid with Blackwell is his daughter and she was used in about fifty porn photos and videos from the age of five. Well, we think she was five, going by the photos. Unfortunately, neither the child nor Keith Blackwell were at the residence. My feeling is that they are with the persons behind the trafficking and the whole set up. And that leads me to our mission this morning ..."

Jen from NCIS interrupted, "What happened to the Lane woman? Is she still an issue?"

"I shoulder shot her after she pulled a gun on me in my room ... long story ..."

Go me. Shoot the nut job.

I frowned then forced the frown away, smoothing my brow with my fingers. I do not need this craziness turning my face into a road map of wrinkles.

"So she's not an issue?" Jen asked, looking over my shoulder.

My heart sank. "She's behind me somewhere, isn't she?"

Jen nodded.

"I don't even care how she was turned loose again, can one of you do the honors, please?" And then added, "Not the UN."

Jen winked. "I got this." She stepped out of the circle and approached Danni. I turned and watched. Something niggled at my gut. Why was Danni here? What could she possibly achieve by lurking near our impromptu outdoor meeting?

We're all together. Ah, crap!

A little yellow duck quacked from the sidewalk by Danni's foot. As I glanced at the duck, I saw the dark shape in her hand. She moved her arm and I saw what I thought was a wire leading into her sleeve. I blinked. It wasn't a gun.

"Jen!" My voice rang out across the expanse of sidewalk and road between us. She half-turned. "Come back." Jen's hand rested on the SIG she wore on her hip.

I felt Sam and Lee tense next to me. Lee stepped back to cover Mitch as I moved forward, gun in hand.

"Don't do it!" I yelled at Danni.

She smiled and shook her head. I had one shot, no mistakes. Had to be clean and hit her before she triggered an explosion.

I aimed and fired and watched as the bullet tore through her forehead. Jen rushed to Danni, she grabbed the black object from her hand before she let it go. She dropped to the ground with the body holding the black object firmly.

"Dead man's switch," she called. "I got it."

There was a collective exhale of breath from around me. Lee got on the phone to the bomb squad.

"Don't move," Kennedy said, running toward her. His voice was muffled but I heard him say, "Let's have a look at the setup."

I tried to move but Kurt grabbed my arm.

"No."

"No?" I queried.

"Stay with us here. In fact, we're moving back to some cover."

Kennedy looked over and gave the same hand signal, three times. The instruction was cover. He followed it with a distance. Two hundred yards. Jeez.

Sam motioned to us then headed across the deserted road. He stopped beside a building. We followed. I made sure Lee and Mitch were in front of me. I didn't want to lose anyone. About three hundred yards down the road was a roadblock, so thankfully, no traffic could come our way.

I spoke to Kurt, "How many of the buildings around here are occupied now?"

"I don't know. We can't evacuate onto this street."

"I know, but we have to clear those buildings."

"Not you," he said. "You will stay here with Mitch." He turned to the rest of the group and started giving orders.

Nagging feelings of doom threatened to overpower me. I saw rubble. I saw smoke. I saw flames. My throat tightened. I couldn't breathe.

"No one moves," I said. "No one."

Mitch's hand touched the small of my back. "What's the matter?" he whispered in my ear. "New explosions?"

"Yes," I whispered back.

Everyone froze. Their eyes on me as I said, "We don't know where she was before she appeared on the street." No one moved or spoke. "There have been too many attempts on our lives. No one moves."

"Bomb squad are five minutes away," Lee said.

"We may not have five minutes. I'm going to Kennedy. No one moves." I can give direct orders when necessary. I shot a warning at Kurt. "No discussion."

Shaking off everything that wouldn't help me I stepped

out of the shade and walked to Kennedy and Jen.

"Can you disable the switch?" I said.

"Yes, or no, we won't know until Jen lets it go," Kennedy replied.

"You ready to run, Jen?" I asked and smiled.

"You bet."

Kennedy never took his eyes off what he was doing with the explosive device. A vest and several long thin blocks of Semtex.

"How much do you think?"

"Enough to bring down a building," Kennedy said. Beads of perspiration gathered on his forehead. He wiped the trickles away with impatience. "I don't know if this will work. Prayers wouldn't go amiss." His hand covered Jen's and the small black unit that contained the switch. "Ready, Jen?"

"Yep," Jen said. She took a deep breath.

"Stand slowly," he said, still crouched on the ground by the body. His hand traveled with hers as she stood. "I'm going to take this switch out of your hand. You and Conway are going to run. I'll be right behind you."

"You better be," I muttered, taking Jen's free hand. "We stay together."

"Okay by me," she said.

I took several deep breaths and reminded myself I run all the time, this is no different. Same ol' same ol'.

"On three," Kennedy said. "One ... two ... go."

Jen's hand was free. We ran. Heavy footsteps behind us told me Kennedy was coming too. As we hit the corner of the building, he slammed into us knocking us down, all the air forced from my lungs. Kennedy's arm was over my head. The ground shook. I turned my head under his arm and watched as concrete, wood, and rubble fell from the air, smashing down behind us. Smoke and dust billowed. Flowing over us, making the air thick and gritty as it fell.

"Holy crap," Jen murmured.

"Yeah," I said. "Kennedy?"

I pushed his arm off me and crawled away using the wall next to me to help me stand.

"Conway?" Kennedy said rolling over. "Jen?"

"We're good," Jen replied. "You hurt?"

"Don't think so," he replied.

From down the alleyway, we heard coughing. Kurt, Sam, Lee and Mitch appeared from the swirling dust. Holmes, Jones and Kathy followed.

"Everyone okay?" Kurt asked, his eyes darted from me to Kennedy to Jen.

I smiled. "Yeah, surprise!"

"Nine lives, Conway. I swear you're running out," Kurt replied with a smile. He took my wrist and checked the oximeter. "Some deep breaths would be helpful."

I took one. Pain shuddered through my rib cage. I took another and another. Pain just meant I was alive.

"How bad is that?" he asked.

"I can cope," I replied. I knew my voice sounded strained. Breathing or talking, seemed to be an either or situation while things evened out. "Emergency services." I took a breath. "Bomb squad. We need the dogs in what's left of those buildings."

"Less talking more breathing," Kurt replied.

I heard Sam and Lee on their phones relaying what I'd said.

Kurt took over. I leaned on the wall. Mitch leaned next to me. His fingers catching mine. No words.

I listened to Kurt and heard Caine's voice in my head reminding me I needed to delegate more. Made me smile.

Kurt separated everyone into teams. FBI and NCIS with the UN.

"What'd you say about the UN?" Holmes asked with a wry grin. "That's how you refer to us?"

Kurt smiled. "Yes. United Nations."

Kennedy laughed. His laugh was warm, lilting and in different circumstances, I bet it was infectious. "United Nations. That's an apt description of the four of us rapscallions."

I turned my head toward Kennedy. "Why didn't you just tell me you were all back together and here for a reason?" Really? We could've been working together from the beginning. "Why didn't you all come to me? We've been here before, yes?"

Kurt leaned closer. "Less talk more breathing."

Kennedy grinned. "Conway, you were injured. With what was going on in D.C, we didn't want to put the abduction on you as well."

"But from what I can tell it's all linked."

"It looks that way now."

"Danni Lane was the bomber, what the hell was that

all about?" I muttered, ignoring Kurt's warning about less talking.

Across the road, I heard sounds of life. Sirens, people coughing and talking, crying, barked orders. I didn't move to look. No need. Not my problem now. My problem was ahead of me. Finding Robinson.

"We're rolling as planned on Robinson's estate," Kurt said. "You're teamed up. I'll have SWAT meet us and air support. We are getting this prick today."

A hand waved in front of my face. I blinked but didn't flinch.

"Conway, you and Mitch are going back to the hotel," Kurt said. "You're sitting this one out. No arguments."

A little duck quacked in circles. Confused. The duck climbed onto some bathroom scales. Scales? Why would a duck need scales?

"Get Troy's friend in legal," I said. "That's the person who has been fucking with my orders."

The duck flapped and jumped off the scales. It waddled away.

"We'll get him," Sam said. "Get going, Chicky."

Kurt talked to Mitch, their voices hushed. I knew what it was about and for once didn't mind.

We walked away, arm in arm.

Chapter Forty-eight.

Master of Puppets

A very long hour after getting back to the hotel and Lee's room, my cell phone rang. Caine. "You're alive?"

"Yes," I replied.

"Good of you to call," he grunted.

"I figured no news is good news," I said, letting my smile infect my words.

"It'll all be over soon."

"Over? They got him?"

"Not exactly. They know where he is. You want to join Delta for the takedown?"

"Do bears shit in the woods?"

"Sending the address now. They're waiting for you."

My phone buzzed as the address arrived.

"Thanks Caine."

"Go. Don't get dead."

I hung up and turned to Mitch. He was already at the door. He jangled the car keys at me and smiled.

"Just tell me where we're going."

I gave him the address. We walked in outward silence to the car. I could hear his thoughts as he shuffled them around but choose to leave him alone. My smashed-up body needed my scrambled brain to focus on the task at hand and not hop in and out of Mitch's skull.

Mitch opened the front passenger door for me then

closed it once I was seated.

"You all right?" he asked as he settled behind the wheel.

"Yep."

My mind ticked. Twenty-three minutes disappeared on a single focused thought. Get Robinson. A sudden onslaught of noise told me we'd arrived and my door magically opened. Mitch held out his hand to help me from the car. We'd arrived.

Kurt's voice rang out, "Gear up, Conway, you're with me. Mitch get back in the car."

"I'll help her with her flak jacket first then happily get back in the car," Mitch replied, matching Kurt's no crap tone.

Mitch delved into the back of the SUV for my bullet-proof vest and FBI jacket. I waited. Groups of men and women, geared up, ready and waiting for orders, stood nearby. I recognized most of the faces. This was a hand-picked group of agents and SWAT, because if we've learned anything at all from past and recent events, it's be careful who you trust.

Sam and Lee waved.

Mitch fastened the Velcro grips on my vest then helped me put my jacket on. "You want it zipped up?"

"No." I flipped it behind my waist, making sure my holster was clear.

"Ready?" Mitch asked.

"Yep. Get back in the car. I'll see you soon."

He nodded. "Be safe, babe."

"You can count on it."

I walked away without looking back and joined Kurt in front of the mob of agents. He gave a short briefing.

"This is a simultaneous operation. We're hitting the senator while Delta C locate and arrest the person in our legal division who has been helping probationary agent Justin Troy. This is a nasty rabbit hole, people. It ends now." Kurt checked his phone then looked out at the group again. "The senator is not a stupid man and it's likely he knows we are coming. Be safe, be alert. We want this prick."

Shuffling silence greeted his words.

People were divided into groups of three and given entry orders.

"What if he tries to escape?" I asked quietly.

"Helicopters are standing by to intercept. Also, we've closed this road and it's the only way in or out."

"Okay."

"You up for a walk?"

Not really. Couldn't say that to Kurt or I'd be back in the car with Mitch.

"Sure."

"You lie well," Kurt replied with a smile. "Stick close, tell me if you need me."

"Uh huh."

We walked half a mile to the entrance of the estate. It hurt.

Standing next to Kurt I watched SWAT use bolt cutters to unlock the gates and start the choreographed assault on the property.

As I passed through the gates and followed Kurt and a three-man SWAT team up the long driveway, a sense of déjà vu enveloped me. I didn't much care for it. Nor did I care for the constant pain in my ribs and head.

Don't need a reminder I'm alive. I'm aware.

A coordinated operation against a senator. My gut churned. Why can't people just play nice?

Two teams hurried past us to the left and two more to the right. Sam and Lee were right behind us with three more SWAT guys. Kurt grabbed my arm as the front door loomed between massive marble columns. Lee and Sam and their escorts took point.

"SWAT then Sam and Lee," Kurt said. "And then us and our SWAT guys on our six."

Taking no chances.

"Okay." I remembered the briefing.

"You feel all right?"

"Yep."

I followed Kurt through the door into a huge entrance way. A sweeping staircase reminded me of *Gone with the Wind*. Expecting Rhett Butler to appear at any second I was surprised when a child flew from under the stairs and stopped in front of us.

"Christ!" Sam exclaimed, grabbing the kid by the arm and pushing her toward Kurt.

We stopped, letting the others go ahead.

"Who are you?" I asked, taking the kid's arm.

"Lily," she said, trying to wriggle from my grip. "Let

me go!"

"Can't do that, Lily," I said, handing her off to a SWAT member who removed her from the house.

Kurt and I caught up with Sam and Lee on the staircase. Pounding boots resounded on the floor below us and floor above. My heart pounded from exertion; each beat vibrated through my ribs. Just when I thought it was going well, gunfire erupted from somewhere.

The pace quickened, the stairs were no place to be with bullets flying around.

At the top of the stairs, Sam pointed to a closed door.

"That just shut," he said.

Kurt nodded. He motioned me to follow him. We moved further down the hallway. Large paintings hung in ornate frames. There was a lot of money hanging on the off-white walls. *Gone with the Wind* came back in full force. I turned my head toward a commotion at the top of the stairs. Scarlett followed Rhett from a room, pleading with him to stay. I listened, leaning over the banister to see Rhett pause at the bottom of the staircase and hear his famous words. "Frankly my dear, I don't give a damn." The front door opened and closed. Rhett was gone. The world was no longer a sound stage.

"Conway?"

"What?"

"What were you looking at?" Kurt asked from beside me.

"Never mind."

I knew I shouldn't be there, and telling Kurt about

Rhett and Scarlett would cause undue worry on his part. I turned to see what was happening in the hallway.

The door where I'd seen Rhett appear was open. I saw the back of a battle-dressed man as he moved into the room and out of my line of sight. A moment later Sam and Lee entered the room. Voices rose and sank from within the room, too muffled for me to make out words.

He and Lee came out walking a handcuffed male between them.

"Who are you?" I called from my position because Kurt wouldn't let me go closer.

"None of your business, bitch."

A smile settled on my lips. I knew who he was. He was the man from the photos I saw when we rescued Anastazia.

"Keith Blackwell, pervert, pedophile, human trafficker, and general asshole. What a resumé."

Blackwall spat in my direction.

Sam's elbow tapped the side of Blackwell's head. "No spitting at the boss, dickwad."

"You know what happens to assholes like you in prison?" I said with a grin.

"You think I'm going to jail. That's cute," Blackwell crooned.

"Your 'get out of jail free' card no longer works."

Running boots hit the marble floor downstairs. Footsteps echoed. A voice rang out, "Agent Conway?"

I leaned over the rail. Lee encouraged Blackwell to walk down the stairs.

"Up here …"

"We need you and Henderson."

"On our way."

Kurt and I hurried past the prisoner on the stairs and joined the agent in the middle of the entrance hall.

"You are?" I asked, scanning his face. I thought I knew him but couldn't be sure.

He smiled. "Claude. We work together."

"Sorry," I said. Really sorry: there was bound to be something hinky happening in my head after the crash. Guess we found it.

The muscles in Kurt's jaw tightened.

"Conway, Claude is the SSA of Delta B," Kurt said keeping his voice low.

"Thank you," I replied, matching his tone.

Claude glanced from me to Kurt and back, then wisely left it alone.

"Follow me. The senator is holed up in his study at the back of the house."

We followed Claude through two wide hallways, past many paintings and occasional tables containing vases full of fresh flowers. Claude stopped a few feet back from a solid-looking set of double wooden doors. An agent stood on each side of the doors. Tweedle Dum and Tweedle Dee. Them, I recognized.

"Do we have eyes in the room?" I asked.

The agent on the left spoke. Tweedle Dum.

"SWAT are working on it."

"Okay. He got weapons in there?"

"No way of knowing ma'am," Tweedle Dee replied.

I managed to keep their names out of conversation. I leaned close to Kurt and whispered. "Tweedle Dum and Tweedle Dee?"

He smiled. "Very good, Conway. Do you know their actual names?"

"Not a fucking clue," I said, grinning.

Kurt nodded, his smile still in place.

I gave Tweedle Dee all my attention. "What do you know, Agent?"

"He locked the door. I heard him talking. We cut the phone lines but the talking continued, so maybe a cell phone."

"Or he's talking to himself? Or there is someone else in the room?"

"I don't know. He was ahead of us and shut the door before we could get a look."

I turned to Kurt. "We need to account for all staff. This place doesn't run itself. Someone puts the fresh flowers in those fancy vases and dusts those freaking paintings."

I just bet he had a housekeeper and cook and several cleaning staff. Maids? Are they still called that?

Tweedle Dum and Tweedle Dee shuffled uncomfortably. Tweedle Dum looked like he wanted to say something.

"Problem?" I asked.

"Ma'am. Yes. Ma'am."

Jeez. Get over the ma'am crap.

"Speak."

"My aunt works for Robinson, she cleans for him."

Crap.

"Where is she?"

"I don't know if she was at work today. Haven't had time to call her."

"Do it now."

He pulled his cell phone from his pocket and made the call. No one moved or spoke. From down the hall I heard a phone ring. I breathed out. At least it wasn't from behind the closed doors.

"What's her name?"

"Akio Uzumaki," he replied.

"Stay where you are," I said.

Kurt and I went to investigate. The ringing grew louder, from inside a door.

"On two," Kurt said, his weapon in his hand.

I swallowed. Breathed out. Turned the handle and pulled. The door swung toward me. Kurt stepped into the doorway. He passed me a cell phone. It was still ringing.

Not good.

I answered Tweedle Dum's call then switched off the phone.

"This is a closest, a janitor's room," Kurt said. "Cleaning supplies. Shelves stacked with toilet paper, tissue boxes, and soap. The phone was on the shelf by the door."

We walked back.

"Sorry, no aunt, just this." I held up the phone we found.

Tweedle Dum's face crumpled. I thought he was going to cry. He sucked it up. Good job.

Claude was on his phone. He ended the call and spoke, "We have two staff unaccounted for. One a maid and the other a gardener."

His phone rang.

"Revising that. The gardener took the day off. One maid is unaccounted for and last seen going into the supply closet in the east wing." He looked around. "Where do you suppose we are?"

"My guess would be the east wing," Kurt said. "We found her phone in a supply closet."

My guess is we have a hostage situation on our hands.

"We need eyes in there A-sap," Claude muttered.

"Is there another way out of this wing or do I have to go back that way?" I asked, pointing back the way we'd come.

Claude pointed down the hall past Tweedle Dum. "Go down there, hang a right, there's an external door."

"Thanks. You three stay put."

Kurt and I hurried off. I had my phone in my hand, already talking to Lee when we found the door.

"Possible hostage situation. Clear the rest of the house then meet us out the back of the east wing."

"Be there in ten, Chicky."

I hung up. Kurt knocked on the glass window in the door and held up his badge. A heavily armed SWAT agent nodded and opened the door for us.

"Where is everyone?" Kurt asked.

"Just around the corner," the agent replied. His voice sounded familiar. He turned to me and grinned. "Hey, Conway."

Think. You know him.

I needed a name to match the voice because his face wasn't triggering anything.

"Kris."

"In the flesh," he said with a small laugh.

"It's about to get messy, get someone else to cover this door and join us," I said.

"Will do."

Kurt walked ahead of me. He leaned against the house and peered around the corner. I heard him call out, "FBI, coming in."

I caught up and we stepped away from the cover provided by the building and into SWAT controlled territory. Andrews walked toward us. I recognized him and felt a relieved smile settle.

"Keep over this way and out of the firing line," he said, ushering us away from the back of the building. We walked about three-hundred yards to the command truck parked at the end of the driveway in front of what looked like a five-car garage. We stood beside the truck facing the house. The study had large windows and a french door that lead to a small lawn and garden. A lavender hedge separated the area from the driveway.

"We've got eyes inside," Andrews said.

"And?" Kurt replied.

"Senator Robinson and an unknown female. We

believe she's staff."

"We have a maid by the name of Akio Uzumaki unaccounted for. Could it be her," Kurt asked.

I felt my breath catch on my ribs. Wishing Andrews would say no and the missing woman would magically appear from a walk in the garden.

No magic.

"Could be."

"Have you communicated with Robinson?" I asked, looking for vantage points that offered an unobstructed line of sight into the ground floor study. I scanned the roof of the garage. It could be done. A glint from the far right told me there was someone up there with binoculars. A large oak tree caught my interest. That would work.

"Not yet. You want us to do that or do you want to try?"

"You do it. I want a marksman in that tree." I pointed.

Andrews nodded. "I've got two on the garage roof."

"I saw one."

Kurt was on the phone. When he finished he had news and it wasn't good.

"Robinson was at a gun range recently with a rifle. He'd just purchased a new weapon and was getting some range time in."

"Do I want to know?"

He shook his head. "No, but you need to know."

"Tell me then."

"SG 550 and he's proficient."

"And there's a weapons safe in that study of his, because that's how our luck goes," I muttered. "Open communication, Andrews. Let's see if he wants to talk. Meanwhile, if anyone gets a clear shot, take it."

"Step into my office, Conway, you can watch the fun on the monitors."

Andrews swung open a side door in the truck.

It was darkish inside and smelled like men. Not unpleasant like a high school locker room, this was more a mix of deodorant and gun oil. Andrews tapped the back of a chair facing three computer screens.

"Here's your vantage point, Conway." He handed me a headset. "You can communicate with the team. If you need to."

"What if I need to be out there, up that tree with a rifle?" I said quietly.

"In a heartbeat, Conway. But I think Kurt here would have something to say about that."

Kurt sat next to me, his elbow resting on the back of my chair. He spoke, his breath tickled as it brushed my ear, "No rifle. No tree. Am I clear?"

"Yeah."

Killjoy.

My eyes settled on the vista before me. Three different views of the same room. The senator sat behind a large desk. I could see his face. He wasn't a happy man. Good, he had no rights to happiness. A woman seated in the chair in front of the desk wrung her hands in her lap. Akio Uzumaki. The complication. I could hear Andrews' team talking via the headset. No resolution. Andrews made a third attempt at getting Robinson on the phone. They'd reinstated the phone line for SWAT use only. I watched as Robinson picked the receiver up off the desk.

Andrews stood behind me, looking over my shoulder at the screens while he spoke. Calm. Controlled. At times jovial. He was good at his job. I gathered from the conversation that the Senator wasn't willing to play nice. Andrews voice grew quieter. He'd moved to the other end of the huge truck.

Kurt pulled a folded wad of paper out from inside his jacket and handed it to me. It was a search warrant for the premises and also the arrest warrant for Senator Robinson. I skimmed the documents and handed them back.

"If he gives himself up, you can slap him with those," I said. I'd like to shoot the bastard and I'm pretty sure I could live with my decision.

My phone rang: Delta C.

Kurt's phone rang. He held his phone next to mine. Same call. We answered together.

"Conway, Henderson, Troy is dead."

"How?" I asked. "He was in custody?"

"Yes. He was. He slit his wrists. His escort found his body in the men's bathroom."

"Find out what he used and where he got it!" I hung up.

Kurt followed suit.

"We need to move on Robinson before he ganks

himself."

"Ganks?" Kurt queried.

I shrugged, and immediately regretted the movement. It hurt. "I've probably watched too much *Supernatural.*" Robinson is a monster. Sam and Dean gank monsters. Gank felt right.

"Conway, explain gank," Kurt said with incredible patience.

"Kill. Before he kills himself."

I signaled Andrews by swirling my finger in the air. He'd stopped talking to Robinson.

"Robinson's not a happy man," Andrews said. "What do you need?"

"We need to get in there, get the woman out, and arrest that bastard. There's a chance he'll try and kill himself. His buddy in the FBI did."

Movement on the screen made us turn. We all watched as Robinson walked across the room took something large from a cabinet and walked back to his desk with the object hanging next to his leg from one hand. He used both hands to lift it and put it on the desk. A rifle. Not that easy to commit suicide with a rifle. Maybe he was planning on shooting his way out.

He turned, reached over his desk, and took something from a drawer. A handgun.

Damn.

A voice over my headset said, "We have a non-fatal resolution."

I answered, "Take the shot."

Watching without breathing.

Robinson's head turned. He frowned. His body slumped onto his desk.

Andrews spoke into his headset. "Entry team. Go, go, go."

Four men stormed the room via the outside door. Watching on the screen, I saw Robinson move.

Crap.

A gunshot rang out.

Red splattered over one screen obscuring the view.

"Andrews, you'll have to clean that camera."

Chapter Forty-nine.

Eye of the Tiger

I sat in the car, Mitch stood outside talking to Kurt. We'd uncovered a lot of information.   Phone call time. I pressed the speaker icon before the phone stopped ringing.

"Ellie. You okay?" Caine's voice sounded uncharacteristically soft.

"Yep."

"You going to tell me ..."

"It's going to take months to go through all the documents found at the estate. Senator Robinson died in a shoot-out with Delta." I figured if I talked fast enough I wouldn't have to think too much about the mess Robinson made. "We located two extra people on the premises, a child by the name of Lily-Ann Blackwell and an adult male, Keith Blackwell."

I closed my eyes and breathed. "Waiting on Child Protective Services to take the kid. We arrested the father," I said.

"And?"

"You won't like this ... half an hour ago Justin Troy took his own life."

"How?"

"Someone gave him a knife," I replied. "That someone was his friend from legal. A lawyer by the name of Craig

Robinson. He got to Troy before Delta C could arrest Robinson."

"Related?"

"Brother to Senator Robinson."

"What a mess."

"You can say that again."

"The Robinson brothers are perverts. They were behind the Blackwell operation. Not only that but Senator Robinson was on the board of a nanotechnology company with a Government contract."

"The girl's parents are in that field?" Caine asked.

"Yes. He approached them. They were about to lose a big contract because they didn't have anyone as good as the Dobrovolný's in their specialized field," I said.

"This was about getting the parents to come on board and work for his damn company here in the USA?"

"Seems that way."

"Excessive?"

"The deal is worth billions," I said. Mitch knew a lot about the company involved and told me more about the contract they were after. Mitch's company was tendering for the same government contract.

Money. The root of all evil? Nah. People are the root of all evil, money is just money.

"While you were busy I did some investigating of my own," Caine said.

"Into?"

"Danni Lane."

"And?"

"She was a nut, working both sides, with her own agenda, which included setting off bombs in D.C. and documenting the results and your reactions for research purposes," Caine grumbled. "You think you can stop attracting these people?"

"I'll do my best," I replied. "There's gotta be more to it than that. She was firmly embedded in the situations as they unfolded."

And Chance told me she was part of it all.

"You're right. There is more to it. We uncovered a connection to Blackwell."

"You what?" I hadn't expected that.

"Danni Lane and Blackwell are related."

"In what way?"

I picked they were first cousins who married but that probably wasn't the case. Maybe their parents were first cousins that married? Focus. Dammit.

"First cousins."

Too good to be true. I doubted my hearing.

"Say what now?"

"First cousins."

"Who married?"

Caine's voice rasped in my ear, "No, but I can see how you'd think that."

"But what about Trudi and Susan, what did they really have to do with any of it?"

"Apart from being convenient scapegoats. Nothing that we have found."

"And the State Department guy, David Krauss, did you

hear from Iain Campbell?"

"Yes, they're dealing with that. Seems he was passing information about you, gleaned from various sources."

"So, it's over?"

"Yes, just the cleanup now."

"No one else is going to try to erase us from the planet?"

"Not today, Ellie." Caine's gruff voice softened. "You can go home. In fact, you are now officially on medical leave."

I didn't argue.

Chapter Fifty.

Enter Sandman

I stood in the doorway to my home office wearing one of Mitch's tee shirts and not much else. He was at my desk, with his back to the door. Watching him work made me smile. I stayed there for a few minutes. I could see the screens in front of him. He was writing a report, his report on Operation Tourist. Two steps closer and I could read the writing on one screen and see the graphs on the other. He was writing about how the hummingbird behaved on its first field test. He hadn't left me since the helicopter crash.

I was in the middle of a familiar and very comfortable scene. Déjà vu? Maybe.

An element of fear crept in. I pushed it aside.

As I walked toward him, he swung around to face me. Smiling. Heart stopping. Yep, he had a heart-stopping smile. Dimples. Sparkling eyes. I slid an arm around his shoulders and sat on his knee. Mitch's arms wrapped around me, his voice ruffled my hair as he spoke, "You all right?"

"Needed a hug."

"That I can do."

I leaned my head on his shoulder, eyes closed, as his hands rubbed my back. Slowly I let go of everything and drifted into Mitch.

"Are you falling asleep?" he whispered.

"No," I replied.

His hand slipped under my tee shirt. Warm against my skin. Each stroke of his fingertips on my back caused a tingle in my spine. I wriggled a little.

"I need to move," I murmured. Wrong angle. It was not making my cracked ribs happy. I stood up and turned to face him.

His smile melted me. Mitch's hands held my waist as I straddled him in the chair. Bare legs against jeans. Wrapping my arms around his neck and burying my face in him. Drinking in his scent. Intoxicating. Ginseng and black pepper. Spicy but not overpowering. I could stay there forever.

And I knew I would.

Post-it notes

Shades of black
Distort the past
None of it's real
Nothing will last

Reminder to myself:
Breathe
Count to ten
It'll be okay
No one has to die today

Shades of orange
Become the flames
A city in ruins
People maimed

Reminder to myself:
Breathe
Count to ten
You'll be okay
No one else will die today

Shades of fear
Filled with pain
Erase the memory
Make me sane

Reminder to myself:
Take a breath
You're not alone
It'll be okay

Repeat after me:
No one is going to die today
Unload the gun
Walk away

About the author:

Cat Connor is a prolific crime thriller author hailing from New Zealand. Her expertise in the genre is reflected in her engaging and suspenseful narratives, which have garnered a loyal following. Her work is known for its intricate plots, dynamic characters, and relentless pace, keeping readers on the edge of their seats until the very end. She has authored multiple books, including the popular "Byte" series, which follows the exploits of an FBI unit that investigates serial crime.

Cat's passion for crime and espionage is evident in her writing, as she strives to create a world that is both authentic and thrilling. Her meticulous attention to detail and extensive research have won her critical acclaim and accolades from readers and peers alike. In addition to writing, Cat enjoys speaking on topics related to writing and publishing. Her talks are known for their candidness, humour, and practical advice. With her unique blend of talent, expertise, and passion, Cat Connor has established herself as one of the most exciting and accomplished authors in the crime thriller genre.

Her other passions include music, reading, tequila, red wine, coffee, and chocolate. When she's not writing she can be found binge watching TV shows and spending time with her much adored animals; Diesel the mastador, Patrick the tuxedo cat, Dallas the tortie Birman, and Jimmy the thug.

You can follow and contact Cat at the following places:

Website: www.catconnor.com
Twitter: @catconnor
Facebook: @cat.connor
Instagram: @catconnorauthor
Bluesky: @catconnor.bsky.social
Threads: @catconnorauthor

Also by Cat Connor:

The Kiwi set Veronica Tracey Spy/PI series:
[Nothing happens here] -2020
[Lure the lie] - 2021
[Leave a message] - 2022
[Whiskey Tango Foxtrot] - 2023
[Foxtrot Mike Lima] - 2024

The FBI based Byte Series:
Killerbyte - 2009
Terrorbyte - 2010
Exacerbyte - 2011
Flashbyte - 2012
Soundbyte - 2013
Snakebyte - 2013 (novella)
Databyte - 2014
Eraserbyte - 2015
Psychobyte - 2016
Metabyte - 2017
Qubyte - 2018
Cryptobyte - 2019
Vaporbyte - 2020 (red)
Vaporbyte -2020 (purple)
Raidbyte - 2021 (collection of short bytes)

Whispers in the water - the poetry of SSA Conway and SA Connelly
Torrent - a collection of short bytes

If I were a carpenter - SSA Kurt Henderson's story (novella)

Array - a collection of short bytes